The Ropemaker

The Ropemaker

PETER DICKINSON

DELACORTE PRESS

Published by
Delacorte Press
an imprint of
Random House Children's Books
a division of Random House, Inc.
1540 Broadway
New York, New York 10036

Visit us on the Web! www.randomhouse.com/teens
Educators and librarians, for a variety of teaching tools, visit us at
www.randomhouse.com/teachers

Library of Congress Cataloging-in-Publication Data

Dickinson, Peter.
  The ropemaker / Peter Dickinson.
    p. cm.
  Summary: When the magic that protects their Valley starts to fail,
Tilja and her companions journey into the evil Empire to find the
ancient magician Faheel, who originally cast those spells.
  ISBN 0-385-72921-9
  [1. Magic—Fiction.   2. Fantasy.]   I. Title.
PZ7.D562 Ro 2001
[Fic]—dc21
                            2001017422

The text of this book is set in 11.5-point Janson Text.

Book design by Susan Livingston

Manufactured in the United States of America

November 2001
10 9 8 7 6 5 4 3 2 1

BVG

The Cost of Living

For Robin

Go then, adventurer, on your vivid journey,
Though once again, of course, I cannot join you—
That is as certain as your happy ending.
The one-armed captain in the pirate harbor
Would know me in an instant for a Jonah.
No gnome would ever speak with me for witness,
And so let slip the spell-dissolving answer
Before you'd even heard the sacred riddle.
I, as it happens, know it from my reading,
But the blind queen would ask it in a language
Not in the syllabus of my old college,
But which your loved, illiterate nanny taught you.

No, I will stay at home and keep things going,
Conduct the altercation with the builders,
Hoe the allotment, fix the carburetor.
I'm genuinely happier with such dealings;
It isn't merely that they pass the seasons
Until I hear your footstep on the threshold.
Then I will sit and listen to your story
With a complacently benign amazement,
Believing it because it's you that tell it.
And when you've done, and I have asked my questions,
I for the umpteenth time on such homecomings
Will say what's happened to the cost of living.

Contents

Asarta

1

The Forest

It had snowed in the night. Tilja knew this before she woke, and waking she remembered how she knew. Somewhere between dream and dream a hand had shaken her shoulder and she'd heard Ma's whisper.

"It's snowing at last. I must go and sing to the cedars. You'll have to make the breakfast before you feed the hens."

Tilja reached up to the shelf beyond the bolster and pulled her folded underclothes in under the quilt, where she spread them along beside her body to warm through. While they did so she lay and listened to the wind hooting in the chimney above her. Anja, beside her, grumbled in her sleep, clutching at her share of the quilt while Tilja wriggled out of her nightshirt and into the underclothes. Then she slid out and hurried into another layer of clothing, tucked Anja snugly in and finished dressing.

The bed was a boxlike structure set right into the immense old fireplace, on one side of the stove. Her parents slept in a larger box on the far side, but that would be empty by now, with Da in the byre seeing to the animals, and Ma on her way to the cedar lake, far into the forest.

Faint light seeped through the shutters, but she didn't open them, and not just because of the savage wind that was battering against them and shrieking into their cracks. She liked to do these first tasks in the dark, knowing without having to feel around exactly where to put her hand for anything she needed.

3

Woodbourne was her home, and this kitchen was the heart of it, as familiar to her as her own body. She had no more need to see to find things than she had to put her finger to the tip of her nose. Relighting the stove in the dark was a way of starting the day by telling herself that this was so.

First, she opened the firebox and carefully riddled out the old ash, leaving just the last black embers, flecked with sparks. Onto these she spread a double handful of straw and another of dry twigs, then closed the fire door, opened both dampers, and stood leaning against the still-warm stove while she repeated the fire charm three times. Ma never bothered with the fire charm, but Tilja's grandmother, Meena, had taught it to her so that she would know how long to wait for the twigs to be well alight before she added the coarser kindling. Usually it took four times, but three would be enough with a wind like this to drag the draft up.

A wind like this? And snowing? That wasn't right.

Once the kindling was in, and had caught, she slid in four logs, sawn and split to fit the stove and dried all summer in an open shed. The flames began to roar into the flues. Now at last she poked a taper in and used it to light the lamp, poured water into a pan and set it to boil, heaved the porridge pot out of the oven where it had been quietly cooking all night in the remaining heat from the old fire, stirred in a little water and set it beside the water pan to warm through.

Next she finished getting up. She rinsed her face and hands, combed and bunched her hair and slipped into her boots, leaving the laces loose, and opened the door into the yard. At once the wind flung a gust of snow into her face, stinging as if it had been a handful of fine gravel. Brando was out of sight, cowering in his kennel from the storm.

This is all wrong, she thought again as she clumped across to the outhouse. The first snow in the Valley should have fallen a month ago, on a still night, huge soft flakes floating steadily down, blanketing yard and roofs and fields a foot deep by morning. These furious flurries weren't *snow*. And nothing was really lying. Any flakes that reached the ground were snatched up by the wind and whirled into drifts in the corners of the yard. When a gust hurtled in from another direction it would catch at these and set them streaming away like smoke.

Worse still, checking by touch in the dark of the outhouse, she found that some of the stuff had found its way in through a crack and made a miniature drift across the seat. With freezing fingers she scooped it away, did what she had to and clumped back in a foul temper to the kitchen. She half thought of sending Anja out with a storm lantern to clear the outhouse and block the crack before Da got back, but in the end she did it herself.

By the time he came in she had the porridge hot and the sage tea brewed and the bacon frying, and Anja was up and dressed and clean.

"Stupid sort of snow we've got this year," he muttered. "I hope your mother's all right."

"Where's Ma gone?" said Anja, through porridge.

"She's gone to the lake to sing to the cedars," said Tilja. "She'll be home to cook your dinner."

But she wasn't, so Tilja started to do what she could. By noon Da had twice gone up to the forest and as far in among the trees as he dared, the second time foolishly far, so that he came out dazed and unsteady with the strange forest sickness that only affected men. Tilja helped him to his chair and pulled off his boots and put a bowl of hot soup into his hands while he hunched by the fire, shaken by sighs and shudders.

Then they heard Brando's silly little yap of welcome for someone he knew, so different from his deep bay of warning to a stranger. Anja ran to the door, peered out, turned and shouted, "It's Tiddykin! Oh, where's Ma? When's she coming?"

Tilja rushed out and saw Ma's pony coming shambling down beside the top meadow. One of her panniers was gone, and the other was dragging and bumping among the snowy tussocks. Tilja was still staring when Da came staggering to the door to look.

Not bothering with boots, she helped him outside, ran to the stable and grabbed a handful of yellownut out of the bin. Tiddykin, who, like most horses, would have crossed the Great Desert for yellownut, limped in after her until the trailing pannier caught behind the door and stopped her.

"I'll see to her," said Da from the doorway. "You go and saddle Calico up and fetch your grandmother. Tell her what's happened. Take a bit of bread to eat on the way—you've not time for dinner, and it'll be long dark before you're back out of the wood."

"Wouldn't it be quicker if I just went straight in? I'm sure I could find my way to the lake. Ma took me last summer."

"I know where the lake is," said Anja, who'd never been there. "I can find it."

"Quiet, Anja," snapped Da. "And you do what you're told, Til. I'm not having you lost too. Off you go. Back indoors with you, Anja, and fix your sister some food while she's getting Calico set."

"You won't go back into the forest, will you, Da?" said Tilja.

"When I can just about find my way across my own yard? Now, get on with it."

Old Calico was much too clever for her own good, or anyone else's. She had seen and smelled the bitter weather, and didn't at all want to be harnessed, let alone with the special horse seat which Da had made for Meena, Tilja's grandmother. Tiddykin usually wore it and it didn't really fit Calico. Tilja bribed her with yellownut while she tugged at straps and adjusted pads, and had her ready before Da, still stumbling in his walk and propping himself against walls and doorposts, had finished with Tiddykin.

"Will you be all right?" she said.

"Have to be, won't I? Get moving. You'll need your coat. Anja's fixed you bread and cheese."

"Suppose Meena's in one of her moods . . . ," Tilja began. (Children in the Valley called their grandparents by their first names.)

"Tell her what's up. She'll come. And take a stick—you'll need to keep Calico moving."

And that was true. It wasn't more than a mile down to Meena's cottage, but without driving Calico would have taken all afternoon. Tilja sat sidesaddle, huddled into her coat and with head bowed and her hoodstrings drawn tight, and every few yards caught Calico a thwack across the rump to keep her moving even at a sulky walk. When she could Tilja snatched a bite at the vast hunk of bread and slab of cheese that Anja had cut for her. Now she had time to think, she was sick with worry. It was so cold. Ma was lying somewhere in the forest, out on the naked ground. Nobody would live long like that in such weather. Before they were halfway down the lane Tilja lost patience, dismounted, and drove Calico on as she might have driven a heifer, while she herself came behind at a stumbling run. At the gate she tied the reins to the post and ran panting up the path and let herself in.

Meena was at her stove, but had swung round at the rattle of the latch.

"Trouble?" she snapped. "Of course it's trouble. You wouldn't be looking for your old grandmother, else, would you?"

"Ma went to sing to the cedars," gasped Tilja. "She hasn't come back, but Tiddykin has with one of the panniers gone. Da wants us to go and look for her. You and me. He says I'd get lost by myself."

"He's not pure fool, then."

"He went too far in himself and only just got out. He looks ghastly, and he's all staggery still."

"Pretty well pure fool. Never mind me—I'm coming. Where's my cane? You catch your breath while I get myself together. Then you can help me with my boots."

She hobbled around, grunting every now and then with the pain of her hip, which was the main cause of her moods. It was obviously bad today, and no wonder, this weather. There was no point Tilja trying to help or hurry her—she hated that, and in any case she had done all she needed in a very few minutes, putting her pots to the side of the stove, closing the dampers, and fetching an extra layer of clothing out of her chest. She let Tilja ease her feet into her ancient boots and lace them and her leggings. By the time she was dressed in her sheepskin coat and hat and swathed to the eyes in scarves you wouldn't have known whether she was woman or man or troll.

Tilja positioned Calico beside the mounting block in the lane, helped Meena climb it, repositioned Calico, who had of course sidled away, and heard Meena groan with the pain of settling herself into the horse seat Da had made for her because of her hip— more like a padded legless chair than a saddle.

"I'll do now," said Meena. "You give me my cane—I'm not standing any nonsense from this stupid creature. Born cussed, and she'll die cussed, like most of us."

In fact Calico made good speed home. She was what's called a barn rat, always ready to head back to her own warm stall. Tilja trotted beside her, and was gasping again by the time they reached the farm, not an hour after they'd set out. Da was watching for them. He looked a little better, his face less ashen behind the black beard, but he'd got his long staff out to help him move around.

"You've made fair time," he said. "It's around four hours till dark. Do you need a rest, Meena?"

"Best stay where I am," said Meena. "More trouble than it's worth, getting on and off this brute. It's Tilja who'll be needing the rest—whole way back, she's run."

"She can rest on Dusty's back. I've put him in the log sled. If Selly's hurt you'll never get her onto a horse. All right, Tilja? Ready to go?"

Without waiting for an answer he took the reins and led them into the barn, where Dusty was waiting between the shafts of the log sled, looking huge and majestic in the dim light. He'd been on the farm less than four months. Da had paid almost twice what he'd meant to for him, and had never before let anyone else handle him. Tilja stared up at the great beast, appalled.

"But . . . but . . . ," she stammered.

"Tiddykin's all in," said Da. "And if she wasn't, she couldn't handle the sled that distance. Calico could, but she won't. Just remember you're master, and Dusty will remember too. Now, listen. You've got rugs on the sled, and a hot flask, a firepot, kindling, logs, a couple of storm lamps, spare oil, a tarpaulin, poles and cords for shelter. That's all just in case. But I want you well on your way out before dark. Whether or not you've found her, you turn back in time for that. You hear that, Meena? For yourself you can do what you want—you will anyway—but I want Tilja home by supper."

Meena glared down at him. The two of them didn't get on, which was why she lived down at the cottage. The farm was still hers, in law, and would be Ma's when she died, but he was the farmer, so he couldn't help speaking as though he had the say in everything.

Without waiting for an answer he gripped Tilja round the waist and lifted her onto Dusty's back. It felt more like sitting on the trunk of a fallen tree than riding a horse. He gave her an instant to settle, handed her the reins, took the bridle and led Dusty out into the bitter flurry of the storm. He clipped a leading rein to Calico's bridle and looped the end over a hook on Dusty's harness.

"I won't come up with you," he said. "Nothing more I can do, and I'm still swivel eyed, and there's the stock to see to. Good luck, both of you. And thanks, Meena."

He patted Tilja's knee and turned away. Anja waved from the kitchen door. Tilja waved back, shook the reins and clicked her tongue twice. Off Dusty strode with Calico trailing beside him, furious and resistant until she got a thwack from Meena, and then plodding sulkily along.

They took the track beside the upper meadow and crossed the spare ground. When they reached the trees Tilja looked back and found that she could no longer see the farm. The wind whined and whistled among the bare branches, and swirled flurries of snow to and fro at ground level, sweeping whole patches bare and gathering the whiteness into sudden drifts. There was no track, but little undergrowth either, and mostly the trees had grown close together and been forced upward toward the light, so that the lower trunks were branchless. Tilja had only once been deep into the forest, on that strange visit to the lake with Ma, last summer. Otherwise they had stayed near the edge, looking for firewood and fungi and setting traps for small game. Though when she and Meena had entered the wood she had had a good idea where the lake lay, now she realized how easily she could have gone astray. Apart from the occasional great cedar towering above the rest, the forest seemed endlessly the same, just pillared trees and gently undulating ground beneath. There was no sun to steer by, and the unsteady wind, buffeting around every which way, was no use either.

Once they were well in among the trees Tilja loosed the leading rein so that Meena could pick her own path. Calico was certainly not going to let herself be separated from Dusty, out here in the forest, but to keep up with Dusty's enormous stride she had to move at an awkward pace, walking for a bit and falling behind and trotting to catch up.

She did so now, and drew almost level. Tilja heard Meena hiss with pain. She reined Dusty back.

"Are you all right?" she said.

"I've been better. Left a bit now."

"Couldn't you just tell me the way? Then you could go back."

"You can't feel it then? Where the lake is?"

"No."

Meena had been gazing up at her with her usual fierce stare, but now she grunted, looked away, paused for a moment and shook the reins.

"Let's get along, then," she snapped. "No point hanging around, chattering."

They rode on, but there had been something in that pause that reminded Tilja of the time she had stood beneath the sweeping branches of an enormous cedar and gazed out over the glistening stillness of the lake.

"Can you hear anything, darling?" Ma had said, with an odd note in her voice, both eager and anxious.

So Tilja had stood and strained for some unexpected sound, but had heard only the whisper of a light breeze through the cedar branches and the steady calling of two doves.

"Nothing special," she'd said. "What sort of anything?"

Ma had looked away. Then there had been just such a pause before she'd said "Never mind," and smiled at Tilja with a sort of pity.

Time passed, both too slow and too fast. It seemed endless, but always Tilja was conscious of the precious minutes dribbling away and nothing else changing, always the same wood, the same wind slapping loose snow and dead leaves hither and thither between the gray tree trunks, and the same certainty in her mind that they were already too late. Then abruptly, the nature of the forest changed. The bare trees gave way to a belt of cedars, whose lower branches swept to the ground and interlaced with their neighbors', leaving no clear way through into the blackness beneath.

"There's a path," said Meena. "A bit to the right, it'll be."

So they followed the line of cedars for a while, and came to a narrow, winding slot in the green thicket. Tilja headed Dusty into it. He didn't care for the look of it and for the first time jibbed, but obediently plodded on as soon as she flicked the reins. Almost at once, though, as they rounded a bend, the traces of the sled tangled into a pine branch and she had to scramble down and clear them. The path was barely wide enough to let the sled through and it was bound to catch again, so she knelt at the front of it and clucked to Dusty to carry on, as Da did when plowing. He heaved forward, and she positioned herself ready to keep the traces clear at the next corner. Despite her efforts, they stuck several times more before she saw open sky ahead of them and caught a glimpse of steely gray water ahead.

Just before they were clear the sled jarred against a hidden stump and she had to back Dusty up to heave it free. She was standing, dizzy and gasping with the effort, when she heard Meena cry out behind her, "Look! Oh, look! There they go!"

Tilja moved to see beyond Dusty's huge haunches but tripped over the runner of the sled and fell. By the time she picked herself up, whatever Meena had seen was gone. Meena herself was sitting bolt up in the saddle, gazing ahead, her lined old face shining with excitement.

"Who'd've thought it?" she said in a dazed voice. "Forty years I came to sing to the cedars, snowfall after snowfall, and never a glimpse, and now I've seen three of 'em. Little wretches."

Astonished out of her worry and exhaustion, Tilja stood and stared at her until Meena shook herself.

"Well, don't stand gawping there, girl," she snapped. "Get that brute moving, and we'll go and look for your mother."

Tilja clicked, Dusty plodded ahead as unconcerned as if he were harrowing the bottom acres, and out they came into a wide space ringed with cedars and almost filled by a long, narrow lake. Most of the way round, the trees grew right down to the shore-line, with their branches reaching out over the water, but to the left of the path a strip of grass the width of a broad lane ran up between them and the lake to a small meadow at the top. Here enough snow had settled to cover the area. Lying in the middle of it was a darker shape.

Tilja dropped Dusty's reins and ran.

The shape was Ma. Her heavy cloak covered most of her body.

Tilja knelt beside her, gasping for breath, and shook her by the shoulder.

"Ma! Ma! Wake up!" she croaked. "Oh, please wake up!"

Nothing.

Her eyes were closed, her face very pale, apart from a single dark mark like an angry bruise in the center of her forehead. Hands and cheek were cold, but not icy. Tilja bent to listen for her breath but the roar of the wind through the cedars drowned all fainter sounds. She couldn't find her pulse.

Desperately she called again, "Ma! Ma!"

Did the pale lips move in answer? For a moment she thought so, then she wasn't sure.

She looked round and saw that Meena had somehow caught hold of Dusty's reins and ordered him forward, and that Calico had then decided to trail along beside them. Tilja rose and ran back.

"I think she's alive," she gasped. "I think I saw her lips move."

"Miracle if she is, this weather," said Meena, as though talking about a frost at apple-blossom time. "Give us a hand down, then, and let's take a look."

Once on the ground she stood with her eyes closed and her face as gray as porridge, then shook her head, let out a long breath, and with Tilja taking as much of her weight as she could, knelt beside her daughter's body. She drew off her glove and with gnarled and twisted fingers felt at the limp wrist.

"Well, maybe there's a bit of a pulse there and maybe there isn't," she said. "She's warmer than she might be, though. Well, we'll be taking her home, dead or alive, so you may as well get started on that. You'll need to make room for the two of us, mind. There's no way I'm getting back on that walking tater-riddle, supposing I could."

So Tilja led Dusty on and turned him to bring the sled close beside the body, but before she reached it Meena called out to her to stop.

"Come here, girl, and look at this a moment. We've messed it up this side, but there—what d'you make of that?"

She pointed. Tilja looked and saw that though there were patches and streaks of snow on the body itself, and a good covering caught in the grass around, all along Ma's further side and the fold of cloak beyond there was only the finest dusting of snow, that might have fallen in the last few minutes. And now that she knew what to look for she could see that it had been the same where she and Meena had knelt.

"Something's been lying here," she said. "Covering her up."

13

"Keeping her warm, too," said Meena. "Little wretches. Who'd've thought they had that much sense . . . ? Well, don't hang about, girl. We've no time for dreamings and wonderings."

Too dazed and exhausted to think of anything beyond what had to be done next, Tilja fetched Dusty, got the sled into place and unloaded it. Ma made neither sound nor movement as Tilja half dragged, half rolled her onto the rough boards and lashed three lengths of cord round her to stop her tumbling about. Meena settled herself at the other end and Tilja packed the rest of the load round them, covered them with rugs, tied all fast and led Dusty back along the strip of grass by the water, with Calico following, loose, behind.

That was easy enough. The extra weight meant nothing to Dusty. But the track out through the cedars was hideous. There was no way now that Tilja could have heaved the sled clear if it stuck, so they had to take one stretch at a time, then halt, position Dusty for the next corner, and let him go forward one or two paces only while Tilja used the logging pole to lever the runners sideways as they moved.

"You're not doing too bad, my girl," said Meena, as Tilja heaved, gasping, at the logging pole and the sled eased forward another foot and a half.

"It's Dusty doing most of it," said Tilja.

"Aye, he's not a bad horse, after all," said Meena. "But don't you go telling your father I said so, or he'll be wanting another one."

And then, at last, they were almost through. Tilja could see the change ahead, and hear the different whistle of the wind between bare branches. Looking up, she saw how the sky had darkened, and for a moment thought it meant that heavier snows were coming, then realized that the darkening was the onset of nightfall. The path widened, so now she could trot up beside the sled and take Dusty's bridle and lead him on.

She was just a few paces out beyond the cedars when the

14

sound hit her. Harsh, wild, terrible, a blast of pure anger. The next instant she was tossed aside as Dusty wheeled to meet the challenge, wrenching his bridle from her hand and barging her over with his shoulder. The noise was still echoing through the trees as he neighed his answer, with his neck arched back and a raised hoof pawing the air. Calico bolted and was gone. Twice the cry was repeated and twice Dusty answered, and then the echoes died away and there was only the shriek of the gale, shredding through the branches.

Tilja picked herself up. The sled had slewed sideways as Dusty had wheeled, but all were still aboard.

"What was that?" Tilja gasped.

"Nothing I've a fancy to meet just now," muttered Meena. "Let's get home, if it'll let us."

Dusty heaved his head away as Tilja reached for his bridle, still trying to face the unseen enemy. Angry with terror, she punched his shoulder and yelled at him not to be stupid, and he gave himself a shake and remembered his business. They trudged on until it grew too dark to see, and she had to stop and light one of the storm lamps so that she could lead the way forward. For herself she was utterly lost, but Meena seemed as sure of her bearings as she had been by daylight. And from time to time Dusty would hesitate in his stride and stare away to the right, so that Tilja, though not herself seeing or hearing anything unusual, began to feel that something large and menacing was moving there, shadowing them on their way.

By now she was deathly tired, too tired to be afraid. All she could do was force herself along, sick with worry that Calico had already come home alone, and Da would have once more ventured into the trees to look for them, and this time he would not come out. But he was waiting for them on the edge of the spare ground. He knelt by the sledge and took Ma's hand, and under the shadowy lamplight Tilja was sure she saw Ma's fingers tighten against his, and then he picked Tilja up and kissed her and lifted her onto Dusty's back and led them all down to the farm.

She could remember no more of her homecoming than dunking bread into the broth that Anja had hot and waiting, and thinking as she did so, *This has got to have something to do with Asarta.*

2

The Story

There was time in the Valley, of course—how could there not be? But there was no history. In all the rich farmland between the northern mountains and the forest there were no wars, or reports of wars, only days, seasons, generations. No kings or other rulers, only parents, grandparents, ancestors. For eighteen generations nothing had happened in the Valley that anyone would have thought worth putting in a book, or setting up a memorial stone to record. So, no history. Only time.

And the story of Asarta.

The story was full of grand magical nonsense, and there was none of that kind of magic in the Valley, any more than there was history. Such magic as there was was petty and everyday, love posies and wart charms and such, which many people said were mere superstition and worked no better than random chance. So very few people believed that there was any truth in the story. Some of them might add that it had been invented long ago to explain why the snow lay year-round upon the mountains so thick that nobody could pass them, and why there was a sickness in the forest that closed off the Valley to the south. It was, admittedly, a strange sickness, affecting only men, first making them dazed and feverish almost as soon as they went in under the trees, and, if they stayed there any length of time, casting them into a stupor from which they did not recover. But that didn't mean that there had to be anything magical about it.

This was the story.

Once there had been nothing but history, and far too much of it. To the south, beyond the forest, stretched a huge, rich Empire. To the north, beyond the mountains, lay endless upland plains, across which tribes of fierce horsemen marauded, fighting each other when they couldn't find outsiders to fight and pillage. The best way between the two realms lay through the Valley, because there was one good pass across the mountains, open all summer. The Emperors, when they remembered, maintained a broad road through the forest so that they could control and tax the Valley and guard the pass beyond. The Valley was large, seven long days' march from east to west and five from north to south. It had fertile soil, which the people farmed well, so the taxes they were able to pay made it worth the Emperor's attention. But every now and then an Emperor would allow the garrisons to weaken, and then the tribes would come swarming through the pass and the Valley, burning and looting and murdering, and sweep on to raid the riches of the Empire.

Slowly the Empire would gather its armies and drive them back, across the Valley, up through the pass, and out into their native plains, where it would attempt to harry and punish them for their impertinence, to no good effect. The Valley made a natural base for these operations, so the armies would quarter there, perhaps for several years, burning and murdering less than the tribes had done, but raping and looting almost as effectively, while the Emperor's tax collectors demanded all the normal taxes again, plus what had not been paid while the tribesmen had controlled the Valley, plus extra sums to pay for the increased level of protection that the Valley now enjoyed. The people of the Valley would have been hard put to it to tell you which state of affairs they liked less.

And then a civil war would break out somewhere else in the immensity of the Empire, or a new Emperor would forget to pay the garrisons, or some other matter of state would intervene, and the soldiers would march south, taking with them whatever and whomever they fancied, and the Valley people would try to piece their lives together again, knowing even as they reaped their scant harvest and stored it in their patched barns that soon the tribes would learn that the pass was once more unguarded.

Nineteen generations before Tilja's time such a period had just ended, with the barns empty, the cattle driven away, houses smashed by soldiers looking for hidden treasures to make up for their unpaid wages, children snatched into slavery. Some people chose to go south with the soldiers, to make new lives for themselves in the Empire, but most stayed where they were. However difficult and dangerous life might be in the Valley, this was where they belonged.

A year passed, and things were better. Another year, and they were better again, and still the tribes did not come. (There was a horse plague raging across the plains.) The barns had new roofs on them, doors were sound and tables laden, and markets began again, with stuff in the stalls worth bargaining for. After market people would sit around, drinking the harsh local cider, and wondering how long the good times would last. On one such evening somebody sighed and said, "If only there were a way of closing the pass."

"Fugon the Magnificent tried that," said someone else. "In our grandfathers' grandfathers' time, wasn't it?"

"No, before that," said someone else. "Fugon the Fourth, he was the Magnificent. It was Fugon the Second tried to close the pass."

They argued about dates and Emperors until somebody said, "Anyway, whoever it was, he didn't manage it. And if the Emperor couldn't do it, who can? No one's stronger than the Emperor."

"Asarta is stronger than the Emperor," said a man. "She could close the pass if she chose."

This man's name was Sonnam, which is not a Valley name, because he had not been born in the Valley, and spoke with a southern accent. He was in fact a deserter from the Emperor's army

19

who had fallen in love with a girl from one of the farms by the river. She and her mother had hidden him for three whole years, but now the garrisons were gone and he was married to her and lived openly.

Because he was not a Valley man they did not take him seriously, and laughed when he spoke. But his wife said, "You are fools. Sonnam has lived in the Empire, and you have not."

"Very well," they said. "Tell us about this Asarta. One story is as good as another at the end of a long day."

"Only what Asarta chooses to be known is known about her," said Sonnam. "But my family are mostly soldiers, and my father's uncle was a corporal in the Emperor's guard. In those days there were pirates raiding along the western coast, and when the Emperor built navies to punish them they banded together and sank his ships before his eyes. Twice they did this, but the third time the Emperor, on the advice of his courtiers, sent to Asarta for help. She agreed on a great price and came. So the navies met once more and the Emperor sat on the cliff to watch the encounter, with Asarta beside him, a small old woman in a gray gown. As the navies bore down against each other she called aloud, and serpents came out of the ocean, six of them, and smashed the pirate ships in their coils and tossed them about and snatched the pirates out of the air as they fell, and ate them.

"Then the Emperor clapped his hands and his servants brought three strong chests and laid them before Asarta, and she looked at them and pointed her finger and they fell apart, so that everyone could see that only the top layer in each was gold, and the rest was lead. The Emperor told her that it was his treasurer who had done this, hoping to keep the gold for himself, and again he clapped his hands and the treasurer was seized and strangled before he could speak. Then Asarta looked the Emperor in the eye and pointed her finger once more, and the Emperor shrank until he was no bigger than my thumb, and Asarta picked him up and put him in a gold cage which she brought out of the air, and hung it on a golden pole.

"At that the Emperor's guard, my father's uncle among them, rushed to the rescue of their lord, but they too dwindled as they came nearer to Asarta, to the size of mice and then of ants, so that they were afraid to come closer lest they should vanish altogether. Next Asarta spoke, a cry so loud that those around her fell to the ground, but the body of the treasurer rose to its feet and walked toward her with its head dangling aside, and she placed her hands round his neck and spoke quietly to him, so that his head straightened and the life came back into him. He gave orders, and more gold was brought, up to the price that had been agreed. Then Asarta vanished, taking the gold and the treasurer with her.

"The Emperor's guards, my father's uncle among them, grew slowly in size, until by evening they were the height that they had been that morning. But the Emperor himself never grew to more than half his proper stature, and spoke always in a thin, high voice, like that of a bird, so that he should not forget that Asarta was more powerful than he was.

"All this my father's uncle saw with his own eyes, but being a prudent man he at once changed his name and his regiment, for few of those that were known to have seen the Emperor dangling in his cage lived many days after."

"Not a bad story," said someone.

"So Asarta is stronger than the Emperor," said Sonnam's wife.

"If she's still alive," said someone else.

"And if the story's true," said another.

"Can't be," said yet another. "All that magic and stuff."

Most of the listeners grunted in agreement. That was how Valley people thought about magic, even then, though there was magic in the Valley in those days, just as there was magic everywhere else in the Empire. Only no powerful magician had bothered to come to so remote a province for many, many years.

More peaceful seasons came and went, as the horse plague continued to ravage the plains, and the problems of the Empire boiled up elsewhere. Indeed, there was such turmoil south of the forest that the Emperor's clerks forgot that the Valley even existed, and for long years nobody came to collect the taxes. It was a full generation before shepherds came running into market one evening with the news. They had been with their flocks in the high pastures and had seen a party of wild-looking horsemen beneath them, at the lip of the pass, looking down at the Valley, and pointing and laughing. It had been clear from both stance and gesture what had been in their minds, before they had turned and trotted away north.

By now those sitting around over their cider were the children of those who had listened to Sonnam telling the story of Asarta. Indeed, there were two of his sons among them, in one of whom the old soldiering blood still ran strong. It was he who said, after they had listened with dismay to the shepherds, "There is nothing for it. We must arm ourselves and fight."

This, with much misgiving, they did. They caught the raiders in an ambush beside the river, but they had no experience of battle, while the raiders were hardened to it, so it was a desperately close affair, but in the end the raiders broke and fled. When it was over they met in council. Some said, "We have beaten them once. We can do so again." Others said, "Next time they will be more, and warier. We must send to the Emperor for help." Yet others said, "The Emperor's help will destroy us as surely as the horsemen." At last somebody said, "We might as well send to Asarta."

This was, or was meant to be, a joke. By now "sending to Asarta" had become a sort of proverb in the Valley, something one said when one was in a fix and couldn't think which way to turn. Then someone said, still joking, "At least it would be better than sending to the Emperor." And someone, joking rather less, said, "Indeed it would." So, gradually, without their noticing how it happened, the joke became a proposal, and the proposal became a decision, and they were discussing how it should be done.

Sonnam was no help. He was an old man now, with his memory half gone, and all he could tell them was, "Asarta? Yes, yes. She demanded a great price."

The thought was dismaying. The Valley was prosperous, but mainly in goods. People had full barns and byres, but little by way of money or jewels, or what counted as wealth in the Empire. But they gathered what they had and chose a delegation to go and see if Asarta would help them. Since half the farms in the Valley were inherited through the female line, they sent five men and five women.

From the first they met with misfortune. One was murdered, and three were seized on false claims of debt and sold into slavery. The rest were cheated and robbed. Moreover, they heard not one word of Asarta, for all their asking. There seemed to be neither tale nor memory of her.

When they had lost almost all that they had brought, four decided to give up and go home, but one man and one woman said that they would continue the search, penniless and hopeless though they were. Their names were Reyel Ortahlson and Dirna Urlasdaughter. These two journeyed on, choosing their roads at random, until they came to a city on the very edge of the immense desert that marked the eastern boundary of the Empire.

It was here one morning, sitting in the shadow of a gateway, they saw two women walking out of the desert. As they passed under the arch, one said to the other, "So that is the end of Asarta. I never thought I should live to see her go. It will be a strange world without her."

The two from the Valley jumped up and caught the women by their cloaks and said, "Asarta? You have news of Asarta? We have journeyed from the furthest north to find her."

The women shook their heads and said, kindly enough, "You come too late. She is gone into the desert to undo her days. An hour after moonrise she will be no more."

"There is still time to find her," said the two from the Valley. "Which way did she go?"

"She went east," said the women. "But you will not find her, not unless she chooses to be found."

Reyel and Dirna filled their flasks from a reeking tank by the gate and set out east across the burning sands. There was no path and no shade. The water was too foul to drink, so they wetted themselves with it and trudged on. A time came when they knew in their hearts that if they did not turn back they would die in the desert, but they plodded on east, and as the sun went down and their shadows stretched far in front of them they came to a rocky hollow with a carved stone slab at its center. Sitting by the slab with her head bowed was an old woman in a gray cloak.

The two went quietly down and stood a few paces to one side, afraid to speak, knowing the place was holy. But the woman looked up and said in a mild voice, "You come on an errand. You have something to ask. Tell me your trouble."

They told her, and she nodded, and said, "You have brought me a fee?"

"We have nothing," they said. "We started our journey with friends and money and jewels, but we were cheated and robbed all the way, and now we have only the clothes we wear."

"Nothing?" said Asarta. "You are asking a great work to be done for nothing?"

"I have half of a stale barley loaf I begged in the city," said Dirna.

"There is a little water left in my flask," said Reyel.

"Give them to me," said Asarta.

They did so, and she moistened her lips from the flask and broke a corner from the loaf and ate it, and then handed them back.

"Very well," she said. "I cannot in any case do what you ask. I have put all that aside. But I can tell you what you must do. First, you must wait here and watch what happens until I am gone, and then you must journey to the city of Talak and find a man called Faheel and ask him to help you. He will demand a fee and you will give him this ring. Keep it safe, and do not attempt to wear it. I trust you with it, because you have shown that you have the will to carry a task through."

She took a gold ring from her finger and put it on the slab beside her. With a twist of her hand she broke off a corner of rock and blew on it and it became fine sand. This she rubbed out between her thumb and forefinger, spinning it into a braided cord which she threaded through the ring, rubbing the ends together so that they joined without a knot. She gave it to Dirna, who slid the cord over her head and tucked the ring down inside her blouse. The cord assumed the color of her skin, so that you would not have known it was there.

Asarta nodded to show that she had finished and sat as they had first seen her. The two climbed to the lip of the hollow and settled to watch. While they waited they ate some of the loaf and drank from the flask, and found that the bread was soft and fresh, and smelled as if it had just now come from the oven, while the water was as sweet and clean and cool as a snowmelt stream in the Valley.

The sky darkened and the stars came out. The moon rose, shining bright across the desert, but the hollow by which they sat was still in dense shade, from which now they heard the whisper of Asarta's voice, old and thin, like dead leaves trapped in a wind eddy. As the moon climbed and began to shine into the hollow the voice became stronger, harsher, like a queen's commanding her armies, or the chant of a priestess with the knife raised for the sacrifice. By the time it shone full down into the bowl there was a tall woman standing beside the carved slab, wearing the same gray robe that Asarta had worn, but with long dark hair flowing around it, so that it could hardly be seen. Her voice was a ringing chant that made the boulder on which they sat tingle and quiver, while flecks of light like crumbled star-stuff darted to and fro across the bowl. Then the stance eased and the voice softened and the chant became a song, while the flecks of light whirled closer around the young woman who stood by the slab so that she was lit by their light as well as by the moon's. The song ended, and she stood in silence, waiting.

Time also waited. The two from the Valley had watched, not understanding what they saw. But they remembered what the women by the gateway had said, and guessed that if they took any step down into the hollow they would be trapped in the backward eddy of the years, sucked into the vortex where Asarta sang. Now that the song was over the eddy stilled.

Asarta threw back her cloak and with her bare arms made a slow ritual gesture, as if offering an invisible vessel to the starlit sky. The shimmering flecks that had whirled around her gathered between her palms, making a shape like the drop that is left at the center of a ribbed leaf after a shower, lit with its own light, paler and brighter than the moon's.

She gazed at it for a while, unblinking. Then, continuing the interrupted movement of her arms, she raised it above her head and it floated away, widening and widening until it seemed to disperse itself into moonlight. Reyel and Dirna watched it disappear. When they looked down into the hollow Asarta was also gone.

The two from the Valley trudged back to the city and asked directions to Talak. It was a long and dangerous journey, but they made it without trouble apart from the ordinary weariness of endless walking. The barley loaf and the flask of water sustained them, not merely staying fresh but renewing themselves, so there seemed always as much of them left when they next needed them as there had been the time before. When armed bandits raided a resting place for travelers and stripped all who were there naked so that they could better search them, they seemed not to notice the two from the Valley where they sat quietly under the wall.

And again, when they came to Talak itself they found lines of travelers at the gateways, where guards questioned and searched each one, demanding monstrous fees before they let them pass. But when the two reached the front of their line the guard was interrupted with the news that his wife had just borne him a son, and in his delight he just waved the pair through.

But once inside the city their troubles began. Talak is very ancient, with the Emperor's palace at its heart, and broad streets leading to it from the twelve great gates. Between these open ways it is all twisting lanes and alleys. People who have lived in Talak all their lives can lose themselves in a strange quarter and take a day or more to find their way home. Furthermore the people of Talak are a suspicious, scurrying lot, and when the two from the Valley asked where they could find Faheel they were met with blank faces or shrugs or, sometimes, a quick, sharp stare, as if the question were dangerous, or mad.

So the two gave up asking and wandered this way and that, loster than they had seemed in the desert, but hoping they might hear a snatch of conversation in which Faheel's name was mentioned, which was how they had found Asarta. Again and again they crisscrossed the city, but however many of the radiating avenues they passed they seemed always each evening to fetch up, by accident, in the same dim street, with only a single door in it, and that bricked up, and no window below the second story. After a while they came to regard this as their temporary home. It was very quiet—indeed not once did they see another person using it—and the arch of the blocked doorway was a convenient place to sleep.

One morning, as they were breakfasting, a small yellow bird flew down to look for crumbs. The two were normally sparing with their water and bread, as if they must not take their magic for granted, but without thinking Dirna broke off a corner of crust and held it out and the bird flew fearlessly up and perched on her finger to peck. The man laughed, startling the bird, which flew off, brushing against the pillar of the archway as it passed. For a moment, brief as an eye blink, the brickwork wavered and was a door. Then it was brick again.

Reyel rose and found the place and laid his hand on it. The door appeared, but it had no handle or knocker.

A voice said, "Whom do you seek?"

"Faheel," they answered.

"What do you want of him?"

"Peace for our Valley."

"You have brought an appropriate fee?"

"Yes."

"Enter."

The door opened, and they went through into a dark, cool hallway. There was no one about. Several arches led toward other rooms, but as they stood wondering which to take, all but one seemed to mist over, so they could see only vaguely what lay beyond the rest. They went through the one clear arch into another such room, where the same thing happened, and the same again. But this third time they saw sunlight beyond the archway, and on reaching it they found themselves in a garden at the center of the house. Here were roses, and lilies, and flowers they had never seen, and also peach trees, apricots and nectarines, with their laden branches neatly tied into place. Clear water whispered through channels in the paving. Birds trilled. Rounding a corner, they found a man intent on his task of lashing a grafted slip into place on a pear tree. He seemed aware of their presence, but unhurriedly finished what he was doing before he turned.

He was a stout, smooth-faced man with a neat black beard. He wore a plain green turban and a brown jacket with pockets for his gardening tools. He raised his eyebrows, as if he had not expected to see them.

"We are looking for Faheel," they said.

"Well, the door knows its business," said the man. "I am Faheel."

"May we tell you our troubles?" they said. He nodded, so they told him about the wild horsemen from the north, and the Emperor's armies from the south, and how all the Valley longed to be rid of both and live in peace.

When they had finished, the man said, "This is a considerable thing you ask. Why should it be worth my while?"

Dirna lifted the cord from round her neck and handed him the ring. At his touch the cord crumbled into the sand that it had been. The ring seemed to move a little and change on his palm, but before they could see quite how, he closed his fingers round it.

"How did you come by this?" he said.

They told him what they had seen happen with Asarta, and what she had told them to do, and to prove that what they said was true they showed him the half of barley loaf that never grew stale or less, and the flask of water that never ran dry.

He listened, and looked for a while at his closed fist.

"I do not know what this means," he said. "For a hundred years I have sought ways to take this from her, and now she sends it to me. Very well. We will use her powers to do what you ask. Take the water and the bread with you and go home. Your house, I think, is close under the mountains. A stream runs past its door."

"That is so," said Reyel.

"Two full moons after the nights become longer than the days, climb to the place where the snow becomes water. Pour the last of your flask into the source of the stream, and as you do so, sing to the snows."

"What shall I sing?" said Reyel.

"Listen to the stream. It will tell you. And your farm, I think, lies next to the forest. A little way off is a small field with a stone barn at its corner."

"That is so," said Dirna.

"As soon as the field is plowed after harvest, take what is left of the loaf and crumble it finely along the furrows. Next spring let the field then be harrowed and sown with barley. Set the harvest aside in the barn. When the first snows fall, take two sacks of the barley and leave them in piles beside the lake nearest your farm in the forest. As you do so, sing to the cedar trees."

"What shall I sing?" said Dirna.

"The cedars themselves will tell you. Do the same each full

moon after, until the barley is finished and the snows are gone. And again next year, at the same seasons, both of you must sing, and Dirna must set the field aside for barley to leave by the lake in the forest. And so on, year after year. You, Reyel, will have sons, and you, Dirna, daughters, and one of each will hear the voices in the mountain stream, and in the cedars. They in their turn must sing the songs and grow the barley and take it into the forest, and one of their sons or daughters after them, for twenty generations. No power, not even Asarta's, can hold time still forever, but during those generations your Valley will have peace.

"And now, since you have asked for nothing for yourselves, take these." He chose two peaches, which he gave to them. They thanked him and left. They ate the fruit for their midday meal, wondering what would happen, but they felt no magical effects. So when they had finished, Reyel threw the stone of his away, thinking that it would never bear fruit as far north as he lived, but Dirna kept hers and planted it at Woodbourne when they returned home, which they did after many more days, but without danger or trouble.

They found the Valley in turmoil. There had been two more raids by the horsemen, in greater force, and though the men of the Valley had fought them off in the end, it had been at the cost of many lives. And then the four who had been on the search for Asarta had come home and told of their failure. In desperation, knowing that the horsemen would come again, and yet again, the people of the Valley had sent to the Emperor for help. So when Reyel and Dirna returned and told their story, nobody was greatly impressed.

Nevertheless the two did as they had been told. Two moons after the nights became longer than the days, Reyel climbed up by the stream that ran by his father's farm and poured the last of his flask into the place where the water dribbled from the snow line. As he did so he listened to the rustle of the infant stream as it tumbled over the boulders. Threaded through the sound he heard a song, one he seemed already to know in his heart, so he straightened and joined in the singing, full voice, and the wind carried the words away and the cliffs echoed them back to him. By the time he had finished, the wind itself had risen almost to a gale, and before he was safely home the first flakes of snow were whirling round him.

For five days the snow fell on the Valley. Never had there been such snows, with houses often buried to their eaves. Throughout a difficult winter it snowed again and again, so when at last the spring came, the little river that had always run from the mountains to the forest had grown to a wide torrent. Shepherds climbing to the upper pastures discovered why. If the snowfall in the Valley had been heavy, that in the mountains had been monstrous. Where the Emperor's road used to climb to the col there was now an immense glacier, from whose melting forefront the waters of the river thundered down.

Meanwhile Dirna had also done as she was told. When the plowing began at Woodbourne she had crumbled her barley loaf into fine pieces, filling a small sack, and with this she had walked along the furrows of the field beside the barn, broadcasting the crumbs like seed. She harrowed the ground and sowed it with the best barley seed she could buy, and waited for harvest.

Now men came through the forest, officials of the Emperor, to choose billets for the soldiers he would send to protect the Valley from the horsemen. While they were at it they taxed the people severely, since no taxes had been raised for many years. When people told them about the glacier, and explained that because of it they needed no protection this year, the officials laughed and started to raise further taxes, on the pretext that since the people were now spared the cost of billeting troops they could afford to pay more. This second round of exactions was savage, with torture for those who could not or would not pay, and children taken to be sold into slavery in lieu of money. But the people of the Valley were now used to their independence. They rose and fought the officials' guards and hanged the officials and threw their bodies in the river.

When the news of this came to far-off Talak it threw the Emperor into a rage. He gave orders for an army to be sent to punish the Valley, every house burnt and razed, every man killed, every woman and child enslaved. But by now it was almost winter in those northern hills, so it was decided to hold back the punishment until spring.

Dirna reaped a good crop of barley from the field, better than anything else on the farm, and stored it separately in the stone barn. When the first snows fell she loaded two sacks of the seed onto a sledge, harnessed a pony to it, and hauled it out to a long, narrow lake, deep in the forest. Here she doled the barley out into piles beneath the branches of the cedar trees that grew all around the lake. As she did so she found that she was already singing. Words and notes, soft and lulling, seemed to reach her, not through her ears, but from somewhere beneath the soft whisper of the wind among the cedars. When she had finished she looked around, but saw and felt no change, so she led her pony home.

A short time after this Dirna's brother went into the forest one morning to set traps, and did not return for his midday meal. Worried, she followed his footprints in the snow and found him only a few hundred paces in, lying facedown and breathing harshly through his mouth. Unable to wake him, she fetched the pony and dragged him home, where she warmed his body and put him to bed, but it was three more days before he opened his eyes, and then he could remember nothing since leaving the farm.

Much the same happened to other men who went into the forest, to hunt or trap or gather firewood. If they turned back soon enough they merely staggered and felt stupid and sick, but if they went too far they fell down and lost consciousness, and unless they were found within a morning or so they died. Women, strangely, felt no such effects, so before the winter was over it was they who were doing the hunting and trapping and wood gathering, while the men stayed home to tend the animals.

At each full moon throughout that winter Dirna took fresh

barley out to the lake, but thanks to the continuing snowfalls she could not tell whether the earlier piles had been eaten, or see the tracks of what might have taken it. When the snows finally melted the barn was empty.

By then, everyone was afraid because of what they had done to the Emperor's officials. They looked for hiding places in the mountains for the men, and they got ready to send the women and girls into the forest, because the sickness there might prevent the soldiers from following them, though they did not truly believe that either of these measures would prevail against the might of the Emperor.

They were wrong. In early summer horses began to come up the road through the forest, in harness, but mostly riderless. In a few cases armored men sprawled in the saddles because they had been lashed there, but all but one of these were dead. This one man was unconscious, and his horse was lathered with hard riding. When he woke some days later, he could remember nothing of his ride, but he told that the army had indeed marched north in the spring to punish the Valley and the advance scouts had discovered the sickness, some dying, some turning back in time. Magicians were sent for, who tried their different powers against the enchantment, for all agreed that the sickness was indeed of magical origin. The wiser ones withdrew almost at once. Those who persisted lost what powers they had had, and some went mad.

Finally, some of the cavalry had tied themselves into their saddles and set their horses to a full gallop, hoping to pass clean through the forest before they were overcome. This man had been one of those. His horse was a headstrong mare, and, he swore, the swiftest horse in the army. He alone had come through, though he had been unconscious for much of the way. Since there was no way back he stayed in the Valley, but unlike the deserter Sonnam he did not prosper or marry, and died in a brawl that he had provoked.

This, then, is the story that is told in the Valley. Or rather it is

33

the version of it that has been passed down in Dirna's family, the Urlasdaughters, who still farm the same land at Woodbourne that Dirna and her brother farmed. Though different versions of the story are told elsewhere in the Valley, with different names for some of the people involved, and different adventures—the tellers feeling free to add or alter as they choose—what does it matter, since it is only a story?—the Urlasdaughters do not change theirs at all, and do not talk about theirs outside the family, because to them it is true, and they don't care to be mocked for their beliefs, and their insistence, year upon year, on setting one small field aside to be sown with barley, which is then harvested and stored in a particular barn, and in winter carried deep into the forest and left for the wild animals to eat.

The Ortahlsons, up in the mountains, still sing to the snows year after year, and take much the same line, keeping their version of the story to themselves. For everyone else, yes, of course there is a strange sickness in the forest, affecting only men, but there is presumably a natural explanation for that. And yes, there is a glacier in the mountains, where there used to be a road, but all that shows is that winters were once milder than they now are. Is that anything to be surprised about? And besides, the story didn't say anything about the great desert that closed the Valley off to the east, just as it always had done, since long before the time of Asarta. (Though perhaps, if the story had all been lies, somebody might have invented a reason for that.)

One other thing. When the Valley had settled into peace again, Dirna planted the stone of the peach that Faheel had given her. A tree grew, and stood for many years against the south wall of a barn at Woodbourne. There seemed to be nothing magical about it, but it thrived despite the climate and bore delicious peaches, so that other families begged grafts, which grew well. When, eight generations after Dirna's time, the barn blew down in a gale, taking the tree with it, the timber of the trunk was seasoned and used for carving small objects, particularly the elaborate wooden spoons which the men liked to whittle on winter evenings, while the women were at their spinning wheels. A tradition grew up that spoons from the original tree could be used for fortune-telling, by studying the grain of the wood, with its innumerable knots and whorls from all those years of training and pruning. The best of these spoons became heirlooms, with their own names, like the swords of heroes, but that didn't mean that anyone actually believed in the fortunes they told, any more than they believed in the story about Asarta.

3

The Gathering

ilja slept almost till noon. She must have fallen asleep at the table and been carried to bed by Da. Now she stirred, feeling strange and lost until the memories of yesterday came flooding back.

"Someone's deigning to move at last, then?" snarled Meena's voice from the far side of the stove.

Tilja heaved herself up. She seemed to be still in her underclothes.

"Where's Ma?" she whispered. "Is she all right?"

"I don't know about all right. She's here and warm and breathing, that's all I can say."

Tilja scrambled up and staggered round past the stove. Ma was lying on her back with her mouth slightly open and her eyes closed. Even in the dim light Tilja could see that her face was not quite ashen; and there was warmth in her hand, but her fingers didn't move to return Tilja's grasp. Meena was sitting with her back to the wall between the bed and the stove.

"And I don't know what that mark on her is, neither," she said. "Only I've never seen anything like it."

Tilja peered. The dark round patch on Ma's forehead was about as large as her thumbnail, and seen close was nothing like a bruise, sharp edged and all the same blue-purple shade, without scar or swelling. It didn't look like a hurt or wound, but more like part of one of the patterns with which the apple pickers painted their faces for the cider feast each fall.

"Do you think . . . ?"

"Not if I can help it," snapped Meena. "You can hope if you want to. I don't know that hoping ever did much harm."

Tilja looked at her and realized that after yesterday her feelings about her grandmother had changed. Though Meena sounded as cross as ever—crosser—really she was worried sick about her daughter but she wasn't going to admit it to anyone, so she covered up by snarling. Now she was glaring at Tilja, her pale blue eyes glinting with seeming rage. Tilja smiled back.

"Glad somebody's got something to laugh about," said Meena. "What's so funny, then?"

"You, Meena," said Tilja. "You were wonderful yesterday. That must all have hurt horribly, but you never said anything."

"No point, was there? I don't mind bearing provided nobody asks me to grin. And while we're throwing posies around I may as well tell you you didn't do so badly yourself."

"Is your hip sore today?"

"Been better. Tickled it up a bit with all that banging around. But I'll do."

"Meena, that thing that bellowed at us when we were coming away from the lake—do you think . . . ?"

"No I don't. I've told you already. And that's enough of that."

This time Meena's snarl was genuine. Her glare was stony. With a gulp Tilja changed the subject.

"Where's Da? And Anja?"

"Feeding the beasts. They'll be starving by the time they've done, so you get a move on and get yourself washed and all, and then you can finish seeing to their dinner. After that you can run down to my place and get the cat fed, or I'll never hear the last of it from him. I'll be staying on here awhile, till I've some idea how your mother's doing."

Ma didn't stir for the next five days. The only change in her that they could see was that the mark on her forehead faded from its dark blue-purple to a deep red and then a fiery orange and a softer yellow, until on the sixth morning it was almost gone.

Meanwhile Tilja had her hands and mind full with helping on the farm, doing all the endless things that Ma usually dealt with, while Anja did her best to take over some of Tilja's tasks, and did them very well, provided someone kept telling her she was doing them marvelously. Tilja was glad to be kept too busy to brood. She didn't want to think about the adventure in the forest, or to puzzle about the "little wretches" that Meena had seen by the lake, or the invisible great creature that had bellowed its challenge at them as they were leaving. The whole episode had been terrifying, but now it was over, that momentary fear was replaced by another, far deeper and more enduring. What had happened in the forest had been something new, something that had never happened before. To Tilja it seemed a sign that her world was changing, a sign, perhaps, that everything she loved—Ma, Da and Anja, Brando and the animals, Woodbourne, the whole Valley—was somehow going to be taken from her.

Tilja was by Ma's bed, feeding the stove, when Ma woke. Tilja heard the rustle of bedclothes and looked up. Ma's eyes were open and she had raised an arm and with her fingertips was caressing the place on her forehead where the mark had been.

"It touched me with its horn," she murmured.

Her eyes closed, her arm fell away, and she was asleep again. When she finally woke that evening she couldn't remember even that. She could recall riding Tiddykin out through the forest in the dawn light, reaching the lake, heaving the barley sacks out of the panniers and spilling the seed in heaps beneath the cedar branches at the top of the meadow, where the snow wouldn't at once bury it. Then she was walking back down to the shore of the lake to start her singing. After that, nothing.

It was a long while before she had her strength back, but in a few days she was up and doing what she could around the farm. It was hard to say whether she was more silent than before, because unlike her mother and daughters she had never been much of a talker, but silent she certainly was, and sometimes Tilja would find her halfway through some task, standing stock-still, with a blank, lost look on her face. At the interruption she would sigh and shake herself and go on with what she'd been doing.

But it was all clearly an effort for her, and Tilja and Anja had to do as much as they could to make up. One day they were up in the forest inspecting and resetting traps, and collecting firewood, when Tilja needed the hand ax and found it was gone, though she was certain that last time she'd used it she'd slotted it back into its notch on the logging sled just as carefully as Ma would have done.

This was a disaster. Metal was scarce in the Valley. For small coins they used counters made from the hard, dark wood of a tree that grew only in one narrow glen in the foothills. Mostly they traded by barter and cooked in clay pots. In the old days iron had been brought in from the Empire, but when the Valley was closed off they could only use and reforge and use again the things they already had, hoarding every scrap. Iron still became increasingly scarce, and now was used almost solely for working tools. Even a small hand ax would be hard to replace.

Tilja tethered Calico to a tree and they started to work back along the way they'd come, scuffling the fallen leaves aside with their feet, but there were long stretches where the sled had left no traces on the leaf litter, and soon Tilja couldn't be sure they were still on their track. She was already miserable and furious with herself when Anja caught her arm. Tilja shook her off.

"No, please," said Anja. "Stop. I want to listen."

With an angry sigh Tilja stood and stared around. No, this was wrong. They hadn't come past this cedar. It must be over there. . . .

"This way," said Anja, and scampered off between the trees. It was the direction Tilja had decided on anyway, so she followed more slowly, scanning the ground for runner marks. Anja had stopped and was standing by another cedar with her head tilted to one side, listening. Before Tilja came up with her she was off again.

And there were the sled marks! Tilja followed them slowly, searching beside the left-hand runner, where the ax notch was. There would need to have been a stump or a root or something to jolt the ax loose. . . . She almost bumped into Anja hurrying to meet her with the ax in her hand. Her whole body flooded with relief.

"It had hooked itself onto a holly branch," said Anja. "The cedars told me."

"That was nice of them," said Tilja, humoring her. Then her heart seemed to stand still. She remembered her visit to the lake last summer. And something Anja had said that day when Ma hadn't come back from singing to the cedars . . .

"Anja," she asked. "Do you know where the lake is?"

"Oh yes. It's over there. But it's too far to go before dinner. Do you want to?"

Anja, who could barely be trusted to find her way down to Meena's cottage, let alone know how long it would take to get there . . .

"How do you know?"

"I just know. It's in my head. It's always been. What's the matter?"

"Nothing. Only you can hear what the cedars say. I can't. And you know the way to the lake. Not me. And one day it'll be you singing to the cedars, like Ma does. Not me. And Woodbourne will be your farm. Not mine."

Anja was staring at her. Of course she'd known she could do those things, but she hadn't known what it meant, hadn't understood. She was too young.

"But you're eldest," she said.

"Aunt Grayne's older than Ma," said Tilja. "I'd never thought about it. Well, at least at first snowfall I'll be able to lie snug in my bed and think of you having to get up and trudge out into the forest and sing to the cedars."

She did her best to smile. Anja didn't try.

"It isn't going to be like that," she said. "Not anymore."

"What do you mean?"

"Singing to the cedars. Something's happening. The cedars keep talking about it, only . . . oh, Til, I'm not allowed . . ."

Anja burst into tears, and wouldn't be comforted. All Tilja could make out was that the cedars had told her something and said she mustn't tell anyone else except Ma.

Next morning, when they were out in the freezing scullery washing themselves before getting dressed, Anja said, "It doesn't mean anything, Til. I won't let it. This is your home too."

"No it isn't!" Tilja snarled. "Not anymore! Don't talk about it!"

She knew it was unfair. Anja was doing her best, and it wasn't her fault, but Tilja couldn't help it, and when Anja started to cry she just stood there, scowling.

Then Ma came in to see what the trouble was, and though Tilja, in her hurt and pride, had made Anja promise to say nothing about what had happened in the wood, she blurted it out. Ma knelt between them, hugging one in each arm, trying to comfort them both, but stiffly and awkwardly, because she wasn't good at this sort of thing. Almost at once Tilja wrenched herself away and shoved her clothes on and went out on an empty stomach to look for a horse to groom. She chose Calico, because she was sure to be in just as bad a mood as Tilja herself, and Tilja could curse and slap her much more satisfactorily than she could have done sweet and amenable Tiddykin.

Still no true snow fell, and despite the incessant gales it was far warmer than it should have been. All winters in the Valley, since anyone could remember and long before, had begun with two weeks of steady, settling snow, followed by almost three months of clear skies and hard frosts, with just a day and a night of more snow now and again. This winter the ponds barely froze, but there was day after day of lashing rain and sleet, and if you saw the sun once a week for half a morning or so you thought you were lucky, and all the lanes were mire, and the animals stood hock deep in the paddocks and got mud fever and worse—a miserable time.

Meena had gone back to her cottage and Tilja plodded down to visit her most days, which she'd never willingly done before. She didn't expect any kind of welcome, and didn't get one, but she knew Meena was glad to see her, and if for some reason Tilja missed a visit she sulked like a child at the next.

Tilja told herself she went because she'd become fond of Meena, but there was another reason she didn't want to think about. While she was at the farm, everything that she saw or felt or heard or smelled reminded her again that it would never be hers. It would be Anja's, and she, Tilja, would have to leave it. Go away and live somewhere else, like Aunt Grayne.

Of course her parents knew how unhappy she was, and did what they could. Ma didn't try hugging her again, but made a point of doing household chores with her instead of sending her off on her own, and Da would sometimes take her with him when there was a job she could help with, and even let her manage Dusty once or twice. But neither of them tried to talk to her about what had happened. It wasn't their way. They weren't talkers.

Meena was different. Tilja got no sympathy from Meena, who only said, "Well, you'll have to make a life of your own like most people do. No point moping about it. Sooner you get used to the idea, the better you'll be."

Despite that, Tilja felt that Meena understood how she was feeling better than any of the others.

———

One afternoon late in the year, when Tilja was wrapping up to plod back to the farm, Meena said, "And by the by, you can tell that father of yours we'll need one of the horses to take us to the winter Gathering. And not that rackety brute, Calico, tell him."

Tilja was startled. One of her parents went to the midsummer Gathering most years, to trade and gossip, and last year Da had taken both her and Anja with him. But no one had been to the winter Gathering since she could remember, and there'd been no question of Meena going even to the midsummer one because of her hip.

"I'll ask him, if you like," said Tilja.

"You'll do no such thing. You'll tell him. From me."

Tilja grinned at her and got a scowl back, but that evening at supper she said, "Meena wants me to go with her to the Gathering."

"Me too," said Anja.

Da frowned, and was starting to shake his head when Ma said, with sudden, unusual firmness, "Yes, they must go. They'll need a horse."

"Not Calico," said Tilja quickly.

"I can spare Tiddykin for a day or two," said Ma. "She's not up to carrying the pair of you, so—"

"Three of us," interrupted Anja, perfectly aware there wasn't any question of her going, but characteristically not missing the chance of a bit of spoiling and petting to make up for it. This time, though, she'd misjudged the mood.

"Anja, be quiet," said Ma. "You'll have to walk the whole way, Tilja, but you won't get there and back in a day, this time of year, anyway, so you can stay with Grayne, and you won't get too tired. All right, my dear?"

Tilja glanced anxiously at Da. She'd scarcely ever heard Ma take charge like this before—that was his job. He didn't look surprised or put out, though, but simply nodded and that was that.

Aunt Grayne looked like a plumper, jollier version of Ma. She had married a farmer's son whose family owned a rich bit of land by the river. His father had died when Tilja was a baby, and he was the farmer now. Their house was larger and newer than Woodbourne, with glass in the kitchen windows, but they didn't give themselves airs.

Despite what Ma had said, it had seemed a weary distance to walk, all the way from Woodbourne, and by the time Tilja led Tiddykin into the yard she was far too tired to pay much attention to what was going on, and fell asleep almost as soon as she'd finished her supper. But next morning, when they were alone in the kitchen, Grayne said, "Tilja, I'm truly sorry for you. I know what it's like. It happened to me, too, you know, having a little sister who could hear the cedars, when I couldn't."

"Oh, Aunt Grayne, why didn't they tell me long, long ago?"

"Because you don't start hearing the cedars the moment you're born, or even as soon as you can talk. You sort of grow into it. I wouldn't know, of course, but that's what your mother says. It wasn't too late for you last summer, even. . . ."

"That's why Ma took me to the lake!"

"Yes, but then, when she realized Anja was starting to listen to the cedars . . . As I say, I'm sorry, Tilja. I know how it feels."

"You really minded?"

"I don't think I stopped crying for a month. There were times when I felt I could have killed Selly."

Yes, thought Tilja. Aunt Grayne had known how it felt.

"But you're happy now?" she said.

"Yes, of course. Very. I often dream about Woodbourne, but . . ."

"But you don't come there. That's why we always have to visit you."

"Yes, I decided if I had to stop loving it . . . I don't know how I can help you, my dear. The best I can tell you is that you're going to have to make a life of your own, and that's good. If you'd been able

44

to hear the cedars you'd have had no choice. You would have be-longed to Woodbourne all your life—just as much as Woodbourne would have belonged to you—more, perhaps. You'd have had to marry somebody and have children, so that there'd be a daughter who could hear the cedars and belong to Woodbourne when her time came. Your grandmother . . . no, that's her story, if you can ever get her to tell you. She's very fond of you, by the way."

Tilja was still trying to think of an answer when they heard Meena's hoarse shout from the parlor, and she hurried off to help her into her boots.

They hadn't far to go now, but by the time they were on their way the road was crowded. For the last few days there'd been a sharp, gusting wind with a few thin snow flurries, but at least there'd been frost enough to harden the road surface, or the throng would have turned it to a quagmire. This was not at all like the midsummer crowd, when everybody, even those with stock to drive, wore their brightest clothes, so they could be seen for miles across the fields like strings of colored beads moving steadily along. And they sang then, and as their paths gathered to the center hallooed to each other, so that the spirit of summer festival seemed to have overflowed the Bowl of Gathering and spread across the Valley.

But now everyone was in winter clothes, browns and grays, like the bare landscape, and the first thing they spoke of when they met was the weather. This was not a normal subject of con-versation, as it is in some countries. What was the point, when the weather was just what you'd expect? You said, "Nice day," or "Cold enough for you?" and went on to something else. But not this year, though all the conversations were pretty much the same, and came to the same conclusion—no one liked it.

The Gathering was held at a place where long ago the river had changed its course and a bend had silted up, leaving a natural bowl, open at one end, with the river running past. The con-venors had, by custom, seen to it that good log fires were burning, round which people could settle and talk. The main trade was in the autumn's pickles and wines and preserves and cheeses, and smoked or salted meat and fish, and also in what families had been making to pass the winter evenings, carved knickknacks and fortune spoons and small furniture, rugs and hangings and winter cloaks and so on.

Tilja settled Meena down with Aunt Grayne by one of the fires, tethered Tiddykin at a horse rail and gave her a nose bag, and started to wander round the stalls looking for a small present for Anja, to make up for her not having been with them. The river end of the arena was already crowded. She overheard at least two people saying that there were far more here than they'd have expected at a winter Gathering.

Then a drum started to beat, a heavy, throbbing note. Tilja knew what it meant, because she'd heard it before at the midsummer Gathering she'd been to. Though people came mainly for the gossip and the stalls, the real purpose of these meetings was to allow matters affecting the whole Valley to be discussed and decided. If someone managed to persuade the convenors that the subject was worth it, they would order the drum to be beaten, and those who were interested enough would gather at the inner end of the bowl and listen, and if they wanted, speak, and finally vote with a show of hands. Most people didn't bother, but at midsummer Tilja had gone along out of curiosity. It had been pretty boring, something to do with preventing sheep scab spreading from farm to farm.

This time, though, almost everyone stopped talking as the slow, menacing thud filled the bowl. At least half the crowd left what they were doing and began to move toward the sound. Tilja went to look for Meena, but met her already hobbling along. Aunt Grayne wasn't with her, but a young woman had taken pity on her and was helping her (and getting no thanks for it, of course). Tilja took over, and they made their way along amid the mass of people until their way was blocked by the throng.

"This is no good," said Meena, and began to barge a path

sideways until she reached the slope that surrounded the bowl. There were a lot of people already standing there for a better view, but muttering and groaning, she forced her way up between them with Tilja trailing behind and smiling with nervous apology at anyone Meena had shoved aside. They stopped at last, and turned, and Tilja found herself looking out over the heads of the crowd to the slope opposite. To her left were the fires and the stalls, with the river beyond them, and to her right the smooth curve of the hill that closed the bowl off. A section of it had been cut away to make a small platform where several people were standing, the drummer with his tall drum, the three convenors with their yellow scarves of office, and an old man leaning on a staff, with a slight, dark boy about Tilja's age beside him. Despite the age difference, the old man and the boy were strikingly alike, with narrow, hooked noses and pointed chins.

"This'll do," said Meena. "Move over a bit, will you? I've got to rest this leg of mine."

Without waiting for an answer she nudged the man beside her off the hummock he was standing on and groaningly lowered herself onto it. She was making far more fuss about her aches and pains than she ever did at home, but when Tilja started to sympathize she was answered with a special blank stare that told her Meena's hip was no worse than on most days. She was just using it to get what she wanted, and why not?

The drumbeat ended with a long roll. The crowd hushed. The convenors stood aside and the old man moved forward, feeling his way with his staff and gripping the boy's shoulder with his other hand. The boy stopped him at the edge of the platform and he leaned on his staff for a while, as if studying his audience, though Tilja guessed he must be almost blind. His body looked slight but not frail under his dark brown cloak, and strong white hair bushed out beneath his fur cap. Judging the moment when the crowd's attention was about to break, he drew himself up and spoke.

"I am Alnor Ortahlson, from Northbeck, under the mountains.

47

It is my task to sing to the snows each year, as my father did, and each one's father before him, since the time of Reyel Ortahlson, who began it. I do so still, despite my age and blindness, because my son is dead, and his son is not yet old enough."

His voice seemed not much louder than a speaking voice, but it was slow and firm, and carried clearly through the come-and-go wind.

"You all know Reyel's story," he went on, "though some of you do not believe it, and most of you are not aware that a man of our family still sings to the snows each year. I cannot make you believe. All I can tell you is that my own father never told me what song to sing, but when my turn came I climbed to the face of the glacier and there the song came to me and told me how I should sing it. Then I went back down to my millhouse, and by the time I was at the door the snows were falling, as they had done for my father and all our fathers before him.

"This is the forty-seventh year in which I have climbed to the glacier and sung. Not the same music always, nor the same words, but still the same song. Each of those years the snows heard me, and fell.

"But not this year. This year no song came to me. I sang what I could from memory, but the snows did not hear me. I knew as my grandson led me down the mountain that the true snows would not fall.

"They did not fall. Which of you has seen true snows these last miserable months? Without them, the glacier will begin to melt, and then what will stand between us and the horsemen of the northern plains?

"Yes, that is all I have to tell you. And yes, the convenors were uncertain whether it was cause enough to have the drum beaten, but I persuaded them. How can snow hear, or not hear, you will ask. If a family take it into their heads to go out and sing to the sun each night, before dawn, does that mean they have caused the sun to rise? Of course not.

"In return I have two questions to ask you. Why are you all here? Why so many, and from so far, at this ill season? What persuaded you to come? Was it a dream, a voice in your head, some vaguer feeling? If so, is it possible that that dream, that voice, that feeling was, without your knowing it, the same thing that I felt when I knew in my heart that the snows did not hear me?

"My second question is this. Is there a woman here from Woodbourne, in the south, a woman of the lineage of Dirna Urlasdaughter?"

"Yes, of course I'm here!" snapped Meena from the ground. "Help me up, some of you. Look sharp! Don't hang about!"

The man she had shoved off the hummock lifted her to her feet and stood her on it, and the people just below her cleared to either side so that everyone could see her. Her head went back and her chin stuck out, as if she were facing down an assembly of unjust accusers.

"Well, here I am," she snapped. "Take a good look at me. I'm Meena Urlasdaughter from Woodbourne, and I'm here to tell you the old gaffer's right. Something's up, and he knows it, and I know it, and if you've got any sense in your heads you know it, and that's why you're here, like he told you.

"I'll tell you how I know it. First snows, one of our women goes into the forest and leaves a couple of sacks of barley under the cedars by the lake, and sings to the cedars. Dirna started it, because Faheel told her, like he told Reyel to sing to the snows, and we've done it ever since. It's what keeps the forest like it is, with the sickness in it, so that men can't go in there, and the Emperor can't get at us like he used to, any more than the horsemen can get past the glacier at us to come murdering and looting. At least you know about the sickness. None of you men who live along by the forest will go in there, not for more than a minute or two, like my fool of a son-in-law tried the day I'm going to tell you about. Went in to look for my daughter Selva who'd gone to sing to the cedars, and came out all dizzy and sick, and stupider

49

than he is by nature. But not so stupid he didn't send for me, which he should have done in the first place, and me and Tilja here had to go in and get my daughter out.

"Wait. There's more to it than that. We found my daughter lying by the lake, unconscious, and we couldn't wake her, so we brought her home on the sled, and she didn't stir for six whole days, and then she couldn't remember anything of what had happened to her, nor why she had this mark on her forehead I've never seen the like of. Since Dirna's day we've sung to the cedars, I tell you, and nothing like this has happened in all those years, only now it has, the selfsame year, what's more, as the old gaffer went up to sing to the snows and they didn't hear him, and we've got this weather no one's ever known to happen before.

"I tell you something's wrong with the forest, just like something's wrong with the mountains, and if we don't do something about it the sickness will be gone, and next thing the Emperor will be sending his tax collectors up here, with his armies to back them up, and they won't just be after this year's taxes either. It'll be all the taxes we've not being paying these last twenty generations! And if you think what we've been talking about, Alnor and me, is all just chance-come things, might have happened any of these years, only now they've all come together, then you're bigger fools than I took you for."

She stopped abruptly, and the man helped her down onto the hummock. The drummer beat a short roll and a number of people put up their hands to speak. The convenors took them in turn. Most of them simply wanted to confirm that they'd had a dream, or some odd feeling telling them to come. One woman said she hadn't meant to until the last minute, but her old dog had tugged at her cloak and pretty well led her to the Gathering. Then a burly man on the slope opposite Tilja said, "This is all very well, and something strange may be happening, if you want to believe in that sort of thing. For myself, I don't, but supposing I did, what then? What are we supposed to do about it? Try if anyone else has better luck, singing to the snows and the trees?

Bit late for that, this year, anyway. We're half through winter already, and the time for the main snowfall is come and gone two months back, so how are we going to tell if something's worked, or it hasn't? That's till next winter, anyway.

"So what I say is, let's see how it all goes for a few months, and what sort of a spring we get, and so on, and maybe talk about it again here midsummer, if anyone's still bothered. And then maybe next fall, after Alnor's gone and done his stuff in the mountains and Meena's daughter's done hers in the forest, we'll get our snowfall like we always have, and we'll know this year was just some kind of freak. Or maybe we won't, and that'll be the time to get our heads together and sort out what to do about it."

There was a buzz of agreement.

"Told you so," growled Meena, though she had done no such thing. "Wait and see, wait and see—only idea in their thick heads. Dolts! This time they're going to wait, and see they're too late."

"What do you think we should be doing then, ma'am?" asked the man who'd helped her.

"Go and look . . . ," she began, but somebody else was already speaking and she was shushed into silence. There was a rule that nobody could speak twice, so she didn't get a chance to tell the assembly what she thought before the convenors closed the discussion. Since nobody had had any other suggestions than wait and see, that was put to the vote and carried on a show of hands. The drum beat three times to signal that it was over.

Meena grabbed Tilja by the arm and dragged herself up.

"All right," she said, "if that's how they want it. Go and find the blind gaffer—Alnor or something. I've got to talk to him."

Tilja hurried off, worming her way as best she could through the crowd as they drifted back toward the fires and the stalls. Halfway to the platform she was almost knocked off her feet by someone weaseling through in the other direction. He muttered an apology without looking, but she managed to grab his arm. It was the boy who'd been with old Alnor.

"Hey! I'm in a hurry," he said. "Leave off, will you?"

"My grandmother—she's Meena—wants to talk to Alnor," she said.

"That makes two of them," he said. "And the old boy's raging. Can you get her across to the platform?"

"When it's a bit clearer. Just don't let him go away, or I'm in trouble."

"Uh-huh—she looks a right handful."

"No, she's all right. She's great."

"If you say so. See you in a bit."

And he was gone, leaving Tilja instantly furious. What right had he? And then not giving her a chance to show what she thought of him? Seething, she made her way back to Meena and found her on her hummock. Most of the others had gone and there was room to move.

"Didn't take you long," said Meena.

"I ran into the boy," said Tilja. "Alnor wants to talk to you, too. He's at the platform."

"All right, then. Let's be going."

With Tilja's help she picked her way down the slope and hobbled over to the platform. They found Alnor just in front of it, leaning on his staff with his blind eyes seeming to stare in fury at the retreating crowd. Everything about him, even his stillness, expressed his anger. He seemed unaware of their coming, and Meena stood and studied him in silence for a little. The boy, Tilja was glad to see, had disappeared.

"So you're Alnor Ortahlson," said Meena abruptly. "I've heard of you. It was your son died rafting, right?"

Slowly Alnor turned toward her.

"That was my son," he said harshly.

"Hard on you, but that's how it goes," said Meena. "Well, I'm Meena Urlasdaughter, and we've one or two things to talk about. Might be warmer by the fires, but there'll be too much chat."

"I have asked my grandson to fetch us two horns of hot cider."

"Just what I fancy. Run along, Tilja, and give the lad a hand.

He'll be spilling it all over the ground if I know boys. Get a couple of mugs out of the saddlebag if you want some for you two."

Tilja didn't want anything to do with the boy, but reluctantly she hurried off, fetched the mugs, and found him at one of the cider stalls. He'd just been served, and sure enough was trying to find a way of carrying two large horns, brimfull of steaming cider, without disaster through the crowd. She took one of the horns and they tipped some of the cider into each of the mugs and carried them all back. They found their two grandparents sitting on a sort of turf bench, with their backs against the timbers that shored up the platform.

"Just what the wise woman ordered," said Meena. "That should put a morsel of warmth into old bones. Now we've got to talk, so you two can make yourselves scarce for a bit. No, first you can bring me my dinner, Tilja, and that rug. Off you go."

Cross with the whole world by now, Tilja moved off to do as she was told, sipping the heady, sweet drink as she went. The boy strolled nonchalantly beside her, seeming to take it for granted that that was what she wanted.

"I'm Tahl," he said. "Ortahl for long, but that's confusing in our family. Who are you?"

"Tilja," she said. She managed to make the syllables sound as chilly as the day.

"Tilja Urlasdaughter, of Woodbourne under the forest," he said, making it sound like some grand title from a story about old heroes. "Go in there much?"

"A bit."

"So what's in there? Apart from trees. Cedars, your grandmother said. And that lake. And squirrels and birds and whatever. What else?"

Tilja paused in her stride. It was as if her body had wanted to halt and confront him, but she'd managed to force it to walk on. She did so in silence, not looking at him. More than anything that had happened since Anja had found the hand ax, this was what had been eating into her heart. Meena knew the answer to

Tahl's question, and Ma, and even Anja. She wasn't sure if Da knew. But she, Tilja, didn't. It made her feel as if she didn't really belong in her own family, didn't belong at Woodbourne, not now, not ever.

"You aren't going to tell me, are you?" he said as they reached the horse lines. "I don't see why not. Sure, you don't talk about it outside the family. We don't, either, about . . . about what we've got. But this is different. We're Ortahlsons and you're Urlas-daughters. We aren't like anyone else. We can tell each other, can't we?"

Tilja was standing beside Tiddykin, unbuckling the strap that held the rolled rug in place behind the saddle. She stopped and stared at the hornbeam buckle, polished with wear, as if it could tell her what to do. There'd been something in Tahl's voice, still the same teasing, unsettling tone at the surface, but underneath a kind of pleading, just as unsettling.

"All right," she said bitterly. "I'll tell you. The answer is, I don't know. I haven't been told. Because I can't hear what the cedars say. I don't know the way to the lake. My little sister, Anja, does. You'll have to ask her."

She glanced at him. He was staring at her. She couldn't bear it and turned away before she started to weep.

"That's rough," he said in a totally different voice, sensible, gentle, as if he meant every word. "That's really rough. It isn't fair."

She unbuckled the rug and got the dinner bag out of the saddlebag through a blur of tears, and they set off in silence for the far end of the arena. When they were about halfway there he said, "Look, we aren't allowed to talk about it, either, but I've thought of a way. They won't want us with them yet, so I'll just get Alnor his dinner and then we'll go over there on the slope where they can see us if they want us, and while we're eating . . . right?"

They settled on the hummock where Meena had sat for the meeting and shared their food between them. Tahl had some little pink fish, pickled in sweet vinegar with herbs, which Tilja had never eaten before and thought delicious. Below them a group of men were setting out a ring for the kick-fighting contest. This was a popular sport in the Valley, and the best fighters were heroes in their villages.

"First," he said, "you'd better tell me your story about Asarta and Reyel and Dirna. It sounds as if it's different."

She did so, between mouthfuls. It took a while. Some of the time Tahl seemed to be more interested in the kick-fighting, but she plowed on. Now and then she glanced across at the platform to check if Meena wanted her, but the two old people were still deep in talk, sitting side by side on the turf bench, sharing Meena's rug. At the river end of the bowl the far-dwellers were beginning to start on their way home.

"That's really interesting," said Tahl when she finished. His eyes were sparkling with excitement.

"I thought you weren't listening."

"I don't listen with my eyes, you know. But fighting's in our blood. Alnor was Valley Champion four years running."

"Can you do it?"

"My da died before I was old enough to start, and Alnor's blind, so there's no one to teach me."

He tried to speak lightly, but Tilja could hear how much he minded.

"I'm sorry," she said.

"I'll find someone. . . . But listen —I think I know what you've got in the forest—stuff in your story that isn't in ours. It's just a guess, but I'm pretty sure. Do you want me to tell you?"

"If you're allowed to," Tilja said sourly.

"All right, we'll play a game. I'm going to ask you questions, and you're going to guess the answers, only I'm not going to tell you if you're right or wrong. You're going to guess that, too. Try it that way?"

The mocking note was back in his voice, but Tilja heard it differently now. It wasn't her he was mocking, or anyone in particular. It was more like a screen, or a mask, behind which he could keep the real Tahl hidden. She'd had a glimpse of that Tahl just now, the glee of guessing the answer to the riddle, the sorrow of never being taught to kick-fight. She nodded.

"First question," he said. "Why isn't there any real magic in the Valley? There used to be, when it was part of the Empire. There was magic everywhere then. Where's it gone?"

"I don't know. Anyway, is magic like that? Isn't it just something magicians do, like shoemakers make shoes? And there aren't any magicians here, so we don't get any magic."

Tahl shook his head.

"No," he said. "It's a sort of stuff. It's like the water that drives our mill. It has to be there to begin with, for the magician to do things with. If there wasn't any leather, I suppose your magician could still make slippers and things out of something else, but they wouldn't be as good as shoes. So people can still do silly little scraps of magic here, telling-fortunes spoons and so on, but it isn't the real thing."

"How do you know?"

He looked at her, but she knew the answer before he spoke.

"The same way that Anja knows the way to the lake, I suppose," she said. And then, after a pause, "All right. Go on."

"Same question another way round. You are a powerful magician. You want to close this whole Valley off. That's going to take a lot of magic. Where do you get it from?"

"I don't . . . oh. Out of the Valley? So that's why there isn't any left here now?"

"And where do you put it? You don't need it in the Great Desert, of course. Nobody can cross that, anyway."

"In the forest. In the mountains."

"And supposing you're right—I'm not saying you are, of course—what sort of things would you find living in a forest full of magic?"

"Oh . . . very magical things. I suppose the cedars are magic."

"Yes, of course. But they don't need sacks of barley fetched out to them as soon as the first snow falls, to keep them going through the winter. What else?"

Everything Tilja had been refusing to think about clicked into place.

"Unicorns," she whispered.

"Interesting guess. What do you know about unicorns?"

"They're supposed to be very difficult to catch. The only way you can do it is for the hunters to take a young woman with them and make her sit down somewhere while the men go and hide. Then the woman starts to sing and the unicorn comes and lays its head in her lap and the men can rush out and kill it. Oh, I see! They're frightened of men and they don't mind women! That's why . . . But I think one of them did something to Ma . . . and later on Dusty wanted to fight it. . . . I didn't see it but it sounded really big, only Meena called them 'little wretches,' and she said they'd been covering Ma up to stop her dying of cold. There can't be two sorts of unicorn, can there?"

He frowned, for the moment as puzzled as she was.

"Let's leave that," he said. "You were just going to tell me, weren't you, why women can go into the forest and men can't."

"Because the unicorns are only afraid of the men, so they make a special sort of sickness. It fills the forest, so that men can't come there. They're magical, so they can do that. Oh, but they like to hear the women singing! Ma's really singing to *them*! Singing to the cedars is just a way of talking about it, so as not to say anything about unicorns."

"She could be doing both—supposing you're right," he said dryly. "There's not going to be only one kind of magic in a magical forest. Alnor sings to the snows, as well as . . ."

He caught himself just in time, and glanced at her.

"You can't have unicorns in the mountains," she said. "You must have something else."

"Sorry," he said, shaking his head. "Too difficult. To guess, I mean. But it wasn't there this year. I take him most of the way up. There's a little cave where I wait for him and he goes on alone.

He says his feet know the path. I think mine do too, but I haven't tried. Anyway, this year I knew something was different already, while I was waiting, and then I saw him coming down the path, feeling his way with his staff, which he didn't usually do, and I went to meet him, and he said, 'Take me home. It is not there. It is gone.'

"And there's something else. Alnor says the magic is running out—getting weaker, or being sucked away—he isn't sure. He says the waters have told him. We aren't farmers. We're right up in the hills, where it's almost all woods. When the timber's cut we raft it down the river. But we've got a small sawmill. It's driven by one of the streams from the glacier, and since he's been blind Alnor's spent a lot of his time sitting out by the mill, listening to what the waters are saying. They talk all the time. I'm just beginning to hear what they say. It's a kind of mutter, the same thing over and over, but changing a little bit each time, so if you listen long enough you've heard a whole word go by."

"Why didn't he tell the meeting that?"

"Because . . . Sorry, they want us. Who's that talking to your grandmother?"

"That's Aunt Grayne. . . . All right, we're coming!"

She stood and waved to show Meena that she'd seen her signal and ran down the slope, feeling far happier than she had for days.

It rained off and on all the way back to Woodbourne. In the worst of the weather they took what shelter they could find. They were about two-thirds of the way home, standing in a wayside barn watching yet another downpour being lashed to and fro by the wind, before Tilja finally forced herself to say what she wanted.

"Meena, listen. This is important. It really matters. You've got to tell me. Please. I know about the unicorns, so I'm not asking you that. I know you're not allowed to tell me. No, listen. What I want to know is why is it that kind of a secret, so that even someone like me can't be told? Does Da know? He can't hear the cedars either."

Meena glared out at the rain.

"Not getting any better," she grumbled. "Might as well be on our way."

"No!" yelled Tilja. "No, no, no! Can't you see what you're doing to me, keeping me out? Treating me as if I were a baby? Or some kind of animal?"

"Stop chattering, girl, and let's be going."

"You didn't tell Aunt Grayne, did you? You kept her out. She decided to stop loving Woodbourne. She told me so. Did she stop loving you, too? I love you, Meena. I don't want that to stop. . . . Please!"

She was weeping, now more with grief than anger. Through the blur she saw Meena turn to her, but it took her a moment to realize that the glistening patches on the lined old cheeks were not rain.

"I'm sorry," she croaked. "I shouldn't have said that. If you can't tell me, I suppose you can't. I'll get used to it, I expect."

"Anything for peace and quiet," said Meena, doing her best to turn her own croak into a grumble.

She paused, still staring out at the weather. Tilja could sense her grimly making up her mind to break a lifetime of silence.

"All right," she said at last. "We don't go talking about the little wretches because that's something the cedars tell us. But there's more sense in it than you might think. There's no magic in the Valley. It's all been taken away, and used to keep us safe. No magic in people's minds, either—you heard 'em yesterday— they'd no idea what Alnor and me were talking about, in spite of everything that had happened to bring so many of 'em in to the Gathering.

"They don't mind us saying we've been listening to the cedars, or singing to 'em, even—that's just a bit crazy, fancying we can hear something in the noise the wind makes swishing through the branches—not that we go gossiping about that much, either. But unicorns—don't be stupid! Supposing I'd talked about unicorns back there at the Gathering, what d'you

59

think they'd all have done? Laughed, that's what. Not listened to a word I'd got to say. The only place for stuff like unicorns is in stories, because stories aren't true.

"But we know they're true, the ones of us that can hear the cedars, and the ones up at Northbeck who can tell what the waters are saying. I can't give you that knowledge, any more than I could give it to Grayne. There's no way I can make you certain sure, or certain sure you're not allowed to talk about it. Suppose I'd told Grayne about the little wretches, and she'd gone off and married that husband of hers she's so fond of—Lord knows why—do you think she wouldn't have told him? Have that happen a few times, and after a while it's all over the Valley, crazy folk at Woodbourne think they've got unicorns, and at Northbeck they go on about their ice dragon—"

"An ice dragon! I've never heard of an ice dragon!"

"Seeing you know one there's no harm you knowing about the other, I suppose. A mighty great beast, Alnor's da told him, and he'd seen it only the once. Wraps itself all round one of the mountain peaks and just by being there it brings our winters to keep the passes closed."

"So it's the same as with us? The waters talk to Alnor and he sings to the snows and that brings the ice dragon? And the cedars talk to Ma, and she sings to them, and that's what keeps the unicorns there?"

"That's right, far as I can make out. No one's ever told us what's really happening, mind you. All we know is what we found out, doing it, mother and daughter, all these years. But my ma told me she thought the real magic was in the cedars. That's why we have to go to the lake to sing to them. The unicorns only do what they do, just by being there and being so scared of men. And if the cedars weren't there, or if they lost their magic somehow, then there wouldn't be any unicorns anymore."

"Alnor says the magic is running out, Tahl told me. Is it the same with us?"

"Why do you think I'm here, girl, this time of year, at my age,

60

with my hip and all? But could I tell them? D'you think they'd have listened to a word I'd got to say?"

Meena stood for a moment, glaring out at the downpour, then sighed with exasperation and turned back to Tilja.

"No reason to load it all on you," she said. "You've troubles enough of your own. But you see what I'm talking about? When your grandfather wanted to marry me I told him about the cedars, listening to them, and sowing the barley field, and singing by the lake—all that. He didn't like it much, but he took it for my sake, I'm glad to say. And the same with your own father. There's no way either of them would have tried to stop us from doing what we know we've got to do. But supposing they'd come to us knowing our heads were full of crazy nonsense about unicorns . . . Your grandfather was specially fond of Grayne. She was always his pet. For all I know your father thinks it's more than hard on you, being cut out by Anja, but they've known the reason. Supposing it was for something they'd grown up not believing in, couldn't bring themselves to believe in . . . Do you see now why it's better like it is, in spite of what it's doing to you? And did to Grayne? I tell you, girl, it's a knife in my heart every time I see her, thinking of it."

"Yes," muttered Tilja. "Yes, I think I see. Thank you, Meena. Look, I think the rain's stopping."

Once back at Woodbourne, Tilja told the others what had happened at the meeting, but not about her conversations with Tahl, or with Meena in the barn. She was, in a sense, no less miserable about knowing that she must one day leave Woodbourne, but at least she knew why, and could accept it as a fact, something that she had been born with—yes, like a kind of birthmark such as her cousin Rinter had on the side of his neck, a great ugly blotch that he wore high collars to cover up, because he didn't like anyone to know it was there.

When she'd finished, Ma sighed angrily and looked at Da, who shook his head and shrugged, obviously uncomfortable. It crossed Tilja's mind to wonder whether, next time she was alone with him, she could ask him how much he knew, but she was afraid to. Neither of her parents talked about anything like that, private stuff. They just got on with what had to be done, and expected you to do the same. She couldn't imagine Ma saying the sort of thing Aunt Grayne had said to her about having to leave Woodbourne, nor talking to her as Meena had, with tears streaming down her cheeks at the thought of the way she had been forced to treat her elder daughter.

Next time Tilja went down to Meena's, the door opened as she reached it. Tahl came out, pulled the door almost shut behind him, then faced her, amused, waiting for her to show astonishment. He was too late. She'd got over that while his back was turned.

"Hello," she said. "Run away from home, then?"

"Come to seek my fortune," he said.

"Here? You'll be lucky. I suppose Alnor wanted to see Meena again. Where's your horse?"

"We walked. He's a tough old thing, but my feet are all blister. I saw you at the gate and came to warn you. Just go in quietly. Meena's reading her spoons."

Tilja nodded, took off her cloak and boots in the porch and slipped through into the kitchen. Alnor was sitting by the stove, his beaky profile dark against the glow from the open fire door. Meena was opposite him, crouching forward over a low table spread with a dark blue cloth. She was always stingy with her oil, and kept the shutters open on the bitterest day until it was almost too dark to see across the room, but this afternoon she had her lamp lit, with her three spoons lying side by side in its circle of light.

Silently Tilja moved to watch. She had seen Meena reading the spoons only twice before in her life, once at the family gathering after Tilja's grandfather, Verlad, was buried, and she was making up her mind whether the time had come to pass the farm on to

Ma, and the second time after Anja was born and she had been asked, as was the custom, to choose a name for her. Both times Tilja had been too small to understand what was happening, but there was nothing specially secret about fortune spoons—reading them wasn't much more than a game to most people—so she knew enough by now to see what Meena was trying to do.

The spoons—two dark ones with a paler one between them—lay facedown, with their elaborately carved handles pointing away from Meena so that she could study the backs of the bowls. The pale one was a true named spoon. That is to say it had been cut from the timber of the very tree that had grown from the stone of the peach that Faheel had given to Dirna. Its name—or rather her name, for these spoons had personalities and genders—was Axtrig. The other two were not named, but they were also very old, and having been kept wrapped in the same cloth with Axtrig all those centuries, had absorbed something from her. A named spoon could not be sold or stolen. Not only would the buyer or thief be unable to read it, but it would bring the worst of luck into any house where it was kept. It could only be inherited, or else given as a gift, and then only if the gift was freely made, without being expected or asked for.

To read a spoon, all that was needed was to unwrap it, wipe it lightly with fine oil to bring out the grain, lay it under a good light and study the smooth back of the bowl in silence, thinking steadily of your need, or the need of whoever was consulting you, and after a while some of the lines in the grain would seem to become more marked. You could then "read" these lines, much as a palmist reads the lines of a hand. It was as simple as that, and as difficult.

So Meena stared at the spoons, snorting slightly with each slow breath. At last she pushed herself upright and sighed.

"Well, all I can tell you is I'm going on a journey, and a long one. I can think of a lot better things to do with my time, at my age, but it's there, and there's no getting away from it. There's a lot of other stuff there besides, but I can't make it out. That you,

Tilja? Just lift the lamp, so I can wrap the darn things up and put 'em safe. Snuff it out, girl! What are you thinking of? I haven't got oil to burn. And then you can nip off home and fetch one of the horses, so Alnor and me can come and have a word with your parents. And take that boy with you before he goes and says something that'll cause him to feel the weight of my hand."

"Want to know what it's all about?" said Tahl, as he hobbled up the lane beside Tilja. "Alnor's going to go and look for Faheel to get him to renew the magic in the mountains and the forest. I'm going with him."

"Faheel! But that was centuries ago! He can't still be alive!"

"The millstream says so. I told you at the Gathering, didn't I? We can hear what it's saying, just like your sister can hear what the cedars are saying."

"But . . . how are you going to get through the forest?"

"On a raft, at snowmelt, when the river's in spate. You remember the story, the Emperor's soldier who got through on a very fast horse? He'd passed out, but he made it. Alnor thinks we may pass out too. That's why we're here. We've got to have a woman to steer the raft, or it'll run aground on a bend, or something. He tried to persuade my aunts, but none of them . . ."

"And Meena's going on a long journey."

"I don't know about long. Whoever it is has only got to get us through the forest, then they can come back. Look, Alnor's going to try it whatever happens, and I'm going with him because somebody's got to, but it'll be a lot less of a risk with a steerswoman. I suppose Meena would do, if we can't find anyone else. What about your mother? Or your aunt who was at the Gathering? It'd be best if it's someone who can hear what the trees are saying, so they can tell her the way back. . . ."

He chattered on about Alnor's plan, but Tilja listened only enough to mutter something in the right places. Meena was going on a journey. A long journey. Much further than through the forest and back. That didn't count as long.

And Tilja was going with her, going away, unimaginably far away. Away from Woodbourne. Not waiting through the dreary years until she could, with luck, find a man on some other farm who wanted to marry her, and go and live with him, and make that her home, and dream of Woodbourne like Aunt Grayne did. Going now.

Yes. Oh yes!

Only her parents would never let her.

Her thoughts were broken by Brando's warning bay at the footstep of a stranger.

Ma didn't seem surprised to see them. She looked at Tahl as if there were something unusually interesting about him, though normally she was shy of strangers and barely met their glances. Tahl gave her stare for stare.

"Your father's up splitting logs in the spare ground," she said. "Anja, you run up and fetch him. You can take Tiddykin down for Meena, Tilja. If Alnor wants a horse too, you'll have to take Calico."

"Alnor's all right," said Tahl. "It's me who isn't. Mind if I take my boots off?"

By the time Tilja had Tiddykin saddled and bridled and came in to look for Tahl he was sitting in Ma's chair with his feet in a steaming basin of steeped herbs, and chatting away to her and actually getting answers more than two or three words long. He turned and grinned at Tilja.

"You'll be all right on your own," he said. "Alnor will hang on to a stirrup. That's what he usually does. He doesn't like riding. Horses aren't much use round us. Too steep."

When Tilja led Tiddykin into the yard, with Meena in the saddle and Alnor walking steadily beside her, they met Da, Anja and Dusty coming down from the spare ground with a loaded log sled.

Tilja helped Meena onto the mounting block and down, then

65

took Alnor's arm and guided him through the farm door, helped him and Meena off with their cloaks and led him to a chair. Then she went and took Tiddykin's tack off, rubbed her down and gave her a feed. She turned to find Anja waiting for her at the stable door.

"What's up?" she asked.

"You've got to come, Til."

"I'm coming."

"No, not there. Up to the forest. They want you. Please!"

"Want me? Who?"

"The cedars. They've got something to tell you. Please, Til! I'll tell Ma."

She scampered off. Watching from the kitchen door, Tilja saw her tug at Ma's apron and start to whisper. Ma bent to listen, straightened and looked for a while almost blankly at Tilja, with her mouth slightly open—that gone-into-a-dream look she'd worn sometimes since the night of the first snows. She shook herself, sighed and looked away.

"All right," she said. "Don't be long."

By now it was getting on toward dusk on a mild, sunless day, with the clouds moving all in one mass, blown by a steady wind. Anja led the way in under the trees to a place where three cedars growing together made a patch of dark green gloom. She stopped.

"Listen," she said.

Tilja did her best. She strained to hear, to listen with her whole soul, but all she could make out was the hiss of the wind through the cedar needles and a faint, pulsing hoot where moving air swirled into a hollow trunk. Almost weeping with disappointed yearning, she shook her head.

"But they're talking to you!" said Anja, astonished.

It was too much to bear. Tilja grabbed at her wrist.

"If they're so clever, why don't they know I can't hear them?" she snarled. "All right, what are they saying? Or aren't you allowed to tell me?"

"Let go! I can't hear them either when you're doing that. Please let go."

Reluctantly Tilja loosened her grip.

"What are they saying?"

Anja drew a breath, waited, and spent it all on the first slow syllable. Another breath for the next, and the next, and the next.

"Go.

  Til-

    ja,

      go.

        You

          go

            too.

              Find

                Fa-

                  heel.

                    Make

                      us

                        strong

                          again."

Faheel

4

The River

Tiddykin went dead lame the day before they left.

"There's nothing for it," said Da. "No chance of finding a decent horse at any price, this time of year. Meena will have to make do with Calico. I'll fix the horse seat to fit her better, and take a look at her harness. Tilja can give me a hand."

Together they went over the worn old gear, buckle by buckle, strap by strap, stitch by stitch, cleaning, oiling, replacing, making good. They worked for a while in silence, but then, without looking up from what he was doing, Da said in a low voice, as if speaking to himself, "I'd give my right arm for this not to be happening. All my married life I've had to accept this stuff. I don't understand it, I don't feel it in my bones, it means nothing to me, but I'm forced to believe in it. It isn't just your mother and Meena saying it's so—Anja too, now. It's because it works. Time and again. You found that when you lost the hand ax. Even when it seems pure nonsense—how can Faheel still be alive, for pity's sake? But the cedars say you've got to go and look for him, so you have to go, and I have to accept it. Accept it, though it means I may never see you again."

Tilja sat blindly picking at a stretch of frayed stitching on the girth. Her thoughts, if you could call them thoughts, were a muddle of astonishment and grief. Why had he never once said anything like this before, never let her glimpse, even, what his feelings for her might be? No, they were secret, those feelings, like the unicorns, yes, private unicorns, deep in the pathless forest inside himself. But to Tilja they mattered more than anything else.

Since that evening when Tilja and Anja had come back from the forest and told the others what the cedars had said, he hadn't spoken a word about her going, apart from the practicalities of it. His only response, on hearing the news, had been to look across the room at Ma, who had silently put on her cloak and boots and gone out into the dusk. When she had come back they had turned to look at her where she stood in the doorway, but she had simply nodded once to him, telling him that what Anja had said was true, and gone back to the stove. From that point on they all had taken it for granted that Tilja was going with Meena, not just to see Alnor and Tahl safe through the forest, but to join them in their search for Faheel.

"I'm coming back," she said now. "Whatever happens, I'm coming back."

"If you can."

"But I was going to have to go one day, wasn't I? Anja will have the farm, because she can hear the cedars. Like Ma did, instead of Aunt Grayne."

"One day. But not yet. You're not ready. And nor am I."

"Anyway, I'm coming back. And that's that."

He grunted, and Tilja realized that though she might have used exactly the same words half an hour ago, on their way out to the tack shed, she wouldn't have meant them in the way she did now.

There was another long pause while they got on with their work in silence. Then, without having to screw herself up to it, but asking the question easily, naturally, she said, "Do you know about the unicorns?"

"Know?" he said musingly. "Well, I've guessed. . . . You *know*?"

"I guessed too. But then I made Meena tell me."

"Made Meena tell you? That's as miraculous as any unicorn. In that case . . . maybe you should ask your mother to tell you her dream. All right, got all those stitches out? Then see what you can do with this while I sew 'em back."

Ma told her about the dream reluctantly, with long pauses during which she seemed to be forcing herself to go on. She didn't know when she had had it. It could have been while she was still lying by the lake, or in her six-day coma at the farm, or even later, in an ordinary night's sleep. She'd only remembered it after the next full moon, when she'd gone out with another load of barley to spread beneath the trees.

"I didn't want to go," she said. "I was filled with fear, a numb, black, griping horror in my chest and stomach. . . . But I went. I made myself . . . and I got there and tipped the barley out and went down to the lake to sing, and . . . and I remembered the dream. I was standing like that in it, just getting ready to sing, when I heard something moving toward me, crashing its way through under the trees. Then it crossed a bit of rock and I heard its hooves. It sounded like a horse, and I thought somehow Calico must have got out and followed us, though she's never . . . and then it came out into the open and I saw it wasn't Calico, or Dusty either—it was as big as Dusty but even through the snow it seemed to be a funny sort of reddy chestnut . . . and then it lifted up its head and I saw the horn. . . ."

There was a longer pause. Eventually Tilja said quietly, "You mean it wasn't one of ours. It's all right, I know about ours. Meena told me."

Ma shuddered and dragged herself out of the pit of remembered dread.

"No," she said. "Ours are white, smaller than Tiddykin. I gather Meena saw them that day. I never have, but I've seen their hoofprints in the snow . . . anyway this—this *thing* . . . it came toward me . . . I was stuck . . . you know, in nightmares . . . and then it stopped and lowered its horn and . . . touched me. . . ."

She raised her hand and felt the place on her forehead where the strange mark had been.

"That's all," she said, forcing a kind of briskness into her voice.

"Are you sure it was a dream?" said Tilja. "You don't think it was what really happened, before you went to sleep, that time we found you by the lake?"

Ma shook her head, but doubtfully. Tilja guessed that though she knew it could have been so, she really wanted it to have been only a dream. But she herself remembered the creature in the forest that had bellowed so terrifyingly at them when they were bringing Ma back from the lake. She remembered how Dusty had wheeled to meet its challenge. There had been something there—something real.

"But what happened the second time?" she said. "I mean when you went to the lake and remembered?"

Ma barely relaxed.

"It started all right," she said. "I realized I could feel them there, in under the trees, waiting for me to sing. So I sang, and they heard, but it wasn't *right*. I mean, it wasn't the way it's supposed to be—like this stupid weather—they could hear me, but they weren't really listening. And I wasn't sure about the song, either, the way I usually am. I had to do it from memory. And it's been like that since then. . . . Anyway, spring's here now and I won't have to do it again this year."

Spring had come suddenly, a normal-seeming spring, though with far less slush and mire than a true snowfall would have left. The wind swung south and smelled of sap and growth, and the swelling leaf buds tinged the gray forest with smoky purples and browns and yellows. Aconites and wild irises sprang open under the mild sun, and within two days the family was out in the fields from dawn to dusk, Da and Dusty with the heavy harrow; Ma behind them with the seed basket on her left hip, broadcasting the seed with a steady sweep of her right arm; then Anja and Tiddykin with the light harrow, burying the seed before the birds could grab it (Tiddykin could pretty well have done the job un-led); and Tilja last of all, with Calico and the roller, watching the repetitive pattern of golden grains arcing out from Ma's hand and falling in a graceful curve, like the ghost of a huge, slowly beating wing.

Tilja was filled with a kind of happy grief that she should be seeing Woodbourne at its most loved season, and family and horses working all together, expressing that love, and their love for each other, in their work, expressing it in a way that her parents could not have put into words, this last time, when she might never see it again.

Last of all they sowed the little barley field by the stone barn. That evening they ate their Seed-in Feast, as if this were a year like any other year, but all knowing that it was not. And next morning Da came in to breakfast to tell them that Tiddykin was lame, and they would have to take Calico after all.

They spent the rest of that day packing and readying. Anja went down to Meena's with the last of the old barley from the little field, so that Meena could bake a loaf to give to Faheel. Alnor was bringing a flask of water from the snowmelt above the sawmill. They had no idea if this was what they were supposed to do, but it felt right.

The six of them left next day, four travelers, Ma and Anja. Da stayed to look after the animals. He said goodbye to Tilja as if she'd be home next week. She set her jaw and didn't look back as Woodbourne went out of sight.

"The river is in our blood," Alnor had said. "It is not in yours. You will need time on the river to learn to work the raft." So they journeyed upstream and spent the first night at Aunt Grayne's.

The raft was already waiting for them, and Alnor and Tahl, and Tahl's two cousins, Derril and Silon, who had built it. Aunt Grayne had beds for them all, so they slept under her roof and went aboard in the morning.

Word had gone round of what was happening, and various rumors of why, so a small crowd had come to see them off. Most thought they were mad, and some said so, but Tilja sensed even so a kind of friendliness and sympathy among the watchers. Anyway, it was just as well that they'd helpers at hand, because it took six strong men to get Calico aboard the raft and into her stall, even heavily doped with the blue hemp mixture that horse copers used to quieten fractious animals.

Ma made no more fuss over their parting than if Tilja had just been staying on a few days with Aunt Grayne. She kissed her and with barely a shake in her voice wished her luck and told her to come back safe. Anja had a good blubber, of course, but Tilja guessed she meant it.

"I really am coming back," she told her. "I promise. And I'll bring you something special from the Empire."

She stepped aboard and found a place for her pack. Derril and Silon poled the raft from the shore and as the current took it away she waved to her family until the bend of the river hid them.

As soon as they were out of sight she looked for something practical to do, to dull the grief of that parting. This raft wasn't like the ones she'd seen before. Those had been just several tree trunks lashed side by side, being floated down the river to where they were wanted, with a post at the stern to hold the sweep that the raftman used to guide his clumsy craft. This one was made of straight poles a couple of handbreadths thick, fitted close together to form a rough deck. There was a slot down either side, into which inflated goatskins had been lashed for extra buoyancy. At the stern were two sweeps, wide apart, with a rail beside each for the sweepmen to steady themselves against. At the bows there was space for the passengers, and their small pile of baggage, and fodder for Calico. In the middle was Calico's stall.

Tilja was really worried about the stall. The Ortahlsons might have had the river in their blood, but they obviously didn't know much about horses. She found Calico already jerking her head resentfully against the short lead, though for the moment the hemp, and her own strong sense of self-preservation, seemed to be keeping her quiet.

Tilja heaped an armful of hay into her manger and turned to see Derril watching her.

"All right?" he said.

"If she doesn't panic or throw one of her tantrums. She'd have the stall to bits, and maybe hurt herself badly, or fall in the river. She might even have us all in."

"They told us she was the quietest horse in the Valley."

"That was Tiddykin. She went lame. This is Calico. Look out!"

Too late. Derril had incautiously reached out to pat Calico's cheek, and Calico had taken her chance to show him her feelings. He swore, and sucked at his hand. Tilja heard Silon laugh from his post at the stern sweep.

"See what you mean," Derril muttered. "Come along aft now, and we'll show you and your gran how to handle a raft. Lay off for the moment, will you, Alnor, so we can give the ladies a bit of practice."

Tilja didn't understand what he was talking about. As far as she could see, Alnor had been sitting on his pack near the front of the raft, with his head bowed, while Tahl squatted beside him gazing ahead and once or twice making some brief remark. But now Alnor raised a hand to show he'd understood, and Tahl turned and grinned to Tilja and then made himself comfortable among the baggage.

By the time she was back at the stern the raft, which had been riding true in the center of the current, had begun to turn its prow toward the left bank.

"See there," said Derril, as the cousins pulled gently on their sweeps to straighten it. "You didn't think she'd been staying straight of her own, did you? She's a lovely little job, this raft, easy as easy, though I say it myself, but left to herself she'll want to slew, one way or t'other. So far Alnor's been keeping her right for us, chatting away to the current, telling it what he wants of it."

Tilja stared, at Derril, at Alnor, at the quietly moving river.

Magic! she thought. *Real magic, here in the Valley!* It didn't seem the same as Anja and Ma listening to the cedars, or Alnor and Tahl to their mill stream. That seemed almost ordinary by comparison. But now Alnor had actually been using his strange power to make something happen in the real world. It was amazing.

"Can you do that too?" asked Tilja.

"Wish I could, but there never seems to be more than just one up at Northbeck has the knack of it. I daresay young Tahl will be doing it when he starts rafting, but the rest of us have to steer the hard way. And looks like that's what you'll be doing, once you're into the forest.

"Now, which of you's going to watch ahead and do the steering? How's your eyes, ma'am, if you'll pardon my asking?"

"You'll be lucky if yours are half as good, my age," snapped Meena. "You see what you make of it, girl."

"Right, ma'am, if you take that sweep there, and the lassie takes this one . . ."

Tilja took the sweep two-handed and put her back against the rail, the way Derril had. She was now facing the right bank, but looking to her left, she could see past Calico's stall, all the way down the river to the next bend. Meena was behind her, facing the same way, so that she could watch what Tilja was up to and do the same. Derril stood beside Tilja with one hand on the end of her sweep, gradually letting her take over as she got the hang of it.

She'd never tried anything like this before, but almost at once her hands, wrists and arms seemed to know exactly what they were supposed to do. It was very much easier than managing Calico in traces. The trick was to keep making constant little adjustments so that the raft stayed straight, and then it actually seemed to want to keep in the center of the current, even on the bends. It wasn't very hard work, but it meant paying constant attention, mile after mile after mile.

When he thought she and Meena had done enough Derril let

her rest, and Alnor took over, while Silon led her up to the front of the raft and showed her, as they rounded each bend, what to watch out for ahead. And then back to the sweeps for another lesson. So they floated on all day, Meena and Tilja taking turn and turn about with Alnor. At one point when she was resting, the main current narrowed to round a bend, running close in beside the right-hand bank. Alnor took them through so near it that she could have reached out and touched the red mud. Silon, the other cousin, was lolling beside her. She heard his sigh of admiration.

"Beautiful," he muttered. "Clean as a whistle. Just look at him sitting there, muttering away. You wouldn't think, to look at him now, that that's the best kick-fighter there's ever been in the Valley. And a wild lad he was too, those days, with the devil of a temper on him, my da told me."

"He looked really furious at the Gathering," said Tilja, "when he thought people weren't taking him seriously."

Toward evening they came ashore to spend the night at a farm. The effect of the hemp had worn off and Calico made a typical fuss about landing, and didn't seem remotely grateful to be loosed into a paddock with real green grass to browse, and friendly horses the other side of the fence. Next morning, at first light, Tilja fed her a double dose of hemp, the farmer sent for extra help from his neighbor farm, and with a great deal of hauling and shoving they manhandled her back onto the raft and into her stall.

"You'd better get used to it," Tilja told her. "I'm not letting you ashore again until we're through the forest."

The cousins came with them as far as the last landing place, in the shallows of the outer bank on the curve that took the river south into the trees. While they were wading ashore with their own kit Alnor turned to the other three.

"From now on I will need your help," he said. "We know that rafts were floated down to the Empire before the Valley was closed, so the journey can be done. But we also know, from memories passed down in my family, that once it enters the forest the river flows in a canyon. And with the snowmelt from the mountains it runs more strongly than it did in those days. In such a place the water will not be quiet. You must tether the horse firm, so that it cannot be thrown about. Then you must take the cords which you'll find coiled by the sweep rails and tie them round your waists, in case you lose your footing.

"Then, Tilja, you must watch me. If the sickness does not affect me—as it may not, out on the water—I will for the most part be able to take us through without help, apart from that of the waters themselves. But at times that may not be enough, and you will need to use your sweeps. If I raise my left arm, you must work to turn the raft that way, and the same if I raise my right arm. If the sickness overcomes me it will also overcome Tahl, and you must do what you can."

Calico was drowsy with hemp, but even in her stupor did her best to squeeze Tilja against the sides of the stall. By the time Tilja had her secure they were in among the trees, and she hurried back to her post at the stern sweep. The river had narrowed suddenly, and now ran between steeper banks, its whole current moving all together without eddies or still places, but sending continuous faint tremors through the timbers of the raft. The trailing sweep fidgeted in Tilja's grip as if it were alive. She kept her eyes on Alnor, waiting for the moment when he lost control and she and Meena must take over. Beyond him she could see the river running dark with the reflection from the hills, and roughening here and there into foam. Nothing happened. All the way down that reach the raft stayed steady in midstream, held there by the waters doing Alnor's bidding.

Until they reached the woods she had barely heard his muttered song, but he was singing more loudly now, so that his voice carried to her above the whispering hiss of the raft, a steady, rippling drone, repetitive, endless, shapeless, but full of intricate little changes, like the surface of a flowing stream. She thought about what Silon had told her, that Alnor had been a wild young man. Yes, she could understand that, wild as a waterfall, where a young river hurls itself down a hillside. She guessed that that waterfall was still there, inside him, but his quiet, slow, formal speech and manner were ways of controlling it.

Now he flung up his right arm.

"Pull," she called, and heaved on her sweep. As she did so, though she had seen nothing different in the rush of the current, she felt the whole raft suddenly trying to writhe sideways against the blade of her sweep. Alnor's arm was still up.

"Again!" she called, raising her own blade clear and stretching forward for another heave.

The raft steadied and swept on. Alnor lowered his arm. In those few moments the hills seemed to have risen more steeply round them, crowding them in with trees. The raft tilted, and plunged down a dark green slope, the surface creased into straining lines, down which they rushed toward a wild pother of foam at the bottom. Then they were rocking and tossing in a roaring jumble of white water, tilting up, steep as a shed roof, with the foam creaming round Tilja's ankles, swooping down into more foam and out into the untroubled reach beyond.

Alnor's left arm was up.

"Push!" she shouted.

Together the three of them caught and straightened the raft as it tried to slew, and they floated into calmer water. At once Tilja hauled her sweep clear, laid it down, untied her safety cord and hurried forward to the stall. Calico was fully awake and on the verge of panic, with her ears flat back and the muscles of her neck bulging stiff as she strained against her head collar. Tilja stayed with her, patting her neck, teasing her mane and talking gently to her until she saw the hemp stupor seep back into her eyes. By then her own heartbeat had steadied, and the great gulp of terror she had felt at the top of the slope was no more than a memory.

Meena caught her eye and cackled with laughter.

"Never fancied dying in bed," she called.

Tilja grinned and went back to her post.

There were cliffs on either side of them now, black, but streaked here and there with falling streams. Time passed. Alnor and Tahl seemed to be all right, the old man sitting erect, as if his blind eyes were staring along the gorge, and Tahl kneeling beside him to tell him what was coming. Alnor was still singing his strange song, though Tilja caught only faint snatches of it through the splatter and rustle of the current. After a while Meena joined quietly in, not the same song, though it had the same kind of strangeness, slow, wavering, wordless, wonderfully peaceful. Turning, Tilja saw a dreamy look on the lined old face.

"Are you singing to the cedars?" she asked.

Meena smiled teasingly, a child with a secret, and went back to her song.

The gorge twisted to and fro. At almost every bend they had to fight to hold their course in the rushing current. Twice more they swooped down roaring slopes into the welter of foam below, but each time Alnor had set the raft dead right at the start so that it came safely through. And something very odd was happening to Calico. Though the effect of the hemp must surely be wearing off, she seemed barely to notice these upheavals. When Tilja went to check her, as soon as they were through the tumbling flurries, she found her with her ears pricked, and with a bright, interested look in her eye, and every now and then she would raise her head and give a whinny of greeting and inquiry, as if she'd spotted another horse somewhere up on the left-hand cliffs.

"Calico seems to think she's got a friend up there," said Tilja, as she came back to her sweep.

Meena produced something between a sneer and a grin.

"Can't see there's any trouble coming, this next bit," she said. "Manage by yourself for a while?"

"I think so."

"Right. I'll just go and see how the old fellow's doing."

There were gruntings and mutterings as Meena untied her safety cord, and then she came into Tilja's line of sight, steadying herself on Calico's stall as she hobbled forward. Tilja saw her stop beside Alnor and say something, and put her hand on his fore-head, but at that point she felt the raft wavering from its course as Alnor was distracted from his task, and she had to hold it steady without his help until Meena left him and came hobbling back.

"Says he's not too bad," she said. "He's feeling it, mind, and so's that boy—they've got a nasty color, both of them, but Alnor thinks they'll do. How we're ever going to get them home again I can't imagine."

That reach ended in a wild bend, another reach, and another, easier curve. All Tilja's attention was concentrated on Alnor, and the rush of water beyond him, so she mightn't have noticed what they were coming to but for Tahl's sudden, astonished gesture. He flung up an arm and pointed ahead, and at the same time called aloud. Tilja looked, and saw.

The cliff on the outer side of the coming turn rose sheer from the water, like a natural watchtower. On its summit, almost at the brink, stood a unicorn.

It was nothing like the lissom white creature of Tilja's imagin-ings. The long horn rose sharp against a dull sky. The beast was big boned, angular, almost clumsy looking, large as a heavy horse. It was a strange, fiery color, between yellow and orange, and when it neighed and shook its head sparks seemed to fly from its mane, though there was no sun to give that glint. Its challenge rang along the canyon, echoing from cliff to cliff, the same fear-some sound that Tilja had heard that day when she and Meena were bringing Ma unconscious home from the lake. The chal-lenge was not to the raft below. It didn't seem to have seen that, but to be staring across the canyon at something above the cliffs on the other side.

It stamped its hoof, once. At the blow a vast boulder split from the cliff and plunged into the water, straight into the path of the raft. Tahl started to speak urgently to Alnor, but broke off, swayed, and slumped against him. Tilja saw Alnor struggling to raise his left arm, but then he too slumped forward. At the same moment Calico came out of her trancelike calm, squealed and started to wrestle against her tethers.

No time for that.

"Push, Meena, push!" Tilja shouted, shoving at the sweep. "Too much! Pull! . . . There! . . . No, push!"

The raft edged across the current, slowly, slowly, away from the onrushing cliff. Meena's side reached the slacker water. Tilja felt it catch, as if on a sandbank, as the shove of the current urged it forward. She yelled to Meena to push and flung herself against the sweep. For that one stroke they held it straight, but as they lifted the sweeps for the next stroke the raft slewed violently and went twirling helplessly on, like a leaf in a running ditch. Dimly Tilja heard the unicorn's wild neigh echoing again between the cliffs, but she took no notice, lost in the futile effort of trying to slow that sickening gyration.

"That's enough of that," called Meena behind her. "We're not doing a ha'porth of good. I've got to go and see to old Alnor, and you'd better do something about that horse of yours."

She was right. Tilja laid her sweep down, hurried forward and grabbed Calico's halter, wrestling to hold her head still and trying to calm her with her voice. No good. The horse was drowning deep in the bog of terror. Tilja's heart began to thunder with the useless effort. Dimly she was aware of Meena groping her way past her, of the cracked old voice starting to sing. Calico gave two more violent heaves and stilled, shuddering.

Tilja stayed where she was, gasping for breath. The raft turned steadily in the center of the stream. The left-hand cliff moved past, and then she was looking back down the canyon. The unicorn was still on its watchtower in the distance. It seemed to have noticed them at last, and to be watching them go. The next bend carried them out of sight.

Meena had stopped singing and was calling for her.

"Come and give us a hand, girl. Got myself stuck."

Tilja turned and saw her half kneeling with her bad leg bent awkwardly aside. She had heard the pain in her voice and rushed to help.

"Just get me down, will you? Gently does it. Aaah . . . that's better. Now, something to lean against . . . that'll do. . . . See if you can roll him over, so his head's in my lap. And I'll have the boy along here. . . ."

Tilja heaved and hauled at the limp bodies. Alnor was alive. Even above the mutter of the river she could hear the ugly rasp of his breath. His face was the color of old canvas. So was Tahl's, but his breathing didn't sound so awful. Bit by bit she levered and dragged them to where Meena wanted them, and stood, panting.

"Little wretches," said Meena, furiously. "Not that it was their fault, I suppose. They can't help making the sickness, like husbands can't help snoring. *They* don't know we're doing our best to help them. You can't see 'em from down here, but I could tell they were up there, following us along. I'd been singing to them, keeping them quiet, telling them there wasn't anything to be scared of. Alnor was a bit on the groggy side, and the boy, too, but they weren't going to pass out. Then that ugly great brute . . . what's it doing in our forest at all? It doesn't belong here. And bellowing at our own little wretches like that, scaring them silly? Doing it on purpose, too. That's what it wants. That's what makes the sickness, them being scared. You didn't feel it? It was like as if they'd just gone and poured a great waterfall of their fear right down on top of us. You saw how sudden Alnor and Tahl keeled over?

"Now you're going to have to manage on your own, best you can, while I see if I can get the little wretches sorted. Don't you bother about that horse of yours. She'll do. Knew they were up there before, didn't she? She'll be happy too, once I've got 'em quieted. So just go and see if you can stop this stupid thing making us dizzy, the way it's doing, there's a good girl, and I'll get on with it."

She was already singing by the time Tilja reached the stall.

Calico was getting ready to panic again, shuddering, tossing her head, and giving anxious little whickers, so Tilja stopped to pet and talk to her, and so actually saw the moment of change, when the shiverings stopped, and the ears pricked up, and the unfamiliar, interested look came into the large brown eyes.

"I think it's a bit much," Tilja told her sourly. "Ma and Anja can hear what the cedars are saying, and Alnor and Tahl can listen to the waters, and Meena can sing to the unicorns, and now you're wanting to make friends with them, and it's just me who's left out. D'you call that fair?"

Calico turned her head away and whinnied toward the cliff top, and Tilja went back to her sweep.

She found that the raft had drifted into slacker water. It was still turning, and still moving down the canyon, though much more slowly now that it wasn't hurried along by the current. Already they were well down the reach, and Tilja could see the curve of the next bend. It looked a gentle one, with the current running close to the inner cliff and a lot of slack water out to the left. There might even be a back eddy there. Silon had told her about that danger yesterday, and told her what to do, while he was teaching her how to pick her course. Caught in a bad one, he said, a raft might circle for a full day. If she let that happen, she realized, Alnor and Tahl would certainly die. Even drifting along as they were now might be too slow. The sooner they were out from among the trees, the better. There wasn't much hope of her stopping the raft from turning on her own, but she might be able to nudge it over closer to the main current.

She heaved for a while and found that each time the raft came to the point where it was facing downstream it seemed to hesitate for one or two strokes of the sweep, hovering almost straight before it swung on. Time after time it turned, hesitated, turned, hesitated, neither better nor worse, and then, without her having done anything different she could think of, slowed before it was pointing directly ahead, and stopped there, no longer turning. Gingerly she continued to edge it back toward the current,

86

watching, and trying to feel with her sweep for any sudden difference which might set it spinning again. As they reached the main flow she thought she'd lost it, but heaving with all her strength on the sweep just managed to hold it and drive it on, and now they were back in the current and she could relax, simply watching the water ahead for signs of change.

Meena was still singing, but she had raised her head and was rocking herself gently from side to side with a faraway, dreamy look on her old face, so that Tilja felt that she could see how her grandmother might have looked when she was a lively young woman. She was mixing her strange, shapeless song to the unicorns in with words, and a tune that Tilja knew well. It was called "Cherry Pits," an old, old song that mothers sang over cradles and children used for counting games, though the words, when they meant anything at all, were about two lovers sharing a bowl of cherries and kissing while they ate. Sometimes as Tilja worked at her sweep she found she was making her strokes to the rhythm of the song, but then it would waver and drift back into the wordless, rhythmless unicorn song and then somehow find its way back to the chorus of "Cherry Pits."

The day wore on. When Tilja felt hungry she chose a smooth stretch and left her sweep and fetched one of the small loaves Ma had baked for the journey, and a piece of cheese, and ate them one-handed. The cliffs dwindled and were gone. The river was far broader, its current less fierce but still easy to see, and they floated steadily on between wooded hills.

There was something else different too. It took Tilja a little while to realize what it was. The trees here were already in young leaf. And the air was warmer, lusher, and at the same time, somehow, drier. They were not in the Valley anymore, not even in a place very like the Valley. They were floating toward a quite different country, different from anything Tilja knew. No one that she had ever heard of had done such a thing for nineteen generations. It was a strange thought.

Late in the afternoon the raft rounded a great, sweeping bend and there this new country was. On either side of them the forest had ended and they were floating between low, rocky hills, dotted with patches of scrub, more waste even than the spare ground above Woodbourne. Meena stopped singing, but instead Calico started to whinny desolately, and Tilja realized that the unicorns must be following them no more.

The new country continued just the same as they rounded each bend of the river, mile on mile of desolate hills, and no sign that anyone lived here at all. Meena stayed where she was all afternoon. It was almost dark before she eased Alnor off her lap and struggled to her feet. She hobbled aft, clutching Calico's stall to stop herself falling, but this wasn't only, Tilja realized, because of her hip. She looked dazed, half-awake, not sure where she was.

"Did you see 'em?" she asked. "Little wretches."

"Unicorns? Oh, where? I was watching the river."

"In under the trees. Right down by the water, some of 'em, so I could see their reflections glimmering off it. Who'd've thought there were that many of 'em? Following us along, come to listen to my singing. All I'd been doing was trying to keep 'em quiet, so they weren't afraid anymore of that great brute."

"With 'Cherry Pits'?"

"Well, it was and it wasn't. It just came to me. I was thinking about old Alnor, and how he must've been a fetching lad once, and then I was thinking about a young man I used to be keen on. Met him at a Gathering, and we really hit it off, only it wasn't that easy, him living right over at West End. I'd've married him too, only there was this farm he was going to come into when his uncle died—really beautiful, it was—still is, I daresay, though I've never had the heart to go back. And I couldn't leave Woodbourne, could I? I mean, maybe I could've gone to live at West End with him for a bit, but I'd always have had to come back, wouldn't I, soon as my own ma was past singing to the cedars? And the worst of it was I couldn't tell him any of that—not that he'd've believed it, supposing I had—so it just came down to he wasn't going to leave West End for me, and I wasn't going to leave Woodbourne for him. Of course he couldn't see rhyme or reason to it, Woodbourne being nothing much of a farm, really, while West End . . . ah, well . . . I don't think he ever forgave me. . . . Be that as may be, we used to sing 'Cherry Pits' together, and that's what started me off, thinking about Alnor when he was younger, and then about my own young man. . . ."

She shook her head.

"And the unicorns didn't mind?" Tilja asked. "I mean, that wasn't *their* song, was it?"

"Not them," said Meena. "I don't know it really matters what I sing to them, provided I know I'm doing it for them, then they make it their song. I've never thought of that before—didn't know I could do any of this, apart from singing to the cedars in the old days, when it was me going out to the lake all those years. Little wretches."

She seemed to have woken herself up by talking, and spoke the last couple of words in her usual grumbling tone. Tilja grinned at her.

"And what do you think you're laughing at, young woman? Nothing much to laugh at, far as I can see—we're never going to get this thing in to the bank on our own, not without Alnor to give us a hand. And I'm all in and I dare say you are too, so here we are in the middle of this stupid great river, and it'll be pitch dark soon and we won't be able to see what's coming and it wouldn't do us much good if we could, either, for all we could do about it."

Tilja looked around. She could still just see the loom of the shore on either side, and the water stretching ahead of them, broad and smooth, reflecting the first few stars.

"It doesn't look as if anyone lives here," she said, "so we may as well stay on the raft anyway. Calico won't like it, but she'll have to put up with it. Let's have something to eat, and go to sleep, and just hope we don't come to a waterfall or something in the night. I don't see there's anything else we can do, so we might as well make the best of it."

"I've seen better bests," said Meena, relishing her grumble.

In the last light Tilja did what she could for Calico. In spite of what she'd just said to Meena, her heart smote her when she heard the cross-grained beast's long, weary sigh. Calico had no idea of what was happening to her, beyond its endless strangeness and discomfort. She was too dispirited even to try to bite or lean against Tilja as she scraped out the floor of the stall and washed it down with a couple of buckets of water. Tilja left her with a full manger and the bucket to drink from and went and groped among the stores for supper. Neither Tahl nor Alnor stirred.

Tired though she was, she woke again and again in the night and raised her head and craned around. Unsteered, the raft was turning slowly in the current, but to Tilja, lying there, it felt as if she was at a center of stillness round which the whole world, and the starry sky, would wheel for ever. The effect made it hard to see how the stars were really moving, until the moon rose and she could judge the passing of time by that. It was long after midnight before true sleep settled on her, soft and warm, and she could settle into it like a hen returning to its nest.

5

The Camp

Something jarred, scraped, lurched. Tilja shot awake and sat up. A light mist veiled the sky, glowing brighter where the moon shone through. That silvery patch was high overhead, so several hours had passed and it must be almost dawn. The mist hid the distances, but nearer the raft she could see open water on one side, and on the other a tangle of dead tree trunks and branches.

"What's up?" croaked Meena.

"It looks as if we've stranded against a sandbank or something. There's a lot of old stuff washed down from the forest."

"That's not good."

"If it isn't an island we might be able to scramble ashore."

"*You* might, and that boy, if he ever wakes up. Give 'em a shake, girl, see how they're doing."

Tilja eased herself out of her rug and crawled across to Tahl. He was breathing steadily, but didn't stir at her touch. Neither did Alnor. Since she was up, she crawled to the stern of the raft for a piss, and once there was struck by a difference in the look of the water. She picked up her sweep and probed down, and discovered that the river at this point was less than waist deep, with a firm bottom. Working her way forward, she found it steadily shallower, until she could actually reach down with her arm and pick up a handful of gravel from the riverbed. She went back to her bedding and waited for daylight.

The mist turned golden as the sun rose, became a haze and cleared away. Now Tilja could see that the river had widened to a lake, blocked at its southern end by an enormous reed bed, but the current had drifted the raft side-on against a great sandspit projecting from the western bank. Wrack from many winters past had piled itself against these obstacles, an immense impenetrable tangle of sun-bleached timber, which the raft had now joined. The bank itself was not all that far away.

She dressed and breakfasted and then experimentally took the pole and heaved against a tree trunk. Using all her strength, she managed to open a gap between the raft and the timber, but as soon as she rested the faint current floated it back. If only Alnor and Tahl had been awake, they might have done it between them.

"Supposing I was to give you a hand," said Meena. "I'm all right, provided I don't have to go skipping around."

"I'll see if I can get Calico into the water," said Tilja. "She'll be a bit stiff, but she should be able to tow us ashore provided it doesn't get much deeper. You'll have to fasten the towlines. And I'll need to borrow your cane."

She stripped off her shoes, stockings and skirt, fetched a handful of her precious hoard of yellownut, showed it to Calico and gave her a few morsels, then let the horse see her putting the rest into the pocket of her blouse. With that incentive Calico backed out of the stall with only a token refusal, and got a scrap more yellownut to keep her interested while Tilja rigged a towing harness of padded rope. Calico started readily enough toward the edge of the raft, but then scrabbled and jibbed as it began to tilt under her weight.

"It's all right," said Tilja mildly. "It's not that deep. Look, I'll show you."

She waited for Meena to hobble into place and took a firm hold of the lead rope, then climbed down into the water, faced the raft, fished out half the remaining yellownut and, standing just out of reach, showed it to Calico. Calico edged forward and craned, bracing her feet against the tilt, but came no further. Tilja moved the nut toward her, closer, closer, and then, as Calico lowered her head to take it, at the last moment started to withdraw her hand. Calico reached the extra distance and floundered in, rearing and kicking, drenching them both. Tilja heard Meena's raucous cackle as she backed clear.

Keeping the lead rope taut, Tilja waited for Calico to steady herself, then let her have the rest of the yellownut, a little at a time, while Meena made the towlines fast to the raft.

"Come on, then," coaxed Tilja. "No, not back on the raft. Last thing you want. Look, we're going ashore. Oh, come along."

For a moment it was touch and go, but then Calico took the strain and heaved, and they were moving upstream with Tilja probing the way ahead with Meena's cane. As soon as they were clear of the timber wrack she turned toward the shore. Once the raft was under way it came easily. The water varied in depth, but by now Calico had seen that dry land lay ahead and made for it with a will, so it wasn't long before they were trudging up the gentle slope of the bank, until the raft grounded in the shallows behind them. Tilja turned to unhitch the towlines.

"Behind you, girl," Meena called from the raft. "I don't like the look of him."

Tilja turned again and saw a large yellow-orange dog watching them from the top of the bank. It was a shaggy, gawky beast, but despite what Meena had said didn't look dangerous, and she stood her ground when it came trotting down toward her, with its long, plumed tail waving gently. It sniffed at her, as dogs do with strangers, but backed away as soon as she reached to scratch between its ears.

"I think it's friendly," she called.

"Better had be," Meena answered. "Hey! Get off! Shoo! You're not wanted!"

The dog paid no attention, but splashed through the shallows and up onto the raft, where it sniffed much more thoroughly at

Meena than it had at Tilja, then turned to the sleeping bodies of Alnor and Tahl.

"Meena! Quick! The food bags!" Tilja called, and ran down the bank.

"Where's my dratted cane? Beat it! There, that's for you!"

Before she'd loosed Calico, Tilja had removed her water bucket and set it down by the side of the stall. Now Meena had snatched it up and flung its contents over the intruder. The dog didn't mind. It backed away, grinning. Then, very deliberately, it shook itself.

The drops sprayed out all round it, drenching the raft. It was hard to believe that a half-full bucket could ever have held so much water. Tilja saw the arcing spray against the light of the rising sun, which made the whole shower seem to glitter with golden fire, with the golden dog glowing at the center of it. Meena was yelling, trying to get at the animal and belabor it with the bucket. Tilja was laughing till she could hardly stand. In the middle of all this Tahl, and then Alnor, sat up. The dog gave one last, tremendous shake, splashed ashore, loped up the bank past Tilja and disappeared.

"Just think," said Meena. "We'd have saved ourselves a lot of bother if we'd thought to throw a bucket of water over the pair of you."

"Perhaps," said Alnor. "I am not sure. For myself, I felt that something came to me in my sleep and made me ready to wake."

"Well, all I can say is you're both of you looking a sight better than you did last evening," said Meena.

They were sitting at the top of the bank eating a midday meal. The dog had come back and was watching them from a little distance away, but made no further attempt to be friends.

It was Tilja who had put her foot down about moving on as soon as they were ashore. It wasn't fair on Calico, she insisted, after what she'd been through. So she gave her a good rubdown and then hobbled her and let her ramble around and browse what she could while the four humans talked. As soon as he'd eaten, Tahl, restless as ever despite the remains of the forest sickness, rose and unlashed pieces of the raft and started to build a frame to help Meena climb onto Calico's back.

"It is time we were on our way," said Alnor. "We will need to buy food tomorrow, and for myself I am still somewhat shaky, and cannot walk far or fast. I propose that we should follow the river. Then at least we will have water."

They rose and gathered their baggage together. Tilja caught Calico and bribed her with a nose bag while Meena, voicing her distrust at every move, climbed the creaking structure Tahl had made and settled herself into the horse seat. Tilja was buckling the last bedding roll into place when Meena said, "At least we're rid of that dratted dog. Where's he got to, now?"

"There," said Tahl. "I think he knows where he's going."

Tilja straightened and looked. The dog was already some distance away, moving at an angle to the river, trotting purposefully toward a low ridge. There it stopped and gazed back at them for a short while before disappearing over the far side.

"The boy's right," said Meena. "He's going somewhere. And inviting us along, by the look of it. Let's go up there, and see what we can see."

Beyond the ridge stretched a plain, visible for an immense distance in the dry, clear air. To the left the reedy lake continued far out of sight. The plain itself seemed almost as barren and rocky as the hills behind them, but at least there were trees there, in scattered clumps, with more and greener trees in the distance. A mile or so away on the right something was moving, slowly, like a small patch of cloud shadow. Sheep? Goats? Too far to be sure, but yes, somebody was walking behind them, herding them along . . . and there, much further off, under the trees, something darker, more solid than shadow. A hut or a tent of some kind.

They watched for a while. The hut thing under the trees was about two miles away. The herd drifted slowly across the plain. Nothing else stirred.

A tied dog yelped, not the one they had seen. A child came out of the low, dark tent, stared at the strangers and ran back in. A woman emerged, told the dog to be quiet and strode to meet them. She was square and sturdy and very differently dressed from the women of the Valley, with a skirt that reached to her bare feet and a long scarf that wound twice round over her head, framing her face, and its tasseled ends dangling at her waist. She held herself like someone used to carrying loads on her head. Halfway to meet them she stopped and waited for them to reach her, her face expressionless.

"Health and good fortune," she said, with a strange, twangy accent.

Alnor was at the head of the party, with his hand on Tahl's shoulder.

"Long life and good fortune," he answered, using the normal Valley greeting for strangers.

"You have come far?" said the woman.

"From beyond the forest," he said.

The woman's face became blanker still.

"All men die in the forest," she said.

"We came quickly, on a raft down the river," said Alnor. "But indeed I and my grandson nearly died."

She nodded, frowning.

"This is not good news," she said. "But you are a stranger and I must welcome you. It is our custom, here in the outlands, though I have little to offer a guest since the soldiers took my husband."

"We would be more than grateful," said Alnor. "We have food, but we are still not well, and need to rest. And perhaps you will tell us some of the customs of this country, for as you see we are strangers here."

96

She shook her head.

"Ask me and tell me no more. Tomorrow I will take you to El-lion. You must talk to him and he will decide. My name is Salata."

Alnor told her theirs, and she led them back to the trees and found water for Calico, and then made them sit down and brought them cheese and goat's milk and pieces of hard, flat, bis-cuity bread, but when they tried to offer her some of their food in exchange, she became offended and insisted it was not the custom.

"Well," said Meena. "It's not my custom to take something for nothing, but at least there's something I might do for you. You said the soldiers had taken your husband. Would you like me to have a go at telling you how he might be getting on?"

Salata's face, her whole attitude, changed completely. She stared at Meena, hesitating, both eager and afraid.

"Oh . . . oh, please!" she whispered. "Anything . . . anything!"

Tilja fetched Meena's baggage roll and Meena opened it and took out the leather bag in which she carried her spoons and the things that went with them. She laid the blue cloth out on the ground, put the spoons on it and told Salata to choose one. Salata chose one of the darker two. Meena poured a drop of oil onto the back of its bowl, gave her a piece of cloth and the spoon and told her to rub the oil well in and put the spoon back between the others. She bent forward until her face was only a few inches from the cloth, and concentrated, wheezing heavily.

"Ah," she whispered. "Here it comes . . . here it comes . . . beautiful . . . my, that's clear. Maybe you can see it for yourself, Salata—this line here—look close, and you'll see it's two lines, really, running side by side, that's you and your husband, I'll be bound, and these little lines branching off and running alongside, that'll be your two little girls getting born. . . . But now, here this one, twisting away all of a sudden and going off into this muddle of stuff over here, that's got to be him getting taken off by the soldiers, and this is you, going straight on but running a bit thin, and no wonder, things being difficult for you without him. . . .

But see, here, this one running back out of that mess, straight as an arrow to where yours is, and fitting in alongside it again as if it's the one place in the world it wanted to be . . . that's got to be him coming back to you. . . ."

"When? When?" croaked Salata.

"Can't say for sure," said Meena, pushing herself upright. "Doesn't look that long, if you measure it off, but that's not really how it works. There's most of a lifetime in a space not as big as half your hand, so it just fits in what's important, best it can. But I tell you it's all clearer than I've ever seen, so that's how things are going to work out, or my name's not Meena Urlasdaughter."

Hesitantly Salata reached out and took the spoon, as if she thought its touch might burn her.

"It's going," she said, peering at it. "Fading . . . I can't see it anymore."

"That's right," said Meena. "And if you asked them again they wouldn't tell you anything special. But you saw it like I showed you, didn't you? It was all there."

Salata nodded, at first unable to speak. "Oh, you have given me a rich gift in exchange for your poor meal," she said at last. "You have given me hope."

She was crying now, holding the spoon and stroking it between her fingers as if its touch still spoke to her of her husband's return.

"There, there," said Meena. "Don't you take on so. It'll all come right in the end, and you won't help nor hinder, making a song and dance."

She managed to sound irritated by Salata's burst of emotion, but Tilja knew her well enough to see that really she was very moved herself, and didn't want to show it.

Salata pulled herself together.

"Since you are strangers in this place, I will say this to you," she whispered. "That is a great power you have. Such things are very dangerous. Even here, so far from people, they are dangerous. Among people you must be very careful."

"What do you mean, careful?" said Meena.

But Salata would say no more.

The elder daughter brought the goats home at sunset to be herded into a corral under the trees and milked, while the younger daughter stirred the pile of ashes in front of the tent and got a fire going. They sat round it and ate again, and talked; that's to say Tahl asked endless questions and Salata answered. She now seemed happy to do so, but still asked none herself. It was clear that she positively didn't want to know anything about the forest, or what lay beyond it.

She told them that her goats and all the land around there, as far as the eye could see, belonged to an official in the court of the Emperor. She made cheese from the milk, and once she had made a certain weight could keep what was left. She could also keep one in twenty of the male kids to fatten and eat, when the rest were driven off to market. Her husband was a trapper, hunting a kind of rock squirrel that lived among the hills to the north, whose fur was prized. Then, two years ago, soldiers had come to look for a way through the forest. Some of them had died of the sickness, and they had made up their numbers by seizing any able-bodied men they could lay their hands on, including Salata's husband. Now she and her daughters had to live on her allowance from the goats and whatever they could glean from the land.

"A bad season, and we will all three die," she said.

"So you're some kind of slave?" said Tahl, in his usual pert way.

"If I were a slave I would be better off," she said, and explained that all land belonged to the Emperor, who then gave the use of it to his nobles, and the officials who ran the Empire for him, to pay them for their services. These were the Landholders, and long ago everyone who lived on the land, including Salata's ancestors, had had to buy the right to do so from them. Since they'd not had the money to pay the price outright, they had borrowed the money from the Landholders themselves. The cheese Salata made and the kids she reared to send to market were the interest she was still paying on that debt, fixed so that it could never be paid off. And under that ancient contract neither she nor her descendants could leave the land until it was.

Salata told them this without anger, just accepting that that was how things were, but Meena became very indignant.

"Well, I say it's a scandal and a shame," she said. "I'd not put up with it, and I'd give this Landholder of yours a piece of my mind, and the Emperor too, if I was to run into him."

Salata, who had been reaching to stir the fire, dropped the branch she was using, stared at Meena for a moment, drawing herself away, then rose and moved round to the far side of the fire, where she knelt and scooped up a handful of ashes and poured them over her bowed head. Her two daughters copied her. All three stayed like that while Salata muttered rapidly, under her breath, what sounded like some kind of charm or prayer.

They rose. At a gesture from Salata the children went into the tent, but she stayed and stared at Meena across the embers.

"Do you wish to bring more misfortune on me and my tent?" she said.

"I'm very sorry, I'm sure," said Meena. "It's just my way of speaking. I didn't mean to offend. Besides, who's to know, apart from us here? There's no one else, miles around."

"A bird may fly to Talagh with your saying. A wind may carry it there. The Emperor keeps great magicians at his court, who listen for all such whispers. If your words come to his ears, you who spoke them, and your friends and I and my daughters who heard them, will be thrown into the furnaces. If you were not my guests I would set my dog on you and turn you from my tent."

She spoke with such hissing vehemence that even Meena was grudgingly impressed.

"Well, I'm sorry," she said. "I see I'd best watch my tongue—it runs away with me sometimes."

Salata nodded, but didn't relax.

"I accept that you spoke in ignorance," she said. "When you came to my tent you foretold good fortune for me and mine. Now, perhaps, you have undone it. How can I feel the friendship for you that I did only a moment ago?"

Meena heaved herself to her feet, hobbled round the fire and took Salata by the hands.

"You've done right by us, and more than right," she said, "and I'm not laying my head down tonight with this kind of feeling between us. Even just now, telling me to my face what a fool I'd been, why, that was a help, or who knows what I might've come out with somewhere, with a pack of strangers listening? Now, listen. You read the spoons just now. You saw what they said was coming to you. It was clear as clear, and there wasn't anything there of the sort of bad luck you're talking about. If there'd been something like that on its way to you, you'd've seen it, just as clear—I promise you that. But if there's anything I can do to make you feel better about it, just tell me, and I'll do it."

Salata gave a stiff half smile and shook her head.

"It is done," she said. "We will do as you say, and lay our heads down in friendship. And tomorrow I will take you to the house of Ellion. He is our Landholder's steward, a good man, who does what he can to protect us. He will advise you."

"That is Ellion's house," said Salata, pointing.

They had started soon after sunrise and walked steadily all morning. Alnor and Tahl had almost recovered from the forest sickness, but Calico was so stiff that she was nearly lame, and in an even worse mood than usual. Now it was early afternoon and they were standing at the edge of the open, half-wild country where Salata and the other herdspeople grazed their animals. In front of them lay mile on mile of farmland, small fields, every inch tilled and sown, and the first crops already green and reaching for the sun. Tilja couldn't see anything that looked like a real farmhouse, though, only a scatter of shabby little huts among the fields, each no more than four windowless mud walls and a straw roof, with a rolled mat above the entrance to act as a door. Three or four miles ahead a mound—you couldn't have called it a hill—rose above the rest of the plain. On it stood what looked like a village, a tight cluster of buildings with whitewashed walls and orange-tiled roofs.

The path picked its way between the fields. In some of them several people were working together, two or three adults and some children, just as you might have seen in the Valley at this time of year. The women were dressed like Salata, though their long scarves were of different colors and patterns. The men wore little conical hats with upturned brims and a tassel, loose brown jackets and baggy knee-breeches without stockings or shoes. They looked up, called their greetings to Salata, stared for a moment at the strangers, and went back to their tasks.

Slowly the village came nearer, and now Tilja could see that it was nothing like the villages in the Valley, where the houses all stood separate from each other with their own garden plots around them. Here, beneath the jumble of roofs, the walls of one building mostly joined straight on to the next, with only a few gaps between them. Perhaps, she realized, it wasn't a village after all. The whole thing was Ellion's house.

Salata led the way to one of these gaps. A man stood there, wearing a loose pale cloak and a red floppy cap with several tassels, and carrying a long staff with a sort of badge at the top. Salata spoke to him. He frowned at the strangers and looked as if he wanted to refuse them entry, but Salata argued urgently with him and he gave way. The gap was the start of a steep alley, so narrow that Calico's saddlebags scraped against either wall. It led into a central courtyard, almost as large as some of the fields they'd passed, with many doors opening onto it, and more onto a sort of balcony that ran almost the whole way round the upper story. Toward one end of the courtyard there was a roofed-over area where three men sat at a table piled with hundreds of scrolls and ledgers. (Coarse paper was made in the Valley and bound into handwritten books. Ma had two, a recipe book and a collection of herb remedies, from which she'd taught her daughters to read and write, but Tilja had never seen anything as huge as those ledgers.)

One or two people stood opposite each of the men at the tables, discussing whatever had brought them there, while thirty or forty others waited their turn in groups around the courtyard. As Tahl and Tilja were helping Meena down from Calico's back a man dressed like the guard at the entrance came over and spoke to Salata. He too frowned at the strangers, cut Salata short, and beckoned brusquely to them. They started to follow, but stopped when they realized Salata wasn't coming with them and turned to thank her and say goodbye. Before they could do so, the guard took Alnor by the shoulder and pulled him away.

"Hey! This won't do—" Meena began, but Salata at once cut in.

"No, you must go with him," she said urgently. "Do as he tells you. Make no trouble. Ellion is not here. His wife is Lananeth. She is a good woman. Tell her all you told me. I will look after your horse. Good fortune go with you."

"And with you," said Meena. "Come on, then. We'll do as we're told, this once."

Without a word the guard led them through one of the doorways, along a dark passage and into a much smaller courtyard, where he told them to wait, and left them. After some while he came back and led them on through several more archways and courtyards, until they reached one where he opened a heavy door and motioned to them to go through. He closed the door behind them. They heard the bolts rasp to.

There was nothing in the room apart from a low table with two unlit lamps on it. A little light came through a barred window high in one wall. All their food and belongings were in the saddlebags.

6

Ellion's House

They sat down with their backs against the chill walls. Time passed. Alnor seemed to go to sleep. Meena muttered to herself. Tahl fidgeted. Tilja thought about Woodbourne, trying to imagine, detail by detail, what her family might be doing at each moment. She wondered if they were missing her. Did it feel very strange without her? Were the cedars telling Ma and Anja what was happening to her? Oh, why didn't she have anything that could tell her about them?

The old bitterness was welling up inside her when Alnor spoke.

"I have a strange feeling," he said. "Now I think of it, I believe I have had it ever since we landed from the raft, but then I put it down to the sickness. Now the sickness is gone and my mind is clear, yet the feeling is still there, like the pressure one feels before a thunderstorm breaks. I dreamed dreams of water all night. . . ."

"So did I," said Tahl. "I often do, but these weren't the usual ones. The water was sort of alive. I was part of it."

"Me, I dreamed I was a tree," said Meena. "There's a lot more to being a tree than you'd think, too. I thought maybe it was reading the spoons so clear for Salata put it into my head."

"What about you, Til?" said Tahl. "What did you dream about?"

"Nothing," she answered crossly. "I must have dreamed, I suppose, but I can't remember what."

"There's no need to sound like that, girl," said Meena. "What's up with you?"

"Nothing," said Tilja, almost weeping now, and furious with herself for the unreasonableness of it, as if not having dreams like the others was the same sort of being-left-out as not being able to hear what the cedars were saying or listen to the waters. And then . . . she didn't know where the idea came from . . .

"I'll tell you what's up," she said slowly. "What you're feeling is magic. And what you're dreaming about. There isn't any magic in the Valley, so you aren't used to it. But there's lots of it here and you can feel it because you can do it a bit yourselves. Alnor and Tahl can do stuff with water and Meena can do stuff with trees. I can't feel it and I don't have that sort of dream because I can't do any of that. But you . . . yes, look how it was with your spoons yesterday. You said it was extraordinary. It wasn't. It's ordinary here."

"Yes, I believe you are right, " said Alnor. "This is the feeling of magic. Perhaps we three are extra sensitive to it, not being used to it."

"And I'll tell you something else," said Tilja. "Magic may be ordinary here, but it's dangerous too. That's what Salata was trying to tell you about the spoons last night, Meena."

"Good thing she didn't pick on old Axtrig, then," said Meena.

Time passed. Voices came and went in the little courtyard, speaking with the same twangy accent that Salata used. Occasionally a man coughed close outside the door, and once Tilja heard soft footsteps approaching, a woman's brief murmur and the man's reply, and the footsteps receding. It must have been well into the afternoon and she was hungry and thirsty and desperate for a pee before there was more of a stir outside and the bolts were drawn. Two guards led them away to the latrines. They returned to find a woman waiting for them in the center of the room, where the light from the little window fell most strongly. She motioned for them to sit, but herself stayed standing. It didn't need anyone to tell them that this was somebody of importance.

She was very short, no taller than Tilja, but twice as broad, with a pale, round face and dark hair. Tilja guessed that she might be the same age as Ma, but that could have been only that she wore much the same slight, permanent worry-frown. Otherwise her expression gave nothing away. Her clothes were in the same style as those of all the women Tilja had seen in the fields, but she wore golden earrings, and several rings on her fingers, and a jeweled brooch to pin her scarf in place. This was longer and more elaborate than the ones that the other women had worn, with a lot of gold thread and a double row of tassels. When she spoke her voice was soft, but clear and even, neither warm nor cold. It too gave nothing away.

"I am Lananeth, wife of Ellion, who is Steward of this estate for the Lord Kzuva, Oversecretary of the Northern Roadways. My husband is away, and I hold his ring and seal in his absence. I regret your treatment, but it has been necessary. If I make you welcome and feed you, I am compelled by custom to help you, and I cannot decide on that until I have spoken with you. Meanwhile the fewer people who see you, the better. So, first, will you tell me who you are, how you came here and what you want?"

"Alnor'd better do that," said Meena.

Alnor didn't answer at once, and then, speaking even more slowly and carefully than usual, he told the Northbeck half of their story, with his decision to come to the Empire and find someone who could renew the barrier of snow that guarded the Valley from the north. He didn't mention the name of Faheel, but only explained that the barrier had first been put in place by a magician in a city called Talak, so that had been where he intended to start his search. He said nothing about the Woodbourne end of the story, apart from the fact that there was this strange sickness in the forest, which was why he had come by the

106

river and brought Meena and Tilja to control the raft if he and Tahl passed out.

"My intention was that they should turn back as soon as we were safely through the forest," he concluded, "but I and my grandson were overcome by the sickness and the women were unable to prevent the raft from being carried on until it grounded on a sandbank. Here at last I woke from my stupor and we came ashore and found Salata, who was kind to us and brought us to you."

Lananeth said nothing for a while, then turned and nodded to the guard, who went outside and spoke to somebody else out there. Several people came in, two carrying trays of food, which they put on the table, three with large cushions, which they spread around it, and two more bringing the saddlebags and blanket rolls that Calico had carried. One of them lit the lamps. They all kept their eyes on the floor the whole time, not once glancing at the strangers, and left in silence. The guard went with them, closing the door behind him.

"Sit and eat," said Lananeth. "Look, I eat with you, as a sign that I have taken you into my house and there is trust between us."

She bent and picked up a little yellow cake and nibbled at it while Tahl and Tilja made their grandparents comfortable at one end of the table and settled themselves either side of them. Lananeth sat facing them.

"I meant what I said just now, " she said. "There is trust between us, because we all five have need of it. We are in great danger. Mine is different from yours, in part, but you can help me with mine as I can help you with yours. When I first came in I told you that I couldn't feed you until I had decided whether to help you, but the truth is that I didn't then know whether I would need to give the order for your throats to be cut and your bodies secretly buried. I would not have given that order easily, but I would have done so rather than simply send you on your way. I couldn't in any case do that. I will tell you why in a moment.

"I am encouraged to trust you not by what Alnor has said, but by what he has not. You must know more than he has told me about the forest, and the nature of the sickness in it, but you seem to have understood that your danger lies in that very knowledge. It is something the Emperor needs. If your coming is heard of, you will be sent for to Talagh and questioned, and when you have told all you know you will be tortured, in case there is anything you have left unsaid. Nobody comes alive from the torturers' hands in Talagh."

She paused, letting what she'd said sink in. Her soft, steady voice had barely changed, but that only made the horrors and dangers she was talking about seem nearer and more real. The silence filled the little room. Footsteps entered the courtyard, crossed it and died away. As they dwindled, Tilja let out a soft sigh, and realized that she had been holding her breath, half certain that the steps had been those of the Emperor's torturers, coming toward the door.

"There are two reasons why I cannot simply send you on your way," Lananeth went on. "The first is that you have no wayleaves. Nobody in the Empire may leave the land to which he is assigned without a way-leave, bearing the Emperor's approval of the journey. If I let you go without them, I would have committed a serious offense. If I gave them to you, which I could do as holder of the Steward's seal in my husband's absence, and you were then found and questioned, that would be far worse for me, because you have come from beyond the forest, and I did not send you at once to Talagh.

"This brings me to the second reason. Every new Emperor, when he first ascends the Opal Stair to his throne, turns at each step and repeats one of the oaths and promises he has inherited with the Empire. These are unchangeable and unappealable. So nineteen Emperors have now turned at the third step and sworn that in the course of their reign they will regain the lost province beyond the northern forest.

"Three years ago a new Emperor climbed the Stair. Two years

ago an army arrived to fulfill that oath. They quartered in our houses, they pitched their tents in our fields, full on the ripening crops. They emptied our barns and our byres, they robbed and they ravished, and on any that resisted they used their swords. But after many deaths the forest defeated them and they left, taking with them the best of our men to make up for those they had lost, Salata's husband among them. When they were gone we counted the cost and found that we had less than half of what we had had before they came, and from that less-than-half we still had to send to our Landholder in Talagh all that we would have sent in any other year. None of our people would willingly reawaken the interest of our Lord the Emperor in his lost province. I don't need to rely on their loyalty to keep your coming secret.

"So you see, I cannot simply send you away from here. You must have a reason to travel, so that I can give you way-leaves, and a story to tell, so that you will not be questioned too closely."

"My, what a pickle," said Meena. "Who'd've thought we'd be causing this much trouble? Look, why don't we just go back to the river, and then somehow get our raft off from where it's stuck, and carry on that way, and all of you can forget you've ever seen us?"

Lananeth shook her head, smiling.

"Wherever you landed you would have the same problem," she said.

"And further from the forest, people wouldn't have any reason not to send us straight on to Talak," said Tahl. "And it wouldn't stop the Emperor sending his armies here again, either."

"I'm afraid not," said Lananeth. "But I've a third reason why we should all do as I suggest. This is where you can help me. First, you have to understand something that may seem strange to you. I have already told you that we may travel only by the permission of the Emperor, but that is not all. We eat, sleep, breathe by the permission of our Lord the Emperor. We live or die at his will. Those are no mere words. When he reaches the highest step of the Opal Stair each new Emperor places his foot upon the Sapphire Stool and recites his final decree, that all who live in his Empire live by his permission and die by his choice, and for any man or woman to do otherwise is treason, for which the penalty is death. At the start of each reign there is a strict census, and all names missing from the previous census must be accounted for."

"Am I hearing you right?" said Meena. "Suppose I lived here and I fell out of my apple tree and broke my neck—might happen to anyone—you're saying I'd be a traitor?"

"Yes, and since you'd be already dead, your heir would either have to pay the penalty in your stead or renounce his inheritance, in which case all your goods would be forfeited to the Emperor. So as soon as they become men or women all who can afford it journey to Talagh and pay the fees and obtain the Emperor's permission to die, renewable by sending a further fee to Talagh each year. If they can, they take with them on that first journey a child of their household, as a kind of insurance, to be sold into slavery and thus pay the penalty in case they should die on the road. Those who can less afford it often delay, sometimes until they feel their end is almost on them, and so at some risk to their heirs save the permission fees. Those who cannot afford any fees travel to Goloroth in the far south when they feel it is time for them to go, but that need not concern you. You are going to Talagh.

"I can see from your faces that you think what I have told you appalling, and you are right. I am sorry to say that we have lived so long with it that we no longer think it even strange.

"Now, we had two old servants, very dear to us, who when they retired from our service went to live with one of their daughters who is married to a substeward of the estate on an outlying parcel of land. They planned, when their time came, to go to Goloroth, but they seemed well and cheerful, so we did not worry. But then the old man died, suddenly and without warning, and the woman, distraught with grief and the fret about the penalty, and the journey to Goloroth without him, climbed a steep hill nearby and threw herself off a cliff. This was no accidental death, but a deliberate flouting of the Imperial decree, entailing a tenfold penalty, and disgrace for all who might have prevented it.

"Worse yet, the daughter and her husband concealed the deaths for a while, thus involving my husband and with him all his household, since the man had been appointed on my husband's recommendation and he had not discovered the crime. Everything we possess, including our own lives, would not be enough to pay the various penalties. When we found what had happened we had no recourse but to continue the concealment.

"Yet worse again. As I told you, the Emperor climbed the Opal Stair barely three years ago. The census on his accession has not yet reached this outlying district, but will do so before the year is out. At that point, further concealment will become impossible. My husband has gone to Talagh on our Landholder's business. While there he hopes to explore what possibilities there are for the purchase of false death permits for the old couple and the insertion of their names in the ledgers. This will be both expensive and dangerous, for he will put our very lives into the hands of unknown officials, who will be in a position to blackmail us for the rest of our days.

"He and I have, of course, often talked the thing through and round and about, and more than once sighed and wished that there were two old people on the estate who had somehow been missed from the last census, who could take the names of Qualif and Qualifa. Now, wonderfully, it is so. You are here.

"It seems to me that neither you nor I have any other choice. What do you think?"

Each waited for the others. Alnor spoke first.

"For me, it is a good offer, and as I told you, the waters of our millstream have said that my grandson should help me."

"Me too," said Meena. "There's got to be two of us, it seems to me, one from Northbeck and one from Woodbourne, like there was when it all started. I don't know about Tilja. It's a lot more than she bargained for, and her parents too, seeing what sort of a place this Empire of yours sounds like. It's all right, girl—you don't have to come. I daresay Lananeth can find a youngster to go along with me to Talak—Talagh I suppose we ought to be calling it now. You ought to be able to find your way back through the forest, just following up along the river. I can't see it's going to be any more dangerous than coming along with Alnor and me, after what Lananeth's told us."

Home, thought Tilja. My own bed by the stove. The kitchen I can find my way across in the dark. She pushed the thought away. It wasn't her home any longer. It was Anja's.

"No," she said. "The cedars told me to come. And anyway, I'm the only one who can cope with Calico."

"Good," said Lananeth. "Now you must eat, and then I will teach you as much as I can of what you will need to know if you aren't to betray yourselves on your journey."

So far, though she had nibbled a couple of morsels, Tilja had barely been aware of the unfamiliar tastes in her mouth. Food in the Valley was always straightforward, however rich the feast. The tenderest, juiciest chicken was still nothing but chicken, with perhaps a few herbs, and though the gravy might be the best gravy in the Valley, it was still just that—gravy, with bread to mop it up and a couple of vegetables on the side. Here there were twenty little dishes and no main dish. Almost the only food she recognized was a bowl of dried fruit, but when she tried a slice of apple it wasn't only apple; there was a whole mouthful of other tastes mixed in.

Lananeth showed them how the custom was to heap a plate with five or six little piles from the different dishes, and eat a bit of each in turn, trying the different tastes, hot or sweet or acid or meaty, against each other in different combinations. Two of them were so strong that they seemed to burn the tongue, but there was a jug of a wonderful pale rose drink that fizzed in the mouth and cleaned the hotness away, leaving only a pleasant prickling. Lananeth ate companionably with them and told them the names of the dishes and what was in them, and the names of simpler things to ask for on the journey.

"Well, we must get on," she said at last. "We have only this evening, as I want you to reach Talagh as soon as possible after my husband, so that he can hear of my plan before he risks anything himself. Your task will not be as hard as you might think. There are about four thousand people on this estate, but I doubt if more than twenty of them have ever left it. Your journey will be little stranger to you than it would have been to the real Qualif and Qualifa. Those are your names from now on, Qualif and Qualifa Jaddo, but there'll be no harm in your calling Meena *Meena*. Most women stick to their childhood names after they marry. I am Elliona on the census forms. Your grandchildren too can keep their own names, as they wouldn't have been born at the last census.

"Now, your status. Qualif was a head servant in the household of the steward to a Landholder, so you, Alnor, will wear the hat of a fourteenth-grade subject of our Lord Emperor, and Meena will wear the scarf. I will show them to you in a moment, and how to recognize the grades of those immediately above you, to whom you must show respect. You are unlikely to meet anyone above twelfth grade, and most will be lower than you."

Hour after hour her quiet voice flowed on, telling them rules and customs and habits and manners and all the ways things were done in the Empire. Tilja listened and struggled to take it in. Their lives might well depend on their knowing these things. But the thought of the Empire itself kept flooding into her mind, and she kept having to push it away. It was all so different from the Valley. That was a place, the place she loved and lived in. But the Empire seemed much more than just a place, more than the hundreds—thousands—of places within its borders. It was a vast, strange creature with a life of its own, unsleeping, suspicious, merciless. And she and the others were going to try to travel along the innards of the monster without its ever once guessing they might be there.

She felt this especially strongly when they were talking about money. Lananeth had brought some coins to show them. Tahl had fetched Alnor's small hoard from one of the saddlebags and Meena had hauled out her purse from under her skirt, where she kept it alongside the bag of fortune spoons. Tahl picked out the old metal coins, with the heads of forgotten Emperors on them, from among the wooden Valley ones. He showed them to Lananeth.

"Yes, these are still good," she said. "No one will question them. There are many old coins around. Things do not change much in the Empire."

Tilja's skin crawled at the thought. Nineteen generations, and the coins were still the same. The monster wasn't just huge, it was old, old.

Lananeth leaned forward and picked up one of the wooden Valley coins, the largest kind made, the size of an oxeye daisy. For a moment she stiffened, as if she were listening to a whispered voice, then turned the coin to and fro, studying it carefully.

"This is a strange wood," she said. "The grain is so marked, and different on each side. It seems almost alive, as if it had been moving until the moment I looked at it."

"Let's have a look," said Meena. "No, don't let go of it—come over here if you don't mind—easier than me coming to you. There. Now, let's see. . . . Well. I'm . . . I don't know what to say—must be because it's been lying alongside my spoons these last few days, but even so . . . my, isn't that interesting—different from how it is on the spoons, mind you. . . . Look, I'll show you. . . ."

She took the cloth out of her bag, unrolled it, laid two of the spoons down on it, and showed Lananeth the third one.

"You see how it's cut along the grain," she said, "so what you're looking for is lines in the wood. But that coin is cut across the grain, and that gives you circles instead of lines. . . . Let's have a look at the other side. . . . Yes, you're right, it's showing you two different things—you'd never think there was so much going on in just a couple of inches of wood. Look, Lananeth, this is your side, all neat and ordered, and here's your house in the middle of it; and see these four little dots, looking like they don't belong somehow, that's us, me and Alnor and the kids, showing up out of nowhere. But see here, right off by the edge, this messy bit. It looks like there's something wrong with the wood, doesn't it, some kind of disease, and it might get bigger and spoil the whole thing—that's the place where Qualif and Qualifa used to live, and now if it's found out they've gone and died without getting leave you're in all kinds of trouble. But—just turn it over now—see here, this side is a real tangle. There's so much going on that you can't make anything out for sure, except this one little bit here, where there's nothing going on at all. And look, if you turn back you'll see that that little bit is straight under this bit your side that's causing you all this worry, like they've both got the wrong side. So I reckon this messy side's got to be Talagh, and what this is telling us is you've got the right idea, Alnor and me being Qualif and Qualifa for a bit, and taking your worries off to Talagh with us. . . . And see now, alongside those four dots I was showing you—wasn't there last time we looked, not to notice, was it?—this is you, right at the center of everything. . . . Why are you so jaggedy, though? If it was on one of my spoons I'd say you're really worried about something, only it's not the old people dying like it was before, it's something new. . . . I've said something wrong, haven't I?"

For a while Lananeth didn't answer, but sat staring at the coin, but, Tilja thought, not really seeing it. At length she put it down on the floor and nudged it delicately away from herself with her fingertips.

"I have taken you under my roof," she said. "I have fed you and eaten with you. If I have brought disaster on myself and my house, so be it. Salata told me that you had a way of telling fortunes, and had promised her husband's safe return, but I thought this was no more than the small peasant magic that many people pretend to. That is unwise, but not for the most part dangerous.

But this is something more than that. And you have brought it here, into my warded room. You should not have been able to do that without my knowing, but only when I picked up the coin did my wards wake and warn me."

No one spoke for a dozen heartbeats. Then Tahl said, wonderingly, "Yes, I think I've felt it too. There's been a funny itchy feeling in here since then. Why's magic so dangerous, though? Can't lots of people do it?"

"Because it is something beyond the control of the Emperor. The Empire is full of magic. It is there, like the sun in the sky, the water in the streams, the trees in the hillsides. Those who are born with the gift could just take it and use it, if they choose. But most are afraid to make that choice. By decree from the Stair, no one may practice magic except in the Emperor's service, on penalty of death. So those who wish to do so must either serve him or practice in secret. Many serve the Emperor, and for some of them their task is to smell out magicians who practice on their own. The most powerful of these are the twenty known as the Watchers, who reside in the Emperor's palace in Talagh, all in their own separate towers, keeping constant watch over the whole Empire.

"But all of those who have the gift, as you seem to, even if they do not practice themselves, can tell when they are in the presence of magic, unless the magician is already powerful enough to set wards around him and thus disguise what he is doing. That is far beyond what I can do, but such people are known to exist. Alnor said you are looking for someone like that, but they cannot be found unless they choose to be. You will need, for a start, to know his name."

"Might as well tell you," said Meena. "Seeing we're trusting each other. All right, Alnor? His name is Faheel."

Tilja didn't understand what happened next. She wasn't deliberately looking at the fortune spoons, merely gazing vaguely at them where they lay side by side on their blue cloth, when Meena spoke the name of Faheel.

Something in the room moved. An instant later there was a crash from outside the window.

She glanced up. No, that had been *outside* and *after*. It was here in the room that something had moved.

No, it hadn't, but . . .

When Meena had shown Lananeth the grain of the spoon she had laid it back neatly beside the other two on the blue cloth, but hadn't rolled them up and put them away. Now the old, paler spoon, Axtrig, was lying at an angle across the other two. Between one moment and the next she had changed. But she hadn't *moved*. Tilja was sure of that. She had no idea what it meant, but it was as if Axtrig had all along been lying where she was now.

She stared at the spoons, frowning. It was a while before she became aware of another change. The others were no longer talking. Silence filled the room. She looked up and saw Tahl staring at something on the far wall—no, beyond it, through it. His mouth was open and his face gray in the lamplight. Meena had her eyes shut, but was pale too, and shuddering. Lananeth was no longer sitting stiffly erect, but had her head bowed, as if she'd fallen asleep, and her hands were clenched so tight that her knuckles showed white between the rings. And Alnor was still sitting upright but had his arms stretched out in front of him with his hands spread wide as if he were feeling for something that hung in the air before him.

"What's up?" asked Tilja.

Her voice woke Tahl from his daze.

"Didn't you feel it?" he whispered. "It was like a thunderclap."

"I only saw Axtrig sort of twist round when you started talking about—"

"Do not say his name!" said Alnor, urgently.

Tilja bit the syllables back and waited, bewildered, through another tense silence.

"There, that's over," said Meena with a sigh. "I suppose we'd better talk about it. Carefully, mind you. What was that you were saying, girl? Something about old Axtrig?"

"She sort of moved. Only . . ."

She tried to explain, but it seemed to make even less sense when she said it aloud, though she could see Alnor nodding encouragingly as she groped for words.

"Knew the fellow's name, Axtrig did," said Meena when she finished. "Think of it! All that time! Nineteen generations, and the peach stone being put into the ground and sending up its shoot and growing into a tree and standing there, season after season, and blowing down at last and the wood being carved into a spoon, and that lying in cupboards and drawers and such a couple of hundred years and more, and her still knowing where she came from, to twitch like that at his name being mentioned."

"No," said Alnor. "It was more than a twitch. Even Tilja felt it to be so, and she heard something fall, so the house itself was shaken. I think perhaps Tahl is right. It was like a thunderclap— or rather it was like the bolt that causes the thunder. When Meena spoke the name something was drawn to this room, to the spoon itself, as the lightning is drawn from the clouds."

"But she must have heard his name before, back in the Valley," said Tilja. "I mean when people are telling the story, explaining about her, and where she came from."

"She's been asleep," said Tahl. "There isn't any magic in the Valley. There's lots here. It's really woken her up. Don't you think . . ."

He broke off. Tilja followed his glance and saw that Lananeth didn't seem to have been listening, didn't seem to have moved when the others had come out of their daze. She was still sitting with her head bowed over her clenched hands, breathing in slow, heaving lungfuls, like someone deep asleep. Tahl leaned forward and shook her gently by the wrist, but she didn't stir.

"Hit her worse than us three," said Meena, "whatever it was."

"But she *is* one of us," said Tahl. "She must be. I mean she was born with the gift, too. Only she doesn't want anyone to know."

"No wonder, after what she's been telling us," said Meena. "Maybe if I put the spoons away . . ."

As she stretched to pick up the three spoons her hand hesitated for a moment; then she seemed to force it on, but fumbled strangely as she tidied the spoons together and rolled them into the cloth. Tilja saw Alnor relax from his stiff posture, and heard Tahl sigh.

"There now, that's better," said Meena. "Didn't want to come, mind you, Axtrig didn't. Felt like that was how she wanted to lie, and no way else. I wonder—"

She was interrupted by a violent snort from Lananeth, who shot erect, shook herself and stared round her with a wild look in her eyes, as if still in the grip of a nightmare that had held her, sleeping.

She gave a shuddering sigh and relaxed.

"I thought my walls would have fallen around us," she gasped.

"Something fell down just outside the window," said Tilja. "Something heavy."

Lananeth frowned, concentrated, shook her head.

"There is nothing there to fall," she said in something like her normal voice. "Only a small tree. But it was in any case nothing of that order. What brought such power here?"

"Meena spoke . . . a name. The name of the man we are looking for," said Alnor.

"His true name!" Lananeth whispered.

"As far as we know," said Alnor. "It is in the story we tell in the Valley."

"I have heard that in the old days, before the Watchers, the names of magicians were openly spoken," said Lananeth, shaking her head. "Now every little country magician, for safety, is forced to take a true name and tell it to no one. My own is not Lananeth. Still, I would not have thought that even such a name was enough. This room is well warded."

"We think the power, whatever it was, came to the spoon Axtrig," said Alnor. "That spoon was carved from the timber of a peach tree that in turn had grown from the stone of a peach given to an ancestress of Meena's by the man she named."

"And she moved," said Meena. "And she didn't want to shift from where she was when I went to pick her up. I'm thinking she knows where he is and is pointing that way—over toward that corner, about."

"Southeast, roughly," said Lananeth. "That way lies Talagh. You said you would look for him there. And you think he still lives—the same man that gave the peach nineteen generations back?"

"So the waters tell me," said Alnor.

"Then he is powerful indeed," said Lananeth. "He must hold Time itself in his hand."

"What did you mean about the room being warded?" said Tahl.

Lananeth hesitated, then smiled her small, tight-lipped smile and shook her head.

"When I said that we must trust each other, I didn't intend it to go this far," she said. "I am one of those who can make use of the magic we have around us. Until I married I knew no one but myself that had the gift, and knowing what the penalties were I was greatly afraid of it and did my best to hide that I had it. But my mother-in-law recognized it in me. This was her room. As I told you, those who practice in this way must take measures to hide what they are doing, so she had contrived wards to seal these walls as best she could. She brought me in here and told and showed me what she could do, and encouraged me to try also, and later taught me as much as she knew. Since she died I've learned more and so built stronger wards, to make sure that what happens in here is hidden. The power that came smashed through those defenses as if there'd been nothing in them. I felt the very stonework was being torn apart."

"That's why it took you worse than it did us," said Meena. "Breaking up all that stuff you'd done."

"I expect so," said Lananeth absently.

She sat in silence for a little while, still breathing deeply, then sighed and shook herself.

"Well, it seems to have left no permanent harm," she said. "As far as I can tell my wardings are back in place, and at least you have been shown how very careful you'll need to be. But you have woken the power in your spoons. They're quieter now, but I can still feel their presence. I'll do what I can to ward them round for you before you go, so that they don't betray you on your journey. But unless you can somehow send them to sleep again you will need to leave them outside Talagh. The city is very powerfully warded, and what I can do will be nothing like enough to conceal them."

"How are we going to find the person we're looking for if we aren't allowed to say his name?" asked Tahl.

"There I can't help you," said Lananeth.

"You had not heard that name before Meena spoke it?" said Alnor.

"No. I know for sure of no one but myself who practices, but as Meena says, many people must have the gift. If I go up into the hills and look out across the plain I can sometimes feel . . . it's hard to describe. It's something like one of the dust devils that we see in the hot season, fierce little eddies of air that suck up loose stuff from the ground and whirl it around as they go. I can feel the loose magic being sucked toward one place and woven into a shape, a shape that has power and purpose, and I'll know that there is someone there—a child, perhaps, who hasn't yet been warned of the dangers or else shown how to hide what she's doing who is practicing magic in some small way. Sometimes I have sensed something more formidable. When the army was here, some of the Emperor's magicians came with them. I felt them testing the magical defenses of the forest, and being defeated by it. I didn't need to go up into the hills to be aware of it. I could feel it from here. But I wouldn't dare risk making myself known to any of these people, or learning their names, or letting them know mine. What I do is all concerned with the estate, helping the crops to grow, scaring away the wild animals that might eat them, caring for our own beasts. My mother-in-law told me that most of those who practice find that their gift is with one particular aspect of the world. . . ."

"Like mine is with trees, far as I can make out," said Meena, "and Alnor's is with water and rivers and such."

"Our river only, perhaps," said Alnor. "I do not know."

"That may well be the case," said Lananeth. "When I travel beyond the boundaries of this estate I feel my powers diminish. I could do nothing in Talagh, if I were fool enough to risk trying."

"Perhaps in our case that is just as well," said Alnor. "We shall not need to be so much on our guard all the time, though I was hoping that we would be able to use the river to travel further."

"No," said Lananeth. "All across the North West Plain, right to the Pirrim Hills, it is barred with reed beds. Tomorrow I will set you on your way by road. You have three days to reach Songisu, where you will have to join a convoy, as there are bandits in the hills. There will not be another convoy for nine days, and every day you delay is danger for my husband. So now we must get on. I have much more to tell you, and it's already late. These are the clothes you will wear. . . ."

To her shame, Tilja was already asleep before Lananeth left. She dreamed not of the dangers of the coming journey, nor of the lost comforts of home, but of a shore where she stood, and an island far out at sea (never before in dreams, and never with her waking eyes, had she seen the sea) and a voice in her head telling her that everything depended on her reaching that island. It must have been sunset in her dream because the whole sky above the island was filled with a glowing cloud that seemed, when she wasn't looking at it directly, to be forming itself into a great fiery shape, but as soon as she turned to see became shapeless again. Only as she woke did she realize that the shape had been that of a unicorn.

1

The Pirrim Hills

our evenings after leaving Ellion's house they reached Songisu. The way station was an enclosed square with a pillared arcade running round three sides, divided into separate booths for the travelers. It was larger than the ones they'd stopped at before, but everything else was the same. Lananeth had warned them what would happen. The clerk took their money—four drin for the fee, two for the bribe and one for the unofficial bribe—and stamped their way-leaves, and then demanded a surcharge before he'd hand them back. Alnor answered with a blast of barely controlled anger and a threat to report him to Steward Ellion, and he shrugged and gave in.

Tilja rubbed Calico down while the other three settled into one of the booths, then joined Tahl to go and haggle for food and fodder at the stalls. All this already seemed easy and familiar.

Waiting for Tahl to finish bargaining, she fiddled with her hair. From the first day of their journey, she had had trouble with it. Ma had always cut it just above shoulder length and tied it in two bunches at the back, but Lananeth said she was too old to wear it like that in the Empire, and she must braid it, secure it with a little beaded tie, and then coil it up at the back of her head and fasten it in place with a pin, with the blue pinhead at the center and the two blue beads below to show that she came from a fourteenth-grade household. Her scarf then went over the top of her head, once round under her chin and over the top again, with

123

the ends hanging down in front of her shoulders. There were two small blue beads and a larger one on the tassels each side. All these beads meant that way-travelers from lower grades could see that they must be careful not to jostle her as they passed.

Unfortunately girls in the Empire wore their hair longer than Tilja's. She could just about braid it, but there was almost nothing to coil, especially as she couldn't see what she was doing, so someone else had to do that and pin it in place, and even then it started to come undone almost as soon as she moved. By the time each day ended her neck was stiff with trying to hold her head as still as possible so that she didn't have to stop every half mile and ask Tahl to coil her up yet again. He did this neatly and without fuss, teasing only a little, but it was a nuisance and made her feel a fool.

Worse, it made her sure that she was giving them all away. Sooner or later some nosy stranger was going to ask about her hair. Tahl had already come up with a story about it getting full of tar and needing to be cut short, but Tilja was certain that as she stammered with the lie the stranger would notice everything else that was wrong about her, her curious accent, and how she kept getting tangled in the ends of her scarf, and didn't look comfortable in her long skirt, and didn't seem to know stuff that even small children knew. The other three looked fine to her. Tahl wore his little blue-beaded hat at a jaunty tilt, and laughed, and smiled, and was interested in everything; Alnor's own natural dignity suited his grander uniform; and Meena would have looked like Meena whatever she was wearing. No, Tilja was the one who was going to let them down.

In fact there was far more danger from one of the other three. For instance, yesterday morning they had passed an area of sparse scrub, with goats grazing for what they could find, and then suddenly they were walking between small fields full of young crops, beautifully clean and tidy, with little one-room huts scattered about, and every now and then a water-filled ditch running as straight as a ruled line on either side of the road as far as the eye could see.

They had come to a bridge over a fair-sized stream. Here Alnor, who had been striding steadily along beside Calico with his left hand on the saddle flap for guidance, halted abruptly. Calico plodded sullenly on until Tilja dragged her to an equally sullen standstill. Tahl took Alnor's hand and led him to the bridge rail, where they stood side by side, leaning on the rail, as if they were gazing into the distance. There wasn't anything special about the place that Tilja could see, only the slow-moving stream, wriggling away between the fields, and every so often someone working an endless rope that dipped below the surface and drew bucket after bucket up the steep bank and tipped them into the ditch at the top. That was how the ditches were filled, she realized, and that was why the fields ended as suddenly they did, because it was as far as the water could be made to flow. Without those hoists, and the hundreds of peasants toiling at them all day long, this great, rich area would have been as barren as the parched plain beyond it.

How long, Tilja wondered, since those ditches had first been cut and the land made fertile? Centuries, she guessed. Again, just as she had in the little warded room in Ellion's house, she felt the size and weight and age of the Empire. All those generations of toilers coming out of their shabby huts morning after morning to spend their days turning the selfsame water hoists, the ropes and buckets wearing out and being replaced, the men and women growing old and dying, never having left these fields, and their children taking up the toil to live the selfsame dismal, empty lives. Standing there, she could feel the Empire around her, above her, below her, before her in time and after, a vast, vague oppression, like a fever dream as huge as the universe.

Alnor woke her from her trance by turning suddenly away from the rail. Tahl led him back to Calico's side.

"What was that about?" asked Tilja as she took the bridle and dragged Calico into an unwilling walk.

"Just listening to what the stream had to say. It was just local gossip, but you remember Alnor said it might be only our river he could listen to or do anything with? It isn't. And I could hear it too. Alnor says it's always easier with two of you, but even so I'm only just beginning to understand ours. Ours giggles and chatters. This one just mutters. But I could hear every word, and it seemed to get clearer and clearer."

"That was you two pulling the magic in, just listening to it," said Meena. "Not that I could hear what the water was saying, but I could feel the power starting to get sucked in round us, just like one of those dust devils Lananeth was telling us about. And if I could, so could anyone else who's got the gift. Strikes me we're going to need to watch our step pretty well all the time, if we can make something happen like that without us even meaning to."

Alnor grunted agreement. Tilja stared around as she walked on. She had, of course, felt nothing, but she didn't doubt what the others were saying. And Meena was right. Yes, now she remembered that just before Alnor had turned away from the rail, she'd been gazing at a woman in one of the fields a couple of hundred yards away, who'd straightened from her hoeing and stared toward the strangers on the bridge. In the daze of her trance Tilja had sensed that the movement meant something. Perhaps that woman too had felt what Meena had felt, an ingathering of magic, starting to swirl into a shape, like a dust devil.

While they were eating, a man came round the booths, stopping at all the occupied ones in turn. He was burly, with a short, square beard, and wore a strange, square hat with a heavy brim. He carried a sort of pike in his hand and had a long knife stuck into his belt—the first real weapons Tilja had ever seen.

"Going south?" he asked when he reached their booth. "To Goloroth?"

"We go to Talagh," said Alnor.

"Good," said the man. "I am Zovan. I lead the convoy. Your place is seventh in the line. The fee is one forin for the token, plus four for the bribe, plus two."

This was, amazingly, the correct amount. Tahl counted out the coins and Zovan gave him a wooden token.

"Be ready," he said. "We leave at sunrise, and those that aren't there get left. We won't be going that fast—there's some on their way to Goloroth—but we don't stop if you fall behind. We don't like losing folk but once you're off the convoy it's not our lookout if you find yourselves dumped at the roadside with empty pockets, and the kids taken off to be sold. Got it?"

"We have it," said Alnor, confidently. The man nodded and moved on.

In the gray dawn light they found their place, about a third of the way from the front of the convoy. Zovan came round collecting the tokens. Eight or nine other men, armed as he was, were scattered along the line. Right at the back came a group of several elderly people and an equal number of children, paired off, old and young. Calico was the only horse in the convoy.

The way station lay between the small town of Songisu and the foot of the Pirrim Hills. Sunrise flung its gold light along their upper slopes, leaving deep-shadowed folds between the spurs. The frontier of light seemed to race toward the plain as the world tilted into day. Zovan shouted. A guard clattered his wooden paddles together. The gates of the way station were heaved open and the convoy filed out toward the hills.

As Zovan had promised they went at an easy pace, and slower yet as the road began to climb. Alnor, born to mountains, strode effortlessly up, but Calico was stupid and balky, trying to stop and browse at every clump of wizened stalks beside the way. Tilja was weary with dragging and driving when at midmorning Zovan called a halt to let the old people at the back catch up.

"That's the worst of the climbing," he told them, "but from now on you've got to stay together. And if you do fall behind, don't give up. Keep going. We'll be stopping a couple more times, so you've a good chance of catching us up, but not if you sit down by

127

the road waiting for someone to come and help. It's a long way to Goloroth, remember, and you've only just started. Those of you that are going south'll get a day's rest the other side of the hills. And now's the time to say good-bye to the North West Plain, any of you that won't be coming back. This is the last you'll see of it."

Tilja rose and looked north. As they'd wound up the hillside the distances had seemed to spread and spread behind them, and now from this height she felt that she ought to be able to see as far as could be seen before the curve of the world hid all that lay beyond. But no. Where were the mountains, that even from the southern fringe of the Valley at Woodbourne seemed to tower above it? Gone, gone beyond sight, and the Valley itself and the forest. You wouldn't have known they were there.

But they are, she told herself. *And I'm not saying good-bye to them. I'm going home.*

The fog came down without warning. At one moment they were under clear skies on an almost level track that had been winding for several miles along the bottom of a valley, wooded with ancient pines. Next, they rounded a corner and could see nothing beyond a soft pale wall of cloud and the shadowy loom of the next few trees. The line jostled to a halt as the cloud rolled over them. Tilja could no longer see the head of the column nor, looking back, the tail of it. Zovan's call echoed through the murk.

"Happens up here, this time of year. Nothing to worry about. Close up and keep up. All here? March."

The guards repeated the orders down the line. The pines and the fog swallowed their voices.

They plodded along through the dankness, Tilja leading Calico with her eyes on the back of the man in front of her. She could barely see the next person along the line. The track was well kept and she wasn't watching her footsteps, so she was utterly unprepared when Calico's bridle was wrenched from her grasp and something massive rammed into her shoulder and sent her sprawling forward and sideways. She broke her fall on her elbow and scrambled up.

Everyone seemed to be shouting. Calico was lying on her side with her hoofs flailing as she struggled to rise, but a piece of loose rope that must have been lying on the path had somehow wrapped itself round her legs and brought her down, and now it was refusing to let go. Meena was lying on top of Alnor on the bank beside the path. Alnor's right foot was trapped under Calico's saddle. Tahl was trying to snatch at the rope. The rest of the convoy was beginning to edge round on the other side of the road, desperate not to get left behind.

Tilja had once seen Ma deal with Tiddykin when she'd caught her foreleg in some loose brushwood and fallen and panicked as she'd tried to kick herself free. Tilja yelled at Tahl to wait, grabbed the bridle, turned and sat heavily down on Calico's head, hissing as loudly as she could between tongue and teeth, and calling her by her name. Calico heaved once more, then gave up as Tilja clung on. Tahl darted in and unwrapped the tangling rope.

Still gripping the bridle, Tilja rose and let Calico scramble to her feet, where she stood snorting and shuddering while Tilja hissed and murmured to her and Tahl ran round to help Meena and Alnor. Meena had rolled herself over and was sitting up, feeling her hips and legs. Alnor was lying on his back, retching for air.

"Meena, are you all right?" Tilja called anxiously.

"Won't know till I stand up," she answered. "Shook myself up a bit, but the old boy broke my fall. Winded him good and proper, by the look of him."

Tahl was kneeling beside Alnor, trying to lift him by the shoulders. Alnor was making feeble motions with his hands to say he wanted to be left where he was. The tail of the convoy, pairs of old and young going to Goloroth, hurried past. Some of them didn't even look, but one old man caught Tilja's eye and shrugged apologetically, telling her he'd have liked to stay and help if he could. The guard at the tail of the line stopped.

"Rough luck," he said. "How's the old fellow? Think he can walk?"

Alnor grunted and somehow rolled himself up onto one elbow and felt for his left ankle with his other hand.

"I'll do," he croaked. "Just winded. Could have been worse. You go on. We'll catch up. We can move faster than you've been going."

"Right you are," said the guard. "There'll be a rest point two, three miles along, but Zovan won't want to hang around there, not with this muck slowing us down. Never seen it this bad."

"One moment, young man," said Meena. "You can help me back up onto this stupid beast before you go. Gently now. My hip's bad enough, best of times, and Lord knows what else I've done to myself."

Good-humoredly the guard hoisted her up to the saddle and strode off into the murk. Tahl found Alnor's cap and put it back on his head. They waited another few minutes while he finished getting his breath back, sat up and felt himself over more thoroughly. Tahl picked up the frayed bit of rope that had caused the accident, stared at it for a moment, frowning, and tossed it into the trees. Alnor rose groggily to his feet and stood, testing his weight on one leg and then the other. With his hand on Tahl's shoulder he took a few limping steps.

"You all right?" said Meena, for once not trying to hide her concern. "I daresay this animal's up to the two of us. Time she earned her keep."

"I'll do if it gets no worse," he answered. "We must move now, or we won't come up with them."

So they started along the path, Tahl and Alnor in front and Tilja leading Calico by the bridle. It felt strange, after the companionable shuffle and chat of the convoy, to be moving through this silent, closed world, the only sounds their own footfalls and the drip of the fog from the branches. Before long Tilja saw that Alnor was limping more heavily, and leaning his weight on Tahl's shoulder at each step, but he still strode fiercely on. His halt was so sudden that she almost allowed Calico to blunder into his back.

There was a man in the path ahead of them, standing straddle legged, blocking the way. He had a cudgel over his shoulder and a long knife stuck into his belt. Then movements either side of the path and five more men, also with cudgels and knives, came out of the trees.

Tilja's heart slammed once, then hammered. Her stomach and limbs filled with the chill of the fog. She half heard Meena muttering fiercely above her. The men closed silently in.

"My grandfather's blind," said Tahl, urgently. "He's hurt his—"

He was cut short. Tilja turned, but before she could see what had happened she was seized from behind, a bag was thrust over her head, a hard hand was clamped against her mouth and held there while someone else grabbed her arms and lashed her wrists behind her back. The hand left her mouth and gripped her elbow while other hands were thrust in under the bag and her scarf was forced between her lips and teeth and the ends tied behind her head.

"Lay off, you goat-get!" snapped Meena, above her. "There! How d'you fancy that!"

Tilja heard the swish and thwack of Meena's cane, a curse from the man she'd hit, a yell of pain from Meena and a slithering thud. A moment's silence, and then more heavings and rustlings, and mutters of command.

"They're the fourteeners all right," said a voice. "Get the old bag back up on the horse, and we'll go."

Now one hand let go of Tilja's elbow while the other turned her and forced her into a blind shuffle back along the way they'd come, jerking her upright when she stumbled. To her immense relief, she heard Meena's muffled groan from behind her. It was not much help, but it was something to cling to as she stumbled on, gagging again and again on the cloth in her mouth.

The man who held her stopped, heaved her onto his shoulders

and carried her up a steep slope. She could hear curses and blows as Calico was forced to climb. Then the ground seemed to level out and she was set down and forced to stumble up a much rougher and narrower path than the one below. The sounds around her changed, and she guessed that they were now out above the trees, with the slope rising to her left and falling away to her right. Sometimes they climbed, but not so steeply that she needed to be carried again. At last she was told to stand still, her arms were retied, and she was pushed down and dragged into some kind of enclosed space and made to sit on a rough earthen floor with what felt like natural rock against her back. Her ankles were lashed together before they pulled the hood from her head and untied the disgusting gag. She retched but couldn't vomit. Her mouth was too dry. Before she recovered a hand grabbed her hair and forced her head back. Something was thrust against her mouth.

"Drink," snapped a voice.

She gulped. Water sluiced down her chin and blouse. The flask was snatched away without warning and instantly the scarf was stuffed back into her mouth. In the few seconds while it was being tied, unable to move her head, she rolled her eyes from side to side, desperate to know where she was and what had happened to the others. There was rock opposite her and rock above, darkness to her right and daylight to her left—a small, low-roofed cave. She could see part of Tahl's legs further in on her right, and Meena and Alnor propped against the opposite wall. Then the hood was shoved back over her head, and she heard the other three being given their turns at the flask.

Footsteps left the cave. Ages passed, in aches and cramps and soreness. She managed to slump herself sideways and by nudging her head against a rock projecting from the cave floor loosen her gag a little. She could hear Tahl wriggling for comfort, and Meena's soft groans. Poor Meena. She must be in agony—Tilja's own intense discomfort would be nothing beside it.

It was almost dark in the cave before the hood was again removed and two men fed the captives turn by turn on some sort of porridge, hooded and gagged them and took them stumbling out, one at a time, to relieve themselves on the open hillside.

Then again they were dumped in the cave, but it wasn't long before Tilja heard footsteps and brusque commands, telling her that another captive had been brought in. This time before the men left, one of them mercifully took the hood from her head.

Not that there was much to see. It was night, with stars showing at the narrow entrance to the cave. Almost at once these vanished as a boulder was rolled into place to seal the captives in, and then, to judge by the sounds, wedged into place with smaller rocks. Footsteps faded into silence.

Still sick with the same unchanging misery and fear, she lay down and wriggled for some kind of comfort. Beside her she could hear Tahl also shifting around, but it turned out he had other ideas. Something shoved against the back of her head, and she gave a protesting grunt. Tahl's grunt answered somewhere in the darkness close by. Clumsy fingers probed among her hair, found the knot of her scarf, started to tug and tease. There were strands of hair in the knot. She winced at the pain. Tahl in his turn grunted as he pricked a finger on her hairpin. She felt the knot loosen, and now he had it free, and she could spit the cloth out and suck and swallow to work the saliva into her mouth and round.

"Thanks," she whispered. "I'll try and do yours."

She worked her back against the wall and managed to wriggle herself up, and then he let himself topple sideways so that she could turn, feel down the back of his head and find the knot of his gag. With endless pickings and pokings she managed to undo it.

"Thanks. That's better," he whispered. "I'll see if I can untie you."

"We'll never get away."

"We've got to try."

They found a position where he could get at the cord that lashed her elbows together, but the moment he started to work at the knot a soft, grating voice spoke in the darkness.

"Wait. Not time."

At the first syllable Tilja had frozen rigid. She stared into the darkness beside the entrance.

"Who are you?" whispered Tahl. Tilja could hear the tremor in his voice.

"Traveler. Like yourselves," came the quiet answer. "Let those fools sleep. Then we go."

Tilja heard a grunt from Meena.

"That's my grandmother," she whispered. "Can I take her gag off?"

"No noise."

Carefully Tilja worked herself across the cave floor toward where the sound had come from. She found a leg by touch, turned herself round and by slithering herself up against the wall managed to reach the gag and untie it. Meena muttered savagely under her breath for a little, then whispered aloud, almost sobbing with pain.

"Get my legs undone if you can, girl, whatever the fellow says. This hip of mine's a nightmare."

"Is that all right?" Tilja asked into the darkness.

"Wait," answered the darkness. "Yes. Now."

Tilja felt her way to the knot, and found it already surprisingly loose. Meena groaned softly as she eased her leg around. Tilja could hear Tahl working at Alnor's gag.

"Wait still," murmured the stranger.

That was hard, with their bodies half free and their minds filled with half hope. At last he spoke again.

"We begin. Stay where you are. Do not be afraid. Make no sound."

For a little while nothing seemed to happen. Then the cord around Tilja's ankles loosened and fell away. She felt a movement at her back, though she was leaning against the cave wall with no room for anyone to reach behind her. She realized that the cord around her elbows had also come untied, and then, with a spasm of shock, that it was now wriggling around, as if it had been a living creature trapped between her body and the rock. She jerked herself away from it and it fell loose. She heard it slithering off into the dark.

The cave was full of those slithering sounds moving toward the entrance. There were moonlit chinks around the boulder blocking it. They changed shape as the cords wriggled out into the night. Something odd was happening to Tilja's clothing. It too felt alive. Yes, parts of it, the cords of her cloak and skirt, the lacings of her blouse, were twitching as if they wanted to follow. Only the lashings round her wrists stayed firm.

"All free?" murmured the stranger.

"My wrists are still tied," Tilja whispered.

She heard his grunt of puzzlement. An odd numbness began to seep up her arms, unconnected with the dull pain of the lashed cord. There was another grunt from the stranger and the numbness vanished.

"Think about it later," he muttered. "Boy can untie you."

Tilja rose and turned to let Tahl get at the knot. He too gave a snort of surprise as the rope came free.

"Don't move," he whispered.

The numbness returned for a moment as something touched the back of her hand.

"No, drop it," said the stranger.

Tahl let the cord fall and it slithered away like the others.

"Don't ask," he whispered. "Explain later."

Yet again they waited in the darkness. Tilja's mouth was dry as her body readied itself for flight. She heard the scrape of rock against rock. Something was dragging the wedges clear.

"Shall we help roll it out?" whispered Tahl.

"No need," said the stranger, not bothering to whisper, but speaking still in his odd, jerky style, with long pauses, as if his mind were somewhere else. "The ropes do it . . . they must tie themselves together . . . find an anchor . . . take strain . . . they are ready . . . ha! Pull, my children!"

At his call the prisoning boulder seemed to leap from the entrance and go crashing down the hillside.

"It is done," said the stranger, with a sudden, startling laugh that went braying out into the still night. "Cave along that way. Rob the robbers, hey?"

A shape moved into the cave entrance, and Tilja almost cried aloud. It was an enormous head, so large that it almost blocked the opening. It was turned sideways, so that she could see the jut of nose and chin near the bottom, and the outline of a shoulder below, but above them swelled a great ballooning growth of skull. The thing crawled out into the open and vanished.

"You go first," whispered Meena. "It'll take Alnor and me a while."

With sick dread Tilja crouched her way to the entrance, hesitated, crawled out and stood. A white mass of fog filled the valley below them, but the moon was high overhead, paling the stars. The stranger was there, a tall, thin shape in the moonlight. At the top of the neck was a normal human face, eyebrows, eyes, a long nose, smiling mouth, pointed chin and wisp of a beard, and above that the monstrous bulge she'd seen from the cave.

She had backed away and was swallowing a scream before she realized that she had misunderstood what she was seeing. The huge mass above the face wasn't part of the head, it was a sort of headdress, fold on fold of cloth wound into a cunning shape, like an enormous patterned knot. The man was smiling at her, a normal human smile. But he was still a strange figure in the bright moonlight, seven feet tall or more with his headdress, but thin, and gawky as some long-legged insect.

"Hurry now," he said. "Out of forest by sunrise."

"I'm not going anywhere much, not without a horse," said Meena from the cave entrance. "My hip's that sore. And Alnor's ankle's not so good, either. Calico ought to be somewhere."

"Horses under the trees," said the stranger. "Cave first."

"I'd better come that far," said Meena. "The so-and-sos found my leather bag, and I've got to have my spoons back. And our money and stuff, too. Give us a hand, girl. Alnor? . . . Then you wait here, but I'll need the boy."

Leaning heavily on Tahl and Tilja and grunting at every step, she hobbled along the hillside. The stranger was already well ahead of them. For a moment they saw his awkward figure lit by something other than moonlight, before he seemed to disappear into the cliff.

"Meena," whispered Tahl urgently. "When he was doing that stuff with the ropes in the cave, did you feel anything? Magic, I mean?"

"Can't say I did, now you mention it," muttered Meena. "But then I wasn't minding much beyond this darned hip. What—"

"*Shhh.* Later," whispered Tahl as a light flared into the darkness from where they had seen the stranger vanish. Reaching the place, they found it was a much larger cave, with the embers of a fire just inside the entrance, and beyond that the stranger holding in his hand a short piece of rope whose frayed end blazed steadily, but with almost no smoke, like a good wick in a lamp. Around him lay the bodies of the robbers, all on their sides, with gags in their mouths, their arms and ankles lashed and their legs drawn hard back behind them and tied to the wrists. Some struggled and wriggled, some lay still. A mound of baggage and other stuff was piled at the back of the cave. From where she stood Tilja could see the saddlebags. She followed Tahl in, stepping over the bodies of the robbers, and picked up the bag they had brought from Woodbourne.

"I can't see your green bag, Meena," she called after a quick search along the pile.

"Hold it. Tell you in a moment," Meena answered.

By the light from the stranger's rope Tilja saw her close her eyes and concentrate. In the same instant she saw the stranger stiffen and look sharply round toward the entrance.

"He's got it," Meena called. "That fellow there. Opposite you and two to your left . . . yes, him."

The robbers had been bound where they slept. Each of them had his own small pile of loot stacked beside him. The man grunted angrily as Tilja sorted through his belongings. She found the green bag, looked inside and saw that the bundle of spoons was there, and the wooden Valley coins, but the metal ones were gone.

"I've got them," she called. "But he's put our Empire money somewhere."

"And ours," said Tahl.

"Wait," said the stranger. "Find what I can."

With the flaring rope held above his head he turned slowly round, and pointed with his free hand at one of the bound men, and then another.

"Cord round his neck," he said. "His . . . his . . . under pillow . . ."

Tilja knelt by the first of the bound figures. The cord was tucked down inside the man's jacket but seemed to be twitching vigorously as it tried to haul itself free, but the man himself was thrashing around, grunting furiously, so she couldn't be sure, and when she laid hold of it, it seemed to be ordinary lifeless cord. She pulled out the purse and moved on. When she and Tahl had finished working their way round the cave, they gave the six purses they'd found to the stranger, who weighed them in his hand, passed three back to Tahl, kept two for himself, and tossed one down onto the floor of the cave.

"Good," he said. "No more time. Cords'll loosen when this burns out."

He dropped the burning rope onto the floor of the cave and led the way out. Tilja gave Meena the green bag, but as she hefted the saddlebag to carry it down the slope she heard a movement from below and saw the dark shapes of three horses coming out from under the trees and starting up. She could tell which one was Calico from the fuss she was making. Then, as they came up the slope, she saw that the first two each had a lead rope wriggling ahead and was following it docilely up, but Calico was fighting against two ropes, which were taking it in turn to snake up the slope and wrap an end round a fresh hold while the other one hauled her on. Even in the thrill and terror of escape Tilja remembered how it had taken several strong men to force Calico onto the raft, and laughed aloud. The stranger joined in with a raucous bellow, more like a donkey's bray than laughter.

"At least someone's happy," said Meena. "Now where's my horse seat? Run down, girl and have a look . . ."

"On its way," said the stranger, as the harness came scurrying up the slope, dragging the horse seat behind it. It stilled as Tilja picked it up and buckled it on, but the other two sets fastened themselves in place without human help.

"Ready?" said the stranger. "Bring the horse, child. Now, madam . . ."

Calico quietened at Tilja's touch and let herself be led up. The stranger's angular, big-boned arms hoisted Meena into the saddle with no apparent effort. Tilja held the saddlebags in place for him while he fastened them on. She had half expected him to do this by magic, but he used his hands, lashing and knotting as anyone else would have done, but very deftly, with none of the apparent clumsiness of his other movements.

By now Tahl had brought Alnor limping across. The stranger helped him onto one of the other horses, then bent and picked up several coils of rope that had somehow appeared, and loaded them onto the third animal.

"All ready?" he said. "Anything else? What, child?"

Tilja started. Unconsciously, from force of habit acquired over the last few days, she had patted the back of her head to check that her coil was in place, and found her hair all disheveled. Now she was feeling hopelessly around for the fastenings. She was oddly distressed by the trivial loss.

"My hairpin and tie," she said. "It doesn't matter. Let's go."

"I put the pin in the back of your cloak," said Tahl. "I didn't feel the tie."

"Wait," said the stranger.

He stood for a few moments, bent and picked something up and handed it to Tilja.

"Oh, thank you," she said. "My hair's too short. It keeps coming undone."

"Give."

She handed the hair tie back. He put it his palm and seemed to stare at it for a moment while he scratched at the back of his neck with his other hand. Then he rolled it briefly between fingers and thumbs.

"Turn," he said.

She turned, and felt his fingers flickering through her hair, and the hair seeming to comb itself out, and braid and coil silkily under his touch. In almost no time at all he slid the pin home. Automatically she put up a hand to pat it into place, but he caught her wrist.

"Don't touch," he said sharply.

"I'm sorry. I . . ."

He stared at her for a moment, frowning, then gave that odd little grunt and let go. She realized that there had been something very peculiar about his grasp, as if she'd been able to feel its pressure but not the actual touch of his fingers. No, that wasn't quite it, but . . .

"New one on me," he said, flexing his hand as if he were trying to ease a stiffness out of it. "But don't you tie it yourself. Won't work. Get your grandma to do it."

"Anyway, thank you," she said. "That's wonderful."

"Sell a lot of hair ties," he said.

His startling laugh was still ringing across the valley as he grasped his horse's lead rope and strode off across the hillside.

At first they hurried along in moonlight bright enough for them to pick their footsteps on the rough path. Tahl led the second horse, ridden by Alnor, whose ankle was now almost too painful to take his weight. Tilja, Meena and Calico came behind. For once Calico was no trouble, with the other horses to follow. She didn't even balk when the stranger turned aside and started down the slope.

As soon as they were in the darkness beneath the trees he stopped. After a brief pause a light flared, like the one he'd lit in the cave. He handed a piece of blazing rope to Tahl and lit another for Tilja. As soon as she touched it it went out. He gave one of his expressive grunts—not of surprise this time, but something else—took it back, lit it with a flick of his wrist and handed it up to Meena without a word, then lit a third for himself and led the way on. The light was just enough for them to see their way but seemed to strengthen when they dipped into the fog. As they reached the bottom path Tilja heard a rustling noise close by her feet. Looking down, she saw several lengths of rope flowing rapidly past her. The stranger stopped.

"Don't wait," he said. "Don't think the fools will follow, but never know. Catch you up."

The knowledge that the bandits were now free gave Tilja's weary legs fresh strength. Hurrying past the stranger, she saw one of the ropes start to climb up his leg like a twining vine while another one was already coiling itself into his hand. As soon as they were well ahead Tahl slowed his pace and waited for her.

"Listen," he said. "In the cave, when I untied your wrists, as soon as I'd got it loose the cord came alive, but when I touched your hand with it it went dead. The man told me to drop it before I could try again."

"He says it's something about me. Just before that he was trying to make the cord undo itself, and I got a funny numb feeling in my arms. I'm going to ask him as soon as I can."

"Be careful. You know the rope that tripped Calico? It felt like the ropes in the cave—alive, I mean, until I'd got it loose. Then it went dead."

"Because you were touching it?"

"No, I don't think so. I think it was because it had finished what it was there for."

"Are you sure of this, Tahl?" said Alnor.

"Not dead sure. I think it was like that, but it was only a moment or two. I just thought . . . Tell you later. Here he comes."

Tilja dropped back and to the side to let the stranger come striding past.

Night and the journey seemed unending, unchanging, the darkness, the dripping trees, the fog. Tired beyond tiredness, Tilja plodded on. For the first few miles fear of pursuit had kept her going, but by now she had used up all those reserves of energy and knew she couldn't travel much further without rest. Then the path dipped, they came out of the fog as suddenly as they'd walked into it, and she saw a vast plain stretching in front of her, with the first pale wash of dawn showing along the eastern horizon. At the foot of the hills a few spots of light pricked the darkness. The stranger halted and they stopped on either side of him.

"Way station," he said. "Be there by sunrise."

"We owe you our thanks, sir," said Alnor. "Without you we would still be prisoners. And yet we do not know your name."

The stranger laughed.

"No name," he said. "Don't use one. Just Ropemaker."

"You must've got one, though," said Meena. "Just you're not saying."

He laughed again.

"Well," said Meena. "Like Alnor says, we owe you a bit, but I've a question to ask you all the same. I know it's dangerous to talk about this kind of thing, but it strikes me we're all in this together. That was a lot of powerful stuff you were doing with your ropes back there up the hill, and none of us felt a thing, not like we'd expect to, Alnor and Tahl and me. When something like that's going on, we get this kind of a feeling . . . doesn't happen where we come from, so we're not used to it, but there's no mistaking . . . you get what I'm asking you?"

He didn't answer at once but turned, not to her but to Tilja.

"You felt nothing, girl?" he asked quietly.

"No. I don't. I can't . . . it doesn't matter."

Perhaps it was just that she was so exhausted, so far from home, so shaken by their adventure, but she could hear the bitterness and sadness in her own voice and knew she was lying, and knew the others knew. It was as though she had been standing under the cedars with Anja all over again. Her inability to feel the presence of magic, in the same way that the others felt it, truly did matter, for reasons she was quite unable to grasp.

The Ropemaker's huge head was a dark mass against the paling stars. She couldn't see his eyes, but he seemed to be staring at her. Then he gave a brief, yapping laugh and turned to Meena.

"Not warded, ma'am?" he asked her.

"Don't know how," she told him. "Like I say, it doesn't happen where we come from."

"Spoon of yours—that's warded."

"Lananeth did that for us. She said it would be safer."

"Right. Won't get it into Talagh with you, though. Need more than that. Might meet someone on the way, too. . . . Only country stuff, those wards. . . . Give it to the girl, ma'am. There's something about her—don't understand it myself. New to me. Don't know if it'll stand up to the wards they've got at Talagh, but it's the best you can do. Strap it against her skin, under her sleeve. May be safe like that. All right? Got to be getting on now, heading north, convoy to catch. No hurry for you—yours goes tomorrow. Day's rest for the old 'uns. And you take that horse, sir. Be more than a day or two before you can walk on that leg of yours. Sell it when you're done with it. Been a pleasure to meet you. Luck be with you, then."

Meena's mouth had barely opened to protest before he had turned and was striding down the slope, waving a spidery arm in acknowledgment as they called their farewells after him.

8

The Walls of the City

alagh. There was no grasping it, no way Tilja could imagine it as just a particular place in the world. It wouldn't fit into her mind. It was like the Empire itself, too huge, too strange, too, somehow, vague.

By the time they reached it even its name had become uncertain. In the Valley it had been Talak; north of the Pirrim Hills Talagh; but in the twenty-seven days of travel since then she had heard it called Talarg and Dalarg and Dhawak and Tallak-Tallak, and Ndalag and several other names, by travelers who had joined the traffic on the Grand Northwest Road by one of the scores of roads that fed into it from north and south.

And the speakers had been just as different as the names they'd used for the city. Tahl, who could make friends with anyone, had hit it off with a boy his own age whom he'd met while he was haggling with a dealer over a price for Alnor's horse at one of the way stations. These were huge by now, with booths for a thousand travelers, more or less grand according to their grade. Tahl's friend, Cinoquo, had a clear, coppery skin, thick lips, a snub, spread nose, and high, prominent cheekbones, just like his parents, who were on their way to a provincial capital to be witnesses in a legal dispute between their Landholder and a rival which had already dragged on through five generations. They were nomadic cattle herders and drove a creaking oxcart—they had no other home—and spoke in an accent so strange that until she was used to it Tilja could understand only one word in three.

But some things didn't vary at all. Cinoquo's father was a chief in his tribe, so he was a fourteenth grader and wore a cap like Alnor's, and Cinoquo's little sister had just started to put her hair up, braided and coiled and fastened with two blue beads and a blue-headed pin showing, and she was having just the same trouble keeping them in place that Tilja used to have until the Ropemaker had done his trick with her hair tie. These were the people who called the city Tallak-Tallak.

Tilja saw it first as a dirty smudge spreading along the southeastern horizon. The Grand Northwest Road truly lived up to its name by now. For the past nine days it had been fifty paces broad, well paved from ditch to ditch and marked off into separate lanes for travelers of different status and speeds, the ordinary traffic plodding along at the outer edges, while imperial messengers, high officials and their like sped through in the middle. (When the Emperor traveled, Tahl had heard someone say, the road was closed to all traffic for a day's march before and behind him, and it took his retinue a morning to pass by.)

For most of the time they had journeyed across plains or among gentle hills; for the last day and a half they had wound up through precipitous valleys, beneath cliffs, over passes, and down by thundering streams until, abruptly, they came round a spur, and there lay Talagh.

Tilja didn't at first notice it, because her eye was inevitably caught by the river. The one by which they had left the Valley would have been a trickle beside it. Nevertheless those waters were here, one of the hundreds of tributaries that mingled into this mile-wide gleaming flood, snaking down from the north, close below the hills, and swinging away east across the plain.

"Talagh," said someone, and pointed. Tilja peered into the distance and saw the smudge spreading along the horizon, a smudge in the clear spring air from the dust and fume of several million lives, a smudge on the patient earth from centuries of such lives building their houses and workplaces and temples and palaces and towers of fortification, and then rebuilding and rebuilding on the rubble of them. A smudge on time itself. From where she stood she began to feel its power.

That was at noon. In midafternoon they crossed the river on one of a pair of wooden bridges built upon massive piles. (What forest of giants must have been felled to provide such timber!) They slept at the last, thronged way station with the city still a few miles distant. From here they could see the low hill at its center, where the twenty spindling towers of the Watchers rose above the haze of dust and smoke, marking the heart of the Empire, the Emperor's palace. Here too, as Lananeth had warned them, they were pestered by touts offering to guide them through the bureaucratic maze of entry and the dangers of the streets to wondrous places of pleasure and profit within the walls of Talagh.

Next morning for a while they saw no sign of any such walls. They walked past fields of vegetables, clusters of shabby houses and barns, more fields, more buildings, and then they were trudging along a tree-lined avenue with pompous statues and fountains, but still with dingy and ramshackle warehouses and yards on either side. Some kind of building blocked the road in the distance.

Nearer, this turned out to be an immense triple archway built of dark red brick. Beyond it they came to an empty space, two hundred paces across and stretching out of sight on either side. Ahead, in the same dark brick, heavy as a thundercloud at sunset, rose the gates and towered walls of Talagh.

They passed under the arch around noon, and joined the lines for entry. Many of their fellow travelers would still be waiting by dusk, and have to camp in their places all night and wait for the clerks to start work again next morning, but Alnor was wearing the uniform of a fourteenth grader, so one of the officials controlling the lines (two drin before he would even look at them) told them to join the shorter line at the left-hand gate. Nobody questioned their identities. The fees and bribes seemed to be all that mattered. Even so Tilja found herself sighing with relief when at last, late in the day, they stepped under the massive arch of the great gate of Talagh.

At once the whole of her left arm went numb. It wasn't ordinary numbness such as she might have got from sleeping on it too long. She flexed her hand and her fingers moved, but it didn't seem to be her, Tilja, moving them. She had two left arms, this strange, new, different arm, full of a kind of glowing chill which blanked out all other feelings, and inside that her own everyday arm, helpless, a sort of ghost. The feeling spread through her whole body, filling it, taking it over, more and more intense. In a moment it was going to come shrieking out—

No! she thought. *This is me! Tilja Urlasdaughter of Woodbourne Farm. No!*

Deliberately she shaped the picture in her mind, herself in the kitchen at home, just having climbed out of bed and now leaning against the stove as she repeated the fire charm and listened to the crackle of twigs and the swelling roar of flames into the flue. Blindly she clung to that image as she forced her feeble Tilja legs to shuffle the alien body forward and out on the other side of the arch, where she halted, sweating and gasping as the numbness flowed back the way it had come, out of her body into her left arm and then down from the shoulder to the place where Axtrig lay against her skin. It swirled into the old wooden spoon and was gone.

Magic, she thought. Yes, Talagh, the warded city. Wards of immense power, built into its walls by the greatest magicians in the Empire. And she, Tilja, had just carried Axtrig through them. The Ropemaker had said he didn't know if she could do it, but she had. The wards had tried to stop her, to break through her own mysterious defenses, and they had failed. Though she was still shuddering with the remembered strain and terror, beneath them she began to feel a strange sort of dazed exhilaration at the understanding of what she had done.

147

"Get a move on, girl! No time for daydreaming!"

Meena's snarl from above her head yanked her back into the everyday world, and she led Calico on.

Again they had to force their way past a mass of touts, keeping close together, knowing what easy prey a blind old man, a lame old woman and two children might seem to these street jackals. Tilja had anything she valued beneath her skirt, and the others had taken similar precautions. Besides, the jackals had misjudged Meena, perched above them, watchful as a house dog. Twice Tilja heard the swish of her cane, followed by a yelp and guffaws from the other jackals, as a hand had reached for one of the saddlebags.

On Lananeth's instructions they pushed through into a court-yard beside the main gate and lined up at yet another booth, where Alnor hired one of the official guides, a silent, unsmiling young man. He seemed quite unimpressed when Alnor asked him to take them to the house of Lord Kzuva, one of the great nobles of the Empire. He took the fee and bribe and extra with-out a word of thanks, told them to keep up, and strode off, using his staff of office to lever a path though the mob. They would never have found their way without him.

In one sense Talagh was roughly what Tilja had expected from the account of it in the story of Asarta. They had entered through one of the twelve great gates and were now on a broad avenue that led, gently rising, up to the Emperor's palace at the center. On either side of her, just as in the story, she could see crooked lanes and alleys running off into the maze of streets that lay between this and the next avenues. She was even prepared, she'd thought, for the crowds and the noise and the smells.

But she wasn't. In her mind, perhaps, but not in her imagina-tion. Not for the overwhelming *pressure* of it all, all those hurrying people, the mass of different lives and purposes, the bellowing vendors, the infants—jackals in the making—wheedling pitifully for a quarter drin but with eyes sharp for anything they could snatch, so street skilled that when some bigwig was borne through, shoulder-high on a chair, with baton-wielding attendants thwacking a pathway, these urchins ducked under the blows without even turning to look. And the rattle of drums and the high bleat of bagpipes calling the scurriers' attention to a troupe of five near-naked contortionists who'd tied themselves into a knot so intricate that no one could tell which arm or head belonged to which body. As Tilja passed, this knot began to dance, rolling itself from foot to foot that stuck out at random from the mass. And just beyond that another raucous ensemble advertised a woman whose gross body was so covered with different-colored scorpions that not a scrap of her flesh could be seen, and every one of them deadly poisonous, so the hawker beside her yelled. And another such sight, and another, and another, every few paces, and the lamplit stalls glittering with trinkets, or great mounds of unknown fruit, or wicked knives and daggers, or sickly-scented salves. . . . Oh, the reeks and odors of Talagh, familiar and strange, honest leather mingling with cloying spices, rots with roses, heady smokes, bitter, cleansing acids, furs and furnaces, people and creatures and stuffs and objects, the very bricks and plaster of the buildings seeming to pour out their own bricky and plastery essences into the dusty, pungent air.

Along its whole length the avenue was thronged from side to side, and at first the going seemed no easier when their guide turned off along one of the broader side lanes. They threaded their way on, crossed two of the main avenues, and came as night was falling to an area of much grander houses than they had so far seen. Here the side streets were almost empty, many of them guarded at either end by men with the tasseled caps and staffs that showed they were the servants of some great lord. At one of these places their guide halted.

"Speak to these fellows," he said. "I go no further."

Tahl offered him the three drin he had ready for the tip, but the guide shook his head.

"My father is also blind," he said. Still unsmiling, he turned and strode away.

One of the guards laughed.

149

"My father has excellent eyesight," he said. "Whose household do you seek, my rustic friends? The Lord Kzuva's? This way, then . . ."

He led them past ornate entrances, beyond which fountains played in lamplit courtyards, and rapped with his staff on a small door in an otherwise blank high wall. Without waiting for an answer, he took his three drin and left. A bored servant opened the door, yawned as he took his bribe, barely seemed to listen to Alnor's message but held out his hand for another three drin before he would open the main gate to let Meena and Calico through.

He told them to wait and slouched off, but almost before Tilja and Tahl had helped Meena down he came hurrying back, accompanied by another man, middle-aged, pale and plump, wearing the braided silk jacket that meant, Tilja knew by now, that he was a fairly important official. This man rushed eagerly up to Meena, threw his arms round her and kissed her on both cheeks.

"My dearest Qualifa!" he purred. "What a pleasurable surprise! And Qualif! And both grandchildren—long way from home, my young friends, eh? And have you grown! See to the horse, Carran, and have the east-court guest rooms made ready. Send food to my room. This way, my friends. Ah, Qualifa, my dear, your hip is troubling you? Shall I send for a litter?"

"I'll do, thank you kindly," said Meena. "And it's a pleasure to see you again, sir."

"Take my arm then, and tell me what's happening at home. You left my wife well?"

He took Meena's arm and led them through a couple of lamplit courtyards, up a few steps and in through a door. The room beyond glowed with colors and had a strange but pleasing smell. On one side piles of cushions ringed a low table. On the other was a work table covered with ledgers and documents. A large caged bird squawked at their entry.

Their guide closed the door and let out a sigh of relief. He shook his head as he studied his visitors. He had, Tilja thought, a guarded look in his eyes. He had stopped smiling.

"And your true names?" he asked in a voice just above a whisper.

Alnor answered just as quietly.

"We are Alnor Ortahlson and Meena Urlasdaughter, and these are our grandchildren, Tahl and Tilja. We came to your house, where your wife questioned us and gave us food. We needed to come to Talagh, for our own purposes. She needed four people, two old, two young, to come to Talagh and buy death-leaves for the two whose names we assumed. She could not get word to you sooner than we could come, but she said you would understand, since you and she had talked of this possibility. Now we are here. If you have no use for us after all, we will go and do the thing we came for, and trouble you no further."

The man stood for a long while, drumming his fingertips on the table.

"She has taken you under my roof and fed you," he said. "She and I are one. You can safely tell me more. Where, for instance, do you come from?"

"Beyond the forest."

"Ah . . . you gave my name at the gate?"

"Yes. Your wife told us . . ."

"Of course."

He stood there for a while, aimlessly tidying stacks of papers, then nodded.

"Sit," he said. "When they bring food they will consider it strange to find you still standing. I must think."

While he paced the room Tilja settled Meena down and made her comfortable, then sat beside her. They waited in silence until he joined them.

"Well," he said with a sigh, "you offer me a way out of one great danger, but into a far worse one. Now not only I and mine, but my Lord Kzuva and all his household stand in peril. Still, I can see no other way than to continue to help you. You have come through the gate, so the names of Qualif and Qualifa are in the registers, recorded as visiting me. Therefore you must be recorded as leaving Talagh, or dying before you could do so. If you had not eaten under my roof, it would have been best for me to poison you two and sell the children for slaves, as the law demands, but that path is now closed. Well, then, I am Ellion, Steward to the Lord Kzuva, and despite all this I welcome you for your own sakes."

"Thank you kindly," said Meena, sharply. "Even if we'd have been more use to you dead than alive."

"Would you really have poisoned them and sold us two?" said Tahl, sounding more interested than horrified. Ellion smiled thinly.

"I am glad to be spared the decision," he said. "And the fact remains that you may indeed be useful to me alive. I find I can no longer do as I intended, and arrange for false death-leaves to be issued, with false entries in the registers, as would have been possible in the previous reign. The man now in charge of the census and registry of subjects is able and vigorous, and many laxities are being swept away.

"Now the main danger lies in your being who you are, and where you come from. My wife has explained to you about this? Good. And of course you are in just as great danger as I am, so it is in all our interests that you should leave as soon as possible. Your gate permit in any case lasts only five days. Can you do what you have come for in that time?"

"We are looking for a man," said Alnor. "Our account of him says that we will find him if he wants us to, and fail if he does not."

Ellion sat very still, staring at the back of his hand.

"That kind of a man?" he whispered. "No, tell me nothing."

"If you say so," said Meena. "Then all I want is somewhere for Tilja and me to go on our own, out in the open would be best, sometime when there's no one else around. I know it's not going to be easy in Talagh, but—"

There was a movement at the door, and a discreet tap. All five froze, but it was only servants with a tray of food. Ellion at once became smiling and easy, fussing over Meena and Alnor and seeing that they were comfortable, just as he might have done over two old friends, but as soon as the servants had left he let out a deep sigh. Tilja could feel his fear. He looked at Meena.

"So you are another of that kind?" he said slowly.

"No, I'm not, sir, I promise you. We don't have anything like that in the Valley, just—what did your wife call it—little bits of country magic. I'll need Tilja here along with me. It'll only take us a moment, and then we'll clear out."

Perhaps if Ellion had known her better he would have refused. As it was, after another long pause and sigh, followed by that anxious smile, he said, "I know an obstinate woman when I meet one. You will do what you plan whether I help you or not. Well, I will need to talk to . . . a friend. Eat now, and then I will send for somebody to show you where you can sleep. When all is quiet let the girl come back here and find me."

A big moon cast dense shadows. Keeping to the darkest places beneath the walls, Ellion led Tilja back the way she had come, round a small courtyard, through an archway and round a larger courtyard, to where Meena was waiting at the foot of the stairway that led up to their rooms.

"I shall not stay for you once we are there," he whispered. "You will need to remember your own way back. Now, come."

He led them on through many windings to what seemed to be the back of the house, and out into yet another courtyard surrounded by large, shapeless buildings which looked more like storehouses than places where anyone lived. Here he unlocked a door and gave Tilja the key. Inside was a musty-smelling space into which the moonlight shone through three small windows high in one wall. Between the bars of silver light everything else was impenetrably dark.

"I will leave you here," said Ellion. "When I am gone, lock the door and hide the key. In the further corner to your right you will find a stair. Climb it until you reach a locked door. Here is that

153

key. Go through, lock the door and again hide the key. Hide it well. You will find yourselves on the inner-city wall. It is not guarded along its length, only at the main gates. But you will see flashes of light here and there, where fragments of loose magic strike against the wards that ring it round. My friend says that the bit of country magic you propose to do should have much the same effect, and so pass unnoticed by any Watcher. Go to your left, until you are well away from this house, before you attempt anything, be as quick as you can, and when you have done leave instantly."

"Well, thank you kindly," said Meena as if she were talking to a neighbor who'd brought her a basket of pears. "I can see you're doing the best you can by us, and we'll do the same for you. Come along then, girl. No point in hanging around."

Tilja closed the door behind Ellion and tucked the key under some sacking that she found by touch down against the wall. She took Meena's hand and with her free hand groping before her and feeling her way with each footstep she worked across into one of the shafts of moonlight and down it to the right-hand wall. There were piles of barrels stacked against it. She felt her way from barrel to barrel to the corner, where she found another door, not locked. She opened it and found the first step with her foot.

"He didn't say how far up it was," she whispered. "Are you going to be able to manage? Wait—there's a hand rope."

"You take my cane, then. Where's your shoulder? Right. One at a time."

Very slowly they climbed eight winding flights. The ones against the two outer walls had slit windows through which Tilja could see the stars, and moonlit roofs, but it was still pitch black inside the stairwell and she had to make sure of every tread by feel. Meena muttered under her breath from time to time, but never groaned nor asked to rest. The ninth flight ended in a door.

Tilja found the keyhole with her fingers, turned the grinding lock and pushed the door open. Beyond it was a battlemented parapet and a wide moonlit sky. She stepped outside and found herself in a kind of alley stretching left and right between the parapet and the much higher wall of the building they had just left. She couldn't quite see over the parapet.

She locked the door as soon as Meena was through and followed her along to the left, looking for somewhere to hide the key. She fully understood the need. If they were caught doing whatever it was Meena was planning, they mustn't be carrying any clues about where they'd come from. There was a small tree growing out of the parapet. Its roots had broken some of the brickwork away, so that Tilja could look over. Below her the wall dropped dizzyingly down to the cleared space that circled the old city, and beyond that the moonlit roofs of the outer city reached away.

Tilja managed to wedge the key in among the roots, then hurried after Meena. Buildings lined the inner side of the walkway, screening the central city, but anyone outside the walls must surely have seen Meena's head and shoulders as she hobbled along through the moonlight. Some distance ahead of them a wisp of pale light flickered above the wall and vanished. Then another, further on. Loose magic striking the wards, Ellion had said. Every hundred paces or so they came to a small watchtower, with a doorless opening onto the walkway. A little beyond the third of these there was a gap in the screen of buildings on their left, with only a waist-high wall to prevent them falling. The gap was wide enough to show them most of the inner city.

"This'll have to do," Meena whispered. "I'll stay back here. Keep yourself down. First thing, we've got to get our bearings. Moon must've come up over there, so that'll be eastish. North's somewhere behind there, then. Drat this moon—can't see a thing this side. You go on ahead, girl, and see if you can spot the Fisherman—he'll be low down this time of night, so he should show up spite of the moon—and that should give you the Axle-pin. Once you've got that you take old Axtrig out and put her down on her cloth—here—and stand a bit beyond, facing this way so you can see me as well as her. Put your hand up when you're ready."

"What are you trying to do?"

"I'll tell you. You remember what happened in Ellion's house when I said the man's name out loud—how Axtrig twisted round and pointed herself toward Talagh, showing us that was the way we'd got to go. Only thing it could mean, far as I can see. What I'm hoping is she'll do it again now, but this time I'll keep myself well clear and just whisper his name. That way maybe it won't hit me as hard as it did back then, but it'll still be enough for Axtrig to move. Soon as you see her twist, you run in and check the line, and then you pick her up and put her away and we'll be out of here as fast as we can go. And if nothing happens, I'll come a bit closer and try again."

"It's still a lot more than country magic, isn't it, Meena, whatever you said to Ellion?"

"Maybe it is and maybe it isn't, but if you was in my shoes you'd give it a try, wouldn't you, girl?"

"I expect so. But one line's not going to be enough, is it? We're going to have to do it somewhere else, and see where the lines cross."

"Well, maybe. But what I'm thinking is this. There's got to be a reason why he gave Dirna the peach in the first place, and why we've kept Axtrig in the family all this time, and why I brought her along without rhyme or reason, just feeling it was important. It's so we could find him when the time came. So maybe when I say his name he'll feel it himself, and he'll know we're here and looking for him, and then either he'll help us, or he won't. Now, don't hang around arguing. Off you go, and let's get it done with."

From the sharpness of her whispered voice Tilja could tell that Meena was as scared as she was herself. Crouching low and keeping in the strip of shadow beneath the parapet, she scuttled along the walkway to the center of the gap. There she turned and gazed out across the dark and jagged roofscape of the inner city, rising in a gentle swell from east and west to the palace at the summit. Each of the twenty fantastic towers that ringed it had one or two lit windows near the top, and everything below was dark and still. Were the Watchers still awake, even at this hour? Awake enough, in spite of what Ellion had said, to notice something different about a flicker of country magic striking the city's wards? A sense of steadily increasing danger filled the night air.

She turned her eyes upward and searched among the familiar stars. Yes, there, faint, because of the moon pallor, and lying on his side, was the good old Fisherman, his rod bowed from the weight of the Fish. She followed the line of the last section of rod, and found the Axle-pin, fainter still, directly over the third tower from the left. So that was due north.

She rolled up her sleeve and with trembling fingers untied the ribbon that for the last sixteen days had kept Axtrig safely against her forearm. She had grown so used to the spoon being there that she seldom noticed her, but now as she took her in her hand, that curious slight numbness seeped across her palm and the pads of her fingers.

Something moved in the darkness beside her.

She froze.

Again, in the utter stillness, the same faint pad. A cat meowed softly. She stared and saw the green of its eyes. As her heart resumed its proper beat, the cat moved into the moonlight and meowed again. It was a large, bony creature, neither starved nor cared for. The moonlight sparkled faintly off its shaggy fur. Automatically her hand moved to stroke it, but it backed away and sat down.

"Off you go," she whispered. "Shoo!"

The cat answered with another meow, but didn't stir. There'd always been cats at Woodbourne, and Tilja felt comforted by its homely presence. She knelt and spread out the cloth Meena had given her, then laid Axtrig down with her shaft pointing east along the wall, so that she would need to make an obvious movement to point to anywhere in the city. Still keeping low, she stepped back, squatted down facing toward Meena and signaled that she was ready. Meena raised her hand in answer. Tilja stared at the spoon.

The world changed.

Light blazed all along the wall, glaring, shadowless. A whirl of movement—the cat streaking away along the wall, leaping past Meena's body where it lay on the walkway . . .

Tilja jumped to her feet and ran, snatched Axtrig and the cloth as she passed, crammed them into her blouse and raced on. Meena was lying on her back, her head facing the way they had come, and her cane beside her. Tilja poked it into her waistband, knelt, worked her arms under Meena's shoulders, heaved her up and started to drag her along the walkway. All this without thought. She only knew that they had to get clear of the place, now, at once. But Meena was far too heavy for her. She was gasping already, her heart pounding. She knew she couldn't go much further. Where . . . ?

Something she'd seen. The fleeing cat vanishing into the darkness of the little tower. It was only a few paces away now. With a last, wrenching effort she dragged Meena in through the opening and collapsed on top of her.

As soon as she could, she mastered her gasping lungs and breathed more quietly, but the thud of her heart seemed still to fill the night. The glaring light was gone. She knelt up and looked toward the tower entrance. Through it she could see only the blank, moonlit wall of the building on the opposite side of the walkway, so bright that the reflected light shone straight into the center of the little tower, leaving a patch of deep shadow either side. Anyone standing there was sure to see her, and Meena too. Carefully she lifted Meena's shoulders again and dragged her into the shadow, close to the curving wall, then rose and stood, knowing it was still useless, hopeless. The tower itself was a trap. Her breathing had eased but her heart wouldn't stop thumping, as it did in nightmares until the terror itself woke her with every muscle locked rigid.

This was just such a nightmare, with the unknown enemy hunting outside, herself hiding, knowing it was going to find her. Except that she was already awake.

Forcing herself out of the paralysis of terror, she edged toward the door until she could see along the walkway almost as far as the next tower. She stared at it. There. It was there that the world had changed, and the nightmare had begun.

An image formed itself in her mind—the spoon, Axtrig, lying on her cloth under that astounding light, with her bowl toward the heart of the city and her shaft pointing the other way. There had been a world in which the spoon had been pointing east along the old city wall. Then there was one in which she was pointing . . . no, not in toward the heart of Talagh, but out, away from it, waking the wards that ringed it, *south*.

She had no time to think about this, to be amazed or puzzled, because now the nightmare became real. Two figures appeared, moving toward her. One was human, a woman she thought, but couldn't be sure because it was wrapped in a wide cloak that reached to the ground. The other . . . she didn't know what it was. It was the height of a large dog, and the human held it by a leash, but it was twice as broad as any dog Lilja had ever seen, with massive shoulders on long forelegs, and a body that then sloped away to squat hind legs. It moved with an awkward waddle and was jet black, blacker than jet. Its blackness drank the moonlight.

As she stared, rigid, holding her breath, trying to silence the betraying thud of her heart, the cat came out of the patch of shadow on the opposite side of the tower and walked to the entrance. It saw the approaching pair, stiffened and arched its back. All its fur stood on end, flecked by the moonlight with pale golden sparks that flickered and changed as it paced rapidly to and fro across the opening, weaving a figure-eight pattern. That

159

done, it came back almost to where Tilja was standing and sat down to watch with her.

Its presence, its ordinariness, didn't belong in the nightmare. For some kind of reassurance Tilja stooped to stroke its back, but again it moved out of reach and sat watching the pair on the walkway.

Halfway between the two towers they halted and the creature crouched and sniffed noisily at the paving. It licked the place vigorously, looked up and gave a purring snarl, its tongue lolling from an enormous, jagged-fanged mouth. It had one eye, in the middle of its forehead. The woman—she had turned her face into the moonlight, and Tilja could now be sure—scratched the back of its head and gazed along the wall, directly toward the tower where Tilja was hiding. She was almost as dark as the creature, a smooth, young, handsome face with no life in it at all. The face of a statue.

She stooped gracefully and held her hands over the place the creature had shown her. Ribbons of yellow light glowed between her fingers and the paving. Tilja's chest started to tingle. Instinctively she put her hand to the place and found that the tingling came from Axtrig, lying between her shift and her blouse, but as soon as her fingers gripped the wood it stopped, and instead the same odd numbness as before flowed into her hand. This time it ran all the way up her arm to the elbow, strong enough for her to recognize it as the terrifying sensation that had almost overwhelmed her coming through the city gate. It came from Axtrig, but it was caused by whatever the woman was doing. Yes, she and her creature were looking for Axtrig—that was the tingling. And Tilja had stopped her when she had laid her hand on the wood— that was the numbness. The magic, instead of reaching out to answer the woman's summons, had flowed into Tilja's arm and away.

The woman stayed where she was. The glow of light beneath her hands increased to a glare, but Axtrig remained inert, while the numbness seeped away. The woman rose, frowning, and looked again along the walkway. Tilja was certain that now was the moment when they were going to come and find her, but then saw that the woman seemed to be looking beyond the tower. It was clear from the way she stood that she was now waiting for something, or somebody, coming toward her.

Soon Tilja heard the pad of shod feet and a man came into view, walking toward the woman. Tilja saw only his naked back, with a wild tangle of hair reaching almost to his waist, muscular arms with heavy bracelets above and below the elbows, a wide belt covered with jewels that glittered in the moonlight, baggy knee-length trousers, sandals jeweled like the belt. Over his shoulder he carried a sort of whip, a short handle with several knotted thongs.

The creature waddled forward and faced him, snarling. The man ignored it. It leaped at his throat. Something in the empty air seemed to cuff it aside. The man walked straight toward the woman as if he intended to do the same with her. Now his bulk hid her completely from where Tilja was standing, so she couldn't see how the woman stopped him, but she must have, somehow.

They faced each other. Tilja could hear low voices, but not the words. It sounded like a language she didn't know. They seemed to come to some kind of agreement. The man took his whip and held it aloft. The thongs fluttered, as if in a lightly gusting breeze, but there wasn't one. The numbness came back into Tilja's hand and arm, and flowed away as before. She could guess what was happening. The man was looking for Axtrig, just as the woman had with her magic ribbons. If Tilja hadn't been clutching the spoon, the thongs would have been straining toward her. As it was, all they responded to was the little currents of ordinary magic wafting to and fro in the night.

The man turned slowly as he searched, until Tilja could see him from in front. The face didn't belong to the healthy young body or the mass of wild hair. It was the face of a very old man, pale and wrinkled, with bloodshot rheumy eyes and cracked blue lips. Surely, with his powers, he could have chosen any face he wanted. Had he chosen to look like that? It was horrible.

His gaze reached the tower and stopped. He shook his whip slightly, as if trying to stir it into action. The thongs rose, straining like weed in a rapid river. But not toward the tower. South, over the outer city. He turned abruptly to look that way. The woman did the same. They stiffened and moved apart. The woman made a sweeping gesture with her arms and her creature threw back its head and bayed. The man brandished his whip. The thongs writhed, grew, and turned to cords of fire streaming out over the wall. From somewhere close below came an enormous, hissing, whooping howl, the howl of a tempest bellowing through a single throat. The glare of light came back, blazing above the wall like a sheet of summer lightning frozen into stillness. The woman, now half again as tall as before, made a whirling gesture to it, and it gathered itself together, spiraling inward, too bright to look at, and then hurled itself down, a bolt of silent lightning, at the bellowing thing beyond the wall. And again. And again.

A hand, massive as a tree trunk but the color of moonlight, reached up and grasped at the swirling curtain of magic, gathering it together. The glow blazed fiercer yet round that silvery fist, but the fist simply absorbed it. Tilja could see the incandescence pulsing away down the veins of the arm. The tower where Tilja was hiding shuddered as a whole section of parapet fell away.

The cat was at the entrance now, its fur again as rigid as a hedgehog's spines. In the lull after the crash of falling masonry Tilja heard a gasping croak from inside the tower.

"You there, girl?"

"Meena . . . !"

"Got to get out of here . . . can't stand much more . . ."

The glare lit all the interior of the tower. Meena was struggling to her knees. Tilja helped her to her feet and gave her her cane.

"I'll just about do," Meena muttered.

The cat moved out of their way as she hobbled, wheezing, to the door. Tilja saw her stagger and almost fall, but she managed to clutch the parapet and worked her way along it, gripping it all

162

the time as if something was trying to wrench her away. Tilja followed. The magical battle raged behind them. A whole section of wall fell thundering into the space below. Nobody seemed to notice their going.

"You go ahead," Meena croaked. "Get the door open."

Tilja ran on. One-handed—the other was still tight round Axtrig—she found the key behind the tree where she had hidden it, opened the storehouse door and looked back. Against the lightning glare she saw Meena forcing her way through the invisible tempest. Behind her came the cat, pacing steadily along, occasionally turning its head to glance back.

At last Meena reached the door and hobbled through. As Tilja was about to follow, something brushed, purring, against her skirt. She looked down and saw the cat. She could guess now why it hadn't let her stroke it.

"Thanks, puss," she whispered, "for whatever it was you were doing."

The cat purred again and stalked off along the walkway. Tilja closed and locked the door. Beside her Meena was gasping in the darkness.

"Are you all right?"

"Don't talk. I'm just about holding on. I'd best go down on my arse. You first. Tell me what's coming."

Slowly they worked their way down, Tilja going backward on her knees, placing Meena's feet on each step and waiting for her to ease her body down, and then repeating the action, all one-handed because of her desperate fear of letting go of Axtrig. When they were halfway to the ground Meena spoke again, her voice less strained.

"That's a bit more like it. They're giving up. My goodness, though . . . Remember that gale we had, two years back when the home byre blew down? It was like being out in something like that, all the magic blasting around. . . . What about you, girl? You don't seem to have turned a hair."

"No, I didn't feel any of that. Only when they were looking

for Axtrig and she started to sort of tingle. . . . Do you think I can let go of her now? If I put her right in under my blouse so she's against my skin?"

"Maybe I can tell you . . . yes, that feels safe enough. Better get on now—the others'll be wondering what's up. They must've heard the racket going on. Stirred up a hornets' nest, I shouldn't wonder."

Meena was right. When at last they had reached the ground and made their way out of the storehouse they found the whole great household in an uproar, with shouts and cries, and the neighing of panicking horses and barking of dogs, and people hurrying about or standing in groups talking in low voices and glancing up now and again at the moonlit sky. No one paid any attention to Meena and Tilja as they made their way back to their room. Despite what he had said, Ellion was already there.

It was well past midnight before they reached the little window-less chamber to which he now insisted on taking them. When he had locked the door the five of them settled onto coarse cushions round a single dim lamp in the middle of the floor. Meena gray with exhaustion and pain and snarling in her determination not to give in to them; Alnor very solemn and calm; Tahl fizzing with interest and excitement, wide awake despite the hour; Tilja al-most too tired to make one word follow another, but still too shaken to think of sleep; and Ellion himself, keeping his voice steady and soft as always, but with his eyes twitching from one face to the next, and starting at every sound that reached them from the still disturbed household.

"This room is warded," he explained. "Every great lord main-tains at least one personal magician. Ours is my wife's cousin, Zara, and they have been good friends. This is her chamber, and no doubt she will have arranged to hear what we say, but it is the best I can do. It is not only for myself. It is for my own house-hold, and my lord and all who depend on him. You have come among us, into the heart of Talagh, and worked your strong un-warded magic. . . ."

"I'm very sorry, I'm sure," snapped Meena. "You think I'd've risked it if I'd known?"

"I accept that you acted in ignorance," said Ellion. "That would not save you from the Questioners, nor would it save me and mine, even if I were to hand you over to them. But as it is . . . I have always tried to know as little as possible about these mat-ters, but now . . . First, tell me what happened on the wall, so that I may try to judge where any safety may lie."

"Tilja'll have to do that," said Meena. "Soon as I'd said the name something hit me and I passed clean out."

Somehow Tilja forced herself to concentrate and explain what had happened on the wall. When she had finished Meena spoke first.

"*South?* Axtrig was pointing south?"

"Yes. I felt the world change. I'm quite sure."

"Then he is not in Talagh," said Alnor.

"He could be in the outer city," said Tahl. "That thing Tilja says came—the one that pulled the wall down—he could have sent—"

There was a soft scratching at the door. They all froze. Tilja saw Ellion's face go white in the lamplight. The lock clicked as the key turned with no hand holding it. The door opened and a woman entered. She closed the door, turned the key in the nor-mal way and came further into the room, then stood and looked at them one by one. Her smile meant nothing. It seemed to Tilja that she spent much longer on her than on the others. She was middle-aged, wearing a dark red robe that completely hid her figure. Despite her smile, her face had the same smooth stillness as that of the woman Tilja had seen on the wall. When she spoke her voice was slow and husky.

"My friend Ellion has guessed correctly," she said. "I had of course arranged to hear your talk. You are in need of my advice,

165

and you can tell me things it would be useful for me to know. I am called Zara. I am the Lord Kzuva's magician. Sit down, and I will explain to you what the girl has seen. . . . Good. From your talk I gather that you are looking for a particular man and that you have brought with you some object that you think will enable you to find him. You name this thing Axtrig. Where is it now?"

They hesitated, waiting for each other. Though Tilja could see a family likeness to Lananeth, this woman seemed very different. Lananeth might have magical powers, but she was human. You could read her voice and feelings and make up your mind whether to trust her, even though Lananeth wasn't her real name. With this woman—Zara, she said she was called, as if that wasn't her real name either—with this woman there was no way of knowing.

"No, you must tell her," said Ellion. "We are in her hands."

"Axtrig is a carved wooden spoon," said Alnor. "Tilja has her."

"Here? In this room? I feel nothing."

"No," said Tilja. "I don't understand, but she's got to be touching my skin. I've had her strapped to my arm most of the journey. Even when I had her under my blouse, with just my shift in between, she started to tingle when that woman was looking for her. I think the woman could feel she was there until I grabbed her handle. Do you want me to show you?"

Zara shook her head.

"Give me your hand, child," she said.

Tilja reached out and let Zara take her hand. She felt the numbness starting. Zara stiffened for a moment and let go.

"Remarkable," she said. "Several others, each far more powerful than I, are searching for this thing. I dare not let you show it to me. The wards of this room are not strong enough to hold them off. And you do it, in pure ignorance. You have no need of wards. I think Silena's beast, the creature you saw on the wall, could not have touched you. To hurt you she would have needed to cause the tower to fall on you, or some such thing."

She laughed, pleasantly human for a moment.

"And this thing is a wooden spoon! I had imagined a sword, at least, or a jeweled rod. Well, then, I was asleep in my room, which is warded like this one, as it needs to be, or I would not dare sleep, ever. Through those wards came a burst, an explosion, of magical power, here in Talagh, in the warded heart of the Empire. The blast threw me from my bed, and I was stunned."

"Me too," said Meena. "It wasn't like fainting, when you can feel yourself going. It was that sudden . . . I don't know . . ."

"But you, child, standing close beside the center of it, you felt nothing at all?"

"No," said Tilja. "Well, there was a sort of blink, and the world had changed, so that Axtrig was lying differently. It was the same that time with Lananeth."

"The world had changed?" asked Zara, more softly than ever.

Stumbling for words, Tilja tried to explain her feelings about what happened to Axtrig when Meena spoke the name of Faheel—how it seemed as if it wasn't the old spoon that moved, but instead the whole world became slightly different. Or perhaps it was time itself that became different, so that Axtrig had *always* been lying the way she now was, though nothing else had changed.

"That is power indeed," said Zara, and for the first time Tilja could hear something like an emotion in the calm voice, a sense of awe. "Well, let me continue. When I recovered, that power was gone, but several other powers were active in the place. I counted, at first, four. Two I felt to be those of Watchers. Those were the two magicians the girl saw up on the wall. We know them as Silena and Dorn. There was another I did not know close by. Then a fourth, whom I also did not know, coming from the outer city below. But it would have been that one who sent the hand that broke the walls."

"The other one up on the wall must've been Meena," said Tahl.

"Me? I was passed out most of the time," said Meena, "and besides, I'm not that sort."

"No, it was the cat," said Tilja. "I don't know what it was doing, but it was doing something. I think it stopped the woman realizing we were in the tower."

"If so, it was a creature with some power," said Zara. "Each of the twenty Watchers oversees a section of the city, and all the Empire that lies beyond it. Dorn is South, the second most powerful of the Watchers, after Varti, who is North. The section Silena watches is next to his. The place at which you chose to do what you did was in Silena's section, but close to Dorn's, so she came first, and he soon after. None of the Watchers are friends to any of the others. They are all in fierce rivalry for power, but will combine to prevent one of themselves becoming more powerful than the rest. By this means the Emperor is able to see that none becomes overwhelmingly powerful. But, sensing a source of power such as you unleashed on the wall, of course both Silena and Dorn wanted it for themselves. . . ."

"And you do not want it also?" asked Alnor.

She shook her head.

"Not yet, and not for many years," she said. "A more powerful magician would take it from me almost instantly, destroying such powers as I have to do so. My guess is that it would also have been more powerful than either Silena could handle, or even Dorn. The magician who came from the outer city is another matter. What you saw him doing was truly powerful, more than a match for Dorn and Silena together. Two more Watchers had joined them in the contest before they could drive him away. I have no idea who he can be, but he is still not the one you want. I think that one is far from here."

"And south, apparently," said Alnor.

"Yes. So it is in your interest to leave Talagh as soon as possible, and it is also in our interest, mine and Ellion's, to have you gone. We have all been extremely fortunate in how this has worked out. The attention of the Watchers will now be concentrated on finding and if possible destroying the magician in the outer city, and it will be assumed that what brought Silena and

168

Dorn to the place was the start of his attack on the walls, and not your doings with your spoon. So, for the moment we are safe. But your presence here with your unwarded magic is intensely dangerous to us, and to everyone under our Lord's roof. Ellion is an honest man, but even so I think he would be tempted to hand you over to the Questioners, if he thought that would save us."

"Yes, I have thought of it," said Ellion. "But I know it would not help, so we must do the best we can to get you away from here. You must remain Qualif and Qualifa until you have left the city, and are recorded as having done so. At first light tomorrow I will send a trusted man with you to obtain your death-leaves and he will bring them back to me while you at once start the journey home."

"But we can't go home yet," Meena burst in. "First we've got to—"

"Wait," said Ellion. "You must be recorded as having *started* on that journey, but only your death-leaves are going home, for me to present to the census takers when they come. Since these will be in order, it is extremely unlikely that they will trouble to check with the records of way-leaves and see whether you in fact made the whole journey home.

"But in fact, once you have crossed the river you will take the Grand Trunk Road south. . . ."

"Meena and I will need way-leaves, surely," said Alnor.

"I dare not give you way-leaves. My name will be on them if you are discovered. Instead I will give you money, so that you can pay the necessary bribes to turn aside from the Grand Trunk Road. Southern officials are notoriously corrupt, so once you are well away from Talagh, you should be able to do that without trouble. But until that time comes, you are traveling to the City of Death. No records are kept of those who take that journey."

9

The Grand Trunk Road

At noon on the fifth day of their journey south, they were sitting in the shade at the edge of a pinewood on a hillside above the Grand Trunk Road. In the far distance they could see the Great River, which had run beside the road for a while, but had yesterday swung away east. Before they saw it again it would have plunged down cataracts, roared through foaming gorges, and almost lost itself in a chain of prodigious lakes, until at last it came back to the road at Ramram, far to the south.

Everything was very still. Once or twice someone went past, people in too much of a hurry to rest out the hottest part of the day. Tilja could hear voices over to their left from where more travelers were also taking advantage of the shade. The only other noises seemed to be the ceaseless hum and click and buzz of insects.

"Might as well get it over," Meena muttered. "Come along, girl."

She heaved herself to her feet and started to hobble up the slope, leaning heavily on her cane. When they were well away from the road she stopped beside a mounded ants' nest.

"This'll have to do," she said. "We're not going to find anywhere flatter. We'll do it like we did on the wall, only we won't try Axtrig straight off. Start with one of the other ones, and don't let go of it until you're good and ready, and grab it as soon as anything happens, supposing it does. I'll go over there."

She fished the leather bag from under her skirt, took out the cloth and laid it over the anthill, and groped again in the bag for one of the nameless spoons. When Tilja took it, it felt like ordinary lifeless wood, no different from any other spoon she had ever handled, but the now familiar numbness seeped into the skin of her left forearm, where Axtrig was strapped against it, under the long sleeve of her blouse. She no longer found it an unpleasant feeling. It was simply something that happened. Not letting go of the spoon, she laid it on the cloth and looked toward Meena.

"I'll count to three," said Meena. "Don't look at me. Just watch the dratted spoon. One. Two. Three."

She saw Meena's lips move as she whispered Faheel's name. The numbness in her forearm exploded through her body. She gasped and staggered. Then it was gone. The spoon on the ant heap hadn't stirred.

"What's up?" said Meena. "Nothing I could feel."

"It didn't move," said Tilja. "Only Axtrig . . . it must have been when you said the name . . . she really wanted to answer, but she couldn't, because I was touching her."

Meena grunted, then sighed.

"Nothing for it, seemingly," she said. "We're going to have to give her a go. Quick as you can, mind . . . no, wait . . . try holding your hand out flat with the cloth on it and laying her down on that—not letting go with your other hand, mind, till we're ready, and seeing what happens. . . ."

Forcing herself into calmness, Tilja rolled up her sleeve and untied the ancient spoon. Through her fingertips she could feel the difference from the other one, the sense of life still there in the grained wood. Holding Axtrig firmly in her right hand, she slid her left hand under the cloth, only to discover that its underside was now swarming with ants, mercifully not the biting kind. She gave the cloth a good shake and then used her teeth to arrange it over her open palm so that she could balance Axtrig there, still keeping her right hand in contact with the wood.

"Ready," she said.

"Sure? Then I'll count again. One. Two. Three."

Tilja let go of Axtrig, keeping her hand poised close above her, watching her, not Meena. For a moment nothing happened. Three or four baffled ants continued to scuttle around on the cloth. Then, all in an instant, they froze into stillness. This time it was different. The world remained the same and the spoon twitched round. Tilja actually saw it move. At once she closed her right hand down on it. As her palm touched the wood the ants resumed their scuttling. Down the hill, she heard Calico neighing in panic. She looked up.

Meena was bent over her cane, steadying herself from falling. She let out a long breath and straightened.

"Could've been worse," she muttered. "Could've been a lot worse. Anything come of it, then?"

"Yes, Axtrig moved. And she's still pointing the way we're going."

"Well, that's something. Let's get out of here, now. I don't know if one of those Watchers or anyone would've picked it up but there's no point hanging around to find out. Just listen to that stupid horse. If she felt it, there'll be others. I'll be starting off while you get yourself sorted out."

Trembling now with the relief that it was over, Tilja strapped Axtrig back against her arm, rolled the sleeve down and put the cloth away. All round her the woods seemed empty and silent. The other party of travelers, further along the hillside, seemed to have stopped their chatter, but as Tilja ran down the slope to catch up with Meena they started again. In their voices there was a note of alarm.

Day after day they traveled on, unhindered and unquestioned. Since they were on their way to Goloroth nothing else needed to be known about them until they reached the city and gave their names to the officials at the entrance, who would then fill in certificates for Tilja and Tahl to take home, showing that their grandparents had indeed passed through those last gates. Not that they actually had any intention of going that far. All that concerned them was to travel south for as long as Axtrig told them. When at last the old spoon began to point in a new direction, then they would turn aside and start to bribe their way with the money that Ellion had given them. Meanwhile, for convenience, they continued to wear the uniforms of fourteenth graders, but used their own names if anyone asked.

The Grand Trunk Road swarmed with travelers, merchants, messengers, officials with their retinues, troops of soldiers, drivers of loaded oxcarts, gangs of slaves being taken to market or to some big task of building or destruction, people of all ages and accents and manners, but always more going south than north. Old and young, pair by pair, made the long journey to the City of Death, but only the young came back.

A section of every way station was set aside for those making that journey. Here free meals were provided, but plain stuff, so that the food stalls still did good business. The atmosphere inside these enclosures was strangely cheerful. Almost all the old people seemed completely to accept what was happening and to face the end of their lives with dignity and not with fear. Tahl, typically, got into talk with some of them and asked bluntly how they felt about what they were doing.

"Much the best way of it," one old woman told him. "Easy for me, mind. I started to get the shakes, which runs in the family, so I knew how long I'd got, and there was time to make all the arrangements and set up a nice funeral party and be gone, and I'm really making the most of it, seeing all these places and meeting all these people, when all my life I've never been more than nine miles from my own front door."

Not everyone felt like this. Some were already in the grip of their last illness, some made the journey with dread, and some with fierce resentment, but most seemed to be going south almost gaily, and these helped to keep the doubters from gloom. When they had collected their evening meals they would settle in groups of twenty or more—people who had been strangers until only a few days earlier—and gossip and sing far into the night, songs of all kinds from all over the Empire, silly or sentimental or stirring, but not often sad.

"Makes me feel a right fraud," Meena said, "seeing them all so cheerful when what's happening to them isn't going to happen to me, ever, not once I'm home."

There was one thing, though, that cast a shadow over everyone. Sometimes in the early mornings a wail would go up from somewhere in the enclosure, announcing that one old traveler had failed to complete the journey and was dead, and the child with them would then be led away by the guards to be sold, while the body would be taken to a side gate to be collected and carried on to Goloroth by specialist carters who had no other trade. At times like that all grieved.

Every few days as they rested for their midday meal, Meena and Tilja would find somewhere hidden from the road and once again put their question to Axtrig. Each time the answer was the same. South.

Now that they knew it worked, the process became less alarming. But it was still a risk. Even damped down by Tilja's two hands, one poised above the old spoon, the other only just below her on the other side of the cloth, the whisper of Faheel's name produced the fierce pulse of magic. Meena needed to find somewhere to steady herself, or a boulder to sit on, while it lasted, and Alnor and Tahl, some distance away and out of sight, also felt the shock of it, and every time Calico neighed with alarm and tried to bolt.

"It's like when you stand up suddenly and bang your head on something," said Tahl. "Except that it doesn't hurt. But everything goes dark for a moment and you don't know where you are."

But nothing else happened. Nobody came to investigate, or questioned them all afternoon as they plodded on to the next way station. The only change as the days went by was that the pause between Meena's whisper and the spoon's reaction seemed to grow longer. It was as if Axtrig, too, was becoming used to the process.

Tilja, strangely, came to welcome these times. Or rather, she welcomed the feelings she had when they were over. The sense of immense, strange power controlled and leashed by her hands and then laid to sleep once more against her arm was something like the feeling she had after a good day on the farm, work that had gone well, in fine clear weather, with larks invisibly high above the fields, pouring out their song. On such evenings she would be tired, of course, but happy, cleansed, with even the mild aches and stiffnesses of toil somehow pleasurable.

On their twenty-second night out of Talagh Tilja woke suddenly out of deep sleep. Something was wrong. There were stars overhead, but no moon. A few lanterns shone here and there around the way station, but otherwise it was almost pitch dark. And still. That was what was wrong. Silence. No noise at all, apart from the whisper of her own breath. Not a murmur or rustle from any of the several hundred travelers in the way station.

Alnor wasn't snoring. Nor was Meena, nor anybody else.

Alnor always snored, gently, steadily, all night. Meena snuffled and snorted. A dozen other old people lying nearby should have been joining in, or muttering in their sleep, or turning over, or getting up to relieve themselves. But no one in the whole enclosure was moving a muscle. Were they even breathing? Were they alive?

For a while Tilja herself lay still, not daring to stir, trying to hush her own breath, the betraying thud of her heart. She was filled with the same sense of nightmare that she had felt on the walls of Talagh. When she could bear it no longer she forced herself to sit up and reach across to where Tahl lay and shake his shoulder.

He didn't respond. She shook him harder. Nothing. She felt

for his face, found his ear and pinched the lobe fiercely between fingernail and thumbnail. Still not a movement, not a whimper. She found his nose and laid two fingertips against his nostrils, almost blocking them. Yes, just, faintly, she felt the come and go of his breath.

Still filled with dread, she straightened and looked around. Something had changed. There was a new light over toward the other side of the enclosure. It was paler and larger than the yellowish glow of the lanterns, like a patch of moonlit smoke. Tilja watched it glide slowly across to the edge of the enclosure and start back. As it turned, part of it blanked out for a moment as something dark came between it and where Tilja was sitting. This thing was also moving.

The patch of light crossed the arena, nearer now, and turned again. Again part of it blanked out as it turned. Now Tilja realized what it was doing. It was systematically searching the arena for something. In her left arm the numbness was spreading from where Axtrig lay. That was what had woken her, and it was still there, steady, not flowing away. Now she knew what the light patch and the dark thing were looking for.

Steadily they came nearer and nearer, the dark shape leading with a clumsy, unnatural waddle that told Tilja what it was, and from that she could make out Silena herself, gliding along in the misty patch of light. Now they were working their way directly toward her. As they passed close by the beast paused and turned. There had been no change in the feeling in her arm. It could not have known Axtrig was there. Perhaps it had sensed her wakefulness.

Still she could not move. Her mouth and throat wanted to scream, but no sound would come. Only when the beast stood right over her and she could smell its sickly hot breath and see the gleam of starlight in its single eye as its muzzle snuffled toward her face did movement suddenly come. Desperately she raised her arms to shove it away.

Her fingers locked into the coarse fur of its chest, and everything changed. There was a sudden convulsion, a sense of things being sucked violently to and fro, her whole self, body and soul, filling with the numbness, something inside her waking, knowing what to do, how to master the turmoil, channel it on, through her, out and away. . . .

She was sitting up, trying to push herself free of the attentions of what seemed to be a small dog which only wanted to get at her face and give it a friendly lick. The voice of Lord Kzuva's magician whispered in her mind, *I think Silena's beast could not have touched you.*

Quickly she drew the dog to her, hugged it against herself and looked up. The patch of light seemed to have changed. Before, it had been as calm and still as moonlight itself, and Silena had glided along inside it steady as a statue, but now the misty stuff of which it was made was covered with confused ripples, like the surface of a pond into which someone has tossed a handful of pebbles. This made Silena seem to ripple too, like a reflection in that pond. Her voice rippled as she spoke.

"Give me the thing you are carrying. Put it in the mouth of my dog and let him go."

"No," said Tilja, hugging the dog yet closer to her. Its whole body had gone rigid at Silena's first word, except for the tip of its tail, wagging anxiously against Tilja's thigh. The light seemed weaker now, but it was still enough for her to see the bodies of her sleeping companions beside her, and Calico standing with her head bowed in sleep just beyond. For herself she felt safe from Silena's magic, but the others wouldn't be. The only thing she could think of was to distract the magician somehow. Still clasping the dog, she rose to her feet and walked directly toward Silena.

Silena was not expecting this. She actually backed away, and her light dimmed yet further. Then she stood her ground and straightened and the light grew strong again. When they were barely a pace apart she twitched the dog's leash. Fire shot along it and reached the collar. The dog yelped as the blazing line ringed its neck, and squirmed so violently that Tilja could scarcely hold it. Desperately she grabbed at the fiery leash, but felt no heat or strangeness, only a tough everyday leather strap, because that was all there was now, reaching from her to Silena, who immediately dropped the leash as if it was she who had been burnt.

She backed off another pace and drew herself up. Tilja could sense her summoning her powers. Her light grew stronger again and the ripples began to die away.

"A magician cannot afford to be overcome," she said. "Unless you give me the thing you have against your arm, I must attempt to destroy you, or else be myself destroyed."

"No," said Tilja.

"Very well," said Silena.

She closed her eyes. Her lips began to move. For a short while nothing seemed to happen, except that the dog's tail stopped wagging. Then Tilja began to hear—no, to feel, rather than hear—a deep, pulsing hum gathering all around her. Out of the corner of her eye she saw one of the distant lanterns starting to quiver, and realized that not only the lights but everything she could see, the black outline of the walls of the enclosure, the very stars in the sky, was shuddering to and fro. The only still things in the whole universe were Silena, and Tilja herself facing her, with the dog in her arms. And now she could feel something try to grasp her, an invisible fist that couldn't quite touch her but had closed all round her, and was attempting to wrench her into that shuddering movement and shake her apart. An enormous energy was battering itself to and fro, stronger and stronger, against her stillness. Soon, soon, something had to give. She willed that stillness, gave it a place and name. Woodbourne—herself leaning on the farmyard gate in the stillness of a summer dawn, looking north across the Valley to the mountains. In that loved landscape she centered herself, gathered it round her. She could see Silena opposite her, pale with ferocious concentration, drawing out of herself all the powers that were in her and focusing them into

Tilja's destruction. The light blazed around her, bright as noon, but now shed no ray into the darkness beyond.

Close by in that darkness a donkey brayed. Tilja's heart bounced with the shock of the sudden harsh clamor, but she knew at once what it was, because there used to be a mischievous old donkey at Woodbourne that liked to bray suddenly in people's ears. But Silena wasn't ready for it. She thought she had put the whole courtyard to sleep. The unexpected bellow told her she was wrong. All her powers were focused on Tilja. She had nothing to spare. She faltered.

The pulse behind the humming lost its implacable beat and dwindled away. The lamps and skyline and stars steadied, and the light around Silena herself died out.

Before it faded completely Tilja saw the proud figure of the magician stoop. Lines creased the emotionless dead face and made it human, the face of an ordinary woman, extremely old, but alive.

Around them sleepers stirred and muttered. There were cries of alarm here and there, as if some had woken from nightmares.

Silena's voice came out of the dark.

"Well, it is I who am destroyed," she said quietly. "The Emperor must find another Watcher. Give me back my dog and I will go. You need not be afraid. It is too late for me to start again."

Tilja didn't need to ask herself if she could trust her. She had both seen and felt what had happened. She set the dog down. Silena called it and it ran to her. Tilja could hear it fawning happily, as any dog might do on a mistress just come home.

"Do you know if anyone else is looking for us?" she said.

"I cannot say," said Silena wearily. "But the Trunk Road lies in the sector that it was my task to watch. I could tell whenever you used the thing that you carry. It shone in my mind like a meteor each time. I could not come before—we watch each other constantly—but this evening I took my chance. None of the others would have had cause to be watching so steadily this way. But to-morrow they will find my tower empty, and their interest will be aroused. That is all I can tell you."

"What about the magician outside the walls—the one whose monster you and Dorn drove away? I think he really wanted . . . the thing I'm carrying."

"You know all this, child?"

"I was there, hiding in one of the towers. You almost found me."

"Ah . . . no, we know nothing of this other man. We searched all the Empire, but he hides himself too well. He has great power. You should be wary of him still, I think."

"Thank you," said Tilja. She felt no fear or hatred of Silena now, this tired old woman who still had her dignity when everything else was gone.

"I'm sorry," she said.

"It was not all your doing, child," said Silena, and moved away into the darkness.

Immediately the whole enclosure was in an uproar. Calico woke with a squeal, answered by a chorus of squeals from around the courtyard. Knowing her nature, Tilja had tethered her securely, but at least two of the other horses broke loose and went charging around in the darkness.

Tahl had woken with a shout, Meena was muttering incoherently, and Alnor rose groaning to his feet and started to stumble away through the dark. Tilja ran and grabbed his arm, but he shook her off, and then blundered into a stranger who came rushing in panic toward him and knocked him aside. Tilja managed to catch him and stop him falling, and then he let her lead him back to the others. By the time she had him settled down Meena and Tahl seemed to be coming to their senses. All three had had much the same nightmare about being hurtled to and fro inside a dark swirling cloud full of explosions of light and faces with monstrous gaping mouths and screaming shapes that swirled by in the storm.

("Only it was and it wasn't a dream," Tahl explained. "It was something else, too.")

From the snatches of talk she could hear around them Tilja could tell that it was the same with everyone else in the enclosure, but they were still all too taken up with their own nightmares to eavesdrop on their neighbors.

"I know what happened," she said in a low voice. "Silena was here. And her beast. They'd come to look for Axtrig. She's gone now."

She told them what she'd seen and done. By the time she'd finished all her fear and excitement were gone. There was nothing left but utter exhaustion.

"A donkey?" said Tahl. "It was still light when they closed the gates, and there wasn't a donkey anywhere around then."

"It was a donkey," said Tilja, yawning and scrabbling for her rug. "Nothing else makes a noise like that. We used to have one at Woodbourne."

She found the rug, wrapped it around her, lay down and was asleep before he'd finished asking his next question.

Usually the first light woke her, but she slept late that morning, and by the time she sat up and looked around most of the other travelers were already getting ready to leave. She couldn't see a donkey anywhere in the enclosure, but it might already have gone.

She was still tired as they traveled on, tired all through, but it was an odd sort of tiredness. What had happened in the enclosure had been extremely frightening and dangerous, and she wasn't at all sure that Silena mightn't have broken through her defenses if the donkey hadn't brayed at exactly the right time. Would she be able to do it again if the need arose? Do what? She didn't even know that. She had broken Silena's power, yes. She had chosen to do it rather than just have it happen to her, but she couldn't describe, even to herself, how. Suppose she were to wake at the next way station and see, say, Dorn, or the unknown magician, stalking toward her through the sleeping wayfarers, she knew she would be just as terrified, just as deep in the nightmare, as she'd been when Silena came.

But that didn't alter the fact that she'd done it, alone and without help, and done it by discovering something totally new about herself. That discovery filled her with a sort of peaceful exhilaration. She didn't want to sing, or dance, or talk to the others about it, only to walk in silence, relishing the feel of it. It was like the new-risen sun on night-chilled limbs, like the smell of rain on parched earth, like the morning, years ago, when she'd gone out before breakfast to look at the little patch of garden that she'd hoed and raked and planted all on her own, and seen that the first bean seedlings had come through in the night, shouldering the crumbs of earth aside and spreading their first two leaves to catch the sun. Hers.

The mood lasted all day. But that night at the way station, at the exact hour that Silena had come (she could tell by the stars), she woke with her heart slamming, her body locked rigid with dread and her palms chill with sweat. And the same next night, and the next, and the next. Usually at least one of the others would be awake at the same time, and they would whisper to each other for a little, and Tilja could hear quiet mutters of reassurance from elsewhere in the enclosure, which told her that they were not the only ones to have woken at that particular time. It was as though Silena had somehow set a clock in all their minds that triggered a danger signal at the hour of her coming. The effect didn't start to fade until the moon had waned completely and waxed again almost to its full, and midnight was no longer dark. But no more Watchers came stealing into the enclosure, with whatever beast or demon they had chosen as their companion, to search for Axtrig.

Those night wakings were the only alarms in all their seemingly endless journey. Steadily the days became warmer, both with the coming summer and the more southern climate. Soon mornings and evenings seemed as hot as noon had been north of Talagh. The landscape changed, and changed again, and yet again, flat miles of fields, green wooded hills, dry and broken ground where immense flocks of sheep and goats were herded, ancient forests full of strange calls and odors, cities, villages, fortresses, grand houses ringed by rich estates.

Only the road did not change. Broad as a fair-sized river, well paved from side to side, it headed on south. Despite the Emperor's decrees it was thronged from dawn to dusk with travelers, all of whom must have proved they had good reason for their journey. The wind swung round to the east and for three long days rain fell, warm and dense, from sagging low clouds. The road became truly a river, ankle deep in places, but then shedding its load into the drowned fields on either side. Through the downpour everyone plodded on. The way stations were cleared each morning, to make room for the next night's travelers, so there was nothing else for it but to endure the drenching. It was the Emperor's will.

After what Silena had said about how she had traced them, Meena and Tilja were even more careful about using Axtrig to point the way they should go. They knew that by now there would be a new Watcher in Silena's tower, who might notice the quick flicker of potent magic, moving further south each time. And perhaps more dangerous still, there was the unknown magician who had sent the great creature to attack the walls of Talagh. He was hiding now, Silena had said, but he had put forth that enormous power for the sake of the old spoon, and he would do so again, if he got the chance. But they had to take the risk, or the time might come when they actually plodded on past the point where they should have turned aside.

So sometimes, though at longer intervals than before, the two of them would slip away from the road during the midday rest, and Tilja would bring Axtrig out from under her sleeve, and Meena would stand well apart and whisper the name of Faheel, and the old spoon would wake and move.

Wake was the right word. Especially since Silena had come to the way station, Axtrig had seemed more and more deeply asleep. It was something Tilja was doing to her with her own increasing powers, wearing her against her skin day after day after day, not destroying her magic, but burying it deeper and deeper in the grained wood, where only Faheel's name would wake it. At the whisper of that name there would be a pause, a stillness, and the strange, eager tree-life would wake and remember itself in a pulse of magic, and point their direction, with a greater sureness each time, as if the spoon heard more and more clearly the summoning voice of the man in whose garden the peach had hung whose seed had become the tree that had grown at Woodbourne.

Then Tilja would touch her with a fingertip and she would sleep again.

On the ninety-third day of their journey, at last, the great river rejoined them. They slept the night at a way station beside it. Here a mile-long bridge crossed to an ancient city, ringed with a turreted wall, and with a huge fortress crowning the rocky hill at its center. The bridge had been widened to make room for market stalls all along its length. Waiting for their dole of food that evening, Tilja heard an old man talking to the boy who was accompanying him to Goloroth.

"See that fort there?" he was saying. "Take a good look at it. You'll be right glad to see it again on your way back. That's Ramram, last city of the living. And that on the bridge, that's the Ramram fair. You want something pretty to take home to your ma from the south, that's the best place to look for it. There's nothing else south of here except the place we're going. That's no place for a child, and it won't have changed much since I came this way myself with my own granddad, this fifty-seven years ago. You'll see what I mean tomorrow morning."

He was right. Almost as soon as they had left the way station the nature of their journey changed. The road was as well kept as before, but less than half the width, and almost no one was using it except the old people going south to die, with their compan-

184

ions, and groups of weary children who had made that same journey earlier now trudging back north.

By that evening the river too began to change, breaking up into a network of reedy channels which spread out to left and right while the road speared straight on, striding from island to island on immense timber bridges.

"We are near the end," said Alnor. "The waters can feel the sea. Can the man we are looking for still be south of here? There is nothing to come but Goloroth. You are sure, Tilja, about the way the spoon was pointing last time?"

"Yes, quite sure."

They had checked their direction only the day before, when Ramram had come in sight. It had certainly looked the kind of place where a powerful magician might choose to live, but Axtrig had unmistakably pointed on past it, south. Still south.

"Then he's got to be in Goloroth," said Meena.

"I bet he isn't," said Tahl.

"Tell you one thing," said Meena. "I don't know how Alnor and me are going to get ourselves back out of here. We're going to stand out like two sore thumbs, the only old folk going north."

"There will be a way," said Alnor, with absolute confidence.

That night's way station was on one of the islands. Despite the steamy heat, braziers were lit all around it and piled with damp reeds whose smoke helped keep the swarming night insects away.

There was a change in the travelers. When they settled down in the dusk, one of the groups started to sing, as usual, but it wasn't the usual kind of song. Tilja had never heard it before, and didn't know the language of the words, but the long sad notes told her that it was a song of farewell, a song of ending. Everybody listened, and when it was over there was silence for a while before one of the other groups began its own song in answer. And so on all round the enclosure, some peaceful and resigned, some full of fierce grief for the bright world that the singers were leaving, but all saying good-bye. Tilja lay down to sleep that night with her cheeks wet with tears.

10

The City of Death

"My, it's getting strong here," Meena muttered as they waited in the still, dense heat outside the walls of Goloroth. She clutched at Calico's saddle to steady herself as if something invisible had suddenly cannoned against her. Alnor was already holding firmly on to Tahl's shoulder, and ahead of them an old man staggered and fell, caught in the same gust. Tilja could feel nothing, and that in itself told her that Meena had been talking about magic.

"It's like a current round a rock," said Tahl. "It can't get in, so it swirls all round. I don't think there's going to be any magic in Goloroth. I bet those walls are warded, like Talagh."

"There's got to be," said Meena. "*He's* in there. There's nowhere else left."

Only an hour before, when the low brown walls of the City of Death—so much smaller than they had expected—had first come in sight, she and Tilja had slipped aside from the road, in among the reeds, and there for the last time asked their question. Axtrig had still pointed south, straight at Goloroth. And Goloroth lay beside the mouth of the Great River, at the southernmost tip of the Empire. There was nothing but ocean beyond it. Unless Meena was wrong about what Axtrig was telling them, Faheel must be inside those walls.

"Perhaps that's why he chose it," said Tahl. "Good place to hide—no one would think of looking for him here."

They were waiting in one of the lines that had formed to enter the city. There were several gateways in the otherwise blank wall. To either side of them officials sat at long tables. As each pair, old person and child, reached the head of the line they waited until a place was vacant at one of the tables and then went up to be interviewed by the official, who spoke to them briefly, wrote their answers in a ledger, wrote again on a sheet of paper and handed it to the child. The child then turned back and the old person went off alone through the gate. Chairs with carrying handles were brought for those who had difficulty walking.

Even here, under the walls of the City of Death, as everywhere else in the Empire, there were traders looking for a profit, selling food and supplies for the return journey, or offering to buy possessions that the travelers no longer needed, now that they had reached the end. Some of these too were sensitive to the gusts of magic. Tilja could see them automatically adjusting their footing as they carried on with their business.

Slowly the line in front of the gate edged forward. As it did so children came walking back, some solemn, some weeping, some seeming simply dazed that the thing was over and now they had to make their own way home, alone. Meena and the others seemed too preoccupied with fighting the invisible buffetings to notice, but Tilja became more and more anxious as she watched what was happening at the head of the line on their right.

Mostly the procedure went smoothly enough, but every now and then either the old person or the child would say something to the official at the table, and perhaps even begin to argue as the official shook his head, and then two other men would come up and lead the pair aside to say good-bye to each other, and though they might cling to each other and weep, before long the men would part them gently and lead them off in their separate directions. Tilja didn't see a single child go on into the city. Neither Meena nor Alnor seemed very put out when she told them.

"I'd been wondering about that," said Meena. "But no point meeting trouble till trouble meets you, I always say."

"I also have been thinking about this," said Alnor. "I am less certain than Meena that the man we are seeking is within the city. If he is here, perhaps he will do what we ask, and then help us to return. If so, well and good. If not, I do not care what happens to me. But if he is not here, then we have no choice but to search further on. Who knows what lands may lie south across the ocean? After all that has happened to us, I am fully convinced that our search will be rewarded, and that in the end we will find him. If I have to travel south on a raft, so be it. He cannot be very far. Every time Meena and Tilja have used the spoon, I have felt the pulse of magic more strongly.

"But let us for the moment assume that we find him here, and he is prepared to help us not only leave the city, but find Tahl and Tilja and return to the Valley. We cannot go home without his help. We would be questioned at every stage. So for the moment the best thing would be for you two to wait here for, say, five days, and then start north. Somehow, I do not know how, we will meet again."

"Best we can do," said Meena.

"I don't want to leave you," said Tilja. Despite Alnor's confidence, she felt that when in a very short time they parted at the gates of the City of Death, she would be saying good-bye to Meena forever.

"Nor me," said Tahl. "And anyway I want to see what happens. I mean, after getting this far . . ."

"I want to come with you," said Tilja, already close to tears.

"Looks like we've got no choice," said Meena.

"We're still going to get in somehow," said Tahl.

"What about Axtrig?" said Tilja. "She's asleep now, but . . ."

"Think she'll stay that way? Long enough for me to get her in, at least?"

"I don't know. When I carried her into Talagh . . . you couldn't have done it then. I only just managed it. But she's different now. She's asleep—like she used to be in the Valley. And you got her in past Lananeth's wards. She didn't really wake up till you said the name."

188

"Well, I'll still be needing her, risk or no risk. Leave it till last thing, and you put her into my bag, and we'll just have to hope. . . . Ah, don't you take it so hard, girl. I'm not like these others, come to the end and ready to go. I've had a good life, and I'm thankful for it, but I tell you it's nothing like over, not yet. Come along then, cheer yourself up and say good-bye like we'd be seeing each other again tomorrow, which very likely we will."

Uncomforted, Tilja fought with her tears until they reached the front of the line. There she watched Alnor and Meena take their turn at the tables, barely noticing the astonishing fact that there wasn't anything to pay, no fee, no bribe, no extra, not one drin.

They moved aside to say good-bye, and the way Meena returned Tilja's parting hug told her that inwardly her grandmother was feeling the same sense of grief and loss. Last thing of all she unstrapped Axtrig from her arm; Meena drew the leather bag out from under her skirt and Tilja slid the old spoon in with the other two. She managed to hold herself together while she said good-bye to Alnor also, and then watched tensely while the two of them helped each other through the gate. As they disappeared a blast of loose magic hurtled by, scattering the waiting lines, but nothing else happened. She led Calico back beside the way the way they had come, suddenly blind with tears.

Someone was speaking to her. A man's voice.

"Thinking of selling that beast, missie? You're from the north, by the look of you, so you've a long way to go, and she's nothing like worth her feed all that time. Much better sell her now. I'll give you a price you won't be sorry for."

Tilja could only shake her head, but Tahl butted in, asking questions as usual.

"What do you do with them when you've bought them?"

"Wait till I've got a string together, then take them up to the market at Ramram."

"We don't want to sell her, but how much to look after her for two or three days?"

"Well, now . . . what's in your mind?"

"We want to see if we can get into the city and be with our grandparents until they actually have to go."

The horse dealer laughed aloud.

"Some people!" he exclaimed. "No accounting . . . I'd have run a mile to get away from my own grandma. Look, sonny, there's a lot of rules in the Empire you can get round, one way or another. But there's one about Goloroth you can't. Man or beast, once you're into Goloroth you don't come out alive, not until you go south yourself on the Great River. . . ."

"That can't be right," said Tahl. "I mean, what about that man there? He's just helped someone in, and now he's come out again. They've got to have someone besides the old people going south, to clean the streets and cook the food and run things. It wouldn't work, else."

"That fellow's not coming out," said the horse dealer. "No more than just beyond the gates. None of 'em are, who you're asking about, not until they go south on the rafts themselves. What do you think would've happened to you two, supposing your old folk had gone and died on the way here?"

"We'd've been sold into slavery," said Tahl.

"Right—but not until Goloroth had taken its pick of you. It's in all the dealers' licenses, they've got to send us a quota of the kids they pick up from the way stations. And the reason you haven't seen gangs of kids on the road alongside of you is that them that run it don't want it getting about that's what happens, so they move 'em at night, and ship 'em in this last bit by the river. Hang around down there till after dark, and you'll see— only I wouldn't try it. You don't want to get taken inside your-selves, now, not after what I've just told you."

He bellowed with laughter at the notion. Tahl caught Tilja's eye and raised his eyebrows. Without thought, she nodded. Any-thing to be with Meena again, right to whatever end was waiting for them.

"How many days' feed do you think our horse is worth, supposing we ask you to take care of her for a bit?" asked Tahl.

"Seven, and that's being generous," said the horse dealer instantly. "It's only because I like your faces."

"Don't be stupid," said Tahl. "She's got years of work in her."

"And a mean eye with it," said the horse dealer. "Look, three days, and I'll be on my way to Ramram. You pick her up before I go and you can pay me for what she's had. Otherwise I'll take her when I go and when she's had her seven days I'll sell her for what I can get. Same with your bedding and stuff if you like."

Tahl looked at Tilja again, and again she nodded, more soberly now, understanding the danger but at the same time sure in her heart that this was not how the adventure was meant to end.

"All right," said Tahl. "It's a deal."

"You thinking of doing what it sounds like?" said the man.

"Don't ask," said Tahl.

"Crazy," said the horse dealer as he took Calico's reins, but this time he didn't laugh.

For days Calico had plodded sullenly south, disgusted with the journey, with the heat, with the food, with everything around her, and clearly blaming it all on Tilja. But now, as soon as she realized what was happening, she gave a wild and piteous whinny and tried to wrench herself away. But the horse dealer was used to difficult animals, and cursed and wrestled her into obedience and led her off, still forlornly whinnying. The sound pierced Tilja through and through. She had never imagined that she actually loved Calico. There couldn't, she'd felt, have been many less lovable horses in the world. But Calico was her last link with Woodbourne, and she was gone.

Goloroth was built of the mud on which it stood, on a headland at the main mouth of the Great River, whose broad, smooth flood swept out beside it. From a spit of shingle Tilja and Tahl watched huge rafts being floated down on the current. Each of these was actually made of a hundred or more small rafts lashed together. Just below the spit they were poled ashore and untied, and the individual rafts were then floated on down a separate channel into the city.

Much further along Tilja could see a jetty with a line of people waiting, tiny with distance. One after another the small rafts were brought to the landing stage, two or three people were helped to board, and men on the jetty then poled the raft along and shoved it into the main current, which swept it swiftly off so that those on it could die outside the limits of the Empire. Beyond the end of the jetty Tilja could see a never-ending line of rafts dwindling away to the southern horizon.

No one paid any attention to her and Tahl. There were a couple of dozen other children watching from the spit, as if in the hope of one last glimpse of the old person they had brought so far. Indeed, it was such a natural thing to do that there was actually a small food stall on the spit, in case those who were waiting had a few spare drin to spend.

"Goloroth's tiny," said Tahl. "They can't keep them here long, or it would be bursting."

"A day and a night and then they're off," said the woman who ran the food stall. "When did yours go through the gate, then?"

"About an hour ago," said Tahl.

"They'll be going south about that time tomorrow, then," said the woman. "Maybe a bit earlier. It's not been that busy. You'll need to sleep out, mind, if you're staying to watch them go, and the bugs'll eat you alive, so I'll sell you a salve. Five drin."

Tahl haggled and got the little phial for four.

"Where will our grandparents be sleeping?" he asked.

"In one of the sheds, great big barns, more like, couple of hundred places in each. They don't treat 'em too bad, if you're worrying. They get supper tonight, and breakfast tomorrow with a bit of poppy juice in the water, so by the time they're floating away they've not got that much idea what's happening to them."

Tilja had been listening with growing anxiety. Now, for a moment, her heart seemed to stop. Meena and Alnor were in Goloroth to find Faheel, who would then, somehow, get them out again. They had no intention of going south on one of the rafts. But what if they were too woozy with poppy juice to realize what was happening to them? She caught Tahl's eye. Blank faced, he gave her the slightest of nods. No need to talk about it. They had to get into Goloroth. Tonight.

But all he said was, "We'd better have some food too," and with a lot of haggling he bought enough for several meals.

The night was heavy and sticky, and barely cooler than the day, but at least it was dark enough, though there would be a moon later. Tilja and Tahl, smeared with the sharp-smelling oil the woman had sold them, lay in shadows a little below the spit from which they had watched earlier. They were as near as they could safely come to the separate channel down which the rafts were floated.

At dusk there had been a lull, but in an hour or two rafts and barges started to arrive again from the north. The work went on by the light of smoky orange torches. As before, the main rafts were broken up into separate smaller ones, but now these were loaded with goods from the barges, sacks and bales and crates, or else the reeking coffins of those who had died on the journey. From the movement of torches along the jetty it seemed that these were sent out on the current by night, so that at least the still living didn't have to make their last journey in such company.

Then, at last, a raft docked from which thirty or forty children were herded up onto the broad wall that ran between the main river and the channel into the city. They waited in silent apathy until a man holding one of the torches started numbering them off, six at a time, onto the line of smaller rafts in the channel. There wasn't an exact number of children, so only three were sent to the final raft. The man on the wall called out, and another man emerged from the darkness at the head of the line, loosing the hawsers as he came. One by one the rafts floated away. The man on the wall didn't stay to watch, but moved off, taking his torch with him.

"Now," whispered Tahl, but Tilja was already moving. Together they scuttled across the narrow strip of shore and leaped for the last raft. It rocked violently as they landed but they hung on and then crawled forward and sat behind the other three. One of these had cried out at their impact, but now they just turned their heads for a moment and stared back through the darkness.

"It's all right," Tilja whispered. "We were just a bit late, that's all."

The three didn't answer, but turned and sat, slumped and uncaring, as they had done before. Ahead, the lights of torches came nearer and nearer, reflected from the water under the archway that led into the City of Death.

There was no magic in Goloroth, none at all. Tahl had felt the change the moment the raft slid through the arch, he said later, but it took Tilja a while to notice, because it was a difference in something she didn't feel with any of her bodily senses, nor in any way she could put words to. But all the time she had been in the Empire, since they had first come through the forest, whatever it was in her that so stubbornly resisted the pervading magic had been at work, and now it could relax.

By the time the revelation came to her, she and Tahl were last in the line of children who had arrived on the rafts, and were being led along a pitch-dark street between the blank walls of two long buildings. There was a man carrying a torch at the front to show them the way, and another bringing up the rear. She was so astonished by the revelation that she relaxed her guard and spoke aloud.

"You were right, Tahl! There isn't any magic here!"

He glanced toward her with a sharp, warning frown, but the man immediately behind them had already heard.

"That's right, lassie," he said affably. "Second-best-warded place in the Empire, Goloroth."

"And you don't mind talking about it?" asked Tahl, instantly.

"What's the harm? The bastards can't get at us here. Death has its compensations, eh? No magic, no Watchers, none of that nonsense. Haven't you got it? You're outside the Empire now. You can die here, and no one has to pay a drin."

"And it's warded like that to keep it out of the Empire?" said Tahl. "I don't see . . ."

"Why should you," said the man, who clearly liked to talk, "seeing the trouble they've gone to keep everyone from getting the idea? You're a thinking lad, by the sound of you. You must've wondered, coming south, about how much all this is costing, the guides, the free stops at the way stations, and now you're here the rafts—couple of thousand a day and working all night when we're busy—and the food and stores, and everything, and the Emperor not getting a drin back out of it by way of taxes. Doesn't make sense once you've thought about it, eh?"

"No," said Tahl. "It's been bothering me pretty well since we started. People don't spend money like that unless they've got to."

"Said you were a thinking lad," said the man. "Well, they've got to, and here's for why. While you've been wondering about things, has it ever crossed your mind to wonder where all the magic is coming from? It comes out of us, that's where. We've all got a bit of it, right? All our lives it kind of settles into us, like dust, and then it comes out again when we die. Some of us find how to take it and use it, and they're the ones who become magicians, but most of us don't even notice it's there. Me, I've not got that much, because I've lived all my life since I was a kid here in Goloroth, where there isn't any magic. But these old folk who come down here to die, they've been living years and years out in the Empire, and they're full of the stuff. Notice how it was blowing around outside the walls?"

"We certainly did," said Tahl. "It was knocking us all over the place."

"That's because the old folk are starting to lose it, soon as they get here. Mostly it blows out to sea—the Watchers back in Talagh look after that. But it's nothing to what they let go of when they actually come to dying. You just think what it would be like if you had that happening all over the Empire all the time.

"And another thing. Suppose I was starting out to become a big magician—where's the easiest place for me to pick up a bit more magic than I've got on my own? There's some of it floating around loose in the air, but it's too much like hard work gathering all that in and making something of it, and I want quick results, so I'll do much better taking it away from somebody else, and the easiest time for that is just when that somebody else is dying and giving up his magic. Right?

"Now, suppose I'm not a magician, I'm the Emperor, and I want to stop this kind of thing happening and a lot of magicians getting more power than I've got myself, what do I do? I make laws against magic, of course, and I hire Watchers who're magicians themselves to keep an eye on things, but most of all I try to see to it that people don't go dying promiscuous all over my Empire, not unless they can prove to me they've got the money to have their deathbeds properly warded, and if they have, no harm in them paying a bit of tax on top of it for all the trouble I'm taking, right? But for everyone else I set up a place they can get to before they die, and then get taken away outside my Empire. That's Goloroth here, and old Fugon the Fifth must've been more than pleased with himself when he thought of it. . . ."

Tilja had been doing her best to listen. What the man was telling them was useful and important, though at the same time almost too horrible to think about, but her mind kept straying. Where were Meena and Alnor? Where was Faheel? What would happen when, in the heart of this warded city, Meena tried to use Axtrig to find him?

". . . only one snag," the man was saying. "Get a lot of old people passing through a place like this all the time, and some of them are going to start dying before they're on the water. And since there weren't that many dying anywhere else, not unwarded at least, you got a lot of magicians hanging around down here hoping for pickings. Started happening pretty well the moment the place was built, which is why after a bit old Fugon decided to have the place warded like it is. And he built way stations everyone's got to sleep at, warded too, in case they go dying on the way. Once you know that, everything else kind of falls into place, you'll find. But the Emperors never wanted it to get about that's how it is, because the only way they can run things is if everybody more or less believes the Emperor's all-powerful, whereas fact is he's only just about in control of it all."

"I see," said Tahl in a tone of delighted wonder. "And—"

"That's enough, sonny," said the man. "We're where we've been going, so there's not time. But just keep your ears open and you'll learn a lot here. You've got the rest of your life for that."

They had come out of the area of large blank sheds and reached a courtyard surrounded by low buildings. Here several women were waiting, and the man at the head of the column halted and called the children round him. Listlessly they gathered.

"Well, my young friends, you've arrived at last," he said, sounding just as friendly as the one who'd been talking to Tahl. "You've had a rough time, but remember that everyone you meet here has been through all that themselves. We know what it's like, and we're out to make it as easy for you as we can. Now the women here are going to show you somewhere to sleep and see you're comfortable, and in the morning they'll—"

He stopped dead. His head began to turn. Every torch in the courtyard went out. Tilja was knocked sideways by Tahl being flung violently against her. She grabbed him and managed to prevent them both from falling. There were shouts and yells nearby, heavy crashes from further away, more cries and screams floating in from further yet, but only for three or four seconds, and then complete darkness and silence, until Tahl groaned and shuddered in her arms.

She reached for his hand and held it tight, and now she felt the same sense of something being sucked or pushed to and fro that she had felt when her fingers had locked into the fur of Silena's beast, and knew that in spite of what they had been told only a few minutes before, the wards of Goloroth had been broken and magic was flooding into the city.

Tahl gave a final, gasping shudder and came to himself.

"What happened?" he muttered.

"I think Meena tried to use Axtrig," she said.

"Yes . . . it was like that time in Lananeth's room, only . . . where . . . ?"

"They'll be in one of the big sheds we came through. That's where the main noise came from. Over there. Don't let go of my hand."

Stumbling and groping, they found their way out of the courtyard. Tilja could see the outline of buildings against the starry sky, but almost nothing at ground level. They felt their way through an arched entrance and saw ahead of them the huge dark shapes of the sheds. There was no conceivable way of telling in which one Meena and Alnor had been housed.

"Try letting go of me for a moment," suggested Tahl. "Then grab me again."

Tilja gripped his collar with her free hand. Cautiously they disentwined their fingers.

Instantly his body went rigid. As she seized his hand he gasped, shuddered and relaxed.

"This way," he said, and led her to the right, then left a block further on. Here they halted and tried again. The third try brought them to a shed, part of whose roof had fallen in. The air was thick with the reek of mortar dust, and the end wall had fallen clean away. Never letting go of each other's hands, they crawled across the heap of rubble and in under the remains of the roof. Here they found themselves stumbling among sleepers who neither moved nor spoke when kicked or trodden on, but then came to a clear patch which turned out to be a path between two long rows of mattresses. By now, despite Tilja's protecting touch, Tahl had begun to move as if he were struggling through a dense and swirling storm that buffeted him this way and that. She felt nothing of it at all, and knew it was there only by the grunting effort of his movements. Slowly he fought his way to its center and guided her hand toward the floor. Her fingers touched and closed upon the familiar rounded shaft of wood. As she picked up the spoon and slid it in under her blouse she felt all round her the shock of change, with herself the stillness at its center. Tahl sighed in the dark.

"That's better," he muttered. "Didn't think we were going to make that. Don't let go, though. There's still a mass of loose magic around."

Others were beginning to stir in the darkness. Tilja heard a familiar groan.

"Meena!"

"That you, girl?"

"Are you all right?"

"Just about . . . just about . . . told you it wasn't the end. Why's he not shown up, then? He must've felt that, if he's anywhere around. Found that dratted spoon, have you? Which way was she pointing?"

Tilja pulled herself together, and managed to re-create in her mind the feel of the wooden shaft as she had grasped it.

"I don't know, in here," she said. "I think I've got the line, but we'll have to get outside where I can see the stars."

"Give us a hand then, getting up. Just let me find my cane and things. . . . Now, where are you . . . ? Got you. Ready? . . . Thanks. Now where's Alnor?"

"I am here," came the dazed mutter. "What has happened?"

"No time for that. I was trying to use old Axtrig, remember? Tilja and Tahl have shown up somehow. But I've gone and let all sorts of stuff in, and someone or something's going to come looking for us. They won't hang around, either. We'd best be getting out of here. Only it's that dark I can't see a dratted thing."

The shed seemed still to be filled with ferocious eddies of loose magic. All round her Tilja could hear grunts and curses as the wakened sleepers struggled to rise. She shifted Tahl's hand across to the one with which she was holding Meena and closed its fingers round her wrist, then groped forward into the darkness and found Alnor and helped him to his feet.

"Good," he said, steadying at her touch. "I will lead. If it is dark, I have the advantage. The door is this way."

Not letting go of Tilja's left hand, and with Meena and Tahl trailing behind grasping her right, he led the way between two of the rows and then sideways toward the outer wall. It was slow going. By now most of the occupants were awake, and full of alarm and confusion, all sensing more or less strongly the storm of magic which engulfed them. Many of them seemed to have marked where the door lay and were staggering in that direction. Others were trying to shove their way toward the only light in the pitch-dark shed, where the roof and wall had fallen in at the further end, and all the time the storm of magic buffeted them to and fro. The throng around the door was apparently so dense that it was impossible to open it. People were falling underfoot, and screaming where they lay as others trampled on them, but Alnor kept his head and managed to force his way out to one side and reach the outer wall, not far from the door.

Here they stood panting, but before they had recovered their breath a light flared just outside, shining fiercely through the cracks of the door. The mass of people fell back, not of their own accord but as if they had been forced to do so. With a snarl of wrenched timber the door burst open and a man stalked into the shed, lit by the web of fire that blazed from the many-thonged whip he carried on his shoulder. He was just as Tilja had seen him that night on the walls of Talagh, the long, wild hair, the naked torso, the jeweled belt and bracelets. Dorn. At his presence the tumult instantly ceased. The throng at the door stood motionless before him, many with mouths wide open in the screams they had started and could not finish. In all the shed, only Tilja and the three whose hands gripped hers could move a muscle.

For a moment she too had frozen, but with shock, not the compulsion of magic. So soon! Far back in Talagh Dorn had sensed the explosion of magic and come, almost in an instant. Now, as he began to turn slowly, studying the crowd and lightly shaking his whip for guidance toward the source of power he was seeking, Tilja came to herself. He had his back to her for the moment, but soon he would be facing her, see her, and realize that she was different. What then?

The obvious thing was to pretend to freeze like everyone else, but she knew in her heart it wouldn't work. It was his magic that bound everyone but her. Like Silena's beast, he would be able to sense the difference. Perhaps, as Lord Kzuva's magician had said, he couldn't hurt her directly with his magic, but he didn't have to use it to get what he wanted. He was far stronger than she was. . . . No, because to use his strength he would need to touch her, and then . . . if she dared . . . No, better, suppose she tried now, when his back was still turned, when he wasn't ready . . .

She was still nerving herself to step forward when an enormous throaty roar shattered the stillness. Instantly the thongs of Dorn's whip rose and streamed toward the further end of the shed. By their light Tilja saw a huge lion standing on the pile of rubble from the fallen roof and wall. Its mane stood stiffly out around its head as its mouth gaped for another roar. At the sound the thongs of Dorn's whip seemed to hesitate, but he shook it fiercely and they surged on, writhing as if they were fighting their way against a gale.

Move now, while all the Watcher's powers are concentrated on the lion! Tilja let go of the others, crouched down and managed to wriggle her way through the trance-held throng until Dorn was immediately in front of her. Still crouching, she reached up and laid both hands on his naked back.

Again, for the third time, but far more intensely than before, body and mind filled with the numbness. She felt that to-and-fro rush of powers being channeled through her. This time they almost overwhelmed her. For a moment she was blind. Her head was full of a strange, drumming darkness. She seemed to be in some other place entirely, or rather a sort of nonplace, an endless emptiness which was draining everything out of her. She willed herself to control it, to cling on to all that was Tilja, while the swirling energies sluiced past. Somewhere in that tumult she sensed Dorn himself being dissolved and carried away into nothingness. Then it was over, and she was back in the shed and scrambling to her feet, and though she still couldn't see, this was because the light from Dorn's whip had gone out and everything was in darkness again.

But the door was open, and the people in the shed were no longer gripped into stillness by Dorn's magic. Like sheep bursting from a pen they surged out into the open and staggered away. Tilja was simply shoved out ahead of them, but managed to twist aside and wait for the others by the doorpost.

They came soon enough, Meena instantly recognizable among the stream of dark shapes by her grunts and mutters. Tilja grabbed her and pulled her aside and Tahl and Alnor followed.

"That's better," Meena gasped. "You do that, girl? I could see a bit of it, but I stuck where I was standing. Don't let go of me again, or I shan't know if I'm on my head or my heels."

"We have to get away from here," said Alnor. "There will be more of them coming, besides the man who came through the door."

"That lion's one of them," said Tahl.

"Where can we go?" said Meena. "There isn't anywhere else."

"Wait," said Tilja. "Over here, where we can see more stars."

They moved down to a wider space between the sheds.

"There's the Fisherman," said Tahl. "I can't see the Axle-pin, but it must be about there, behind that roof."

Tilja looked back and checked the lie of the shattered shed.

"Then Axtrig was still pointing south when I found her," she said.

Alnor grunted, as if this was something he had been half expecting. Tilja remembered him talking about it outside the gates of Goloroth. And she herself felt strangely unsurprised. She knew nothing about Faheel beyond what could be learned from the story of Asarta, but of one thing she was certain. Now that she had seen it, she knew that the City of Death was no place for him.

The others seemed to share her thoughts.

"That man told us they weren't too busy just now," said Tahl. "They should have finished with the coffins—there weren't that many. There mightn't be anyone there. We saw them pushing the rafts out this afternoon, Alnor. It's this way."

For a moment none of the others spoke.

"Well," said Alnor. "It would be good to be on the water again."

The spaces between the sheds were full of old and frightened people stumbling about in the darkness and the eddying magic. There seemed to be nobody trying to take control, or to shepherd them back inside, let alone stop and question anyone who seemed to know where they were going. So they made their way eastward, awkwardly, with Tahl and Alnor leading, each with an arm reaching back to grasp Tilja by hand and wrist, and then Tilja with the fingers of her other hand twined into Meena's as she helped her hobble along. So protected, they could proceed erratically through the tumult, except when part of the panicking throng blundered against them and forced them apart, and whoever had been knocked loose had to stand and fight not to be swept into the same panic until Tilja could make contact again.

Twice from all around them, and from as far as they could hear across the stricken city, fresh wails of terror rose and died away.

"I suppose that means another Watcher's showed up at the shed where we found you," said Tahl.

"Doesn't need to be a Watcher," said Meena. "There's others, remember, looking for Axtrig. Just have to hope they've no way of finding her, long as Tilja's got her safe."

"I think one of them may be following us," said Alnor. "I am not certain, but last time I was separated from Tilja—"

"It's getting lighter," Tahl interrupted. "There'll be a moon soon. And look, that'll be the channel they send the rafts down."

He was right. They had reached a strip of water, embanked with masonry. A paved walkway ran beside it. Beyond the channel, faintly visible, lay the dark expanse of the Great River. To her left Tilja could see the outline of the walls of Goloroth, and the archway through which they had entered the city. The workers who had been unloading the cargoes earlier in the night were gone. There were no lights moving on the jetty.

They turned south and hurried along the pathway as fast as Meena could manage. When Tilja glanced back she could see nothing following. Nobody else seemed to have thought of leaving the city by water. All the tumult lay behind them.

Now there were rafts in the channel, ready for use next day, a long line, jostling against each other, kept together by the current. At the head of the line the stone jetty reached out into the river. Seen close to, the system was very simple. The current in the channel ran out through sluices beneath the jetty, and thus kept the line of rafts in place, but the masonry was so shaped that the front raft was nudged round the corner to the foot of a shallow ramp and held there. The passengers boarded it down the ramp, the workers on the jetty poled it away and the next raft was automatically pushed into place.

Tahl picked up a coil of loose cord and tossed it aboard the first raft, then chose a pole from the dozen or so leaning against the jetty.

"We'll manage from the raft," he said. "If Tilja gets us all aboard Alnor and Meena can sit down and then she can just hang on to me while I shove us along. The river will do most of the work."

He was right. Again, the jetty had been carefully shaped to turn some of the current outward, and all he needed to do was to use his pole to keep the raft from scraping against it. Soon they were sweeping along beside the dark stonework, and shore and city were sliding away behind them, sharply outlined now against the pallor of moonrise.

"Hold fast," called Tahl. "We're going to bucket about a bit round the end."

But in fact the raft barely tilted as the side current they had been using met the force of the main stream. The jetty rushed away. Ahead lay the open sea.

"Look at that!" cried Meena.

She was staring back along the way they had come. Tilja turned. The first sliver of moon was showing above the horizon beyond the walls of Goloroth. Right at the end of the jetty, black against that brightness, stood an enormous lion. Its shaggy mane was rimmed with sparkles of moonlight. It did not move. Its head was turned toward them. It seemed to be watching them go.

11

The Island

ilja woke, already screwing her eyes up against the blaze of light. She was lying on a hard, slanting surface that was tilting slowly, becoming level, beginning to tilt the other way so that her head was lower than her feet and she seemed to be slipping down, down, steeper now, with a rushing sound in her ears. . . . And then light spray whipped across her, drenching her face—drenching it again, for it was already wet, and so were her clothes on her upper side, and still she couldn't force her eyes open against the glare and look around and see where she was.

All she could remember was staring back at an enormous lion, black against a rising moon. In her mind's eye she could see the moon sparkling on its mane. Odd. Fur didn't sparkle like that—not ordinary fur. Except . . . yes, the cat on the walls of Talagh . . . magical cat . . . magical lion . . . She was too tired to think about it.

But there was something else odd about the way she remembered that lion, not magical weird, like its hugeness and its suddenness and the way it seemed to be watching her, just homely odd. Yes, it was odd in the same way as the old plow horse at Shotover, the next-door farm to Woodbourne, which never looked as if it had been put together quite right; legs and body and head seemed to belong to different horses. Or lions.

The combined memory of horse and lion pieced everything

together. The lion was of course the same one that had appeared suddenly at the end of the shattered shed and roared at Dorn, and it must then have followed them down to the pier—yes, Alnor had said that he sensed something following them—but it didn't seem to have tried to catch or stop them, it had just been standing watching them go.

And then something had happened to Tilja herself. She was tired and she had fallen asleep, but it hadn't been just that. The tiredness was like nothing she had ever felt before. It came as if she had been fighting, all alone, for hours and days and months and years, against an enormous invisible something, keeping it out, or sometimes, if it became too strong for that, letting it in and channeling it through and away, away, to an unknowable somewhere, and she was the only one who could do this, so she'd had to keep on doing it, hours, days, months, years, but now it was over and she could allow the great calm wave of tiredness that had built up all the time she had been fighting to pick her up and carry her along in its softness and darkness and forgetting. . . .

But something had woken her, or she might have slept on forever.

More fighting.

She wasn't ready.

Groaning, she tried to sit up, but couldn't. She was being held down.

"Hello. Do you want to wake up?"

Tahl's voice.

"No . . . where . . . ? what . . . ?"

"Hold it. I'll untie you. We didn't want you rolling overboard in your sleep."

Hands moved. The pressure against her chest eased. That was what had woken her. . . .

No, it wasn't, but it had been there, against her chest. A pulse of numbness. Axtrig. She clutched at the place through her blouse and lifted the spoon clear of her chest. The moment the wood lost contact with her skin she felt the handle trying to twist itself round, until she let it fall back against her chest.

The pulse of numbness came and went.

"Meena was trying to use her?" she muttered.

"We were just talking about it. Meena's not feeling too well. Some people get sick even on the river, if it's a bit rough. You can sit up if you want. You've got a safety cord round you."

Barely able to see for the dazzle, Tilja sat and stared around. Meena was lying by her side. Her eyes were closed and her face was a nasty yellowish color. Her lips were moving in silent, angry mutters. There was a dribble of fresh vomit from the corner of her mouth. Tilja forgot everything else and crawled to the edge of the raft so that she could dip the end of her head scarf in the rush of water, then crawled back and wiped the old face clean.

"Thanks, girl," came the sick whisper. "I'll live. Better had, after all this to-do. What about the spoon, then? Not doing much out here?"

Before she could answer, Tilja became aware of what was happening inside her blouse, unnoticed by her in the urgency of tending to Meena. As she had crawled to and fro the spoon had fallen into the fold of her blouse and now seemed to be trying to nudge and nuzzle, blindly but insistently, against the fabric, like a newborn pup searching helplessly for the unknown thing it wants, until its mother noses it toward her teats.

"She's not just turning," Tilja whispered in astonishment. "She wants to go somewhere. Over there. Is that south, Tahl?"

"Hard to tell. The sun came up over there, if the line of the waves hasn't shifted, so where you're pointing is a bit east of south, maybe."

"We are still in the flow of the Great River," said Alnor. "The water is almost fresh. Let me listen. Tahl, come and help."

So Tahl joined him and they sat side by side in silence, with bowed heads. After a little while they started to sing, the same sort of quiet, wavering, almost tuneless chant Alnor had used to control that other raft when they had left the Valley. Tilja strapped Axtrig safely onto her arm, crawled back to the side and scooped water into her mouth. There were old stories in the Valley, going back to the times before it had been closed off, and some of them were about the sea. They all said that seawater was too salty to drink, but this had only a faint refreshing tang to it. She got a mug from her bedroll and gave Meena a drink, then she ate one of the flat cakes Tahl had bought on the sandspit outside Goloroth.

After that she lay down, pulled her head scarf over her eyes, and for a short while listened to the song as it mingled with the rippling whisper of the waves brushing along the timbers of the raft. The sound filled her with a sort of vague amazement. They were so far from home, out in the blank ocean, where there was no magic at all and all waters are lost in the end, but Alnor and Tahl could still persuade the current to carry them where they wanted to go. Then the great wave of tiredness took her again.

This time she woke and knew where she was as soon as Tahl shook her shoulder.

"We're moving out of the current," he said. "We may have been doing a bit of good, but we can't keep it up now. Can we have another fix?"

With a groan Tilja sat up, crawled to the edge of the raft and rinsed her face. The water was now too salty to drink. To judge by the sun, it seemed to be about midafternoon.

She untied Axtrig and wrapped her in a fold of her skirt so that she could keep her grip on her without touching her when she let go with her other hand. When she did so, the shock of the spoon's attraction to her unseen target was so strong that it felt that if Tilja had let her she would have slithered across the raft and gone swimming off sidelong across the slow, rolling swell. The direction was unmistakable. So was the need, and the power behind the need.

"There," she said, pointing.

"Not too good," said Tahl. "We're still in some kind of

current, but far as I can make out we're heading well south of that. Not much we can do about it, either."

They tried twice more as the afternoon wore on. Each time the line Axtrig longed for slanted slightly more across that of the waves, so that they all could tell that if the current carried them on as they were going they wouldn't ever come to the place they had journeyed so far to reach.

By the time the sky was red in the west the waves had eased, and Meena was feeling better and sitting up.

"We're not doing much good so far," she said. "We're going to go sailing right past unless we try something else. What about if I say the man's name? Then maybe he'll hear us and give us a hand or something."

So Tilja knelt with her back to the sunset, facing the way Axtrig seemed to want to go. Her left arm was already numb to the shoulder, as if the spoon understood what was happening and was readying herself for the moment, and when Tilja took her in her hand she was like a living force. Tilja shifted her grip so that the bowl was toward her, and with her other hand wound the end of her shawl round the handle as Meena counted, "One. Two. Three . . ."

Tilja let go of the bowl of the spoon and grabbed for the handle, so that she had it in both hands. She heard the whispered name begin. A violent jerk pulled her flat on her face against the timbers of the raft, almost jarring the spoon free, but she managed to wedge the handle down into the cleft between two of the logs and pin it there. The whole raft seemed to be shuddering. She realized that she had heard cries from the other three, and looked round.

Both Meena and Alnor had tumbled onto their sides, and Tahl was on his hands and knees, shaking his head like a sick dog.

"What happened?" she gasped.

"Magic . . . the raft . . ."

He collapsed on his face.

Tilja stared around. Nothing else had changed in the huge

emptiness of ocean. Behind her the fuzzy orange disk of the sun seemed to rest on flame-streaked wave tops, and ahead lay the darkness of night. She was helpless, trapped by the need to keep Axtrig pinned in place. It took her a while to discover that that need was gone.

The first inkling came from the feel of the raft when she tried to shift her position. She had been kneeling on her skirt, but now her left shin touched timber. For a moment the familiar numbness spread along it, and she realized that every timber of the raft, infected with Axtrig's desperate need, had been faintly quivering with eager life, until her touch had stilled it. When she tucked her skirt back under her knee she felt the life reawaken.

Cautiously she raised her other hand an inch above the cleft, ready to grab again, but Axtrig lay content. Even so, careful to keep the spoon in contact with the raft all the time, she managed to shift her along the cleft and wedge the shaft tight under one of the cords that bound the logs together, then knelt up and looked around.

The sun was down and night looming ahead. Ahead. No longer directly into the waves, but slanting across their northward march, slanting in a rush of foam down the back of each one, across the hollow, and up the slope of the next one to its crest, and then slowly down again.

In the last light she made the others as comfortable as she could, drawing their clothes around them and wedging the garments in place, trying to see that no flesh came into contact with the magic-infected timber. When she lay down herself she did the same for herself, but for the opposite reason—to keep the magic active in the timber, and so carry them all wherever it was that Axtrig was determined to go.

Light woke her, stiff and cold. The sky in the east was pale with dawn. Dark against it rose an island, ringed with cliffs.

The other three lay as she had left them, but when she tried to wake them they didn't stir. She couldn't find their pulses, or hear

211

their breathing above the sound of the waves. And yet their bodies were still as warm as hers beneath their clothes, so she tried to hope they weren't dead. She was too worried to eat, but simply sat, watching the island draw nearer. There was nothing to see but the cliffs and a rocky shore, with waves breaking gently against it. The top was hidden.

Slowly her fear for Meena and the others left her, and she began to feel strangely calm, confident that whatever had brought them so far would see them safe to the end. A kindness was in the air. She seemed to smell it in each breath she drew, and to sense that even in their tranced sleep the other three were blessed by the same faint sweetness. There was peace in their faces. So as the dangerous-seeming shore drew nearer, with the long ocean swell being tumbled and shredded by jagged rocks, she felt no tension, but rose and watched, ready.

The raft headed for a sloping shingle beach lying in a fold of the cliffs. It was moving—Tilja could now see, with the motionless island for comparison—as fast as a cantering horse. At the last moment a wave added to that speed, lifting the whole raft up, laying it with a heavy crunch far up the beach, and withdrawing down the shingle in a pother of foam.

Tilja knelt and worked Axtrig out from beneath the lashing and tied her to her forearm. Faint numbness flowed into her flesh, but the spoon now felt peaceful, with the calm of a cat sleeping by its own hearth. When she laid her hand on the timber of the raft she could tell that the magic was gone from there. Hopeful, she waited for the others to wake, but they slept on and neither her voice nor touch would wake them. Still with that strange sense that all was well she left them and looked for a way up the cliffs.

She had been half expecting to find a stair, so easily had the last few hours gone for her, but there seemed to be only one possible place in the sheer rock, where a thin dribble of water trickled down a kind of slot, with a few juts and crannies on either side for handholds and toeholds.

She started up it, and soon found herself wondering whether there wasn't a stair because it was not in the nature of the cliff to carve itself so, but it was doing what it could to help, all the same. There was always something to climb, provided she trusted it. When she looked down she could see the plain rectangle of the raft below her, with her three companions lying asleep on it. Rest after weary days—on this island it could be nothing else. She smiled and climbed on.

It was midmorning before she dragged herself out onto smooth turf. Three rabbits glanced up, then went back to nibbling, unperturbed. Ahead of her stood a low stone wall, with what looked like a garden beyond it. She walked to her left and found a gate, opened it and went through, closing it carefully behind her because she could see that wall and gate were there to keep the rabbits out.

This vaguely surprised her. The man they had been looking for surely had no need of such things. He could point out a line with his finger, and no creature—except perhaps an even more powerful magician, and the rabbits didn't look that—could come beyond it. But now she thought of it she sensed that, apart from Axtrig, whom she carried sleeping against her arm, the only magic on the island was its own magical calm. And . . . and . . . a curious faint buzzing close beside her right thigh. Not an audible buzz, a buzz of feeling. But otherwise just like some tiresome insect.

Automatically her hand had moved, brushing her skirt to get rid of it. The buzzing shifted but continued. She patted around. It was coming from inside her pocket. She felt and found her hair tie, and the buzzing stopped.

Her first thought was that the two things had nothing to do with each other—her movement had driven the buzzing thing away and her touch had emptied the hair tie of its magic, but it hadn't. Not quite. A trickle of numbness seeped out of the hair tie into her palm. She stood and stared at the trivial little object, and for the first time realized how strange it was that her hair had stayed in place, without one strand drifting free, ever since Tahl had last put it up for her while they were waiting for darkness before they could find their way into Goloroth. It had stayed in place in the heart of the warded city, and through the turmoil of the breaking of those wards, and again through the long journey out across the magicless ocean, until she had woken that morning and found her hair tumbling down to her shoulders and the hair tie wedged between two of the timbers of the raft. Tahl had been deep in his tranced sleep and there'd been no point in her trying to tie it herself, so she'd slipped it into her pocket.

She gazed at it, puzzled. Morning after morning she had held it, ready for Tahl to finish braiding and coiling her hair, so that he could then tie it into place, but had felt nothing in it but the feel of any other hair tie. Now, though, as it lay cupped in her hand, the unmistakable numbness in her palm told her that it was very, very different, a tiny magic object, even smaller, even more everyday-seeming, than a wooden spoon. But still full of its magic, on this island where no magic came.

Close ahead of her a voice spoke, softly creaking, and seeming to share something of her own bewilderment.

"So who are you . . . ? And what brought you here?"

She looked up, unalarmed, still sure that nothing bad could happen to her in this place. A grassy path stretched in front of her, and a short way down it an old man had emerged from between two rows of vines. He wasn't dressed in any of the fashions of the Empire, but wore a broad-brimmed straw hat, a plain unbleached-linen garment that fell from his shoulders to below his knees, sandals, and a brown apron with pockets for garden tools. He might once have been tall but was now stooped. His face was lined with innumerable wrinkles, but his white beard was combed and clean and his pale, yellowish eyes were much clearer than they should have been at his age and barely blinked at all.

"I'm looking for a man," she said.

"You must answer my questions first," he reproved her.

"I'm sorry. My name's Tilja Urlasdaughter and I came here on a raft from Goloroth."

"Alone?"

"No, but my friends—the magic was too strong for them, and—"

"What magic is this? There is no magic here but mine."

"It happened yesterday evening. It was something to do with Axtrig."

"Axtrig?"

"She's just a wooden spoon, but—"

"You have it? Show me."

Tilja rolled her sleeve up, untied Axtrig and held her out toward him. He peered at her.

"Just a wooden spoon," he said, nodding his head, as if amused by a puzzle. "I have been wondering . . . from time to time, you see, something that I made long ago still finds its way home to me. Last evening I felt this thing coming, but did not know what it was, and now I see it I still do not remember it. Indeed, it seems to me to have no magic in it."

"That's because I'm touching it."

He peered at her with sudden intensity, his face unreadable.

"You had better tell me about it," he said quietly. "Where did it come from?"

"From the Valley, in the far North. I'm afraid it's a long story, but ages ago two people came from the Valley to get help from a magician. He did what they asked, and gave them peaches from his garden. When they got back the woman planted the stone from hers at the farm where I live, and it grew into a tree, and years later when it blew down they used the wood to carve things from. Axtrig is one of them. We didn't know how magical she was, because there isn't any real magic in the Valley. She just told fortunes."

"Yes, I see. The Northern Valley. The Lost Province, beyond

215

the forest . . . And now, what you said about yourself. The spoon has no magic when you are touching it. That is why you had it tied to your arm?"

"We met a magician who told us it was a good idea, because otherwise people might sense we'd got her, and we'd be in trouble. I don't really understand, but magic doesn't seem to do anything to me—in fact I sort of undo it some of the time. Mostly I don't do that on purpose—it just happens—it's something about me. I didn't even realize how tiring it was until we were out in the middle of the sea, where there isn't any magic."

He stood looking at her for what seemed a long while, but perhaps not really seeing her. Then he sighed.

"Yes," he said. "Tiring. Tiring beyond belief . . . Will you please let me hold the spoon for a little?"

The numbness shot up Tilja's arm as he reached forward. Axtrig seemed to leap from her hand into his. For some while he stood silent, holding the shaft between his clasped palms with his head bowed over them and his lips lightly touching the bowl. Then he straightened and handed the spoon back to Tilja. The moment she took it Tilja knew that the magic was gone. The shaft was still wonderfully carved, the grain of the bowl still intricately beautiful, but it was all just dead wood. Axtrig was "her" no longer, only "it." With a pang of loss she slid it into her pocket and without thought dropped the hair tie in beside it.

She stared at the man. He seemed to be standing a little taller now, and when he spoke his voice was stronger than it had been before.

"I have taken back some of my powers from your spoon," he said, smiling at her surprise. "It is remarkable how they have grown over the years. . . . Well, I think I am the man you are looking for. My name is Faheel."

Already, with a sinking heart, Tilja had guessed this was so. So old, so feeble and unsure of himself. So quiet and peaceful too. How could he wield powers enough to hold back the might of the Empire from the Valley for twenty more generations? Was all their long and dangerous journey for nothing?

"Th-that's wonderful," she managed to stammer. "We hoped you'd let us find you, somehow. . . . Can you do anything about the others? They're asleep on the raft on the beach. I couldn't wake them up. Strong magic does that to them, but I've taken Axtrig away and it feels as if there isn't any other magic here. Anyway, Meena and Alnor are the ones who want to talk to you. Tahl and I just came to help them."

He shook his head, smiling as if he knew her thoughts.

"Best let them sleep," he said. "Nothing will harm them. And you are both right and wrong. There is no magic here, except one, and that prevents all the others. And it is very strong. Your friends could not endure it, waking. In spite of what you say, it is still astonishing to me that you are able to. Well, you must come in and tell me the rest of your story, and then we can decide what to do."

He turned and started to lead the way along the path, but then stopped and turned back, frowning.

"I think you are carrying something else besides the spoon," he said. "The force of the spoon hid it earlier. What is it?"

In the astonishment, relief and dismay of meeting Faheel, Tilja had forgotten about the hair tie, though it was still producing that faint, insectlike buzz beside her right thigh. She fished it out of her pocket and showed it to him.

"I don't understand," she said. "It's just something a traveling magician gave me to keep my hair up. Somebody else had to do that for me. If I touched it the magic didn't work. But since I came here something seems to have woken up, and it's much stronger than the plain hair-tie magic. I can feel it even when it's me holding it."

He took a pair of spectacles from one of his pockets, put them on and bent over her hand, peering at the hair tie. He straightened. There was a different kind of interest in his voice when he spoke.

"I shall need to know about this magician. What is his name?"

"I don't know. He told us to call him the Ropemaker."

"Ah . . . time is a great rope," he whispered.

He removed his spectacles and smiled at her.

"Indeed you must tell me your story," he said. "You may have brought me more than you had thought."

Again he turned and led the way through the garden. Tilja looked around her with surprise as she walked beside him. Like Faheel himself, this was not at all what she had expected. A magician's garden should have been extraordinary, surely—extraordinarily beautiful, extraordinarily neat, every plant not only wonderfully strange but doing precisely what it was supposed to. Instead, Faheel's garden, though certainly beautiful, was beautiful only with a kind of heightened ordinariness. There were gardens almost like this in the Valley, despite the harsher climate, gardens crammed with all the various plants their fanatical owners could fit in. Here were fruit trees and vegetables in straight rows, healthy and strong, though some of the rows needed hoeing, and there were masses of different flowers, and marvelous wafts of their scent floating in the mild, warm breeze, but often they sprawled among each other and some could have done with deadheading, and a few weeds poked up among them, and there were even patches that seemed to have been let go wild.

They came to a sheep, cunningly tethered so that it could nibble the grass on the path without getting into the beds. Faheel patted it as they passed.

"My garden has become rather more than I can now manage," he said, pausing to wipe greenfly from a rose shoot with his thumb. "But I do what I can."

His house, when they came to it, was like the garden, ordinary. Tilja had seen dozens just like it on the journey south, larger and better built than the hovels of the peasants, but very far from grand. A low white building with a vine-shaded terrace; small square windows with green shutters, mostly closed; large, curved, loose-looking orange red tiles; beyond it, the empty sea.

The door was covered with a bead hanging to keep out the flies. Inside was a low, tiled room, cool and dark, with a few coarse wooden cupboards and chests, a low table with two unlit lamps on it, and a pile of large cushions in one corner.

"You will be hungry and thirsty," said Faheel, "and I may as well eat with you."

Out of cupboards he fetched common pottery mugs and platters, dark bread, sheep cheese, oil, honey, fruits both dried and fresh, and a pitcher of water from a corner. Cross-legged on one of the cushions, Tilja told her story, pausing to collect her thoughts while she chewed or drank. Faheel, half lying on one elbow on the other side of the table, ate slowly and didn't interrupt at all. When she finished he shook his head and sighed.

"Well," he said, "you bring me both news I had long been hoping for and news I had long feared. I will explain later, but let me for the moment be sure about this. Apart from when your grandmother used the spoon to point the way, the only time any of you spoke my name, once you were in the Empire, was when your grandmother named me in Lananeth's warded room?"

"Yes."

"And you had not then met or seen this Ropemaker?"

"No."

"You saw him only between the time when you were in the robbers' cave and when he left you at the end of the road through the hills?"

"Yes. And we'd have spotted him at once if he'd been there—he looked so odd."

Faheel took a cloth and carefully wiped his lips and beard.

"Still, I think you may be mistaken," he said, rising. "We have work to do. You say it is not your mere presence that is destructive of magic? Your physical touch is needed?"

"Yes, I think so."

"Good. Then come with me. Bring the hair tie, and keep good hold of it."

He led the way into the next room and with some difficulty, making Tilja even more aware of his great age, climbed a fixed ladder into the attic. This had one large window facing out over the sea, and was full of light. The light showed up the dust, covering everything in a fine, even layer, undisturbed for months, perhaps for years. Faheel stood and looked round while Tilja climbed up beside him. He shook his head, ruefully.

"Well, it is time," he sighed. "You have been disappointed in me, I think, Tilja. I was not what you expected. As you see, I have had to lay my powers aside. The powers themselves are no less. They do not age. It is I myself, in the end, who am mortal. I could not afford to wear this body out any further, if I was to accomplish what I must before I go. I did not even dare use my powers to find out how long I must wait. Instead I withdrew to this island and nursed my strength, using little more than ordinary country magics to support my needs.

"But now, unmistakably, this is the moment. As I say, you bring me bad news as well as good. The whole of the next age is poised in the balance. So if you are not the one I have hoped for, then all is lost. Now, stand where you are, and do not move."

He went to a shelf, opened a small black box and took out a ring. As he carried it between fingertip and thumbtip to the center of the room Tilja saw it clearly—a simple gold circle engraved to look like fine cord. When he stopped, the dust around his sandaled feet slid gently away and she saw that the floor was polished wood, dark green, inlaid with a pattern of red and black. Faheel stood exactly at the center of the pattern, with two twined serpents, one red, one black, ringing his feet.

He turned toward the window and bowed his head. Tilja could feel his concentration. With a slow, ritual movement he slid the ring onto the middle finger of his right hand, and Tilja sensed the pulse of magic around her, instant and immense, drawn from great distances into the silent room. It didn't touch her, didn't swirl round her in a storming chaos, but spiraled smoothly into the center where Faheel stood waiting to receive it. For a moment everything vanished in a blinding whiteness, then returned, changed.

The window was the same, with the same sea beyond it, but the room itself seemed larger, and the dust was gone, and every surface shone or glittered with jewels or glowed with intense color. It wasn't, Tilja realized, that everything had been magically swept and dusted in that dazzling instant—no, the space between these four walls was now ageless, outside time. No dust would settle in *this* room, ever.

And in the middle of it stood a man wearing a dark blue robe of some rich fabric with a lacy golden collar sewn with seed pearls. His hair must once have been jet black but was now streaked with gray. He had his back to her, but his arms were raised as if in blessing, so that she could see a dozen great rings on his left hand, but on his right, on the middle finger, only a plain circle etched to look like fine cord. With a slow movement, like a dancer's, he drew it off, then turned toward her.

She gasped.

"Fa—"

He stopped her with a gesture. She stared. She had seen but not felt the room shudder.

The eyes were Faheel's, and the strong black beard was what Faheel's might well have been when he was younger. Faheel's wrinkled old face, too, could have become what it was from a face with this shape and these features. Except that these all belonged to a different order of being, not human, ageless, living stone. Like Silena on the walls of Talagh.

He fetched the box from the shelf, put the ring in it and dropped it into a pocket.

"Yes," he said. "I am the one you would have named. You should not have been able even to begin to do so in this place. Now, first, I will see to your friends, so that you do not distract yourself with worrying for them."

He closed his eyes briefly. His lips moved.

"Good," he said. "They sleep in the room below. Nothing can

harm them under this roof. Now, look at your hair tie. You see the gold hair? Tease it out."

Tilja peered at the little object and spotted a golden glimmer among the interwoven colored threads. What Faheel asked looked impossible without unraveling the whole tie, but she took one of her hairpins and picked at a strand. A loop of gold hair freed itself, and when she pulled with her fingers the whole strand slid smoothly loose.

"Remarkable," said Faheel. "The magic that bound that in place was far more than a village charm. Now give me the tie and bring the hair to the table. . . . Wait."

The table seemed to be made from a single block of polished black marble, an ornate stem supporting a round top, smooth as a mirror, so that Tilja could see the brightly decorated ceiling reflected in its dark depths. As Faheel leaned over the table the reflections faded and the darkness seemed to become bottomless, until up from those depths there floated a curious irregular shape. At first Tilja couldn't make out what it was, but when it reached the surface it became a delicate inlay of colored marbles, making a map with rivers and roads and mountains, and minuscule pictures of cities, and in a blink she realized it was a map of the Empire, from Goloroth in the far south to the tremendous mountains in the north. Yes, and there, ringed in between the forest and the snow peaks, was the Valley. Screwing her eyes up, she even persuaded herself that she could see a tiny dot close in against the forest edge. She pointed at it, careful not to touch the magical surface.

"That's where I live," she whispered. "That's home!"

The map changed. The pictured mountains and trees grew larger and moved apart. The trees reached the edge of the map and the mountains disappeared on the other side, and the dot itself was more than a dot, growing and still growing, until she could see Woodbourne with its fields around it, and Ma and Da side by side hoeing beans in the Home Field and Anja trying to coax an escaped cockerel back into the safety of the run. She stared until her eyes were too misty to see and she had to wipe them with the end of her head scarf. When she looked again the table once more showed the map of the Empire.

"Now," said Faheel, "without touching the table lay the hair somewhere on the map."

Tilja chose an empty-looking area northeast of Goloroth. The hair, when she dropped it, curled itself together into a neat spiral, as if it had been trying to regain the shape it had held in the hair tie, but then lay still.

"A curious color," said Faheel. "I have seen nothing like it. Have you, Tilja?"

She peered. A single hair doesn't usually declare its full color. You need at least a ringlet for that. But this one fine strand seemed to shine not only with the reflected brightness of the room, but with an inner fire of its own, shining through the gold. Yes, indeed strange, but . . .

"The unicorn!" she whispered. "And the dog! When we landed from the raft! They shone like that! And the lion at Goloroth! I didn't see its color, but the way its fur sparkled in the moonlight . . . and that means the cat—the one that helped me on the walls of Talagh . . . do you think the donkey . . . when Silena came to the way station? She said something about it not being only my doing."

Faheel nodded, as if she had confirmed something he'd already guessed.

He stretched his hand for a moment above the map, and it began to move once more, enlarging itself at the same time, flowing away off the edges of the table, but mainly toward the south, so that the coil of hair appeared to float rapidly north over it, straight as a rule, with the Great River and the Grand Trunk Road streaming past to the west, then across the river where it curved away east at Ramram, and on, north between road and river, all the way Tilja and the others had tramped those ninety-three days, to Talagh itself, at first no larger than a drin coin, but growing and growing until it filled the tabletop and then stilled, with the coil of hair floating over the forecourt of the pinnacled palace at the center of the city.

Faheel grunted, as if with mild surprise, and picked up the hair, wound it round the hair tie and put them into a small purse. The map started to grow again, until it showed only the palace. Minuscule people began to appear, as they had at Woodbourne, but stopped growing before Tilja could make out more than that they were human figures arranged in a pattern of rectangles. Other figures ringed the courtyard. A parade of soldiers, with spectators, she guessed, the sort of thing that Emperors did in courtyards. Faheel grunted again.

"We can come no closer," he said quietly. "The place is well warded. I could overcome the wards, of course, but at more cost than I can afford. This will take thought. . . ."

As he turned away from the table the map vanished. For some while he stood at the window, gazing out over the sea. He sighed and returned to the table. He took the box from his pocket, removed the ring and placed it on the gleaming surface, then stood back.

"Hold your finger above the ring," he said. "Do you feel anything? Move closer. Stop as soon as you feel anything. Closer. Still nothing? Touch it and withdraw. . . . Still nothing? Touch it again and hold your finger there. . . . Pick it up. . . . Put it in your palm and close your fingers round it. . . ."

"Oh, I can feel something now," she said. "It isn't the usual sort of feeling I get when I touch something magical. It's a sort of hum. Like a noise when it gets so deep that you can't hear it anymore, but you still know it's there. It's as if everything else was humming with the ring. Except me."

Faheel spread his hands and held them a little apart on either side of Tilja's clenched fist.

"Astonishing," he said. "I sense nothing at all of its presence. I do not know how you do this—it is something I have never before encountered. Give it back to me now. Thank you."

Tilja put the ring into his cupped hand, where he weighed it for a moment or two, then put it away and sighed.

"Well, we must take the risk," he said. "The thing that you have come for will have to wait. My problem is this. I would prefer not to make use of a power I do not understand, but I have lived too far beyond my time, and I cannot hold back my death much longer. Before I die, I must destroy the power of the Watchers. I brought them into being in the first place, at the Emperor's behest, to help me control the chaos of magic flooding through the Empire, but my cure turned out in the end to be worse than the disease. So now I must undo what I did.

"But I cannot afford to do that until I have passed the ring to a new keeper, or chaos will come again. Twice over the years I have chosen one. Both became Watchers, and both then failed me, corrupted by their own power. Now you come with news of another, this Ropemaker. From things you have told me, and from the single hair you brought me, I believe that he has great natural powers, so far uncorrupted. But what the map showed us tells us that he is at this moment present at a grand parade in the courtyard of the Emperor's Palace, and this almost certainly means that he has been chosen to take Dorn's place as a Watcher, and will be installed in the course of the ceremony. Then it will be too late for me to pass the ring on to him."

"That's the bad news, I suppose," said Tilja. "You said I'd brought you bad news as well as good. . . . Oh, no, that was before you'd used your map to find where the Ropemaker was, so you didn't know then."

"No, that is not what I meant," said Faheel. "It is in fact part of the good news. It means that everything is coming together to my advantage. Many of the Watchers will be present at the ceremony, and not in their towers, so they will be more vulnerable to the attack I have long prepared. The Ropemaker will also be there, so when I have done I will be able to give him the ring and go, for my task will be over.

"The bad news . . . no, I have no time now, and if all goes well it will no longer be my problem. What matters now is that I must go instantly to Talagh. I do not dare wait, or the chance will be lost. The Ropemaker will be lost. He is in far more danger than he can understand. But there is a difficulty. I could go to Talagh between a breath and a breath, but I must take the ring for what I may have to do, past the warded walls of Goloroth, and stand, unnoticed, with twenty Watchers around me, whose task it is to detect the existence of such things as the ring in the presence of the Emperor.

"I still have power to do all this, but that would leave me no strength for what else I have to do. Moreover, if I were detected and it came to a magical battle, the power I would need to defeat twenty Watchers would destroy me also. You understand?"

"I think so. Would it help if I came with you and held the ring? I got Axtrig past the wards, and I think I'm stronger now."

"That is what I was about to suggest, but there is a further difficulty. Because you are what you are I cannot take you instantaneously to Talagh, as I could take myself. You must be carried there, physically, mile by mile, minute by minute. By the swiftest means I can devise this will take too long. So what I must do is ask the ring to hold all time still for everything but you and your immediate surroundings while you are carried to Talagh. There will be a sort of bubble of moving time inside an unmoving universe. The bubble will be centered on you. Our journey will seem to us to take several hours, but when we reach the palace at Talagh the parading soldiers will not have moved a step. Asking the ring to do this will take strength from me, but it is in the nature of the ring, once asked, to deal directly with time of its own unmediated power, and I will then be able to rest while we are carried to Talagh. Will you do this?"

Tilja was too astonished and overawed to do more than nod her head. Faheel smiled at her.

"Good," he said. "Now you had better go back downstairs while I do what I have to. Your friends are there. Do not try to wake them."

Tilja climbed down the ladder and found Meena, Alnor and Tahl each asleep on a separate pile of cushions, but still in the exact attitudes in which they had lain when she had last seen them, far below her, from halfway up the cliff. All three faces had the same look, Meena not sharp and touchy, Alnor not proud and angry, Tahl not eager and inquisitive, but all of them full of deep, quiet content. Tilja smiled at them and went and leaned on the windowsill, gazing out over the garden and the sea to where she guessed the Empire must lie.

Her mind was full of a jumble of thoughts about the Ropemaker. They didn't seem quite to fit together, in the same way that the Ropemaker's own gawky body didn't . . . and the animals he'd been didn't either, if Faheel was right, the lion, the donkey perhaps, the cat on the walls of Talagh, the dog by the river, the unicorn on the crag, guarding them, helping them all the way south. . . .

Except for the unicorn. The unicorn was one of the things that didn't fit. It had been different, menacing, dangerous, almost an enemy, nothing like the Ropemaker himself, strange but friendly, not frightening at all—until she remembered what Tahl had said about the bit of rope that had wrapped itself round Calico's legs in the pine forest . . . and . . .

And—she really didn't want to think about this—Ma's dream. *It touched me with its horn.* What else could she have been talking about . . . ?

Tilja was jolted out of her wonderings by the appearance of the bird. A little to her right, beyond the nearest flower bed, was a small meadow cropped by a pair of sheep, each tethered to a single peg so that they mowed a series of circles. The bird appeared in what must have been one of yesterday's circles. At one moment there was just a patch of short-cropped grass; the next it was filled by an enormous brown bird, far larger than the elephants Tilja had sometimes seen hauling loads of timber on the journey south. It had a fiery red crest and a black, hooked beak, which looked as if it had been designed for tearing at meat, but

227

the two sheep merely glanced up at it and went back to grazing. The bird put up an immense, taloned foot and started to scratch itself under the chin, like a farmyard hen. A moment later a large, cushioned litter appeared on the grass beside it. There were poles at each corner with a striped canopy stretched between them and what looked like a sort of carrying handle lying loose on the cloth.

Before the bird had finished scratching, time stopped. Tilja both saw and heard it happen. The bird stuck, motionless, with its claw against its chin and a look of idiot absorption on its face. The sheep stuck with their mouths against the turf. The gulls wheeling above the cliffs stuck in midglide on slanting wings. All over the garden the birdsong stilled in an instant, and in the same instant the endless faint rustle of leaves and hush and shush of waves against the cliffs became a silence so intense that Tilja could hear not only her own breath but, at last, that of the three sleepers in the room.

She frowned. Time ought to have stopped for them. They shouldn't still be breathing. Then wood creaked on wood behind her and she turned and saw Faheel, now back in the shape of an old man, climbing shakily down the ladder.

"Ready?" he said. "We will need food and drink, if you will carry the basket."

With trembling hands he fetched stores out of a cupboard and she stowed them neatly away.

"Why hasn't time stopped in here?" she asked.

"Because you are here. Your friends will stop breathing as soon as you are out of the room, and when you are close to the roc it will wake and carry us to Talagh. Now, if you will let me lean on your shoulder . . . I shall be stronger after a rest."

As they passed the nearer sheep it began grazing again as if nothing had happened. A few paces further on, the bird woke and went on with its scratching. When they reached the litter Tilja put the basket down and helped Faheel settle onto the cushions, where he lay back with his eyes closed while she found a place for the basket and made herself comfortable at the other end. The bird—a roc he had called it—seemed to know what was expected of it. It rose and settled its feathers into place with a thunderous rattle, so huge, standing, that that she could see only its scaly, yellow lower legs beneath the canopy of the litter, and then only one as it reached out with the other to grasp the handle above the canopy. With a deep thud of its enormous wings it drove itself into the air.

The litter lurched across the grass, almost spilling the passengers before the flight had begun, then swung wildly forward and round as they rushed into the air. Tilja grabbed one of the corner posts and clung to it. Faheel spread his arms wide but stayed where he was, still with his eyes shut. By the time their flight steadied they were already far into the air, and Faheel's island was dwindling below and behind them. The spume against its rocks neither rose nor fell, but stayed poised in the instant when time had stopped for it.

And still they rose, and the air shrieked past them, fiercer than any winter gale. Now Tilja could see a change in the northern horizon, a darker, grayer, fuzzier line than the blue curve of ocean to east and west, and knew she was looking at the shore of the Empire. The sky was mottled with small clouds that came nearer and nearer as the roc continued to climb. The steady pulse of its wings boomed in Tilja's ears like strokes upon a monstrous gong. When she tried to shut the sound out with her fingers the bones of her body still rang with it.

Faheel's eyes were open, looking at her. She saw him beckon and crawled forward against the clawing wind. He put a hand into the fold of his overshirt and drew out the black box in which he kept the ring. Careful not to touch his flesh with hers, she put her ear close to his mouth so that she could hear what he was saying above the wind-shriek and the thud of the wings.

"We go high. It will be cold. Cover me, and then yourself. But first, take this and put it in safety. I must sleep."

So Tilja took the box and stowed it in the bottom of the

basket, and wedged that well with cushions. Then she chose furs and rugs from a pile and spread them over Faheel, and did the same for herself, but sat up for a while and watched the Empire draw nearer. By the time they crossed the coastline they were above the clouds. Between them, over to their left, she could see the innumerable channels of the Great River delta, and so was just able to make out Goloroth, but only its largest details, the wall, the big sheds, and the launching pier. As it slid away behind them she realized how fast they must be going.

It grew colder, and her eyes were watering too much to see, so she coiled herself down into her bedding and pulled a cushion over her head to muffle both wing thunder and wind wail, and closed her eyes. She didn't expect to sleep, but lay for a while wondering at the strangeness of what was happening—far stranger, she thought, than anything else in her adventure, from the unicorns in the forest to the roc in Faheel's paddock, stranger even than her gradual discovery of the power that lay in her own lack of any magical power—this business with time. Suppose in the wild hurtle of the start of their flight she had fallen out of the litter, but landed unhurt, what would have happened? Would the roc have stuck in its flight between wing beat and wing beat? Or would Faheel have found the strength to wear his ring again? And if neither of them had been able to do that, what then? Would *she* have been stuck, moving and breathing, in a world forever still?

She need not have been alone. She could have gone to Faheel's lower room and Meena and the others would have started to breathe again and she could have waited for them to wake, but they would have needed to stay in her presence in order not to be stilled once more. They could have walked in Faheel's garden and picked grapes from his vines and eaten them, but fresh grapes would not ripen, ever, unless she stayed near enough to draw them back into time. . . .

But of course, Tahl would have worked out a way of getting her back up to the roc.

Smiling at the thought, she fell asleep and dreamed of Woodbourne in a winter storm, with a gale shrieking through the thatch and a strange, deep booming in the chimney.

She woke, and automatically looked to see how far the sun had sunk west, so that she might guess how long she'd slept. It hadn't, of course, moved. The tearing wind was no less, so she constructed a sort of tunnel from which she could spy out eastward while still lying in shelter. Almost at once a soaring vulture swung past, woke into time, saw the roc, jerked itself into a spasm of escape, and stilled again, motionless wings wrenching at the motionless air.

Most of what slid by below was too far off for Tilja to see any sign of its changelessness, but once they skirted a mountain range over which a thunderstorm was raging. Time must have stopped in the instant of a lightning stroke, which stood there, a blazing vein of light, branching into twenty side veins between the dark sagging cloud layer and the darker crags below. She had to screw up her eyes against its brightness and even so couldn't look at it for long.

After a little she eased herself out of her nest and crawled forward to see how Faheel was doing. He was awake, and looked rested. She fetched him bread and fruit and cheese and a little flask of wine, and then crawled back, found what she wanted for herself and took it in under the rugs and nibbled peacefully. The litter was very comfortable, so when she'd had enough she let the weariness of all those days of travel overcome her, and slept again, and was only woken by the mild bump of landing, and the stilling of the sounds of flight. She looked out and saw that they were in the cleared space before the gates of Talagh.

12

The Palace

Faheel had slept too. He was standing straighter and looked much stronger. He took what looked like a handful of rubies from his pouch and offered them to the roc, which neatly nibbled them one by one out of his palm with the point of its huge beak, swallowed them in a single gulp, closed its eyes with an expression of total bliss, and belched. It then settled down, ruffled its feathers and fell asleep.

"Won't one of the Watchers see it?" asked Tilja. "It's magical, isn't it?"

"To perceive something takes time, however short. They are all fixed in the instant when time stopped for them, a little while after you saw the parade in my table. Now, bring the box that holds the ring and keep it in your hand. Good. Over here."

The roc had landed in a space to one side of the entrance gate, with nobody near enough to be affected by the flow of time that enclosed Tilja wherever she went but was frozen still for the rest of the universe. Now as they picked their way between the citizens who had been coming and going until the moment that the ring did its work, some of them woke into movement and took a pace or two as Tilja went by, then returned to their stillness. When they reached the throng by the gate Faheel halted.

"We cannot go through the city like this," he said. "The streets are too crowded. People will wake round you and push us apart. Will you open the box? The egg of the phoenix is the catch. Good. Hold it in front of me and keep it steady. When I have touched the ring, lay your hand on my wrist."

The inside of the box seemed to have no bottom. It was a pure blackness, like the table in Faheel's room. The ring simply floated in that blackness, resting on nothing. Taking a firm grip on Tilja's shoulder, he put out his other hand and lightly touched the ring for a moment with the tip of his middle finger. She felt a shudder run through him. His hand rose a fraction and he stiffened into stillness. With a gulp of fear she realized that she was now alone, the only moving thing in a timeless world, but the moment she touched his wrist he relaxed and sighed.

"Once it would all have been so easy," he murmured. "Now I cannot spare the strength to exempt myself from the power of the ring. Well, from here on only you and what touches you is not locked into the moment. Let me just move my hold so that you have both hands free. If something causes me to let go of you, you must take me by the hand again. Close the box and keep hold of it. When I tell you, take the ring out and grasp it in your bare hand, and its effect will cease. Now we must find this Ropemaker."

So, slowly, with Faheel leaning heavily on Tilja's shoulder, with his hand firmly against the bare skin of her neck, they made their way past the motionless lines waiting for entry to the city, and under the archway. Again she felt the force of the wards that guarded the city, powerful still in the instant into which time was locked, but it was very different from when she had first come through. There was no numbness, but an intense, strange feeling, as if the hand that enclosed the ring box had been a wine glass round whose rim somebody was rubbing a moistened fingertip, setting up a note that in a moment would shatter the glass.

No, she told it, and raised her fist in defiance. The finger withdrew and the note stilled.

"Well done," murmured Faheel as she led him into the crowded street beyond the archway.

233

Remembering what that had been like when she had first come to Talagh, Tilja was worried about how she was going to pick a path through the scrum without waking anybody into life. Fortunately some great lord had been just about to leave the city when time had stopped, and his servants had already cleared a way for him to the gate. She came to the lord himself a little way up the street, riding a beautiful spirited horse which must have been frightened by the tumult and was shying aside, with its rider fighting to control it, when the instant had come, fastening them into the same unchanging, impossible pose. As she edged past, Tilja was tempted to lay her hand on the glossy flank and wake the horse into life, just to see what happened. With a shock she realized that she was experiencing something she had never imagined, a sense of absolute power. All these people, even a great lord of the Empire, even the Emperor himself, were under her control. They could move, or not, as she chose. The thought was oddly frightening. If you had that power you wanted to use it. This must be what magicians were like, all the time. This was why some of them had tried so hard to get hold of Axtrig.

They passed the ball of contortionists, poised on one foot, the woman smothered in motionless scorpions, jugglers with arcs of flaming torches or daggers hanging in stillness above them, barkers and stallholders with their mouths gaping in the shout they had started and never finished, sneak thieves with purses half cut, the smoke from roasting grills fixed in the windless air, all the bustle and frenzy of Talagh halted, as if forever.

It was slow going, but Faheel could not have gone much faster if the avenue had been empty. Three times he needed to rest, and each time he rose his face seemed grimmer and grayer, like Meena's when the weather changed and her hip was hurting her worse than usual.

"Are you all right?" said Tilja, anxiously.

"I will manage because I must," he said. "It is the last chance. Foolishly I thought too much of the magical effort I must make, and forgot the ordinary physical cost of walking from one place to another."

"Couldn't we have got the roc to take us the whole way?"

"Perhaps, but it is a powerful center of magic in itself. It will wake with everything else when you take the ring out of the box and hold it in your hand, and there will then be more than enough magical forces around us for me to contend with."

At last the slope became steeper as the avenue rose to the palace gate. On either side the fantastic building stretched away, walls of white and pink marble carved with the wars and triumphs of forgotten Emperors; balconies and arcades dangling with huge-flowered vines; pinnacles and towers, banners and emblems; all the work of generations of master craftsmen toiling to please rulers who expected a fancy dreamed up over supper to have become fact by breakfast time.

The gate appeared to have been carved from one immense block of jade. It was guarded by two bronze dragons, each six times the size of a horse. They looked like real dragons, but Tilja couldn't be sure. They might have been statues. The living sentries beneath the archway stood just as motionless.

The wall and the buildings behind it were just an outer shell. Inside that stood another palace, even more ornate. From it rose the soaring towers of the Watchers. It was too dazzling to look at long, like a jeweled crown for a giant king, a giant the size of a mountain. Its roofs were lapis lazuli and gold, all set with precious stones. Around it lay a scented garden, with fountains flinging jets of different-colored water far into the air. Directly in front of it was a large open space. It was here the soldiers were paraded.

At first Tilja could only glimpse them between the motionless spectators who ringed the parade ground, but Faheel looked around and then led the way to a door of a tower beside the gateway they had just come through. An enormous soldier with a fierce mustache blocked the entrance.

"Take his hand in yours," murmured Faheel.

At Tilja's touch the man came to life. For a moment he stared at her in furious astonishment, then looked up at Faheel. An odd, blank look came into his eyes and he backed slowly into the room behind him. "You can let go now," said Faheel.

Tilja did so, and the man froze. They walked on past him, and found three soldiers squatting on the floor, gambling. One of them had just thrown the dice, which hung suspended beneath his hand.

Tilja felt an extraordinary impulse to interfere. What possible harm would it have done to leave Faheel for a moment, step across the room, pluck the dice out of the air—her touch moving them into the flow of time—and lay them down as triple sixes on the floor for the men to find when they were woken? Only the urgency of what they were doing stopped her.

There was a winding stair in the corner of the room, too narrow for Tilja to climb beside Faheel so that he could lean his weight on her. He had to go up it on hands and knees, resting every few steps, while Tilja followed, gripping his ankle so as not to lose contact.

At the top they found a small room, richly furnished, where several women stood by a pierced screen that looked out over the heads of the spectators. There were dice on a low table, with cushions around it. Some of the women must have been gambling, like the soldiers below. One had a purse in her hands and was paying another. She'd dropped a gold coin, which hung halfway to the floor. Tilja had never seen such clothes, glorious silks and velvets, brooches, necklaces and earrings. What any one of them was wearing looked as if it might be worth half the wealth of the Valley. On Faheel's instructions she moved along the line of them, touching their hands, waking them for a few moments before he murmured a word to them. One by one they sank to the floor in a different kind of sleep.

"What would have happened if I'd changed that man's dice throw?" she asked while he rested again.

"Who knows? Nothing. The whole world. Suppose one man loses a bet he would have won. He needs money to pay. He steals and is found out. He is punished and loses promotion. So he does not become the Emperor's favorite, does not get to rule and ruin a province, but another man governs it well—why, then, you have changed the happiness of many hundreds of thousands of people. Or the other way round. Time, I tell you, is a great rope. Wearing the ring, I have stood outside it and seen how its strands weave into other strands, back and forth, far beyond the instant in which we all live.

"Now, come, and we will see what we can see."

The whole parade that Tilja had seen in Faheel's table was now visible through the screen, rank beyond rank of soldiers, all in glistening armor, with banners and standards and pennoned spears. They had their backs toward Tilja, so she could see nothing of their faces. Beneath their spiked helmets they wore head scarves, something like the women of the Empire wore, different colors for the different companies. Almost all of them must already have been standing still when time had stopped for them, but to one side and toward the front Tilja could see an officer with his head thrown back and mouth open, in the act of shouting a command, and on the opposite side of the parade there was a group of people who must have been on the move when they were halted. A double line of soldiers, bearing drawn scimitars across their shoulders, had just rounded the end of the rank. They were picked men, a bodyguard, fierce and bearded like the ones below in the tower, and a head taller than the men on parade. Whoever they were guarding was still out of sight beyond the rank, but Tilja could see an ornate canopy, followed by the helmeted heads of further guards.

Something was puzzling her, something she'd seen only just before, but for a moment couldn't quite lay her mind on. Frowning, she glanced back at the officer giving the command, young, slight, beardless . . . a blink, and the thing became obvious . . . all of them! The head scarves, their smallness compared to the men, the very way they stood and carried themselves . . . a whole regiment of them!

With a flash of intuition she realized what they were for.

"They're women!" she gasped. "They can go through the forest! The Emperor's going to use them to retake the Valley!"

"Yes," he said quietly, as if his thoughts were elsewhere.

"Can't you do something?"

"Later, perhaps. Look now. Over there beyond them. By the gateway, on the right."

Unwillingly Tilja did as she was told. On either side of the doors of the central palace there was a raised terrace, from which groups of people, fantastically garbed, were watching the parade. Some had great plumed headdresses, or steeple hats with floating veils. Some wore jeweled masks, or the skins of exotic beasts with their fanged heads snarling above their own. Others had robes so voluminous, so weighted with jewels, that it took several slave children to carry their hems.

The group directly opposite Tilja were stranger than any. Several of them looked hardly human at all, though they wore clothes and stood like people. One woman—was it a woman?—seemed to have six arms. Another had no face at all, only a pale, smooth blank beneath a plain black velvet cap. Tilja knew who these creatures were before Faheel spoke.

"Fifteen Watchers," he muttered. "Four still on watch in their towers. Dorn is dead. When the Emperor has finished his inspection of the regiment, a new Watcher will be installed. Do you see your Ropemaker? My table showed us that he is in or near this courtyard."

The wonder and excitement of the last few hours had driven Tilja's worries about the Ropemaker from her mind. Now, at this last instant, they came rushing back

"The Ro-Ropemaker?" she stammered. "But . . . I . . . I meant to ask you . . . if . . . if he was the unicorn, then he almost killed Ma!"

Faheel nodded.

"We all make mistakes," he said sadly. "The more powerful we are, the worse they will be. I have no time now to explain. I must ask you to trust me when I tell you that this was a mistake in innocence. But once your Ropemaker accepts the powers of a Watcher he will be lost beyond recovery. Some of those who stand there now were once honorable magicians. Dorn had been my own pupil."

He waited. Tilja realized he was allowing her, even now, to decide to refuse to help him. That itself decided her. She nodded and turned to the screen.

"Do not stare at them," he muttered. "They may sense your attention. Look for the Ropemaker."

Tilja searched along the terrace. Could she have missed that extraordinary headdress among all the other fantastic costumes? No, not on the right-hand side. Wait. Under the little door, close to the inner end . . . The top half of the figure was in deep shadow, but she could see a trousered leg, as far up as the hip, the leg of a tall man with a curiously gawky stance, both awkward and powerful. . . .

"There," she whispered. "He was just coming out of that door."

"Good," said Faheel. "Then we are ready. I will tell you what I am trying to do. My object is to prevent your friend being installed as a Watcher, and perhaps, if all goes well, to destroy the whole system of the Watchers. In passing I may be able to do what you ask for your Valley.

"These woman warriors are not here by choice. They have been snatched from their homes at their Emperor's will, and trained to recapture your Valley. That is not their only purpose. The Emperor has peculiar tastes. He is delighted by women dressed in uniform, so he holds these parades often, and takes any that catch his eye for his own use. The women are furious about this, and long to return to their homes, but they are afraid. The punishments for desertion and mutiny are unspeakable. Now I propose to make use of both his lust and their anger.

"But I dare not use more strength than I must. Whatever I do will wake the Watchers, and I shall need to hold them off for at least a little time, or we will both be destroyed and all will be lost.

"So, when I tell you, you will take the ring out of the box and clasp it in your hand. The world will move on its course once more. After a little while I shall work a very ordinary bit of village magic, a love charm, as it were, beneath the notice of the Watchers. When this has had its effect I shall wake the anger of the soldier women. What then happens should be enough to distract the Watchers on the terrace, and I will use what strength I have left to hold off those in the towers until events have taken their course, and then I will tell you to put the ring back in its box, and time will stop, and we will go as we came.

"And if I should fail . . ."

He paused, and she looked up, waiting. More strongly than ever now she could feel his immense age, his frailty, his weariness. His voice became little more than a whisper.

"If I should fail, you must put the ring back in the box and go by yourself. The roc will wake at your presence and carry you to my island. As you pass between shore and shore, take the ring and throw it into the sea. In the time that would have been a day and a night for you, had the sun still moved through the sky, the effect will cease and your friends will wake. You will be safe enough on my island."

He straightened and spoke more strongly.

"Now we begin. Take the ring out of the box."

Fail? With the whole of the next age poised in the balance? Now, as soon as I take hold of the ring?

Tilja almost froze at the thought, but then a quite different thought steadied her, ordinary, everyday, but as important to her as the balance of the whole next age.

I promised Da I'd get back to Woodbourne.

Her hands didn't shake as she opened the box and closed her fingers round the ring. At once she felt the strange deep humming that she had felt when she had held the ring in her hand in

Faheel's room, the long unchanging tremor that seemed to be vibrating through all creation, apart from her own body. The women on the floor of the room didn't stir from the enchanted sleep into which Faheel had thrown them, but the gold coin finished its fall and went rolling across the floor. Beyond the screen the parade flowed smoothly into movement. Drums and gongs, pipes and trumpets thundered, blared and whistled as the soldiers came marching round the end of the rank, followed by two resplendent court officials, and then the leading pair of slaves who carried the portable throne beneath the canopy, and then the throne itself, more bearers, dignitaries and soldiers.

Tilja got a clear look at the man on the throne as it turned the corner. He was wearing a small crown with three golden feathers at the front. Beneath that his face was pale as a mushroom, fleshy, with a snub nose and pale lips showing through a weedy little beard. He didn't look any older than the young men Tilja had watched kick-fighting at the Gathering, but his body was so fat that she wondered whether he could have walked even a few steps without help. Where had she seen that shape before? Yes! The inflated goatskin floats on the raft that had brought them down the river! Despite the glittering surcoat that enveloped it, the gross shape looked more like one of those than anything human.

So this was the Emperor. In all her life Tilja had never seen anyone looking so bored. He could have anything in the world he pleased, but nothing in the world could please him. Seeing him for that brief moment, she felt a shudder of horror both at him and for him. Then, as the throne vanished behind the next rank, she thought, *And he wants to reconquer the Valley. No!*

She looked at the terrace. The Ropemaker had come through the door and was moving behind the group of Watchers. He stopped a little beyond them, turned and stood waiting. He hadn't changed. He had the same fidgety, inquisitive look he'd had in the Pirrim Hills, the same laddish awkwardness, as if he hadn't ever quite grown into his adult shape.

Faheel must have been watching him too. She heard him murmuring to himself, "No, not too late. Not too late."

Nothing else happened as the little procession moved along behind the next rank. As it neared the end Faheel gripped the metalwork of the screen, as if to steady himself. She heard him draw a deep breath. The procession stopped with the throne once again just in sight. A dignitary came forward and bent to hear the Emperor's command. He straightened and walked round and back along the rank, where he spoke briefly to one of the woman soldiers and led her back toward the Emperor. As they came fully into view Tilja saw that he was leading her by the wrist, and she was following reluctantly.

"Now, be ready," said Faheel in a far stronger voice, and Tilja poised her clenched fist over the open box.

He clapped his hands. The sound was like a crack of thunder close by, that went rolling away across the parade ground, while Tilja's head still rang with it. She saw the woman soldier flinch and stagger, and then turn her head and call out to her comrades. Instantly they broke rank and swarmed toward the Emperor like a bee swarm clustering round their queen. Scimitars flashed in the air. The canopy tilted, toppled and was gone. The guards struggled a little longer and then they too went under. And now, as Tilja's hearing returned to her and she could hear their wild high whoops and yells, the whole enraged regiment was streaming toward the terrace.

Even the Watchers seemed to have been taken by surprise. When Tilja looked, they were struggling in a mass of panicking courtiers rushing for the door beyond them. A great beast rose amid the crush, squatting on its hind legs and batting everyone around it out of its path. Two fiery shapes and a shadow-thing burst away upward and soared on wings of flame and darkness toward the towers of the Watchers. And then everything gave a sort of shudder, and changed.

At first Tilja thought something had gone wrong with her

eyes. What they were seeing didn't make sense. The towers rose straight and true still, but they weren't straight with each other. Each of them made the rest look crooked. And the same with everything else. Palace and spectators seemed to be floating, not above the ground, but loose, as if they were somewhere else, and the courtyard walls and towers seemed to get larger as they reached away into the distance. And the people too. The further away they were the more gigantic they became.

But the sky beyond was too near. It was much too near. It was nearer than the towers, inside out. As the dark and burning magicians fled toward their towers the sky wrapped itself round them and they disappeared.

Tilja could actually see the bottom edge of the sky, where it touched the ground. That edge swept across the terrace, and Watchers and courtiers were gone.

Then, as it closed on the towers, it seemed to pause.

All this in an instant, or in a different kind of time.

Tilja heard a mutter from Faheel. She glanced up and saw that he was in his magician's shape, tall and strong. His spread hands were raised beside his shoulders and his face was set and pale with concentration. She realized that this was the final effort, the moment for which he had been saving his powers so carefully, and when it was over he would have almost nothing left. The four Watchers still in their towers may have been taken by surprise, but they were in the places where they were strongest and they'd had a moment or two to rally their powers. Now they must be fighting back.

She looked again through the screen. The center of the parade ground was empty, apart from a few bodies lying around the toppled litter. In the midst of them was a bulging golden object, like an outsize float for a raft. The Emperor. Dead.

Tilja stared. It was difficult for her to take in. What had Lananeth said? *We live and die at his will.* No longer. He was dead himself, not at his own will, but Faheel's. And Tilja's too, perhaps. Faheel couldn't have done it without her, and if she'd understood what she was doing she'd still have chosen to do it. For the sake of the Valley.

Too shaken to think clearly, she forced herself to look away and see what else was happening. All around the parade ground the massed spectators were streaming for the entrance gate, and beyond it the regiment of women was charging toward the palace. Tilja could hear their whooping war cry, above the yells and screams of terror from the spectators.

Her eye was caught by a patch of stillness, of difference, not part of the strange, sickening, lurching inside-out world that Faheel had created to do his work. In the middle of it stood the Ropemaker, alone on the terrace. Somehow the sky had managed to leave him behind. Now, instead of trying to escape, he had climbed onto a low stone platform against the palace wall and seemed to be gazing at the confusion as if it had been a show put on for his amusement.

Something was happening to the towers above him. Still, if Tilja looked at any one of them directly, it seemed to stand upright and motionless, but the ones at the edge of her vision were tilting away at unbelievable angles. Some now bent sharply in the middle, as a stick seems to when thrust into a pond. Others stretched away out of sight, endless.

The sky closed round the palace, and closed again. There was an immense, tearing crash, and a shudder that seemed to shake the world. Tilja staggered against the wall and managed to push herself upright.

When she looked again the sky was in its rightful place. Out of a billowing cloud of mortar dust the stubs of twenty broken towers rose straight and true toward it. What was left of the palace rested on the ground. The Ropemaker no longer looked different from everything else, but was still gazing around as if waiting for something else to happen to amuse him.

"It is done," said Faheel. "With your help I have broken the Watchers."

"Are they all dead?"

"No. Some fled before we had finished, and still have many of their powers, but they are Watchers no more. Now we can give the Ropemaker the ring and go. I will tell him you are here."

Tilja looked, and saw the Ropemaker stare toward the tower from which they were watching. He raised a hand in cheerful acknowledgment, but then stiffened and stared again, not at the tower this time, but beyond it. With a quick movement he untucked an end of his turban cloth. At a flick of his wrist the whole elaborate structure unraveled and his hair tumbled around him.

Hair? The flaming orange cataract covered his whole body, hiding him completely. A shake of his head and it floated out, hair no more but a blazing ball of fire which grew, became a shape, became solid, an immense flaming orange lion, a lion the size of a barn. It turned its head and stared again for a moment beyond the tower, then swung away and raced off, clearing the outer wall of the palace at a bound.

Puzzled, Tilja glanced up to see why Faheel hadn't stopped him. She gasped with astonishment and horror. Faheel was staggering back from the screen. His hands were up in front of his face, and his mouth was working. A faint groaning mutter came from his lips.

One of the women on the floor writhed and screamed. The light dimmed as a darkness closed around the tower.

No!

Tilja unclenched her fist and dropped the ring into the box.

Everything stopped. The woman's scream cut short. Her writhings froze. The darkness stayed as it was. And Faheel, who was already toppling away from the invisible blow, hung suspended in midfall, but when Tilja seized him by the hand he crumpled to the floor and she had to ease him down. He didn't stir.

She couldn't think what to do next. With a thundering heart she took the rings from his fingers and put them into the pouch at his belt. As she pulled the last one off he changed into an old man, lying half on his side, looking desperately frail and tired, and he still didn't wake.

"If I should fail," he'd said, "you must go by yourself."

No, she told herself again, *you're not going to fail. And I am going to get back to Woodbourne.*

How long had she left before time started again for everyone else, and the powers that had overwhelmed him came swarming down into this room? And the roc still had to fly them home. Faheel couldn't weigh much, but he was far too heavy for her to carry or drag that distance. If she could find a horse or a donkey, or even a strong man. A strong man. One of the soldiers below? But how . . . ?

There was a gold coin on the floor beside Faheel's left hand, the one that had fallen from the air and rolled across the floor when time had restarted. Tilja picked it up, found the purse itself and took it, then hurried down the stairs. It was very dark in the windowless room. The guards were as they'd left them, sprawled on the floor, held by the power of the ring and by Faheel's enchanted sleep, and she wasn't sure if her touch would overcome both forces. But at the moment when she'd dropped the ring back into the box, several other soldiers must have been running into the room to escape the magical encounter in the courtyard. She chose the one in front, took three gold coins from the purse and gripped the man's hand. She had to hang on while he dragged her a couple of paces across the room, still in the frenzy of escape. He halted and stared around.

"Wha . . . What . . . Wha . . . ?" he gasped.

"It's all right," said Tilja. "Look."

She held up the coins.

He stared at them, and at her. His mouth gaped soundlessly.

"Listen," said Tilja. "This is magic. It's done with a ring. I didn't do it. Someone else did. But it means that everybody and everything is stuck fast, except me, and anyone whose hand I'm holding."

He obviously didn't understand, but continued to stare to and fro between her and the coins.

"Never mind," she said. "I want you to help me. I'll give you three gold coins if you'll carry an old man out of Talagh. He doesn't weigh much. Nobody's going to know what you've done. The Emperor's dead, and everything's different. Here's one coin to be going on with. All right?"

She put it into his palm and he stared at it, nodding dumbly. She left him in midnod and went and cleared the other soldiers out of the doorway by touching them briefly so that they ran another pace and then froze again. Despite the urgency, doing this, so easily, so confidently, brought back that extraordinary sense of pure, secret power. She could, if she had chosen, have gone upstairs again and stolen every fabulous jewel that those women were wearing, and no one would ever have known how it was done. The idea was thrilling. And dangerous—a danger that came not from outside herself, but from within. A Tilja who gave in to it would have become a different Tilja from the one who had flown to Talagh on the back of the roc. Now she could understand why it had mattered so much that the Ropemaker didn't become one of the Watchers.

She went back to her helper and brought him into time. Dazed but unquestioning, he let her lead him up the stair. Here they found a problem. When the man bent to lift Faheel onto his back he couldn't budge him. He couldn't even lift a fold of his cloak. It was like iron, fastened in time. The effect that Tilja had on the soldier didn't seem to reach any further out from his body than the clothes and armor he was wearing. So Tilja had to use her other hand to release Faheel while the soldier heaved him up. She was afraid she might have to go the whole way out of Talagh like that, which would have been extremely awkward, but she found she could walk along beside the man, with her right hand touching both of them where he gripped Faheel's wrist to hold his body in place across his shoulders.

Slowly they made their way down the stairs and into the open. The further side of the courtyard was still in brilliant sunlight, but around the tower it was like late dusk. It wasn't cloud that made this darkness by casting its shadow, it was more like a patch of night gathering there. Tilja had no idea what could have caused it. But whatever it was, however powerful, the ring now held it locked into the instant.

But for how long? Full of fresh urgency, Tilja hurried out of the palace and down the long avenue. All the way the soldier stared around, muttering his astonishment in half-heard curses. From time to time Tilja had to leave him frozen with his burden while she cleared a path for them through the crowds. She now found that the thrill of power was gone, and what was left was an unpleasant task, oddly shameful, because she was using people as if they were just things, to do what she wished with. When she snatched a couple of savory pies from a stall for herself and the soldier, she wasted a few seconds leaving money to pay for them.

Just beyond the gate, where Faheel had changed the rules to let Tilja take him through the crowded streets, they now changed back. Once again Tilja was moving at the center of a bubble of time, so that she could let go of the soldier, while anyone she passed close by woke for a moment into time and then fell still. The roc was where they had left it, but it must have used the period when Tilja had been holding the ring to start preening itself, and now was stuck with one vast wing half spread while it nibbled at an armpit. When Tilja came within a few paces it woke, saw her and closed the wing. Its eye had an odd look of affront, as if she'd invaded its privacy.

The soldier halted at the movement, cursing more loudly.

"It's all right," said Tilja. "It won't hurt us. Will you put my friend in the litter? Then I'll pay you the other two coins. The roc's going to take us away, and then you'll go to sleep for a bit, and when you wake up we won't be here. But you'll know it wasn't a dream because you'll have the money."

He laid Faheel down and she covered the old man over and then paid the soldier and thanked him and wished him luck.

"And good luck to you, miss," he said, gazing up at the roc. "Well, I never! Well, I never!"

Apart from curses, those were the only words she'd heard him speak.

She wedged the ring box safe and nestled herself in down beside Faheel, hoping to help keep him warm with the heat of her own body. The roc stood, stared at Talagh and crowed, a sound in Tilja's ears like victory fanfare. It spread its wings and hauled them into the air. Before Talagh was out of sight behind them she was asleep.

13

The Common Way

Tilja woke in the same unchanging daylight, as the roc, with three last booming flaps, settled in front of Faheel's house and folded its wings. Almost the whole way from Talagh she had slept too deep for dreams, the same ocean-deep sleep she had slept on the raft on the way to the island. Once again, without her realizing, her strength had been drained from her by her own power to channel and control magic, this time the enormous magic of the ring.

Her right arm was numb with Faheel's weight. He was still asleep, but the movement of his breath seemed steadier and stronger. She hesitated whether to leave him. She felt it must be better for him to keep breathing the magical air of the island, but if she went more than a few paces from him his time would stop, and even his breath and his heartbeat would be stilled until she returned, or time resumed its course.

When? A day and a night, he had said. And then . . .

The power of the Watchers was broken, but there was still an enemy, whoever or whatever it was that had sent the darkness to the tower. Had one or more of the Watchers, instead of fleeing into hiding, returned and taken Faheel by surprise, and almost destroyed him in the moment of his triumph? Or was it someone or something else? Tilja had no idea, but she was sure of one thing—such an enemy would not give up. As soon as the ring withdrew its influence, he, or it, would come to the island.

A day and a night. How long had their two flights taken, to Talagh and back, since the ring had cast its spell? She had slept both ways and could only guess. It was a long way. The roc was a magical creature, but it had flown in real time, pounding the real air with its huge wings. There couldn't be much of that day and night remaining before the sun started to move again.

The roc by now was standing beside the litter, preening the thick-laid golden feathers just above its scaly leg, but as soon as Tilja started to ease free of Faheel and straightened the rugs over him it looked up, with an eager gleam in its eye.

"I don't know if it will work for me," she said, and using the ends of her scarf as gloves, pulled out Faheel's pouch. It felt completely empty, but when, awkwardly, she managed to undo the tie and tilted it toward her other palm, out fell a handful of jewels. They were a wonderful deep wine red, more beautiful than any that the women had worn in the tower from which she and Faheel had watched the parade. She tipped half of them back into the purse and offered the rest to the roc, which pecked them delicately off the scarf, swallowed them one by one, and then stared pointedly at the purse.

"In a minute," she said. "When you've carried the litter to the door, please."

The roc tilted its head, puzzled. Tilja reached up and grasped the loop of the carrying harness, which was dangling over the edge of the canopy. When she held it out the roc took it obediently in its beak and straightened up, so that the litter rose clear of the grass. Steadying it with one hand, she led the way to the door of the house and swung it round so that the end was in the doorway, where the roc lowered it to the ground. The roc must have been a lot brighter than it looked, because when Tilja released the catches that fastened the canopy poles and started trying to haul the litter into the house it bowed its head and carefully butted it in through the door.

"Good bird," said Tilja, as if she'd been talking to a dog. She gave the roc the rest of the rubies and it turned and settled down,

251

blocking the doorway. But instead of going to sleep it just sat there gazing fixedly north toward the Empire.

Comforted by that powerful presence she moved further into the room and found Meena, Alnor and Tahl sleeping as she had left them. Then, realizing how hungry she was, she got out a meal for herself and for Faheel when he woke. Everything in the storage bins seemed fresh, and the bread still smelled of the oven. From time to time she glanced out of the window at a swirl of gulls that had been frozen into stillness by the power of the ring, but she was washing her plate and mug when she heard their first cries, startlingly loud and sudden in the enormous silence. So the day and the night were over.

The sound seemed to wake Faheel. He stirred and opened his eyes for a moment, then closed them. His old face seemed more peaceful even than it had looked in sleep.

"Tilja?" he whispered.

"I'm here. I got a soldier to carry you out of the city and the roc brought us home. I've still got your ring."

"Well done."

He spoke the words so quietly that Tilja could barely hear them. She thought he had gone back to sleep but then he whispered again. A question. She didn't catch the words but guessed his meaning.

"The roc's guarding the door," she said. "But . . . whatever it was happened at the end . . . that darkness . . ."

He didn't answer for a while, but then spoke more firmly.

"I will tell you what happened. You remember, before we went to Talagh, I told you that you had brought me both good news and bad?"

"Yes, but you didn't have time to tell me that bad news."

"It lay in your description of the contest on the walls after your grandmother had spoken my name and the spoon had moved. The magician who came from the outer city . . ."

"Zara told us he was very powerful—she's the Lord Kzuva's

magician. She said that in the end it took four Watchers to drive him off. And then they were all trying to find him."

"They did not succeed. He was there, in that darkness. He came for the ring, and now that he has woken he will try to come again. If he did so, not even the roc could hold him back. Nor could I, as I am now. You yourself might withstand him—I do not know. But I have even more powerful friends, who will protect us until I have said my farewells to them, and for a little while longer. By nightfall I shall be gone, and so will you and your friends. I will rest now, and then eat. And then we must work. I will tell you more later."

"Can we wake my friends up?"

"Not yet. But before we go. Now, while I rest, go to the upstairs room, put the box with the ring back on the shelf from which I took it and open the silver box beside it. Take out the jewel it contains and give that to the roc, with my blessing and my thanks."

Tilja did as she was told. The room at the top of the ladder was as she had first seen it. She could tell exactly where the ring box belonged by the circular patch in the dust on the shelf. The jewel in the silver box was an egg-shaped ruby as big as her two clenched fists. It was warm to the touch, and there was something inside it that seemed to be moving in sudden little spasms that changed the way the light shone into it. As she carried it down the ladder she could sense, faintly against her palm, the same tiny movements. She had felt something like that so often at Woodbourne that she understood at once what the jewel must be. She forgot all about the enemy who might come, all about Faheel, all about Meena and Alnor and Tahl and her own adventures. For the moment this mattered more than anything else in the world.

She edged out past the roc, laid the jewel between the immense yellow, black-taloned feet, and stood back and waited. The ruby doubled in size, and doubled again, and again. With a bubbling, crooning sound far down its throat, the roc bowed its head and pecked at the glowing surface, precisely but firmly, studying the movements inside the jewel each time before it pecked again. At the seventh peck the jewel cracked. The thing inside gave a convulsive heave, the ruby fell apart and the fledgling roc struggled to its feet with shreds of crimson yolk sac patterning its fluffy golden feathers. It cheeped, just like any new-hatched chick at Woodbourne.

The roc crooned over it, delicately picked the yolk sac away, and then lifted the chick, twisted its own head round and settled it into the hollow between its shoulders. It turned back and stared at Tilja. There was a question in its eyes.

"Faheel sends you his blessing and his thanks, and says you can go," she said. "And I'd like to say thank you too."

Perhaps it understood her tone, for it bent its huge head and nibbled gently at her ear, and in unthinking response she reached up and teased her fingers among the soft plumage beneath its neck.

Her hand froze. This great magical animal, and she, Tilja . . .

But no, nothing had happened, no flow or pulse of power out of that fullness into her emptiness. The roc was different. Its magic was of another kind. She must ask Faheel.

It raised its head and she stood aside to let it pass. It walked a few paces, glanced back at her, then hurled itself into the air. Two small golden feathers came floating down as the wings pounded out their rhythm and it sped away. Tilja picked them up and went back indoors.

Faheel was up and sitting by the table, sipping the orange juice she had found in his store cupboard. He had peeled an apple and cut a slice of bread and was eating slowly.

"Yes, you are right," he said when she asked him about the roc. "There are different kinds of magic. Almost all human magic is made magic, made like a clay pot or a wooden chair. The wood and the clay are not chair and pot until the carpenter and the potter make them so. The air is full of wild magic, gusting around, so that a magician can gather it into himself or herself and give it shape and purpose. That is made magic. Your power appears to be to unmake that making. It is as if you could put your hand on a chair and return it to the tree from which it was shaped. The roc is not of that kind. It is natural magic, magical of its own nature. If you put your hand on a tree it would not change. It is itself already."

"You made the roc do what you wanted."

"No, I asked it. It owed me a favor. Many great magicians would risk everything they have won to possess the egg of a roc, but as well as there being two kinds of magic there are two kinds of magician. Once, like all who have held the ring, I was of the first sort, using made magic. But the ring is of both sorts, magic both made and natural. That is why it is so powerful. From it I learned to be of the second sort, and thus made friends with the creatures of natural magic, and was given new powers by them. So it was safe for the roc to give her egg into my keeping until it was due to hatch."

"Look, I've got two of its feathers."

"Keep them well hidden, or they will betray you. Tie them to your arm, as you did with the spoon. They have power—and purpose, for all I know."

"This island—what makes it so peaceful—is that natural magic? Is that why I could feel it?"

"Yes, it is inherent in the island. It was here before I came and will remain when I am gone. I could live here not because I have magical powers, but because I have the friendship of the island."

"Are unicorns natural magic too?"

"Indeed, yes. That was what finally persuaded me that I must prevent your friend the Ropemaker from becoming a Watcher. To transform oneself into an animal is not very difficult, though it has its perils. But to transform oneself into a magical animal, and even more to return to one's human form, requires immense power and is still very dangerous. Even when I had all my strength I would never have tried it except for the greatest cause. But he did. He cannot have understood what he was risking.

That was why my hope was that his powers were both untaught and uncorrupted, and why part of my reason for going to Talagh was to give him the ring. I failed. So now I must ask you to take it to him. Will you do that?"

Tilja stared at him. The Ropemaker?

"I . . . I'm not sure he *is* my friend," she whispered. "He . . . he almost killed my mother, if he was the unicorn."

"Yes. I told you it was dangerous to transform oneself into a magical animal. That is the main danger. One may take on too much of the nature of that animal. A unicorn such as you saw would not have ordinary human sympathies. But remember, your mother went to sing to the cedars again, and he did not try to stop her."

"I . . . I'll have to talk to the others when they wake up," she said.

He shook his head.

"I'm afraid not," he said. "If you do, the knowledge will be in their minds, unprotected. While the ring is in its box and the box is against your flesh, and you alone know that, not even the man we fear will find it. If your friends know, then he may well be able to use that knowledge. I think I know who this man is, Tilja. Like myself, long ago, he was one of those who tried to take possession of the ring while Asarta still held it. He was much older than I was, and I was certain that he was dead, but somehow he is not. Or perhaps he is, but . . . No, that does not bear thinking about. Tilja, I tell you, he must not have the ring. With it he could live forever. I dare not let you tell your companions."

"But . . . but if I've got to go looking for the Ropemaker . . . I'll have to tell them what's been happening."

"Yes, you can tell them that, apart from what has happened to the ring. I will give them reason for looking for the Ropemaker themselves, though I shall not tell them that is what they will be doing. No doubt he took the shape of a lion and fled from the palace because he recognized that our enemy was too powerful for him. He now knows of the ring's existence, and of your connection with it. He tracked you on your journey south, so he will know which way you will return. All he need do is watch the road. He will choose a place you must pass and be waiting for you there. That is our best hope. It is not perfect—I had not planned for this, but I have neither power nor time to make other arrangements."

"But suppose he doesn't find us . . ."

Faheel felt in his pocket and fished out the little purse into which he had put the hair tie, took it and unwound the Ropemaker's hair from it, and gave them both to Tilja.

"Then I'm afraid you must risk sending for him," he said. "Wind the hair round the roc feathers before you fasten them to your arm. When the time comes, lay the hair down on a firm surface, take the ring out of its box and put it beside the hair. That is all, and it need only be for a moment. But wait until the last possible moment before you do this. The Ropemaker will be compelled to come. If our enemy is on the watch he will do so too, but until that moment, provided that no one but you knows that you have the ring, I think you have nothing to fear from him. He will not believe that I have not taken it with me.

"Now we must work, or we will not be gone by nightfall. First, will you go out into the garden and pick a bunch of grapes and bring it to me? You will find a sharp knife in one of the baskets by the door. If you want grapes for yourself, take them from another bunch. The small dark ones to the left of the central path are best at this season."

Tilja went out into the garden in a daze, trying to understand what Faheel had told her. She ought to have been afraid—unable to think for fear—but she wasn't. She guessed this was something to do with the island. Fear would come later, perhaps. But now—perhaps it was the island again that caused this, trying to help her—in her mind's eye she saw a great brass balance, like the cunning wooden scales Ma used to measure ingredients when she was baking. There was a bowl at either end of a bar. The bar tilted at the center, one way or the other, depending on which bowl held more weight. But the bowls Tilja saw in her mind weren't polished wood, like Ma's. Each of them was half of the world. A small figure stood beside each bowl, waiting for the bar to tilt his way. One of them Tilja couldn't see clearly. He was darkness in the shape of a man. The unknown magician, the enemy. His bowl was full of the same darkness. The other one was the Ropemaker, unmistakable, that gawky figure, topped by the monstrous headdress. There was nothing to tell her what was in the Ropemaker's bowl, but whatever it was it had to be better than the darkness.

At the center of the bar was a small golden ant. The bar hid it from the two magicians. As she watched, the ant started to crawl along the beam toward the Ropemaker's end, and she realized that when it reached the bowl its tiny weight would be just enough to tilt the balance that way—provided the other magician didn't realize what was happening, and reach out with a magical hand, pick up the ant, and drop it into his own bowl. Then the darkness it held would spill out and smother everything.

The ant, she realized, was herself, Tilja.

When the vision cleared she found herself standing in front of the vines Faheel had told her to look for. She cut herself a small cluster to try. They had an intense, sweet, wild taste that seemed to linger in her mouth long after she'd swallowed. She chose the best bunch she could see and carried it back to the house. Faheel was just finishing his meal.

"Good," he said picking up a small green purse from his pocket. "First, give this to one of the others when they wake—it is no use in your hands. It is just a convenient toy. Open it, and you will find it holds two gold coins. Take one out and close it, and when you open it next day you will find it again holds two gold coins, and you may again take one out. But take both out in one day and the magic is gone, and it will thenceforth be just an empty purse.

"Now I may need you to help me up the ladder to my room. Bring the grapes with you, but do not come through the trapdoor. Hand them through to me and I will close it. Then take two of the baskets, fill one with all the roses you can find and the other with whatever fruits you and your friends will need for the start of your journey home. Do not overburden yourself. There is no magic in the garden, so its fruits last no longer than those in any other garden. When you hear a bell come indoors. Stay in this room with your friends so that what is about to happen will cause them no harm. Fill another basket with stores for your journey. When your friends wake, you and the boy must come up the ladder and find me."

"I'm sorry. Just one more thing . . . when my friends wake up . . . we came here to ask you . . . Oh, I see. *That's* going to be their reason for looking for the Ropemaker."

He smiled.

"Yes, of course," he said. "There is more to the magic that protects your Valley than you imagine. While Asarta held the ring, I and others did our best to wrest it from her, and she had to use some of her strength to keep it from us. When my turn came, I decided to do as your two ancestors asked me to, and by doing so to seal all knowledge of the ring away in your Valley. I then sought out everyone who knew of the ring and either took the memory of it from their minds, or if they resisted, destroyed them, all but the one I have told you about. Tell the Ropemaker this when you give him the ring, and he will see the use of it and do the same for you. But when your friends wake and ask me . . . Wait. You will see. Now I must go."

As it turned out he climbed the ladder without help, though with several pauses for rest. Tilja passed the grapes up to him and took the weight of the trapdoor as he lowered it into place, then wandered round the garden filling the baskets. She did the roses first. It wasn't a sad task, though Faheel had talked of making an ending and she guessed that they might be part of that ending. He had been so calm about it, so ready and accepting, that she was sure of its rightness. There might have been no magic in the garden, but the roses by their own nature were magic enough, wonderfully shaped and colored and, as the basket filled, scenting the air around her with a richness so intense that it should have been cloying, but wasn't.

That done, she chose her fruit carefully, grapes, peaches, nectarines and apricots, and a spicy yellow berry she had never seen before. She didn't think it could be poisonous if it grew in such a garden. She also found a row of carrots and pulled a good bunch. The bell rang just as she was finishing and she went back indoors. None of her three companions seemed to have stirred.

While she was choosing her stores the room darkened, as if in a thunderstorm, though the sun had been only halfway down a cloudless sky when she had left the garden. Through the window she could see nothing but swirling colored mist, brownish but flecked with purple shapes that seemed to be made of a solider kind of mist and flickered as they swept by. She saw the walls of the house judder, though the floor on which she stood stayed steady. A moment later a booming voice called from outside and Faheel's voice, loud and firm, answered from above with a name and a greeting. Other voices followed, not human or animal, the voices of mountains, perhaps, of forests and of stars. Once it sounded as if the whole sea were singing. The mist came and went outside the window. Sometimes it was dark night, with shimmerings and bolts of brilliance, sometimes day so bright and shadowless that there might have been several suns in the sky. All these beings, forces, spirits, or whatever else they might be, Faheel welcomed into his attic room by name. When they were gathered the window cleared and there was silence.

Tilja stood and waited. She could sense around her a continuous flow of movement through it, into and out of the room above her, as though Faheel's house had become a great fire in a dark forest, a fire from which flames and sparks and lit smoke swirled endlessly upward, but not in random eddies—in shapes, shapes that had meaning, shapes that somehow held the balance of the world in place. Faheel was at the heart of the uprush, giving back to his friends the powers they had loaned him, as they blazed round him. And so was she too, Tilja. For the powers weren't only here to say farewell to Faheel. They had come to welcome her. It was as if her gift had hidden her from them, and now they could rejoice in her finding. Though she didn't yet know what use they had for her, she felt that there was such a use, and that one day she would learn it. For the first time since she had become aware of her strange gift she felt that she wasn't having to use it to fight against the forces around her, but to accept them, just as they were accepting her, and accept that they and she were part of something larger, all of which belonged together and needed all its parts, balancing each other, to make it what it was.

Time had no meaning, but it must have continued to move because there was a change, and she knew that the rite was ending. The visitors gathered themselves into the attic room, and then one by one withdrew, calling their farewells as they left. When the last had gone the windows cleared and the garden lay outside, the sunlight already golden with evening, and the shadows long across the grass.

"You there, girl?"

"Meena!"

Tilja swung round. Meena had struggled up onto her elbow and was staring round the room, for once too astonished to pretend to be angry, or to push Tilja away when she rushed to hug her.

"Expecting someone else, were you?" she said. "Where's this, then?"

"Faheel's house. On his island."

"Be careful how you say his name," Alnor said sharply.

"I don't think it matters anymore," said Tilja. "He said it wasn't safe for you to wake up because there was going to be too much magic here, but it's all right now. It's almost all gone."

"Gone! I hope you told him what we came for before he let that happen."

"Yes, but I don't know . . . there's been other things going on. Now he wants me and Tahl to go up and help him down the ladder. Then we're going home. Are you awake, Tahl?"

"Sort of," said Tahl's voice, sounding much more dazed than Meena's. "We were on the raft, and then . . . I've been talking to the ice dragon. It told me all sorts of stuff. Funny. It didn't feel like a dream. It doesn't come from this world, you know. There's a world made of ice somewhere else in the sky . . ."

"Its name is Manzal," said Alnor. "I too spoke with the ice dragon. With my blind eyes I saw his face, that I had never hoped to see."

"And there's a Queen of the Unicorns," said Meena. "I never knew that! Maybe I'll tell you someday. For now, I just want to think about it. . . . Well, girl, don't just stand there! Tell us what's going on."

"I don't think there's time," said Tilja. "We've got to get away from the island by nightfall, Faheel said, and it's almost sunset now. Ready, Tahl?"

She led the way up the ladder and pushed the trapdoor open. When she poked her head through she saw that the attic was empty and bare. Faheel lay facedown at its center. She scrambled through and with Tahl's help turned him gently over. His body seemed to weigh so little that she could almost have lifted it on her own. His lips moved. She bent her head to listen.

"Take me down," he whispered. "Come back and fetch the things on the shelf."

Tahl ran Tilja's long head scarf under Faheel's arms so that she could take some of his weight from above while he took most of it on his shoulders, and they eased Faheel down the ladder and made him comfortable on a pile of cushions. Tilja went back upstairs to find what he'd left on the shelf—the ring box and the bunch of grapes she'd brought in from the garden. The ring box had a cord attached, which she slid over her head, and then tucked the box down inside her blouse. She took the grapes and climbed down the ladder. This time, when she stepped off the last rung, the whole thing vanished, and the trapdoor too, leaving nothing but a plain, bare ceiling.

"It is over," said Faheel, still speaking with effort. "Now we must go. First . . . First I must ask you to help me down to the shore. Once there, I will explain to you what you will need to do to return to your Valley."

With Tilja and Tahl on each side of him carrying the two baskets of stores, and his arms around their shoulders, he led them slowly toward the western cliffs and down a series of steps to a sandy beach. Meena hobbled along behind, leaning on Alnor's arm. In his other hand he carried the roses. The raft on which the four travelers had come from Goloroth floated in the shallows, and beside it a strange boat that seemed to be made out of seashell, with a broad stern and a high, curving prow. Faheel asked them to help him sit, and they lowered him onto the sand.

"Now," he said, "listen carefully. I have given back all my powers . . . given them back to those who first loaned them to me, and should any enemy come I could not defend us. . . . But I still have friends, some of whom will tow me out westward into the current of the Great River, so that I may make my last journey by the common way, like my parents before me. . . . Others will take you back to the southern shore of the Empire. Once there . . . Tilja, you have the grapes from the shelf?"

"They're in the basket."

He nodded and straightened his back. Tilja sensed him gathering his last energies for what he now had to say.

"Set them apart and do not touch them until you are safely ashore tomorrow. Then Meena and Alnor must eat them, one at a time, turn and turn about. Eat nothing else until they are gone. But keep the stem carefully and take it with you. When you are safely home you must build a fire and burn it, to undo the magic the grapes did for you. This is most important. Fail to do it and your whole journey fails. Now we must go. Will you help me stand?"

"Is that all?" Meena burst in. "I'm sorry, sir, seeing how tired you are, but I can't help asking. I mean, isn't there anything else we've got to do? Here we've been sowing our barley field all these years, and trudging out winter after winter and singing to the cedars, and Alnor's lot have been doing the same sort of thing up at Northbeck . . . and I've brought a loaf I baked from my field, and Alnor's got a flask of water from his stream. . . ."

"Ah, yes," murmured Faheel, smiling and shaking his head, as if he'd forgotten all about it. "Of course. Show me."

With trembling fingers he broke a few crumbs from the loaf and ate them, and sipped from the flask.

"Honest bread," he whispered. "Sweet mountain water. I bless them both, but that is all I can do. Asarta's powers are still there, my friends. Somewhere on your journey you will find another to wake them. Or rather, he will find you—it would be dangerous for you to seek him out. . . ."

His voice trailed away in weakness. He closed his eyes, as if he were about to die where he lay. Meena clicked her tongue in frustration. Alnor was frowning and shaking his head. Part of Tilja felt like laughing aloud. The cunning old man, waiting till now, pretending he'd forgotten, making it seem a little thing. But even as she suppressed her smile it struck her that this was the start of something very uncomfortable. From now on, day after day after day, she would be keeping the secret of the ring from her friends. So far, they had all trusted each other, absolutely. But from now on, day after day after day, she was going to be lying to them.

Faheel's lips moved.

"Now, if you will help me onto the raft . . . ," he whispered.

"You're not going in the boat?" said Meena in astonishment.

"That is for you. It is safe from Tilja's touch. I go the common way."

They lifted him to his feet and he raised his head and spoke rather more loudly, apparently calling to the empty sea.

"Friends, we are ready."

By now the sun had touched the horizon, and the water stretched its reflected light into a rippling golden highway across a great reach of fiery ocean. Out of that brightness, just beyond the raft and the boat, rose two dark figures, man-shaped as far as Tilja, screwing up her eyes, could see, but twice the size of any human. They called a deep-voiced greeting to Faheel and then, in a flurry of foam, started to wrestle with something just below the surface. Having so often needed to back the unwilling Calico between the shafts of a cart, Tilja recognized at once what they were up to, and soon she could see at times the gleaming dark backs of the creatures they were struggling to harness to the boat and the raft.

When they were ready they backed off and waited with only their heads above the surface. Tahl and Tilja helped Faheel onto the raft, where he lay down.

"My roses," he whispered.

All four of them stood round the raft with the wavelets lapping up to their knees and strewed the roses around him. He smiled and closed his eyes. He looked so peaceful that Tilja found herself weeping, though still not with sadness.

He beckoned, and she bent to catch his words.

". . . the Ropemaker's name . . . I broke his inner wards to call to him . . . Ramdatta . . ."

Ramdatta

14

A Bunch of Grapes

aheel's raft was a small dark shape dwindling toward the sunset. By the time the last sliver of the sun slid below the horizon it was no more than a dot, which disappeared in the brief dusk, and then there was night, with innumerable stars. None of them spoke for a long while as their seashell boat skimmed away north from the island, towed by the unseen team beneath the surface.

"Well, so we're going home," said Alnor at last.

"And somewhere along the way we're going to find a magician who'll tell us what to do about the Valley," said Meena. "Fat lot of sense it makes to me, I must say."

"Nothing's going to make much sense unless Til tells us what's been going on while we've been asleep," said Tahil. "It's bad enough missing it all, but not even knowing . . ."

"I'm starving," said Meena. "May as well eat while she's telling us."

All Tilja wanted to think about was the beauty and sadness of Faheel's going, so she started reluctantly, but then found it somehow comforting to relive the day and a night and less than a day more that she had spent in his company. By the time she had finished, the moon had moved halfway across the sky, and she lay down to sleep still full of the peacefulness of the island.

———

When they rose and looked around them in the morning the island was out of sight astern and the dark shore of the Empire lay ahead. Alnor woke in a bad mood and sat hunched and sullen, but gave no sign of what was troubling him. Tahl on the other hand was full of chat, still thrilled and fascinated by everything Tilja had told them the night before, especially what might happen to the machinery of the Empire with the Watchers gone from their towers and the Emperor himself dead.

"You may not even need way-leaves," he said as they breakfasted. "Perhaps the whole system's broken down. If it hasn't, we're in trouble. You two can't go anywhere without them, except back to Goloroth."

"How'm I going anywhere without a horse, if it comes to that?" said Meena. "All this sleeping on rafts and boats. My hip wasn't that bad yesterday, but it is now."

"We can buy a horse, can't we?" said Tahl. "We've got Faheel's purse. You can get a good enough horse and still have change from a gold coin. There's horse merchants at Goloroth— we sold Calico to one of them—though perhaps that's not happening anymore, either."

"I'll tell you one thing it'll mean," said Meena, with relish, "it'll mean robbers on the roads, and the rascals in charge of way stations grabbing what they can squeeze out of us with nothing to stop them."

They argued it to and fro. Tilja listened without much interest and said nothing. All her real attention was elsewhere, inward. When, last night, she had told the others about her adventures, she had described in detail their arrival at the island, her meeting with Faheel, the journey to Talagh and back, and everything she had seen and done there, but had said only that after they had come back Faheel had gone up to his attic and given up his magic while she waited with them in the room below. She had said nothing about what she had then seen and felt. One day, perhaps, she might tell Meena, but not yet. She wasn't ready. She still needed to understand and come to terms with her own discovery—deliberately shown to her, she now felt, by the spirits that had come—that her lack of magic was not in fact a lack, not an emptiness, but a power, a gift—a gift which, if she nurtured it, practiced it, learned all she could about it, might one day be as powerful in its own way as the gifts of a great magician like Faheel. A gift which was a kind of magic in its own right, a flow of power, but in the reverse direction. A gift she must, one day, use. Faheel had said there were two kinds of magician, those who worked with made magic, and those like himself who had discovered natural magic. Perhaps there was also a third kind. Herself. Though who was to say if she was the only one?

Thinking about it as their seashell boat whispered across the empty ocean, thinking about how she did whatever it was she did, she discovered in herself a need to find a place where it belonged. Not Woodbourne, to whose remembered image she had clung as she had fought her way into Talagh, and again when she had faced Silena. She couldn't cling to Woodbourne any longer. She had changed. Now she needed a new place, somewhere that would always be hers, which she could explore and learn to know, as she knew her way round Woodbourne, every cranny in the house and outbuildings, every yard of the fields and meadows.

She closed her eyes and an image filled her mind, so strongly seen that it was hard to believe that it hadn't been there already, waiting for her to find it. A lake, calm and clear, and deep beyond sounding. Nothing like the cedar-ringed lake in the forest, but set high among mountains, whose white unreachable peaks were reflected from its still surface. Cataracts poured down their slopes in roaring foam and plunged into the lake and became part of its stillness. Perhaps the image meant that she was like that lake. Her gift was to take the raging, demonic forces of made magic and channel them down into a central calm where they would be unbound from their making and loosed into their simple elements, and then perhaps breathed back into the world, rather as the lake on warm days breathed its water back to join the clouds.

But the lake was more than that, more than a way of thinking about what she did. It was real, as much part of her as her heartbeat or her breathing. She would have it until she died. With closed eyes she gazed at it, seeing it in detail. It wasn't like a dream image, shifting, unreliable. Shoreline and cataract and peak remained firm. Only the clouds and their reflections moved.

But everything else was changed, all Tilja's hopes and fears and expectations, all her life to come. Yes, she was going home with the others, if she could. She was going back to Woodbourne. But she wasn't staying there. There was no magic in the Valley. Her gift was no use there.

The shore of the Empire neared. From time to time now the seahuman controlling the unseen creatures that hauled the boat would rise from the surface as far as his waist and stare around and plunge below. When a cluster of fishing boats appeared almost directly ahead of them he changed course to avoid it. Now they could see fields and a small harbor as he skirted the shore, and then a range of barren-looking hills, and then a stretch of marshland. Where the hills met the marsh he turned shoreward, unharnessing his team before they reached the shallows and himself gripping the stern post and driving the boat up onto a muddy beach with powerful thrusts of his tail. Seeing him full length, Tilja discovered that he was at least as much fish as man, with dark green scales almost up to his shoulders and a ridged fin running the length of his spine. They rescued their packs, climbed ashore and turned and thanked him. He nodded briefly in acknowledgment, then scooped up a handful of mud from the seabed and tossed it into the boat. Instantly the hull split apart, shrinking as it did so. In the space of a couple of heartbeats all that was left of it was several fragments of gleaming seashell lying on the dark mud. He waved farewell, turned and slid out of sight.

They plodded up the beach with Tahl guiding Alnor, and Meena leaning heavily on Tilja's shoulder and wincing at every step. As soon as they were beyond the tide line she halted.

"That's enough for me," she said. "I'm giving my leg a rest."

"We cannot stay here," said Alnor, without any scrap of sympathy for the pain in her voice.

"Then you'll just have to leave me here," she snapped.

Even Alnor had to see that this wasn't possible.

"Well, we can rest while we eat the grapes, Meena and I," he said.

"I don't know I'm that hungry," said Meena, arguing for arguing's sake, because of her hip.

"We must do as he said, exactly," snapped Alnor. Something in his tone gave Tilja a clue to the reason for his foul mood. He resented not being in control of things, in the way that he could control a raft on the river; he resented having set out on this difficult journey, by his own independent decision, despite everyone else's advice, and then . . . Yes, against all the odds they had actually found Faheel, but once they had left Talagh hardly any of that had been Alnor's doing. He had been swept along, helpless in the rush of the current, and finally lain asleep on Faheel's island while far away in Talagh the whole Empire was shaken apart. Now he was determined to take control again.

So they found a clean patch of ground and settled down. Alnor and Meena passed the bunch of grapes to and fro between them, and Tahl and Tilja each ate a nectarine to keep them company.

"Now, that's what I call a grape!" said Meena as she swallowed her first one.

"A grape is a grape," said Alnor.

"That all you can say?" said Meena. "You tell me when you've eaten a better grape! Go on. Tell me."

They continued to squabble about the grapes as they ate them. Tilja, still thinking about what had happened to her on the island, paid no attention; they were just two old people, tired and anxious and disgruntled, arguing like children in the way old people often do. The first thing she noticed was that Tahl had stopped eating. She glanced up and saw that he was sitting stock-still with his mouth open, ready to take another bite at his nectarine.

She looked to see what he was staring at, and stared too.

Alnor and Meena were still sitting side by side, engrossed in their squabble as they passed the half-eaten bunch back and forth. But they themselves had changed. Alnor's snow-white hair was flecked with dark streaks. His lined old face had fleshed out, and his slight body seemed sturdier. While Meena . . . when they'd settled her down she'd made herself as comfortable as she could, half lying against a tussock of reedlike grasses, but now she'd straightened up and drawn her knees sideways under her. . . .

There was no way, even on one of her best days, that Meena could sit like that!

And lean and reach across to take the grapes!

And her face and hair!

She leaned further to snatch the grapes as Alnor withdrew them.

"Now, then, turn and turn . . . What's up?"

"I can see," said Alnor in a wholly different voice, soft and full of wonder. "Shapes in a mist, only, but . . . it was like this when my blindness began."

"How's your hip, Meena?" said Tahl.

"Not as bad as it might be. Matter of fact . . ."

She twisted herself up, stood and felt at the joint. Gingerly she lifted her foot clear of the ground, balanced and moved the leg around. She put it down and blew her breath out.

"Now, there's something I never thought I'd do again," she said. "What about it, you old fool? Now try and tell me these aren't good grapes!"

Alnor actually smiled.

"I may be a fool," he said, "but I think I am not as old as I was."

"Nor me," said Meena. "My, I'm sorry I didn't get to know your Faheel a bit better. He's a really thoughtful old gentleman—

unlike some I could name. Now I'll be walking back to the Valley, after all."

"And I, perhaps, shall be seeing my way," said Alnor.

"Hey! Me first," said Meena, as he started to pull another grape from the bunch. "Turn and turn about, he told us."

Even in the wonder of what was happening to their grandparents, Tahl couldn't help thinking of the practical uses of it.

"It's better than that," he said, as Alnor grudgingly handed the grapes over. "You've got to eat the whole bunch, Faheel said. At the rate you're going, you won't be much older than us by the time you've finished. So you won't need way-leaves going north."

Meena had a grape halfway to her mouth. She paused and stared at it.

"Perhaps you'll be younger," said Tilja with relish. "Then I'll be able to tell you what's what, for a change."

"May I live to see the day," said Meena, and popped the grape into her mouth and gave the bunch back across to Alnor.

"They tell me you were a handsome young fellow once," she said. "Let's have a look at you then."

For a while they almost gobbled in their excitement, while their grandchildren stood and watched them shed the corrupting years. The wrinkles vanished from their faces, apart from the laughter lines at the corners of Meena's eyes. Her hair grew and thickened, losing all its gray until it was a soft, light chestnut, with a slight wave in it, reaching down to her shoulders. Her figure changed with almost ridiculous speed, swelling to serious stoutness and then shrinking again to comfortable plump curves. Alnor on the other hand stayed much the same, a slim, wiry, muscular man with almost jet black, short, curly hair and a look of fiery pride.

Meena glanced at him as she started to hand the grapes across, and jumped to her feet.

"Tell you what," she said. "It's frustrating watching you getting so likely looking. Let's see if we can't find a pool I can see myself in."

They picked up their packs, but Alnor didn't at once move off to explore along the edge of the marsh. Instead he closed his eyes and slowly turned his head, as if listening for a distant call. Tahl copied him. They opened their eyes at the same moment and side by side led the way slantwise up across the dry and dreary hillside, halting at last in a place as barren seeming as everywhere else. But when Meena and Tilja came up beside them they found at their feet a rocky ravine, which here widened into a steep-sided basin with a waterfall tumbling down at its upper end. Below the fall was a pool.

They scrambled down and settled on the rocks beside it for Meena and Alnor to finish the grapes. The water was creased with ripples below the fall, but smooth enough where they sat for Meena to make out her own wavering reflection as she shed the years. She finished as a plump-faced, smiling, lively girl, a year or two older than Tilja, with a mass of glossy chestnut hair that Tilja would have given her soul for. Alnor might have been a year or so older, unmistakably an Ortahlson, absurdly handsome, much more so than Tahl, though they could easily have been brothers. Unlike Meena, who had studied her reflection in the pool every time she ate another grape, he had refused even to glance at his, but from the way he stood and moved Tilja was quite sure that he knew how good he looked.

Meena ate her last grape kneeling by the water, watching her rippled image, then rose to her feet and took Tilja's hands and drew her to her and hugged her, cheek to cheek, laughing with pleasure. It was such a natural gesture that Tilja hugged her back, laughing too. Then she stiffened and pushed away and stared at her.

"What's up?" said Meena.

"You didn't feel anything? No, nor did I, but I was afraid of undoing the magic, like I did with Silena's dog. You can't be that kind of magical."

"I'm not magical at all, thank you very much. He may have used magic to get me here, but I'm me. Guess what day it is?"

"What *day* it is?"

"It's my fourteenth birthday," crowed Meena, laughing at Tilja's bewilderment. "Look."

She held out her left arm and showed Tilja an angry blistered patch on the inside of the wrist.

"I got that just yesterday," she said. "Helping Ma with the baking for my birthday tea."

They picked up their packs again and climbed the hill. The stream ran out of a boggy plateau that stretched away north. On its further side, two or three miles away, they could see a group of low buildings, and knew at once what they were, having seen so many on their way south.

"Where there's a way station there's got to be a road," said Tahl. "This must be a side road, from another part of the Empire. Problem is, which way's Goloroth? We've got to get there to reach the Grand Trunk Road."

"The other problem is, all four of us are young now," said Alnor. "We're supposed to be coming away."

"You and Meena could dress up old and hobble along," suggested Tahl, teasing.

"Don't be stupid," snapped Alnor. "We'll travel at night. It can't be that far."

"Isn't that a couple of kids?" said Meena. "Look. There. And they're going that way. So the other way must be to Goloroth."

There was a three-quarter moon, clear enough to show some distance along the empty road. Nobody in the Empire traveled by night, because who knew what other creatures might be about?

"I think we should be all right," said Tilja. "If anything like that comes, you'll just have to hold on to me, and then it can't touch you."

She felt completely confident about this. She had held Faheel's ring in her hand and blanked out its magic. She didn't believe that all the Watchers together could match that power.

277

Along with that confidence came a feeling—more than a feeling, almost a certainty—that what she had seen and done in the last few days had given her strengths that she had not had on the journey south. As much as Meena and Alnor, though in very different ways, she had changed.

Despite that, none of them was quite ready for what happened almost as soon as they had set foot on the road. They were walking abreast through the silvery dark. Nothing stirred. There was barely a breath of wind, only a delicious waft of smells, dewy and earthy, drawn out by the night-cooled air. Tilja's head was full of the knowledge that they were now going home, back to Woodbourne. She wanted to sing.

She felt nothing, but Tahl was flung against her as if he'd been buffeted from the other side. She staggered and almost fell, but caught herself and grabbed his wrist as he fought with something she couldn't see. He steadied. On her other side Meena and Alnor were sprawled in the road. Meena had her arms braced in front of her chest as if she was trying to push something away from her neck. Alnor was on his face, bucking to rise, but pinned down.

Tilja bent and thrust her wrist into Meena's grasp.

"Hold on to me," she yelled, kneeling and reaching across to touch the back of Alnor's hand where it scrabbled at the dust.

They rose gasping. The night was as peaceful and still as it had been only seconds before.

"Loose magic," muttered Alnor.

"Bad as outside Goloroth," said Meena.

"This had *things* in it," said Tahl. "No wonder people don't like moving around in the dark."

"The power of the Watchers is broken," said Alnor. "It will be worse now."

"And you didn't feel anything?" said Tahl.

"No," said Tilja. "Not even that funny numb feeling I get. Wild magic must be different. It looks as if we're going to have to hold hands all the way."

They adjusted their positions and walked on, tensely at first, but then more easily when nothing frightening happened, though all except Tilja could feel gusts of loose magic swirling around them with, as Tahl had said, *things* in it. The road wound down the hill they had climbed and ran for a while almost directly beside the marsh. Along the way two more roads joined it from the north, and as dawn was breaking it crossed the Great River on a bridge and joined the Grand Trunk Road. With sighs of relief they turned north.

It was strange for Tilja, making friends with a girl her own age who was also her grandmother, an old woman with a bad hip and a dodgy temper. But Meena didn't seem to find it anything like as strange when Tilja asked her about it.

"Mostly I don't think about it," she said. "I suppose it's like remembering a dream, except it doesn't go shifting around the way dreams do."

She paused for a moment, thinking.

"There, now," she went on. "I can remember what it's like, my hip hurting, and I can remember what Faheel told us, and going back a bit I can remember things like speaking my mind to your da about buying that stupid great horse . . ."

Another pause.

". . . but mostly, like I say, I shut it away. No. It shuts itself away, more like. It's a different room from the one I'm in, and the door's closed. I can get up and go through, but the door's the sort that shuts itself soon as you let go. And, anyway, I *like* this room."

She laughed. Her laugh hadn't changed at all, but Tilja heard it a lot more often now. And she could be sharp as ever still, mostly just teasing, but also speaking her mind with vigor when anything annoyed her. It was all part of the sheer gusto with which she lived, so brimfull of the pleasure of the moment that the surplus spilled over. That made the change easy for Tilja. Anybody would have wanted to be Meena's friend.

Tahl had a much harder time with Alnor. Though they looked

so like, they were very different. Tahl was outgoing, interested in everything, always ready to talk to passersby. Alnor was withdrawn, touchy, stiff with strangers on first meeting, as if they were somehow a challenge to him. He spoke to them in much the same formal manner that he had used as an old man, but less naturally, as if this was a style he had not long ago chosen for himself and was still getting used to.

On their second morning they were walking in pairs, Meena and Alnor leading the way, and Tahl and Tilja not quite in earshot behind. Meena was chatting away, with Alnor laughing as he answered. Tahl, on the other hand, had been unusually silent so far. Now Tilja heard him sigh.

"What's up?" she said.

He shook his head and sighed again.

"I want my grandfather back," he muttered.

"Oh, no! This is wonderful! It's thrilling!"

"For *them*. Have you heard him talking to me? As if I were some kind of *henchman*. I'm not anyone's henchman."

"Why can't you just be friends? That's how I feel about Meena—as if she were my elder sister. I've never had an elder sister before. I've always been eldest. I'm really enjoying it."

"I'm not. And I wouldn't if he *were* my elder brother. He'd be like this anyway. It's all right in a grandfather—and anyway he needed me then. He doesn't now. Besides, just look at the two of them! Next thing, they'll be falling in love! They've started already!"

"That will be fun for them. Meena will really enjoy it."

"They're our *grandparents*, Til!"

Tilja laughed, but watching the pair ahead of them for a minute or two, she could tell he was right.

A day and a half north of Goloroth they came to Ramram, the small city lying along the other side of the river, with its immense fortress built long ago to defend the Empire against raiders from the south who had never come. The famous fair on the bridge was in full swing.

"Let's just have a look," said Meena.

"There's nothing we need," said Alnor.

"Who said anything about need?" said Meena. "When d'you think I'm going to get another chance to come to Ramram? With money to spend? Right, Tilja?"

(Alnor had put himself in charge of Faheel's purse, and taken a gold coin out of it each day since they had landed. When Tilja touched one of these it remained a gold coin, so they knew that the magic was not in it, but in the purse.)

Ramram, thought Tilja. Calico . . .

"I'll never hear the last of it if I don't bring something home for Anja," she said.

Meena frowned, puzzled for a moment, until she went into her other memory-room and found the name.

"Nor you won't," she said. "Come on, Alnor. I'll buy you a belt buckle or something."

"We'll be quicker if we go two and two," said Alnor when they stood at the entrance to the bridge. He squinted for a moment at the sun. "We'll meet back here when the shadow of that column reaches the drinking trough. Don't lose sight of each other."

Tilja smelled the familiar reek of sun-dried dung before she saw the horse fair, lying along the near bank of the river, invisible from the road, but she didn't drag Tahl off at once to the horse lines. What she'd said about Anja was true, and this was the best chance she'd get to find something for her. The bridge was as busy and crowded as the streets of Talagh, but felt very different. Though hugely larger and richer than the stalls at a Gathering in the Valley, it had the same kind of feel, friendly and businesslike. Tahl bought himself a hunting knife and Tilja found a mother-of-pearl hair comb for Anja and a plainer, tortoiseshell one for Ma. Satisfied, she started back.

"We don't have to go yet," said Tahl. "There's lots more . . ."

"I want to go and look for Calico. The man said he was coming here."

"Why on earth? You could get a much better—"

"Calico belongs at Woodbourne. Like your dog you told me about at Northbeck. She was useless, but you kept her there till she died."

"Oh, all right."

"Course I've still got her," said the horse dealer. "I'm a man of my word, I am. Besides, d'you think anyone would have bought her off me? You sure it's her you want? I've a sweet little pony, now, five years if he's a day. Purebred Harst Mountain, and they're tough as they come, but good tempered with it. Had a kick from one of the others a couple of days back, so he's going a bit lame in his off fore—"

"Spavined, you mean," said Tahl, unable to resist a haggle.

"Shut up," said Tilja. "Look, I'm sure he's lovely, but I just want Calico back. I'll pay you the full seven days, if you like."

"Well, if you're sure, though I reckoned I'd be giving her away at the end. She's along this way. . . . And while you're here, young lady, there's something I may as well ask you. You were trying to get into Goloroth that night, right? I'd've said you couldn't've made it, but seeing you're here . . . well, did you?"

Tilja nodded. The man lowered his voice.

"There was something happened inside the city that night, big enough to make 'em close the gates all next day. Some of the racket you could've heard back here in Ramram. And now there's all this loose magic blowing around. Devil of a time I had of it, bringing my beasts up north, though every one of them's got an amulet in its mane. And now you've got into the city and out again. . . . So what's up, supposing you know?"

Tilja hesitated. To tell anyone anything about what they'd

done might be dangerous. To refuse to tell might be just as bad. She glanced at Tahl.

"Yes," he said easily. "We sneaked in with the slave children. We found our grandparents in one of the big barns. Somebody'd brought something magical in—"

"But it's warded to hell, the city!"

"Yes, I know. But they managed it somehow. And a couple of magicians came to get it for themselves and fought over it and there was an explosion and lots of screaming and running about, so we managed to get out. That's all I know. I've no idea what it was all about. You haven't heard anything else, have you? Nothing from Talagh, for instance? I'd have thought they'd send somebody down to sort things out."

"If they did, it's not the sort of stuff folk like us get to hear about. Nor anything else. Better off that way, like as not."

He shrugged and spread his hands, accepting the appalling whims of the Empire.

"What about Calico?" said Tilja.

"Well, young lady, seeing you're set on it, we'll call it six days and leave it at that. Here she is, then. Looks pleased to see you, too."

"That'll make a change," said Tilja, but for a moment it seemed almost true. As the dealer led her out of the line Calico sidled up to Tilja like any normal horse greeting its owner, but as soon as Tilja reached to pat her she flattened her ears and turned away. Forgiveness was no part of her scheme of things.

Meena laughed when she saw Calico, but Alnor was furious. He couldn't complain of the waste of money, when a single gold coin from Faheel's purse would have bought them at least two decent horses. And Calico could carry their packs, and Tilja would deal with her moods. But in his own mind he was in command, and buying Calico back was something he hadn't had a say in. So both he and Calico sulked all afternoon.

———

Next morning Tilja was walking with Tahl when he said, "This fellow who's supposed to find us somewhere, and make it snow properly in the Valley again and so on—did Faheel say anything else to you about that?"

Tilja shook her head. She'd been expecting the question and had decided that was the best she could do—not quite lying because she might have meant only that she couldn't answer, which was true.

Tahl looked at her with his bright-eyed stare, making her very uncomfortable. He started to say something, changed his mind and began again.

"It sounded as if he'd forgotten about it, but he'd thought of everything else. Tiny things. That purse . . . and he must have asked you why we'd all come to his island in the first place. Didn't he?"

"Well, yes, but . . . I told him we'd come from the Valley, because he wanted to know about Axtrig, but then I said he'd better wait for Meena and Alnor to wake up, because they were the ones who wanted to talk to him."

"You mean he knew what Meena wanted before she told him, but he'd just forgotten about it? He didn't forget anything else, though. He remembered about the way-leaves, for instance."

"He was very tired by the end."

Again the look of doubt.

"I suppose so," Tahl said discontentedly. Tilja walked on with shame in her heart and a chill in the pit of her stomach—shame for her half-truths told to someone who trusted her, and the chill of dread about what else Tahl's bright and restless intelligence might tease out. *Oh*, she thought, *let the Ropemaker come and claim the ring soon, soon, so that this can be over!*

15

The Road North

It was curious how slowly the news seeped through of what had happened at Talagh. The Emperor was dead and the power of the Watchers broken, but the body of that strange great beast, the Empire, still twitched with a kind of life, like a headless chicken running round the yard at Woodbourne. In the evenings at the way stations Tilja heard people talking in anxious voices about the amount of loose magic gusting around, and complaining in guarded tones about the Watchers falling down on their job. It was clear that something had gone wrong with the system that had always ruled their lives, but no one knew what. It was nine days before any other signs came through.

Then there was a flurry of grander travelers on the road, horsemen at a rapid canter carrying the message staff of their Landholder with a bell at its top clanging to clear a path; and once or twice the Landholder himself with only half a dozen outriders for retinue because he too was in a hurry. All this could only mean that something important was happening high in the upper reaches of the Empire.

The news, when it seeped down to the lowest levels, where those who made the journey to Goloroth and back had their existence, was still only rumors. Some said the Watchers had killed the Emperor and were fighting among themselves, others that he had dismissed them and they were revolting against him, others yet that one of his regiments had mutinied and killed him—a regiment of women, according to one version.

"Women soldiers!" Tilja heard a man saying. "It'll be a long time before anyone tries that again!"

"Let's hope he's right," said Tahl later. "There's going to be a new Emperor one day. We don't want him getting the same idea."

Despite these upheavals, for a while nothing much seemed to change for the ordinary travelers. The same laws ruled their lives that had always ruled them. The same bribes had to be paid. And so far Tilja and the others had had no trouble. They had no fees to pay, they were just children going north from Goloroth, like tens of thousands of children before them. Meena was the first to notice the oddity.

The Grand Trunk Road was as busy as ever, with travelers of all kinds moving at different speeds. With their strong young legs and their longing to be home the four of them went faster than most, and kept going later, so they often passed others who had already settled down by the road to rest out the worst of the heat. Tahl, typically, insisted on greeting these as they went by, though the conversation seldom got further than an agreement that it was hot.

They were walking along, four abreast for once, when another such group came in sight, two women and a man. One of the women had peeled an orange and was passing the segments to the other two, who were gazing blankly at the road.

"Just keep an eye on their faces when Tahl says hello to them," Meena whispered. "Don't stare. You don't want them to notice."

"Hello," said Tahl as they came up. "Hot, isn't it?"

The man started slightly. The woman with the orange looked up. The other one's eyes widened and her mouth half opened. The expressions lasted only a moment, then the women smiled emptily and the man said, "You can say that again," and reached for another segment of orange.

"See," said Meena, as soon as they were out of earshot. "It's like they'd never seen us coming. There we were, out in the middle of the road, no one else in sight, and they hadn't so much as noticed us till Tahl said something to them. You remember the story, how Dirna and Reyel never had any trouble after they'd talked to Asarta and she'd sent them off to look for Faheel, because she'd worked it so that people didn't seem to notice they were there? Old Faheel's done the same for us now."

"He can't have done it for Til," said Tahl. "Magic just runs off her."

"Her being with us does it, maybe," said Meena. "It mightn't work supposing you were alone, though, Til. . . . You may as well be a bit careful about that."

She was right, as they found out a few days later. By now they had seen definite signs of the system's breaking down. At one way station the women who were doling out the free meals for those going the Common Way insisted on being paid. They said they needed the money, because their official allowance hadn't come through. At another somebody caught one of the guards stealing from his baggage, and when he complained to the warden he was laughed at. And next day, where the road crossed a tributary of the Great River, there had been armed men on the bridge demanding a toll from all travelers, but by the time Tilja and the others reached the place enough furious people had gathered to overpower them and throw them into the river.

It was almost dark by the time they reached their way station that evening. As usual Tilja went and bought fodder for Calico while the other three fetched supper from the food stalls. She was on her way back when she sensed that someone was following her and looked round.

"Hold it right there," said a man's voice.

She dropped the bag of fodder and started to run but he grabbed her by the shoulder. Her shout was stifled by a gritty hand.

"You got some money," he growled. "Don't try and pretend

not. Just seen you buying stuff. Get it out and drop it on the ground and you'll not get hurt."

She tried to jerk herself free. His other hand grabbed her wrist and wrenched it up behind her back, twisting to cause more pain, and again as she bit at his palm.

"Let go," said Alnor's voice.

"You keep out of this, sonny."

"Let go."

"If that's how you want it . . ."

She was flung violently aside, and fell. As she picked herself up she saw the man, with Alnor facing him and Tahl and Meena a little behind, all silhouetted against the line of lights on the far side of the courtyard. The man was squat, with a bulging belly. He didn't look like a fighter, but he had a knife in his hand. Alnor walked toward him, slightly up on his toes, like a dancer.

The man gestured with the knife to stop him. Alnor moved as if meaning to dodge the thrust but instantly twisted the other way, swinging his body to the left while his right leg slashed up and caught the man cleanly on the wrist.

The man shouted with pain and let go of the knife. It looped upward and fell. Almost before it hit the ground Alnor had twisted again, on his right foot this time, with his left foot scything round to strike the man in the back of the knee, toppling him to the ground, where he lay groaning. Alnor turned away.

"Are you all right?" he asked Tilja. "Did he hurt you?"

"My shoulder's sore," she said shakily. "I . . . I think I'm all right. Thank you. . . . I had some fodder."

"I've got it," said Tahl. He sounded much more excited than Alnor, who had now turned back to the man.

"Keep away," he said, prodding him in the neck with his toe. "That's what I'll break next time."

"Meena noticed him following you," explained Tahl as they went back together.

"Can you do that?"

"Kick-fight? My da died before he could teach me. And by then Alnor . . ."

"Oh yes. You told me at the Gathering."

"Well, now's your chance," said Meena. "Alnor, why don't you teach him kick-fighting? He ought to know how. And seeing how things are going, it might come in handy if he could do it too."

Alnor frowned. His face went blank for a moment, just as Meena's did whenever she went into her other memory-room, something he did very seldom, as if hating to be reminded of the helplessness his blindness had cursed him with. He nodded.

"Yes," he said. "We'll do that from now on. And from now on, Tilja, you'd better keep close to us all the time."

Soon they were moving through an Empire in turmoil. Half the way stations were deserted, and those that functioned demanded triple or quadruple fees. Robbers and looters were everywhere.

Nor were those the only dangers. Now that the Watchers were gone, magicians who had been practicing in secret began to do so openly, and not all of these were benign. At one way station the story came of a well-armed convoy that had been traveling without a hired magician to protect it. Two great scaly creatures had attacked it and had wantonly slaughtered, but not eaten, man, woman and child, gurgling with pleasure as they did so.

For a while the four from the Valley joined one of the armed convoys that were now operating on the Grand Trunk Road. It moved more slowly than they had been doing on their own, but the road had become a dangerous place, despite Tilja's powers and the near invisibility that Faheel had given them. They saw one or two weird beasts in the distance; and at two rest camps they found, hanging from improvised gallows near the entrance, the bodies of thieves who had been caught sneaking around in the dark; and the hired magician traveling with the convoy claimed to have earned his wage twice over, warding off unseen enemies.

The convoy tended to stop for the night at least one way station sooner than the four might have done on their own, giving the boys a chance to get on with the kick-fighting lessons before they were tired with travel. It was typical of Tahl that he didn't mind being watched making a fool of himself, as a beginner; but, surprisingly, Alnor didn't try to make him look one. Perhaps, Tilja thought, kick-fighting was too serious for that. Anyway, the lessons went far more easily than she'd hoped.

"Notice how much better they're getting on together now?" said Meena one evening while she and Tilja were sitting watching a practice bout. "Funny how they weren't making out as just friends, the way you and I are. And it wasn't all Alnor's fault, either. But teacher and pupil, that's something they're comfortable with.

"And pretty to look at, isn't it, now Tahl's getting the hang of it? Alnor, specially, of course. I daresay that's what won him his championships, it wasn't just winning the fights, it was how he did it. Look at him now, just standing ready for Tahl to have a go at him, graceful as a cat."

"No wonder you're keen on him," said Tilja.

It was the first time she'd brought the subject up, but Meena laughed, without even a trace of a blush. Then she sighed.

"It's not going to last, you know, Til," she said. "D'you blame us for making the most of it while we've got it?"

"Of course not. I think it's lovely for you."

"We've got to get home, mind. In time for the winter, latest. But I shan't say no to taking a few days longer over it than we'd've done traveling on our own."

Meena's wish was not to be granted. Only a few nights later the convoy was given horrible reason to doubt the boasted powers of its hired magician. They had halted at a way station where the warden was a jolly little man who, most unusually, came fussing around in the dusk chatting to his customers and asking whether they had all they wanted. Like everyone else he might have passed the four from the Valley unnoticed, if Tahl hadn't spoken to him. Then he picked up that Meena and Alnor had something going on between them, and teased them about it. Meena gave as good as she got, but Alnor was still simmering with rage when they lay down to sleep.

Tilja woke in the middle of the night, already knowing what had woken her, the same quiet tension that she had felt when Silena had brought her beast to that other way station on the journey south, looking for Axtrig. Again she didn't at once sit up, but lay where she was, listening to the unnatural silence, not a snore, not a stir, not even a breath from any of the hundred or so sleepers. She knew that something powerful had come into the courtyard, since neither the wards around the way station nor the convoy's magician had been effective against it.

Carefully she raised her head. There was no moon, but the stars were bright overhead, and a few dim lamps ringed the courtyard. At first she could see and hear nothing, but then, a little way off, a dark hummock rose, straightened and became the shape of a man. He, or it, moved closer. Tilja eased her arm free of her rug, ready to stretch out and touch the thing as it passed—better, she guessed, to take it by surprise than rise and confront it—but it stopped just before it reached her, and turned away. It moved its arms and a pale glow came out of its spread hands, showing Meena asleep, with her rug pulled half over her face. With the extra light Tilja could see that the thing was a man. Though his back was toward her she recognized him from his shape. It was the warden of the way station. He knelt, twitched the rug aside and bent over Meena.

Tilja jerked up, flung herself forward and grabbed at his ankle. But he had heard her coming. Quick as a cur in a dogfight he twisted round, hissing. His face was black, a beast face, blunt snouted and scaly, with rubbery lips and needle-like fangs. His mouth dripped blood. The light went out. His hand grasped her by the hair and dragged her toward him. She reached up and caught him by the wrist.

She was ready for the sudden numbness, and the rush of energy, into her and away. It was different from the time when she had laid her hands on Dorn's bare back in the dormitory at Goloroth. That had been a whole complex tangle of powers surging through her. This was a single blast, strong but simple, there for an instant, and gone.

The hissing stopped and the beast-man stood rigid, but only for a moment or two before he snarled in purely human fury and started to shake her to and fro by her hair. She screamed with the pain of it, and then the other three woke and together they grappled him to the ground.

The rest of the courtyard was awake by the time she had staggered to her feet. The guards lit torches at their brazier. By their light the travelers caught five more of the creatures, a woman and four children. The warden had changed back into his human shape at Tilja's touch, but these others had beast faces. They wailed like pigs as they were hunted and caught, and wept black tears. When the guards led them away and ran them through with their swords they died, or seemed to.

The so-called magician was dead, his throat slit. Four girls and a boy, all about Meena's age or younger, were dead too. All their flesh was gone from their bodies. Folds of wrinkled skin wrapped their bare bones.

So the convoy was forced to travel on unprotected as far as the next roadside fair, where the captain hired a plump, homely little woman and explained to the travelers that she was the only magician to be had, and was demanding twice the fee he had paid to the man they had lost. If they wanted her protection, there would therefore be a surcharge.

A man stood up and asked for proof of her powers. She stared at him for a moment and a violent gust of wind came out of nowhere, twisted round him and dragged him into the air, high as a tall tree, and there dropped him, leaving the air still. The man fell headlong, yelling. Just before he reached the ground invisible

hands seemed to catch him and set him on his feet. He came tot-
tering back to the gathering and agreed to pay the extra fee.

That evening at the way station Tilja and Tahl went to buy
roasted honey sticks and were strolling back to their booth—
slowly, to allow the other two a little more time alone together—
when the magician appeared in front of them. She gazed silently
at Tilja and then laid her hand briefly on Tilja's bare arm. For
that moment, as Tilja felt the numbness flicker and fade, the
woman changed, became taller, slimmer, white-skinned, ageless,
with the stone look so strong that she might have been born with
it. Then she was the unimpressive little housewife again.

"Yes," she said, "my friend Zara, Lord Kzuva's magician,
spoke of you. So you have done what you set out to do, it seems."

"How did you know?"

"I will trade information."

"All right."

"I did not know, but guessed. Before you came, there was
nothing in the Empire that could have destroyed the Watchers.
But the power you loosed on the walls of Talagh was of a different order. I was in the city that night. All my wards were shat
tered by the strength of it, though I could tell that it was
operating far from its source. That source, I think, could have
done it. Yes?"

Tilja hesitated. *What if this woman asked about the ring?*

"Yes . . . I suppose so," she said.

"And the source was a man? A woman? Something else?"

"A man," said Tilja firmly, but very aware of the *something else*
hidden beneath her blouse.

"And where is he now?"

"I don't know. He was dying. He told us to put him on a raft
so that he could go the common way. He'd been waiting to destroy the Watchers before he went. It was up to him, he said, because he'd set them up in the first place."

"*That* man," said the magician meditatively, and fell silent.

"Is that why there's so much crazy magic loose?" asked Tahl. "Like the warden's family at the way station last night?"

She nodded.

"Things were not always as you have seen them," she said. "We are taught that long ago, before there were Emperors, there was a balance. Magic came into the world, and those who knew how could use it, and the rest flowed away south. But as the Emperors established their power they hired magicians to take control of the magic. No one foresaw that one result of their work would be that they gathered all the magic they could into themselves, so that now less of it flowed out than came in. The difference was only slight, but the balance was lost. Gradually, over the generations the pressure has increased.

"And, of course, the magicians became ever more powerful, but there was always some man or woman with powers different from and greater than those of any of theirs, who could keep them in check. When each of these grew old they passed the task on to a successor, whom they had themselves chosen. Last but one of these was a woman called Asarta, who in her turn chose a man called Faheel—the selfsame man, I imagine, whom you helped onto a raft and launched upon the common way to die."

She spoke the name calmly, without any hesitation, and looked enquiringly at Tilja. Tilja nodded. The magician stood, pondering.

"So, as you say, he finished what he had begun," she said at last. "He destroyed the Watchers he himself had set up."

"I thought you said it was the Emperors who did that," said Tahl, who of course by now had taken over the questioning.

"They had hired the magicians in the first place, but it was Faheel who set them up as Watchers, as much to control and counter each other as to control the magic. Naturally he saw to it that the Emperors should think it was their own doing. But in the end the cure proved worse than the disease."

"So what happens now?" said Tahl.

"Now things are very dangerous. The Emperor left no heir,

and the Landholders are struggling for the Opal Throne. My own was fool enough to think he could make a move. His house is destroyed, his servants scattered. The Lord Kzuva was wiser. He retired to his own estates, and my friend Zara went with him, while I am forced to hire my talents along the road. Worse yet, there is an unknown force in the land, something that one by one is seeking out and destroying those Watchers who escaped from Talagh. Five times I have sensed the dissolution of a Watcher's powers. I do not know how many are left. I had imagined this must be the work of whoever had broken the towers at Talagh, completing his task, but you say he is gone."

"Yes, I'm sure it wasn't him," said Tilja, barely managing to keep her voice steady, knowing what that force must be. She was remembering things that Faheel had said. *He came for the ring. . . . He will try to come again. . . . You yourself might withstand him— I do not know. . . . The whole of the next age is in the balance.* She was remembering a fist the color of moonlight rising above a parapet and grasping great eddies of raw force as if they had been cobwebs dangling from a beam in a barn. She needed a name for the enemy, a way of thinking about him. *Moonfist.* Yes, that would do.

The magician was staring at her. She was saying something.

". . . why Faheel never chose his successor . . . Do not tell me, child, that *you* are his chosen successor."

"Oh, no! Of course not . . . but . . . I think it may be all right."

Again, for an even longer while, the magician stood deep in thought.

"You do well to be careful," she said. "Well, I have a message for you to pass on, perhaps. If there is work to be done, I am willing to help. So, now, I wish you well."

She smiled an unmeaning, purse-lipped housewife's smile, nodded and turned away. *She's frightened too,* Tilja thought. *She isn't just hiring her magic along the road to earn a living. She's hiding from Moonfist.*

"Chosen successor?" murmured Tahl, as soon as the magician was out of earshot.

Tilja shook her head unhappily. She could almost hear the fizz of Tahl's brain as he tried to piece what the magician had told them into what they already knew.

"I want to get home," she said, desperate to distract him. "If things are as dangerous as she says . . . we aren't going fast enough."

The next day was miserable for Tilja. In the middle of the night a hideous thought had come to her. She had woken with her own words buzzing in her mind, like a bee she had once seen buzzing against one of Aunt Grayne's glass windows, trying to find its way through. *We aren't going fast enough.* She had spoken the words almost at random, but knew in her heart they were true. And now, waking, she knew why.

Somewhere along the road, Faheel had said, the Ropemaker would be waiting for them. But now Tilja had learned that Moonfist was systematically seeking out and destroying other magicians. He already knew of the Ropemaker's existence—he had seen him change himself into a giant lion in the palace court-yard. He would be looking for him, surely. So every day she and the others spent on the journey put the Ropemaker in greater danger. The sooner they reached the place where he was waiting for them, the sooner she gave him the ring, the better.

She spent the rest of the night wondering how she could persuade the others of the need to hurry. All she could think of to tell them was that she'd had bad dreams about what was happening in the Valley.

They didn't agree.

That wasn't enough. Alnor in particular was adamant.

"Not worth the risk," he said. "The road gets more dangerous every day. We've had the luck to pick up a good convoy. The guards are honest, and this new magician knows her business. We'll be home before winter with time to spare, and that's all that matters. There's nothing I can do before the first snow falls, and Meena won't be sowing her barley until next spring. I'm sorry,

Til. You'll need to produce a stronger reason than just a ~~feeling."~~

"He's right, Til," said Meena. "So let's enjoy the journey whi~~~ we can, eh?"

She didn't glance at Alnor as she spoke, but there were layers of meaning in her smile. She was quite open about her love for him, and her determination to make the most of it for the few weeks she had left to her in this young body. Even Alnor had mostly given up trying to pretend he didn't feel the same.

And Tahl was relishing the journey for different reasons. He liked traveling in company, making friends, giving a helping hand here and there, asking questions all the time, so easily and unashamedly that people told him the answers, laughing as they did so. If a newcomer joined the convoy one morning, by nightfall he'd know all about them. At one point he even persuaded a glassblower to set up his kiln and show him how it was done, and thus became the proud owner of a small misshapen flask that he had blown himself.

And against these powerful arguments all Tilja had to offer was some dreams she hadn't really dreamed, and a real, strong reason that she wasn't allowed to tell them. She tried several times during the day's march. Soon Alnor refused to listen, and in the end Meena lost her temper, and in a brief flare of the old anger that reduced Tilja to tears told her she was as tiresome as Calico and it was time to stop being a stupid baby wanting its own way and blubbering because she couldn't have it.

From then on Tilja walked in silent unhappiness, vainly trying to think of some new reason the others might listen to. Tahl walked beside her, for once not chatting but keeping her company, seeming to understand that it was no use trying to cheer her up. In the end he broke the silence.

"You know something you can't tell us, don't you, Til?"

She shook her head, not looking at him, but knowing the intelligent, questioning glance that would have gone with the words.

…nd there's a good reason, of course," he said, just as though
…d told him he was right. "Difficult for you."

She couldn't pretend any longer.

"Try not to think about it," she muttered.

He laughed, and she knew why, and managed to laugh with
him. Tahl, of all people, not thinking about something that was
puzzling him.

"All right," he said. "I've thought of something else just worth
trying."

The convoy halted well before nightfall and settled into a busy
way station. It was still too soon for supper when the boys had
finished their kick-fighting.

"Why don't we go and see if the river's got anything to tell
us?" said Tahl. "There's just a chance we might pick something
up from the Valley, and set Til's mind at rest."

"With a hundred other rivers talking away?" said Alnor.

"Oh, go on," said Meena. "You're dying to, really. It's ages
since you had a good chat with one of your wet friends."

Alnor grunted agreement and rose to his feet. They walked
down to the river, a good half mile wide at this point, a great
smooth expanse of water moving southward under the darkening
sky. The first stars were out. One or two lights glimmered along
the further shore. A little below the way station a sandspit ran out
from the bank.

"That'll do," said Alnor. "You two wait here."

So the two girls settled down at the edge of the water and
watched the boys moving out along the sandspit and wading into
the shallows where it ended until they were almost waist deep
and needing to steady themselves against the press of the current.
It was dusk, with the Herald rising bright in the east, and a few
other stars faintly showing. The boys stood awhile with bowed
heads, motionless dark shapes against the moving flood, then
turned and came slowly back along the sandspit and up the bank,
deep in serious talk.

"Well," said Meena. "How are things back home, then?"

"The voice of our river was there indeed," said Alnor, speaking as he'd used to when he'd been an old man. "It was loud, because the glacier is melting fast, and our river is in spate. There has been fighting beside it. It has carried the bodies of slain men."

"That means the pass is open," said Tahl.

The four of them stood in silence. The boys' drenched clothes dripped steadily onto the ground.

16

Lord Kzuva's Tower

From then on they traveled alone, making the best speed they could, but limited always by Calico's needs and their own endurance. Nobody noticed them unless they chose to be noticed, though the further north they traveled the busier the great highway became. Every scrap of possible forage by the roadside was already grazed bare, but there were plenty of well-stocked forage stalls along the way, where they could buy enough for Calico to eat while they took their midday rest. Such was their apparent invisibility that they sometimes wondered whether they could simply have taken what they wanted, unobserved.

But they weren't certain how far Faheel's magic protected them from the other magical powers that were now loose in the Empire, especially at night, so for safety they continued to sleep at well-warded way stations, slipping wearily in in the dusk, and away again as the sun rose, unquestioned by anyone.

Opposite Talagh they left the river and turned northwest. Resting on the first foothills they looked back over the plain. There lay the great city, the wounded heart of the Empire. Even at such a distance they could see how it was changed, with the spindling towers from which the Watchers had controlled the great tide of magic now mere stubs, or fallen completely.

Tilja and the others had joined a group of travelers, resting under some shade trees. As they gazed out at this symbol of the enormous change, they were talking in hushed and apprehensive

300

voices about what else might now happen, and swapping stories of the dangers and marvels they had seen.

As it turned out, little of that kind awaited the four on the road to the Pirrim Hills. Nor did the Ropemaker, though this was where Tilja had been expecting at last to meet him. *He will choose a place you must pass*, Faheel had said, *and be waiting for you there*. Not the Grand Trunk Road—that was far too thronged— but now that they had turned off toward home, and there were fewer people on the road . . . Indeed, the way stations became less and less busy as travelers reached the turnings to their own destinations. Still the Ropemaker was not among them.

The way station beside the last town before the hills was completely deserted, apart from one lame old man and the chickens he had started to rear in the empty booths.

"No point your going on," he told Meena.

"You're telling me there are robbers in the hills?" she asked.

"Nah. They'll have gone south. Richer pickings for them there. But the Lord Kzuva—he's Landholder up the other side of the hills—he's shut off the whole of the North West Plain. He's not letting anyone in, barring those as belong there or as got business with him. Doesn't want a lot of strangers crowding in because they've heard things are quieter there."

"We're on our way back from Goloroth," said Meena. "We live there."

"You'll be all right then," said the old man. "With Lord Kzuva, anyway . . ."

He hesitated and went on in a lower voice.

"Better warn you. My wife's sister—she's got . . . gifts. She says there's some weird stuff moved into Pirrim Forest these last few weeks."

Tilja slept and woke, slept and woke, slept and woke. Each time she opened her eyes she expected to see the gangling figure with the enormous headdress looming above her, outlined against the stars. It didn't happen. *In the Pirrim Hills, where we first met*, she told herself. *There, at last, surely.*

301

In view of the old man's warning they did a short stage next day rather than face the pine forest in the dark, and camped at the deserted way station immediately below the hills, taking turns to keep watch while the other three slept close together, within easy reach of Tilja. Next morning they started at dawn, for three long hours toiled up the steeply winding road, and around midmorning reached the pass. As soon as they were in among the pines Calico shied and bolted.

Tilja wasn't ready. For the last few days Calico had been unusually biddable. In her stupid horse mind she might even have realized that at last they were on their way home. Now, instantly, she was crazed, wrenching her lead rope from Tilja's grasp, squealing and rearing like a stallion. She whirled round. Her hindquarters slammed into Tilja, stunning her briefly as she grabbed at Alnor for support.

Tilja came to with something pressing on her chest—Alnor's arm clasping her tight against his body. Meena and Tahl were holding her hands. Calico, at full gallop, was disappearing round the corner ahead. She realized that the other three were standing very still and all breathing in slow, gulping lungfuls. She could feel the thud of Alnor's heart against her shoulder blade.

"Wh-what happened?" she stammered.

"Don't let go!" Meena gasped. "Can't move unless you're holding us! The forest's come alive!"

Another terrified squeal rang out, and again, and again. Awkwardly, holding hands, the four of them stumbled forward and round the corner. Calico was lying on her side in the middle of the path, while a sort of gray net that seemed to be growing out of the ground was wrapping itself around her in billowing folds.

"I need that hand!" Tilja yelled. "Hold somewhere else, Tahl!"

With the other three trailing she flung herself forward and grabbed at the gray stuff. It stopped growing, but didn't otherwise change or loose its hold on Calico. There was a slow, strange pulse in the numbness of her arm, a sense of some vague, large thing resisting her power. She concentrated, forced her willed attention onto it. Now, instead of rushing on through her and away, the thing withdrew. The net shriveled in her grasp, became powder and fell away. Calico started to kick herself to her feet, still squealing, but unbalanced as Tilja grabbed her by the bridle, forced her head down and sat on it, then laid her free hand against her neck and worked her fingers down against the skin. Shuddering, Calico quietened, and as soon as Tilja let her got shakily to her feet. A heavy, earthy reek filled the air.

"What was that?" said Tahl.

"Bull's-ears, by the smell of it," said Meena.

This was a poisonous toadstool that grew out of rotting stumps in the forest near Woodbourne. All summer these stumps would become covered in a fine gray mesh, dewy with little droplets that stank of moist mold. Then, later, as all the leaves changed color, brown and white fungi would emerge, looking exactly like the ears of cattle.

"It's not just the bull's-ears," said Meena in a low voice. "It's the whole dratted forest—it's come alive. I can feel it. Watching us, somehow. It wasn't like this when we were going the other way."

"We must be through here by nightfall," said Alnor. "Suppose Tilja rides, with Meena behind. Then Tahl and I can walk either side of her with our hands on her ankles. It's either that or go back."

"We've got to give it a go," said Meena. "Should be all right if we all hang on to Til."

At first this seemed to work well enough. Calico wanted nothing more than to be out of the forest, and seemed to have realized that she was safe nowhere except under Tilja's protection, so she plodded steadily on.

But Tilja was deeply troubled. There had been something wrong about what had happened when she had shriveled the fungus in which Calico was trapped. She felt it shouldn't have worked, because the magic of the forest was surely natural magic, against which she had no power. And at first the fungus indeed had seemed to resist her, in a way that not even Dorn had done. That was the forest magic, surely, holding her back. But then, when she had concentrated, the fungus had shriveled. So, somehow, the fungus must have been made magic. She didn't understand it at all.

And now, after a while, she realized that something like that was happening again. The silence of the forest was more than an absence of sound. It was a thing in its own right, dense and oppressive. Tilja saw Tahl holding his hand to his mouth, rather than break it with a cough. A dense fog was closing down. Tilja could feel the thing that caused the silence all around them, filling the long valley up to the invisible tree lines on either side. It was far more than just a huge number of trees. It was the living forest, a great, strange power. A natural magic.

Still, somehow, and with increasing effort, she seemed to be holding it back. No. It wasn't the forest itself that she was holding, but something else, some kind of made magic that was *using* the power of the forest to try to crush her. It was the same thing that had controlled the fungus that had almost trapped Calico. Again she concentrated, and again the thing seemed to yield.

But this time there had been nothing for her to lay her hand against and shrivel, and after a brief respite the pressure returned, closing in on her like a gradually tightening fist. The others were feeling it too. Alnor and Tahl, who had at first walked easily beside her, now had their shoulders pressed against Calico's flanks, and the fingers that grasped Tilja's ankles felt like iron shackles. Meena had her arms around her, hugging her so close that it was hard to breathe. Calico had shortened her stride and was moving as if she were leaning against a horse collar, with a full load behind her.

Faheel, Tilja thought dimly, had known powers like this. He had made them his friends. She remembered waiting below through a timeless afternoon while those powers had gathered to say farewell to him, calling to him as they had come. Perhaps this forest had been one of them.

With an effort she straightened her back and called aloud.

"Faheel sent us. He is our friend. We are doing his work."

The dead silence absorbed her voice. Nothing happened. The pressure grew and grew.

"This won't do," Meena croaked in her ear. "I'll try and tell 'em. Maybe they'll listen to me. They're trees, aren't they?"

She drew a deep, gasping breath and, faintly, creakingly, started to sing.

The song was at first wordless, no more than a humming in the throat, slow and wavering, but after a little while Meena began to repeat the name of Faheel, drawing it out into a dozen floating notes.

Her voice grew stronger. Little by little the pressure began to ease. Steadily Tilja concentrated her will against the thing, whatever it was, that she had felt using the forest's power. There was a sudden moment of change, of breakthrough, a rush of release. Tahl moved away from Calico's side and looked around, interested. Alnor let go of Tilja's hand and took Meena's. The fog became palely golden and a little while later they were walking along a track with the sun already westering ahead of them so that it lit the tree trunks on their right almost as far as the ground. Meena stopped singing.

"Done it!" she said, triumphantly. "It wasn't the forest's fault, mind you—there's no real malice in trees. Something was making it act that way, but it didn't really like it. But that's better, isn't it?"

The silence was silence still, but they weren't afraid any longer to speak. They knew that the forest had fully withdrawn its menace when Calico stopped in her tracks to sample a patch of grass growing beside the road.

The sun was full in their faces by the time they came to the end of the pass. Only on the long descent to Songisu did it cross Tilja's mind that the Ropemaker, after all, hadn't been waiting for

305

them in the hills. She felt strangely unworried about this. Of course there was still time. Though she hadn't known it, he had been with them on their way south, in the shape of one animal or another, all the way across these northern plains, ever since they had landed from their raft. He would be waiting for them here.

The stars were out before they reached the way station at Songisu. To their surprise this was manned, and running, much as it had been on the outward journey.

There was a guard dozing at the entrance, wearing what Tilja recognized as Lord Kzuva's livery. They might have slipped in unnoticed, as usual, if Tahl hadn't spoken to him.

The guard looked up, blinking.

"Where you from, then?" he asked, yawning.

"We are on our way back from Goloroth," said Alnor.

The guard frowned and sat up.

"Try another one," he said. "Forest's not letting anyone through no longer. Lord Kzuva, he got his magicians to see to it."

"We told the forest what we were doing and it let us through," said Alnor.

"Did it, now?" said the guard, impressed. "All right, then, make yourselves at home. You're the only ones here. You're lucky to find us still going—we'll be closing right down any day now. Stalls are closed already, but we'll find you a bite."

He and his wife joined them as they ate and questioned them eagerly about what was happening in the Empire, so Tahl and Meena joyfully fed them their fill of wonders and horrors.

"Well, you'll be finding things easier, now on," he told them when they'd finished. "The magicians have got things pretty well under control up here. It's only a couple of women, mind you, but they're making a real go of it, I give them that."

It was strange to be back in something like the old Empire. Strange to find it a relief, order instead of chaos, the grip of strong rule instead of the whirling free-for-all of loose magic and lawlessness. Soon, perhaps, they would have found this as op-

306

pressive as they had on the journey south, but now it simply meant that they could relax their guard and hurry on.

The traffic increased, though the way stations were less busy than they'd been on the outward journey. The wardens asked no more than the fee and the official bribe. The talk in the evenings was cheerful and ordinary.

But every mile they walked Tilja became more and more oppressed and withdrawn. A new and terrible fear had begun to obsess her. What if Moonfist had already found and destroyed the Ropemaker? Then, when at last she took out the hair tie and laid the ring beside it, only Moonfist would come. *No,* she told herself, *I won't believe it. There's still time. He'll be here, somewhere, waiting for us.*

Just after they had left the way station on the third morning after the Pirrim Hills she stopped to watch a golden cockerel scratching in the dust by the road. It was almost the right color, but not gawky enough, she decided, and was about to move on when a man came up and spoke to her. He was wearing the Lord Kzuva's livery, and she had half noticed him studying the groups of travelers as they came through the gateway.

He looked at her for a moment and nodded.

"Yes," he said pompously. "You were with them. Five months back you came with"— he studied a clay tablet—"Qualif and his wife to the Lord Kzuva's house in Talagh."

Tilja recognized him now.

"That's right," she said. "You let us in."

"Where is your friend?"

"They're just there."

The other three had seen what was happening. Tahl came hurrying back.

"Three?" said the man. "Yes, this boy, and the horse, but . . . there was a blind man and a lame old woman. You were taking them to Goloroth, I was told. Who are these others?"

"They're our cousins," said Tahl. "They went south before we did."

"I've no instructions about them," said the messenger.

"What do you want?" asked Tahl. "We're in a hurry. We've got an urgent message for the Lady Lananeth."

"She's the one sent for you. She's at the Lord Kzuva's house. Your cousins can carry on home."

"She'll want to see them too," said Tahl calmly. "They're the ones with the message."

The messenger hemmed and hawed, for the sake of it, but then, to Tilja's relief, nodded.

The side road along which the messenger eventually led them dipped into a wooded valley with a sluggish river winding through. They came round a bend and there was the Lord Kzuva's house. They stopped in their tracks and stared.

"My, that's something!" Meena gasped.

Tilja thought it was the most beautiful building she had ever seen, not a house but a small palace, intricately varied and ornate, built on a series of massive bridges across the river. Workmen were busy adding another story to a structure of bamboo scaffolding that already rose well above the tallest pinnacle. Others at the center of the network seemed to be building some kind of column.

"What's that for?" said Tahl.

"It is His Lordship's pleasure," said the messenger. "That is reason enough."

He led them down to the entrance, where a groom came and took Calico. Then he showed them into a pleasant room with cushions strewn around and fruit and drinks on small tables for those waiting to see the Lord Kzuva or his officials. They could hear the river whispering below them, and feel its coolness through the stone floor.

There were a dozen other people already there, but they had hardly settled before the messenger came back and beckoned them out. This time he led them through several grand apartments and up a noble flight of stairs to another, larger room.

Here a whole crowd of people were waiting to do their business. The messenger whispered to the official sitting by the doorway, nodded a haughty good-bye, and left.

Tilja assumed that this time they'd have to take their turn, but the official glanced at them, checked a list, glanced up frowning, shrugged bafflement, rose and led them not to the handsome doorway opposite the entrance but to a little door in the side wall, where he showed them into a much smaller room and told them to wait. They stood around uneasily until the hangings on the far wall stirred and two women slipped quietly in.

For a moment Tilja didn't recognize either of them. Then she saw that the shorter one was Lananeth, and from that made the leap to seeing that the other was Zara, the Lord Kzuva's magician. But the change in them both was shocking. There was that unnatural stillness and smoothness about them which all powerful magicians seemed to have—that look of a statue brought to life. Zara had already had something of it when they had met her in her warded room in Talagh, but then there had still been something human about her. Now even their smiles of greeting were stone smiles. The change was far greater in Lananeth.

"Our Lord Kzuva bids you welcome," said Zara.

"How did you know we were coming?" asked Tahl.

"The forest told us. It has no language, but we could sense it struggling to master someone who was draining its power away, and guessed that could only be Tilja. But we were not expecting . . . you two are Alnor and Meena?"

"That's us," said Meena. "Fa . . . I think it's all right to say his name now—anyway Lananeth knows it—Fahcel gave us a bunch of grapes to eat to make us like this, so we could travel home with the other two and nobody'd ask any questions. And very nice too, it's been."

Exactly together, as if moving in time to unheard music, Zara and Lananeth stepped forward and each raised a hand and held it close beside Meena's cheek, then Alnor's, and after a moment or two, still exactly together, lowered their hands and backed away.

"We do not know how this is done," said Zara. "You are in our warded room, where we are at our strongest, and still we cannot feel that you are not just what you seem."

"We are, too," said Meena. "Tilja touching us doesn't make any difference, either."

"He has changed time, not you. Somehow he has brought you out of your past and put you into this time."

"Like Asarta undoing her years in the story, you mean?" said Tahl. "After she'd given the ring to Reyel and Dirna to take to Faheel?"

The magicians lost their smiles. Tilja gulped with sudden tension. She'd never imagined that the existence of the ring might slip into a conversation like this, and anyway she couldn't have warned the others about it without telling them more than she dared. Tahl was staring at her, frowning. She shook her head in warning. He nodded and looked away.

"Ring?" said Zara softly. "Indeed, there was once a ring, but Asarta took it . . . or so it is said. Perhaps you should tell us the story. And your own."

The four from the Valley looked at each other. Tilja could sense that the other three were feeling her unease by now. Alnor took charge.

"I think you'd better tell us something first," he said aggressively. "How do we know you're the people we met before? You've changed. You're doing everything exactly together. Lananeth has not said a word. And you keep talking about 'we' as if Lananeth had not got a mind of her own. Is she in your power? Or are you both in someone else's?"

The two smiles returned, but now Tilja was certain she didn't believe them.

"We are one, joined," said Zara. "It became necessary when His Lordship asked us to wake the forest. This was a very big undertaking, far too great for either one of us alone. Joined, it was just within our powers, but the effort itself changed us, wove us into each other's mind, so now, though our bodies have separate existences, our thoughts are one thought."

"And what's happened to your feelings, if you don't mind my asking?" said Meena. "Or haven't you got any, anymore? All the thoughts you'll ever think, they aren't any good without feelings."

Still with the same stony smiles the two women gently shook their heads. Tilja had been unhappily watching Lananeth while the magician spoke, looking for some hint of the strong and friendly human who had welcomed them to Ellion's house. For a moment that Lananeth seemed to be there, a sad and desperate glimmer in the depths of the calm brown eyes. Yes, she was sure. Quite deliberately Tilja took a pace forward, put an arm round Lananeth's shoulders and kissed her on the cheek.

The numbness exploded through her. Lananeth juddered and went rigid. Zara too, standing beside her. Zara became a sort of thick mist, which became taller and thinner, then solidified, and now where Zara had been, a man was standing, tall and skinny, dressed all in black. His eyes had no pupils. They were the color of ice. They blazed fury, but he too, for the moment, was locked rigid. Before he could break the spell Tilja reached out and took him by the wrist.

He was strong, far stronger than Dorn. Though she had taken him by surprise, he fought her with his fury, gathering it together, building it into a focused power.

She took Lananeth's wrist in her other hand and with a huge effort closed her mind, shutting out the man, the fury, and searching into her own depths to find her central, secret lake among the mountains. Now the three of them stood on its shore. But its surface was torn by a mountain storm. Unheard winds shrieked between the snow peaks. The whole slope opposite was covered by the menacing dark shadow of the man, with Lananeth's and Tilja's shadows small beside it. The shadows were not thrown by any sun. There was none. Never again. No sun.

Still grasping both wrists, Tilja stepped into the raging water. There was no bottom. She sank, dragging the other two with her. Down they went, and down. The man melted into the water, dwindling away. She looked up and in the dim, watery light saw it was Zara and Lananeth she was dragging behind her. She could live in this water as long as she chose, but they would drown. She let go of their wrists, put an arm round each of them, and simply by choosing to do so rose to the surface, pulled them out and laid them on the grass. The storm was gone. Sunlight glittered off the glaciers, reflected in the barely rippled surface of the lake. Reluctantly she turned away and came back into the outer world.

She was in the warded room in Lord Kzuva's castle, holding Lananeth and Zara by the wrists. A black-clad body lay at their feet. Tilja could see the back of the head, an old, bald cranium, yellow and blotched and shiny. When she let go of the two magicians they both crumpled to the floor.

All this in an instant. Meena, Tahl and Alnor were still picking themselves up after being buffeted aside, as if by an explosion in the middle of the room, when, from somewhere outside, came a tremendous series of crashes, dwindling away amid the yells of human voices.

Tilja barely heard them. Shuddering with exhaustion and relief, she too collapsed and buried her face in her hands, gasping for air.

When she straightened and looked around, Meena was kneeling beside her, holding her close, Alnor was crouching and feeling for Lananeth's pulse, and Tahl was staring at the body on the floor. Outside the room the tone of the voices had changed from alarmed shouts to bellows of command.

"She's alive, at least," Alnor whispered. "Wait. She's coming round."

"Grab hold of Til in case she tries something," said Tahl.

Huddling together, the four of them watched the magician slowly straighten her body and lie still for a little. She groaned and pushed herself up onto her elbow, shook her head slowly from side to side and gazed round the room.

Seeing Zara's body, she jerked herself to her knees, crawled across and laid her hand against the ashen cheek. With a gasp Zara sat up, and they helped each other to their feet. They stood for some while face to face, holding hands and studying each other in silence, like old friends who haven't met for many years. They were both very pale, but most of the stony look was gone.

At last Zara breathed a quivering sigh and smiled weakly.

"Are you much hurt, my dear?" she whispered.

"The worst pain I have ever known," said Lananeth. "But it's gone now. And you?"

"The same."

They fell silent, still looking at each other with the same amazed relief.

"But what happened?" asked Tahl. "Who is this, anyway? One moment he wasn't there, then he was, and then . . . Did Tilja do all that?"

"I do not know," said Lananeth. "I remember nothing since I came into this room."

"Nor I," said Zara. "Only the pain. Did you do this, child? Did you have any idea what you were doing?"

Tilja pulled herself together.

"I—I'm sorry," she stammered. "I ought to have asked. I—I just couldn't stand it like it was. It was all wrong."

"Yes, it was wrong," said Lananeth. "I fought against it still, but Varti was far too strong for me."

She gestured toward the body on the floor.

"This was Varti," said Zara. "He was North, most powerful of all the Watchers. My Lord Kzuva asked Lananeth to try to close the hills against all comers, which was beyond her powers, so she came to me for help. It was still too much for us, far too much. Then Varti came. He told us that if we all three joined our powers then we could do as My Lord asked. He had good reason, he said. There was a powerful, unknown magician at work in the Empire. This man had first destroyed the towers of the Watchers, and half the Watchers with them, and was now hunting down the rest. Varti hoped to close the hills against this enemy. So we agreed and between us we closed the hills, but Varti then possessed us, as you saw, until Tilja set us free. . . .What is happening?"

Tilja realized that the sounds from the antechamber, and beyond, had quietened. Now they broke out again in a wailing cry that rose and fell in slow pulses. Somewhere a deep gong began to sound, keeping time with the wailing. Lananeth had her hand to her mouth and a look of horror on her face. Zara was standing rigid. Her eyes were dull as pebbles. Then the light came back into them and she bowed her head.

"My Lord was building a tower for Varti, thinking it was for us," she said somberly. "It has fallen. My Lord was beneath it."

They stared at each other in dismay.

"We shall be blamed," whispered Lananeth. "Who else is there, if it was magic that destroyed the tower?"

Zara nodded somberly.

"We must go at once," she said. "You four also. Come."

She led the way out by a small door behind the hangings through which she and Lananeth had entered.

By the time they reached the bottom of the narrow stair that led down from the warded room, both magicians looked like menials of some sort, with different faces and wearing coarse clothing. Zara led them out through back passages. None of the frightened servants hurrying by questioned or even noticed them. They found the stables by the squeals of panicking horses. Some of them had broken loose from their stalls and were cantering wildly round the stable courtyard. Zara quietened them with a gesture, allowing Tilja to enter the stables, find Calico and lead her out. Tilja returned to the courtyard to find that the two magicians had each chosen one of the loose horses, which was now standing placidly beside her, unharnessed and unbridled. When Zara led the way on they followed as if on invisible halters.

As they crossed the bridge Tilja halted to fiddle with her shoe, sure that Tahl would stay with her.

"Whatever you've guessed, don't tell the other two," she whispered. "I think Lananeth and Zara have forgotten. Try not to think about it. It's dangerous, anyone knowing, even you."

He stared for a moment, then nodded. They hurried to catch up.

At the bend in the road from which they had first seen Lord Kzuva's palace they turned and looked back. The gaping hole into which the unfinished tower had fallen was invisible from where they stood, so the wonderful building seemed almost unchanged, apart from some tangles of smashed scaffolding in among the turrets and spires. The slow throb of the gong reverberated along the valley.

"He will never now set foot upon the Opal Stair," said Zara, as if speaking to herself.

"He wanted to do that too?" asked Tahl.

"Too? You have met with another?"

"There was a magician we hired for our convoy," said Tahl. "I think she knew you. She said that's what had happened to her Landholder."

Zara nodded.

"Every Landholder in the Empire has the same dream," she said. "Only some go about it with more patience than others. Yes, Aileth was my friend. Where did you meet her?"

"Our convoy captain hired her on the road five days south of Talagh," said Alnor. "She was going on north with the others when we turned off to come here."

"She has twice my powers, and she has come to that," said Zara, and sighed and shook her head. "Well, my friends, now we must leave you. You already have a warding round you, so that you are not noticed unless you choose to be, and I do not think you will be closely sought. But it is otherwise with us. Lord Kzuva's heirs will want vengeance for his death."

"That wasn't your fault," said Meena. "It was Varti's."

"Yes," said Lananeth, "but who will believe that? My life, and my husband's, and all his household are forfeit, so we must go to him, and go quickly. There are no other magicians of any power this side of the Pirrim Hills, so between us Zara and I can perhaps defend us all. And I would like to defend our people still against what is loose in the Empire, just as we did with Varti, though he was doing it for his own purposes."

"I doubt we will be strong enough for that on our own," said Zara.

"What about the magician we met on the road?" said Tahl. "Aileth, didn't you say her name was? She told Tilja that if there was work to be done, she would help."

"I will send to her," said Zara, "but now . . ."

"One moment," said Alnor. "We've been hoping to meet a magician somewhere on the road who'd help us to close our Valley off again, as it used to be. We were told whoever it is would find us on the road, but they haven't so far. Is it either of you?"

"It is neither of us," said Zara. "We do not have that kind of power. I do not know about Aileth."

Alnor turned to Tilja, an unspoken question in his eyes. And in Meena's too, now. Tahl was deliberately not looking at her, but she knew the same thought was in his mind.

"No," she said sadly. "It's supposed to be a man. Faheel talked about 'he.' "

"Well, good-bye, my dears," said Lananeth. "What has happened is no more your fault than it is ours, and if ever you return you will be welcome under my roof, if it still stands. But you must not come there now. Go straight to Salata. Her husband, Gahan, has returned. He knows the hills to the north, and will guide you as far as the old road to the forest."

They all said their farewells and then Zara and Lananeth moved a little way up the road, followed by the two horses. They turned and faced the animals head-on. The horses bowed their heads. The two magicians, Lananeth glancing from time to time at Zara, like an apprentice following a master through some unfamiliar task, placed their hands on either side of the long skulls and lowered their own heads until the brows, horse and human, touched. Tilja felt nothing, but Meena and the boys reeled with the rush of magic as the human shapes shimmered, faded and vanished. The horses swung round, switched their tails and raced away up the road while Calico whinnied with distress at their going.

17

The Forest Edge

In their haste to be home they made long marches, and in no more time than the shorter outward journey from El-lion's house had taken them they reached Salata's en-campment. She and her daughters ran to meet them, full of welcome, and then of confusion when Salata found not the Meena she knew and longed to thank, but a lively girl less than half her own age, so her thanks were confused and doubtful.

Her husband, Gahan, was a square, sturdy man who had been with his regiment in some western province at the time of the Emperor's death. Like most of his comrades he had taken advan-tage of the confusion to desert, and had made his way home through the turmoil that followed the fall of the Watchers, and come through the Pirrim Hills before the waking of the pines. On the way he had seen enough horrors and marvels to be able to accept anything, so he could thank Meena more simply. He said he would be glad to take them as far as the old road that the Em-perors had built before the sickness in the forest had closed the way north.

Salata told them that a third magician had already reached El-lion's house, and so it was safe from any attack for the time being.

"It can't be Aileth already," said Tahl. "She's right out on the Grand Trunk Road, and that's days and days away, even for a gal-loping horse."

"It must depend on the magician," said Tilja. "Faheel told me he could have gone to Talagh in an instant without me, and Zara said Aileth had twice her powers."

"You know what," said Meena slowly. "I'm getting a feeling about all this—what's been happening to us since we left the Valley. And before, I daresay. It's felt like just one thing after another, no connection, but it wasn't. It's been all connected, like it was *meant* to happen. And the same with those three women at Ellion's house. They haven't just come there all on their own. They're *supposed* to be there. I don't know what for, no more than they do, but that's what's happening."

"Why don't you ask your spoons?" said Salata. "I'd love to see them again."

Meena looked at her and sighed and shook her head. All the way north she had carried the spoons as before in the bag beneath her skirt. It would have been dangerous, of course, to try to use them, but she had never once even mentioned them. Partly, Tilja guessed, this was because they belonged in what Meena called her memory-room, and she didn't go in there except for some definite purpose; but also, perhaps, there was a kind of grief involved. Axtrig had been alive, like a person, an old, old friend of the family. They had called her "she." Now there was just this "it." The old friend was dead.

"Oh, please, Meena," said Salata's younger daughter. "I want Da to see."

Meena sighed again, shrugged and pulled out the bag, laid out the cloth and set the spoons on it. She picked up each of the darker ones and put them back, hesitated and picked up Axtrig. With another sigh she unstoppered the flask and rubbed a drop of oil onto the bowl. She laid the spoon down, leaned forward and concentrated.

"Yes," she whispered, "yes . . . just a little something . . ."

It was a long time before she straightened and put the spoons away.

"I don't know," she said. "It wasn't like when we were here before, clear as clear. It was more like it used to be in the Valley,

319

little bits of stuff you've got to decide what they mean. Anyway, far as I can make out, somebody's coming. Or something. And there's people waiting for him. Or her, or it, but somehow I think it's a him. Waiting in two places, it looks like, but . . ."

Her voice trailed off. Tilja bowed her head, trying to hide the shock of recognition. *The three magicians at Ellion's house*, she thought. *And me, here. And Meena and Alnor and Tahl. All waiting for the Ropemaker.*

And then, with a great surge of relief, *He's coming. He's alive. Moonfist hasn't found him yet. And I won't need to send for him.*

She felt the silence and looked up. Everyone's eyes were on her. Even the two dogs were staring. But there were differences. The bright look of interest in the dogs' eyes was just that, interest because they were aware of Tilja's being the center of attention. Salata and her daughters were simply puzzled by the reaction of their visitors to what Meena had said, or rather started to say and not finished. Tahl had his head bowed and was gazing steadfastly at his own clenched fists, but Alnor and Meena were staring directly at her, all with a look that said, *Now, surely, at last, you're going to tell us.*

"I . . . I . . . ," she began, and bit her lip and turned away. She didn't dare. All three were already far too close to the deadly knowledge. Soon, soon, the Ropemaker would be coming, and then they'd understand.

If Axtrig was right.

It was not yet dawn when they rose next morning and said goodbye to Salata. They reached the old road a little before dark, and there they built a fire and camped, Gahan staying the night to see them safely on their way next day.

The road wound north through barren scrubby hills. Despite its age, it was almost as easy going as the one they had traveled from Talagh, because the Emperor's engineers had put it in order less than three years earlier, when he had sent his army north to try to fulfill his vow to recapture the Valley. The bridges were sound and the wells and rain cisterns held water for an army on the march.

On the second afternoon they climbed a low pass and saw the dark mass of the forest stretching away east and west, in the full glow of its autumn color. Already there was a smell of winter in the wind. Beyond the treetops, a little above the horizon, or so it seemed, ran a wavering white line, and they knew that they were looking at the snowy peaks of the northern mountains. The sight made Woodbourne seem so near that Tilja felt that she could almost have reached out over the trees and stroked its roofs. The thought steadied her for what she had to do.

The wind, which for many days had blown dry and gentle from the east, had swung unnoticed to the north, and had a new feel to it, colder but softer. Above the snow peaks clouds were massing.

"Looks like we're in for a wet night," said Meena.

"We'll find a place to camp," said Alnor. "Then, if there's time before dark, we'll go a little way in among the trees and see whether Tahl and I feel the sickness."

"Best let me go in on my own first," said Meena. "See if I can find a cedar, tell me what's up."

"Take Tilja along," said Tahl. "It's just the sort of place bad stuff might be hiding. All right, Til?"

Tilja hesitated. Meena should be all right in the forest, surely. The trees were her friends. And she ought to stay with Tahl. He was their danger point. But once again she couldn't explain. *At least*, she thought, with something like relief, *this is the last time. Tomorrow I'll be able to tell them everything. If we're all four still alive.*

But perhaps it would be easier for Tahl if she wasn't anywhere near him, and he could think about something else.

"All right," she said.

"We'll build a shelter while we're waiting for you," said Alnor.

This turned out to be unnecessary. Shortly before they reached the trees they found several tumbledown buildings beside the road, temporary storehouses, they guessed, for the army that had come. Most were already ruinous, while those whose roofs were still sound were dark and rank with the stench of lairing beasts. Small creatures scuttled into hiding as they stood in the doorways.

"I'd sooner get wet," said Meena, turning away. "What's that over there?"

The strange little circular hut stood all on its own, well away from the road. It was walled on three sides but open toward the forest. Birds had roosted in the rafters and the floor was spattered with their droppings, but the roof was sound. At the center of the hut was a flat stone on which someone must have lit a small but intense fire, hot enough to redden and crumble the surface, though no ashes remained. They eyed it suspiciously.

"Anyone feel anything?" said Alnor.

"Nothing special," said Tahl.

"Looks like something's been going on here, but not that recent, judging by the mess," said Meena. "There was magicians came with the army, Lananeth told us. It'll be something to do with one of them. Why don't we just clean it out—we don't want to be doing that in the dark—but not move in here unless it comes on to rain? Then Tilja and me can have a go at the forest while you do your kick-fighting. And you may as well get stuff for a fire together, too."

There was, for once, a decent patch of grazing just below the hut, so Tilja hobbled Calico and left her with the boys while she and Meena returned to the old road and followed it to the edge of the forest, only to find that the place where it had entered the trees was an entrance no more. Three years ago the Emperor's engineers had started to hack a broad gouge into the forest, and had thus let in the light. Dormant seeds had sprung into growth all across the opening, even between the cobbles of the road itself. A mass of brambles tangled through the dense array of saplings.

"We'll not do any good here," said Meena. "And besides, if they've gone and cut everything down, where'll I find a cedar old enough to talk to me? They need to be a hundred years old and more before they start that, and a couple of hundred before they say anything worth hearing. There's got to be a way in somewhere along here. . . . Now look at that! What's been happening here? That's never woodmen who did that!"

They were now a little beyond the road, staring at a tangled jumble of smashed timber. Many great trunks had been snapped like twigs twenty feet above the ground. Trees that still stood had lost half their branches. Then, as they walked on along the edge of the forest, the damage ended as suddenly as it had begun and they could pick their way through the fringe of undergrowth to ancient standing woodland, like that above Woodbourne, shadowed leaf litter between the soaring trunks, with only here and there a shrub or smaller tree that could thrive in such darkness.

"What do you make of that?" said Meena, gazing back to the ruin they had passed. "That's never a storm did that, just all in one place. That's got to be magic, like I was saying back at the hut. Now, just stand still a moment, will you . . . ? Don't tell me there's none over this side . . . not a whisper . . . you'd've thought . . ."

"Can you tell where the lake is?"

"Should do . . . let's try a bit further on—maybe it's something to do with you. You just stay here . . ."

She ran off between the trees, halted a moment and waved to Tilja to join her.

"Got it," she said, pointing. "Still a long way off, though. I was right, too—I can't feel it now with you being so close."

"I didn't seem to do that to you that time we went to fetch Ma out of the forest."

Meena paused, frowning, while she went to fetch the memory from the other room.

"Wasn't the same, then. You've changed. Found yourself, if you know what I mean. There's a lot more to you now. And that'll be why I couldn't hear the cedars. So if you'll just keep a bit behind me . . ."

Again she ran off, but this time didn't stop until she turned aside and disappeared. Tilja found her standing at the foot of one of a group of enormous cedars, their boles as broad as haystacks, their spires way out of sight above the canopy. She watched while Meena laid her hands against the ridged red bark, bowed her head and stood motionless. After some while she straightened, turned and came slowly back. Tilja had never seen her, either young or old, look so stricken.

"Just mumbles and mutters," she said sadly. "Like when you wake someone up only they don't want to be woken. The magic's dying, Til. It's dying!"

"Perhaps they'll wake up when . . . What about the unicorns? Are they still there?"

"If they are, they're hiding. Ah, well, there's one way to find out. Let's go and fetch the boys in before it gets dark."

The answer came clearly. Barely twenty paces in under the trees Alnor stumbled and would have fallen if Meena hadn't caught him. Close behind them, Tahl halted, swaying, and closed his eyes, waiting for Tilja to turn him and lead him back into the open. Her touch seemed to have no effect on the sickness. Calico watched the proceedings with a bored sneer.

"That's the unicorns being so scared, and they've good reason," said Meena when they'd helped the boys out and settled them down to rest beside a small grove of sweet chestnuts that stood separate from the forest.

"You mean they were there? Somewhere close by?" said Tilja.

"Don't have to be," said Meena. "It fills the whole forest, what they're feeling. Maybe it's worse when something's happened to scare them, but they've no need of that just now. Like I say, they've reason enough without it. The cedars aren't talking, and what that means is the magic's dying out of the forest. Not just the sickness—that's worse than ever, like you've just seen, but it's not going to stay like that. Once the magic is gone, the unicorns can't live here anymore, and they know it. That's why they're so scared right now. And when they've gone the sickness will go too, and anyone will be able to come through the forest—soldiers, tax collectors, anyone. That's why we've got to get back, see it doesn't happen."

"There's got to be a way through," mumbled Alnor, lying with his head in Meena's lap. "We've both got to get back, he said, and he'd have known if I couldn't."

"Oh, there'll be a way all right," said Meena, running her fingertips along his bare forearm. "We just need to find someone who knows where it is."

She paused, and glanced sideways at Tilja.

"And tell us what to do when we get home," she added.

There was a silence. Tilja shrank into herself. Tahl was looking directly at her now, and didn't glance away when she caught his eye. Now that the moment had come, he had allowed himself to think it all through. He knew. She swallowed.

"All right," she said. "He told me not to tell you, in case . . ."

"Then don't," said Alnor.

"Only if there's anything we can do," said Tahl.

"You'll have to stay right away," said Tilja. "And . . . and if it goes wrong . . . he said it might . . . no, there won't be anything."

There was another silence.

"He told you to try this?" said Alnor.

"Yes . . . if . . . I can't tell you that either."

"Then it'll be all right," said Meena firmly. "If it's something you've got to do, you'd better get it over. And just smell that wind—it'll be raining in a couple of hours. You'd best take Calico. We'll stay here and look for chestnuts. Don't you worry about us. They're good honest trees, these. They'll look after us."

Tilja settled herself by the strange burnt slab in the little circular hut. She wanted privacy, secrecy, for what she had to do. Everywhere else was too exposed.

Ten seconds, she told herself. That should be enough.

Her fingers were covered with sweat as she rolled up her sleeve, unwound first the lashings that held the roc feathers in place and then the Ropemaker's hair from their quills. She slipped the feathers into the pocket of her blouse and laid the hair on the rock beside her. Then she hauled the box out, opened it, laid it down beside the hair and started to count to ten. At three the hair tie burst into flame. Instantly the flame was a raging blast of fire straining toward the forest. At the hut's edge it became a roaring gale. She could see the bushes outside being lashed about, and hear the crash and creak of falling timber mixed with Calico's squeals of panic. She smelled her own clothes and hair beginning to scorch in the heat, but felt nothing on her skin. The flame was a made magic and could not harm her. Grasping that knowledge, she forced her hand into the heart of the blast, found the box by touch and picked it up. The flame died instantly.

The Ropemaker's hair tie had vanished. The ring floated in blackness, as she'd first seen it. The box seemed untouched. She closed it, ran the cord round her neck and slid it in under her blouse.

Calico in her panic had tripped on her hobble and fallen. She was still struggling to her feet when Tilja found her. Shakily Tilja helped her up and stood with her for a while, soothing and calming her, and at the same time soothing herself with the homely feel of horse. Then she left Calico to graze and went and sat, in front of the hut, waiting, in a tangle of hope and dread, for the Ropemaker. Or Moonfist.

A wall of cloud was looming to the north—the rain must already be sheeting down at Woodbourne—but overhead the sky was clear, and the setting sun, hardly lower than when she had gone into the hut, colored the cloud mass with heavy purples and fringes of gold. Time passed. Nothing happened until Meena, Alnor and Tahl came cautiously up the slope, just as the last fiery streaks were dulling in the west. Meena had her skirt held up in front of her, full of the chestnuts they'd been collecting.

"Is everything all right?" said Alnor.

Tilja could hear the anxiety in his voice.

"I . . . don't know yet," she said. "I'm hoping someone will come and help us, but there may be other things. . . ."

"D'you want us to keep away still?" said Meena. "I don't fancy leaving you here alone in the dark."

"Nor us being away from you, either," said Alnor, "if that sort of stuff's going to happen. Let's get a fire going. We'll need it anyway if we're going to get the chestnuts roasted before it rains."

Nobody wanted to talk about what had happened or might still happen. Alnor used his tinderbox to light the dry branches that he and Tahl had already laid in while Meena and Tilja were in the forest. By the time it was fully dark the embers were hot enough for the chestnuts. They were fat and full of flavor, but Tilja could barely eat for tension. In her mind the conviction grew and grew that Axtrig had been wrong and the Ropemaker wouldn't come after all, would never come, because Moonfist had already found and destroyed him. And if Moonfist himself came . . . She felt utterly drained, certain that she would lack the strength to deal with him. When a chestnut popped or a burning branch collapsed, her heart leaped like a rabbit. And if anything beyond the circle of firelight stirred—a leaf, a settling bird—she froze with the hair on her nape erect while she waited for the intruder.

What came in the end was a little mouselike creature. She saw it first as a pair of glistening eyes at the edge of darkness. She froze. It crept forward, nose twitching. Now Meena saw it, and whispered to the others to sit still. Very slowly she leaned and crumbled part of a chestnut into the animal's path. It hesitated, then came on in short, nervous darts. When it reached the crumbs it sniffed at the largest one, picked it up between its forepaws, sat back on its haunches and nibbled rapidly. The fire-light sparkled off its fur. There was something odd about its movements, a kind of gawky deftness, as if it had not really been born as a whole mouse, but had been somehow assembled from several other mice. Like the unicorn, the dog, the lion . . .

You have eaten our food, Tilja thought. *Now you must deal well by us.*

She smiled and waited for what it would do next.

Without warning it turned and flipped away into the darkness.

Nobody said anything. For a moment she assumed they hadn't recognized the mouse-thing, and were waiting for it to re-cover its nerve and return. Then she became aware of their still-ness. She looked. All three were sitting rigid, gazing straight ahead of them, unblinking. At the edge of darkness she could see Calico, motionless.

Something moved on the far side of the fire. A man was stand-ing there, behind Alnor, watching them. She knew at once he was Moonfist. He came round the fire and faced her, looking down. She scrambled to her feet. He was about Da's age, but broader and shorter, and clean-shaven, not dressed in the fashion of the Empire, but wearing a soft cap, short cloak, jerkin and leggings, with a belt of large silver links at the waist. He carried a sturdy wooden staff with a leather bag tied to it at the top. There was nothing about him to tell her she should be afraid, but she was. Fear seemed to beam out of him. Fear held Meena and the others rigid in its nightmare. She was outside the nightmare. She could move and think. And be afraid.

He glanced at Alnor. Alnor jerked and strutted forward, stiff as a doll, and faced him. Moonfist studied him for a moment, then laid his hand on his shoulder. Instantly Alnor became a little mannikin, only a few inches high, dangling from Moonfist's hand. Moonfist slipped him into the leather bag at the top of his purse. He did the same to Meena, but when Tahl stood in front of him he paused.

"Too clever," he murmured. "Too clever for your own good."

He tapped him on the shoulder, put him in the bag and turned to Tilja.

"You have my ring," he said. "Give it to me."

"It isn't yours," she whispered.

"It is mine," he said calmly. "Faheel should never have had it. Give it to me."

"No."

"You destroyed Varti, who was last of the Watchers," he said. "All powers are now mine. I could destroy you, but choose not to. You will be useful to me. Give me my ring, and I will give you back your companions unharmed."

"No."

"Very well."

He glanced at the leather bag and it became a transparent globe, lit from within. The three mannikins were awake now, alive, looking around, seeing her, staring at her with terrified, pleading eyes. Moonfist glanced at the fire. A white flame shot up at its center and steadied, gently roaring. He gripped his staff by its lower end and swung the globe toward the flame. The mannikins shrank away from the heat, covering their heads with their arms. He stopped the movement and looked at her.

She put her hand into her blouse, drew out the box, opened it and took out the ring. Gripping it lightly between the forefingers and thumbs of both hands, like a priestess laying an offering on a shrine, she held it toward him. He reached out his cupped hand to accept it. At the last moment she let go with her left hand and snatched at a finger, while her right flung the ring into the darkness where the mouse had gone.

"Ramdatta!" she cried.

In the shadows something moved, began to explode. Then she was in darkness.

Again, but hopelessly, she sought the lake. She was still

holding Moonfist's finger. He strode beside her in the darkness, untroubled. She had to take him to the lake. She couldn't have let go, even if she had wanted, but she didn't. To take him was the only hope. If he was with her, with all his powers, he was not by the fire, and the Ropemaker would have a few moments more to find the ring.

They were there. In the starless blackness she could feel the icy wind sweeping down from the glaciers, hear the rattle of wavelets at her feet.

He stretched out an arm and called. Four heavy syllables. Four blows on a great gong, echoing and reechoing from the mountains. Avalanches slid bellowing toward the lake, and with a vast, sucking roar the water started to drain away, down through the chasm that Moonfist's cry had opened beneath it.

It was happening to her. Everything that was in her, everything that made her Tilja, thoughts, memories, loves, hopes, dreams, terrors, was draining away through the hand that held Moonfist's finger, into him, becoming part of him.

No, I will not, she thought. *I am Tilja, Tilja, Tilja, Tilja.*

There was nothing to hold to, nothing to stop the awful slither of herself into the man's otherness. She had to have something to hold to. Her free hand clutched uselessly at her own body, as though that would do, and brushed against the roc feathers in the pocket of her blouse. Yes, there! Not the actual feathers, not the memory of the roc, but the place, Faheel's island, where, while his unseen friends had danced their dance of farewell, she had discovered who and what she was, the innermost Tilja, her true self.

She seized the moment and clung to it, as she might have clung to a rock in a raging torrent. The outflow faltered, ceased. Moonfist turned toward her. She felt him summoning up further powers and knew that this was the end.

Everything changed. The finger she was grasping melted from her hand. With a shudder the chasm below the lake sealed itself shut. She felt warmth, heard the mutter of a human voice, opened her eyes and found herself swaying with exhaustion by the fire in front of the hut. Hands took her by the shoulders before she could fall and lowered her to the ground, where she crouched, shivering, her whole body bathed in sweat.

"Near thing," said the Ropemaker's voice. "Did it between us, just."

He was standing beside her, much as she remembered him, a skinny, gawky figure topped by his immense turban. A body lay at his feet. The head was away from her but she recognized the silver links of the belt chain. The hand that protruded from the sleeve beside it was fleshless bone.

Meena, she thought. *Alnor. Tahl.*

She looked toward the fire. Moonfist's staff lay half across it. The end to which the bag had been fastened was blackened embers.

Numbly, through her sobs, she was aware of being lifted, carried, set down. A voice spoke. She didn't take it in. She must stay where she was. He was going to do something. She was alone with her horror and grief, and the knowledge of failure. All useless. Alnor dead. Tahl dead. Meena, whom she loved more than anyone in the world, dead, horribly, horribly dead. Nothing else mattered. Nothing ever would.

Something changed. She didn't feel or hear or smell the change, but there was a sort of inward flicker, and the world was different, just as it had been when Alnor had spoken Faheel's name in Lananeth's warded room. She looked up. Through the gray blur of her tears she could see the entrance of the hut, but nothing beyond. She wiped her eyes. There *was* nothing beyond. The hut floated in grayness, lit by a vague light that came from nowhere. As she stared the grayness changed, becoming paler at the center and darker to either side. Faint shadows appeared in it, acquired dim shapes, five people standing in a group. The man on the left moved his arm and touched one of the others on the shoulder. That figure vanished. The man moved his hand and did something at the top of the staff he was carrying, then moved it back to touch the next figure. And the next. Now the girl on the right faced him alone, and Tilja understood that she was looking back out of one time into another, watching herself a little while ago confronting the magician she called Moonfist.

They stayed motionless. Tilja knew what they were saying, but could not hear the murmur of their voices. As the time she was watching came nearer to the time in which she watched, the figures became clearer. She couldn't breathe for the sudden intense hope and intense fear. Now, as Moonfist swung his staff toward the fire, she could see the transparent globe at its end. The movement paused. The girl moved her arms to draw something from under her clothing and offer it to the man. He reached to take it.

She saw the spasm of violent action, her own grab at his hand, her other arm flinging the ring into the darkness; heard, like a far whisper, her own cry, *Ramdatta!*; saw the staff toppling into the flame . . .

Now, Ropemaker! Now!

At the edge of the darkness on the right the Ropemaker exploded into his shape. His arm moved, flicking something toward the fire. The staff was twitched clear. The Ropemaker was bending, picking the ring up, sliding it onto his finger . . .

For a long moment he stood rigid, then turned and strode toward the motionless pair by the fire, locked in their desperate inward conflict. He seemed larger than he had been, no longer gawky and misshapen in his monstrous turban, but all of a piece, commanding, magnificent. Briefly he considered the magician, then raised his hands in a firm gesture and held them over the magician's face. Something invisible grasped Moonfist's body and battered him violently from side to side, like a terrier killing a rat. It let go. He collapsed and lay still.

The Ropemaker turned to the girl and far more gently made the same gesture. The invisible hands caught her as she crumpled and lowered her to the ground, where she crouched, hiding her face in her hands.

Tilja understood what she must now do. Sobbing with relief, she huddled down into the same posture as the girl. She heard the pad of the Ropemaker's feet on the hut floor, felt herself lifted and carried. The Ropemaker waited for the exact instant at which the time that he was in caught up with the stilled moment from which Tilja had been watching. When the two times became one he lowered her into herself.

She let her sobs die, rose and looked. The staff was lying beside the fire. The cord that the Ropemaker had used to twitch it clear was still wrapped round its shank. The globe lay well away from the embers. The three mannikins were standing up, waiting to be released.

"Got that box?" said the Ropemaker.

She drew it out and handed it to him. As he slid the ring off his finger and put it away he changed, shrinking to the odd, slightly clownish figure she was used to, but sagging with weariness. She looked at the globe.

"What about the others?" she asked. "Can you . . . ?"

"Your turn," he muttered. "I'm done for."

Uncertainly, feeling that all her powers were exhausted, she bent to pick up the globe. It vanished at her touch. She held out her spread hand to the mannikins. Each reached and grasped a fingertip. Between instant and instant they rose to their true size.

"Don't ask me to go through that again," said Meena, with a shuddering half laugh. "I really thought we were down to be toast. My, was I cross about it!"

18

Roc Feathers

"Is there anything else out there?" said Alnor, peering into the darkness. Even he was unable to conceal the horror in his voice.

"Nothing much left," said the Ropemaker. "Just small stuff. Won't bother us. Fellow there was the last."

He sounded just as exhausted as Tilja herself felt. The long, angular face was gray and lined.

She turned and gazed at the figure of Moonfist lying beside the fire. A skeleton. Yes, she thought, that was his real body, dead already, dead long ago. He had been even older than Faheel, so his real body had died. But by magic he had made himself a seemingly living body, and waited for the moment when Faheel gave up the ring and he could take possession of it. Then he would use it to do for himself something like Faheel had done for Meena and Alnor, bring his own young body, living, into the present, and when that in its time wore out do the same again, and again, forever. That was what Faheel had said couldn't bear thinking of. No wonder Moonfist had so wanted the ring.

"Who was he?" she asked. "Faheel told me a little about him, but he didn't know his name. I've been calling him Moonfist, because of the magic he used when he tried to get hold of Axtrig on the walls of Talagh. You saw it too, didn't you? You were the cat."

She'd taken him by surprise. He stared at her. She saw the other three stiffen, and guessed that he was putting up some kind of magical defenses, but felt nothing herself. Then he made a rueful grimace and relaxed.

"No use against you, anyway," he said. "Talk about it later. Moonfist, you say? That'll do. Don't know that much about him. Spent my time keeping out of his way since he showed up. Glad to see him gone . . . Ah well, let's get rid of him."

He drew a deep breath, squared his shoulders, gazed at the fallen body and muttered. The body crumbled to a pile of pale dust. He muttered again. A breeze sprang up, concentrated, became a swirling dust devil which danced across the clearing, picked up the ashes and swept them away in a swirl of dead leaves and other trash. The first huge drops of rain started to fall, laying the dust, cleansing the place with the sweet smell of damp earth, until the Ropemaker pointed out a circle around the fire and made a gesture of ending. Within the circle the rain stopped. He nodded and relaxed.

"Any chestnuts left?" he asked.

They settled round the fire in their own little patch of calm, while all around them the rain sluiced down and the wind battered to and fro. Tahl was bursting with questions, but none of the others felt like talking. Alnor sat with Meena, their arms round each other's waists, using their free hands to hold and peel the nuts and taking turns who ate them. The Ropemaker sat cross-legged, lost in thought, though every now and then his long arm would snake out as if of its own accord to take another chestnut, which then peeled itself at his touch. However many they ate, there always seemed to be a few left waiting to be roasted.

And Tilja relived her encounters by the lake, absorbing the horror of them and letting it go, until she could simply wonder at the strangeness of them, and her discovery of the size and power of the inward landscape that she had only just begun to explore. The lake must be the center of it, surely, but she felt that there were other places waiting for her to find, and creatures who lived in them, friends like Faheel's friends, an inward world, a world of power, whose measures were not our measures, whose times were not our time, just as her long and battering struggle with Moon-fist had been packed into a few of our instants, time for the Rope-maker to find the ring and come to her rescue.

There were dangers too in that world, she realized. You could lose yourself there if you let it happen. Deliberately she pulled herself out of her half trance, peeled a handful of chestnuts and took them to Calico, who was standing still half-asleep, apparently unaware that anything strange had happened, or that there was now a wall of rain rattling down just beyond her. She ate the chestnuts grumpily and gave Tilja no thanks.

"You must be the least magical horse in the world," Tilja told her fondly, and went and fetched her rug, rolled herself up in it and lay down by the fire.

She woke late next morning to the smell of roasting meat. The rain had cleared away and the whole world sparkled. The fire was glowing hot. Meena had spitted the body of a small animal on a stick and was twisting it to and fro over the embers. Alnor was skinning and gutting another. Tahl was looking for dry firewood. The Ropemaker had vanished, but almost at once a heavy wing beat broke the silence and a large orange bird settled into the clearing with the body of a hare grasped in its talons. It dropped its burden beside the fire, strutted to the hut and pecked at one of the coils of cord that lay by the entrance to the hut. Rapidly the cord wove itself into a string bag. The bird glanced at Tilja with a mocking eye and heaved itself clumsily into the air. When it next came back the bag was full of sweet yellow plums.

"Couldn't you just have made us a magic breakfast?" asked Tahl.

The Ropemaker chewed for a while at the tough hare meat, and swallowed.

"Enjoy hunting," he explained. "You're an animal, do what it does best. Good sport. Besides . . ."

He glanced enquiringly at Tilja.

336

"I don't know," she said.

"Find out?" he suggested, and held out his hand. An earthenware platter appeared between his fingers, piled with dark brown biscuits. He handed them round. The others crunched theirs up and reached for more, but the one Tilja tried to take vanished at her touch. *No*, she told herself. *Not this time, please*. It made no difference.

"Do you think I could learn not to do that?" she asked.

He shrugged, then smiled at her surprise.

"Don't know all that much about any of this," he said ruefully. "Better explain."

Slowly, his jerky manner of speech still further interrupted while he chewed, he told them his story. He had been born in an isolated village far out on the eastern coast. The food was fish and edible seaweed, but very occasionally somebody found a pearl and became rich enough to leave. From the first he had hated the life, knowing he was different, though he didn't yet know how. To get away, he had apprenticed himself to a traveling ropemaker. This man knew a few simple magics, bindfasts and so on, which the Ropemaker had learned—"Picked 'em up as if I knew 'em already," he said. "Knew at once this was what I wanted, what I was *for*."

From there he'd simply gone on, talking to anyone he could. He'd met a young woman who knew about wards and could turn herself into a cat, and with her he'd experimented and started to piece things together until they'd attracted the attention of one of the eastern Watchers, who had then sent a horrifying sending to scare them off. It had worked with the woman, but it had merely excited the Ropemaker. He had managed to track it to its source, and so come to Talagh.

Once there, he'd spent most of his time not getting picked up by the Watchers, but in the process he'd learned about the lost province to the north, and the magic forest that defended it against the most powerful magicians the Emperor could send. This, of course, had made him want to go and find out for himself, with the added notion that if he came up with an answer he could return to Talagh and win the Emperor's favor, and so be admitted to the innermost magical secrets of the Empire.

The forest had fascinated him. It was a different sort of magic from any that he'd come across before. For a long while it had simply baffled him, but he had refused to give up. Then, in a flash of intuition ("Don't know how I do that," he said. "Happened before. Things just come to me.") he'd realized that the magic had something to do with unicorns, and had decided to try to turn himself into a unicorn in order to get into the forest.

"Don't tell me you were that dirty great unicorn!" Meena burst in. "What did you think you were up to, scaring our own little wretches that way? And doing what you did to my daughter Selly by the lake? What harm had either of them done you?"

He spread his hands in apology.

"Mistake," he explained. "Made a lot of them in my time—bound to, doing it all on my own. Never tried that before, being a magical animal. Took a lot of doing. Then, once you're there, different. Let's say you're a mouse, you think mouse and feel mouse—quick, scared, inquisitive—but you're in control. Mouse does what you want, spite of the mouse bit. Magical animal—unicorn anyway—haven't tried dragons—if you don't watch out, it takes over. Happened to me. Knew what I wanted—to get your unicorns out—forgot why. Tried doing it unicorn fashion, scaring 'em out, stopping your daughter feeding 'em. Didn't work with her, and I'd felt bad about it, under all the unicorn stuff. Didn't try again. But I was still stuck there, being a unicorn, when you came by on your raft.

"Saw you, but wasn't interested. Only interested in the unicorns. Then Meena there started her singing. Wasn't singing to me, of course, just to the little white fellows on the far side of the canyon, telling 'em what you were up to, going out into the Empire to find this man who'd make their forest right for 'em again. But it did the trick, reminded me what I was there for, just enough to get myself clear of the forest and stop being a unicorn—and was that a palaver!

"Followed you down, of course. Meena's song had told me you knew some of the stuff I was after. So I was hanging outside Lananeth's window, just clear of her wards, minding my own business, being a bat and listening to what you were saying, when Meena there pops out with some fellow's name—Faheel, right? Never heard of him before, but bang, I'd lost my shape and fallen into a rosebush. Cut me to ribbons—never noticed. Got to know about *that*, I was thinking."

His braying laugh shattered the morning silence.

"So you followed us to Talagh," said Alnor. "And on the way you arranged for the bandits to kidnap us in the Pirrim Hills, so that you could make our acquaintance."

"Not like that. They'd a spy at the way station—spotted you for fourteen graders—going to cut you out anyway—not difficult, convoy all strung out, but one of you might've got hurt. Better arrange for it myself. Worked out all right, didn't it?"

"You mean we wouldn't have got to Goloroth without you?" said Tilja. "You were the dog that woke Tahl and Alnor up when we landed from the raft, and the cat on the walls of Talagh, and the donkey in the way station when Silena came, and then the lion at Goloroth."

He nodded as she named each creature.

"Ah," he said. "Suppose this Faheel told you, so you spotted me for the mouse. Told you my name, too, did he? Been wondering about that."

"Yes, and I saw you change into the lion when Faheel was fighting the Watchers at Talagh."

Again he stared at her in astonishment, then shook his head and dragged on his chin, grinning ruefully.

"Lot I don't know," he said. "Look, I'll finish off, then you tell me your side. Keep things straight that way. Right?"

Yes, he said, he'd been able to follow Tilja all the way because she'd been wearing his hair tie. He'd been the cat on the walls of Talagh and done what he could to stop Silena finding them in the tower, but he wouldn't have been a match for her and she'd have broken through his screen if Dorn hadn't arrived. And yes, he'd been the donkey at the way station, and though Tilja had done most of the work, when Silena had lost her powers they had somehow settled into him. He hadn't been expecting that at all, but the same thing had happened when he and Tilja, between them, had destroyed Dorn. He had come out of the barn at Goloroth far stronger than he had gone in.

Then, knowing he couldn't follow Tilja and the others to Faheel's island, he had returned to Talagh, with the idea that he might be taken on as a Watcher in Dorn's place, now that he possessed Dorn's powers, and so watch for the travelers' return. He'd been accepted for the post, but realized almost at once that it was a mistake. This wasn't what he wanted, at all. Quite the opposite.

"That was why Faheel came—to stop you becoming a Watcher," said Tilja. "He said you'd be lost if that happened, and he wanted you to have the ring."

"Got to ask you about that," he said. "Better finish first."

He hadn't dared try to back out. The Watchers now knew of his existence, and if he refused to join them they would destroy him, sooner than let someone with his powers loose in the Empire. So he'd decided to go through with the installation ceremony and then leave when he got the chance. The chance had come sooner than he'd expected, at the ceremony itself, but then he'd been too fascinated by what was happening to leave at once. Only when the darkness had started to gather behind the tower from which Faheel was working did he recognize the peril and make a bolt for it. Since then he'd been in hiding, knowing that a very powerful magician was roaming the Empire systematically destroying all possible rivals.

"Thought it was the same fellow that had done for the Watchers," he said. "Couple of things didn't fit, mind, but that was the best I could make of it. But if it was your friend Faheel did for the Watchers, and then this other fellow—Moonfist—sneaked in and did for him . . . yes . . ."

340

"He knew about the ring," said Tilja. "In the story we tell in the Valley, Faheel himself knew about it while Asarta still had it. He'd been trying to take it from her for three hundred years. So when Asarta used people from the Valley to take it to Faheel he decided to seal their knowledge of the ring inside the Valley. He told me that himself.

"But Moonfist knew already. He'd been trying to get hold of it too, and he thought Asarta should have given it to him. He's been waiting all these years for when Faheel had to pass it on to someone else. He must have recognized the power in Axtrig and attacked the walls to try and get hold of her, but then he lost her again because I was holding her, and the same with the ring on the way back, right up until Tahl guessed I'd got it. Moonfist felt that—Faheel said he might—and came."

The Ropemaker sat nodding slowly, thinking about it.

"Right," he said at last. "Now one more thing. Why me? Ignorant fisherboy—clutching at straws, eh?"

"No. It was realizing you'd managed to turn yourself into a unicorn that decided him. But really he was interested the moment I told him you were a Ropemaker. . . . He said time was a great rope."

"That's right," said Tahl excitedly. "I've often thought of that. Millions of twisting threads, all holding each other in place. You can see back along it, not forward. There must be a sort of mist. But it goes on beyond. Forever."

"That's about it," said the Ropemaker.

"If you could change one thread, you'd change everything," said Tahl.

"Right," said the Ropemaker. "Went back last night, for instance, two, three minutes only, fiddled with a thread, let me pull you three clear of the fire, that's all. But more than I could chew, almost. Out beyond where I could see, felt the whole rope bucking and heaving around, all of time to come weaving itself fresh. Had to hang on, all my strength, to what I'd got fixed this side, stop it being messed up by stuff happening beyond, till it went

341

and calmed down. Only just made it. Rocked me, that did, badly. Lucky to get back out."

He shook his head again, remembering the struggle. No wonder he was so exhausted last night, Tilja thought. Both of us. Only just made it. But given those two or three changed minutes, Alnor and Meena were alive instead of dead, and could go back to the Valley and remake the old magic, and all time to come would be different, utterly different.

"Your turn now," he said. "Anything you know—any of you. Going to need it."

It took them until well into the afternoon to finish, breaking off at midday to rest and eat. The Ropemaker turned some of the breakfast scraps into a succulent meal, and a twist of dried grass into a pile of juicy hay for Calico, who munched it as if it had been only her due, which perhaps it was. Tilja ate what was left of the scraps. She barely noticed.

She was thinking about the story. Inevitably she had done most of the talking. She had a strange feeling that it was all there coiled inside her—every minute of every day, every word spoken, every breath breathed, almost—ready and waiting for her to reel it out. She wondered if perhaps this was something else Faheel had arranged. There had been this great strange beast called the Empire. Now it was mad and sick and dying. Only the Ropemaker had the power to heal it, which was why he had to have the ring. But as well as the ring he needed to understand the causes of the sickness. That was what the story was for.

Tahl butted in from time to time, but Alnor didn't try to take over, and Meena too said less than she might have. Neither of them, Tilja guessed, much enjoyed staying longer than they had to in their memory-rooms, reminding themselves of what they had once been, and soon would be again. Only when they reached the point at which the two of them had become their young selves did all four really share the telling round. Even then, somehow, the story held to its shape and purpose.

The Ropemaker interrupted very little, sitting with his head bowed, his long, bony fingers absentmindedly spinning wisps of grass into a fine silk tassel. Once or twice he asked a question about one of the other magicians they had met, but that was all. When it was over he tied a twig to the knot of the tassel and it became a short ivory rod. He rose and stretched, blowing out a long breath.

"Been a near thing," he said. "Lot of luck around. Worked out all right in the end. Now what? Got an empire to put to rights, you tell me. Get you home first, though. Still have that bread and water?"

Meena undid her pack and fished out the barley roll she had baked all those months ago. It was battered and shrunken with age, but the moment the Ropemaker's long fingers touched it it seemed to swell, and the air was filled with the aroma of fresh baking. He broke off a corner and munched with gusto, then took the flask that Alnor handed him and drank from it before passing both offerings back, smiling and shaking his head.

"They'll do," he said. "Given them a bit of a stir-up. Not what matters. Give me your hand, Meena. You too, Alnor. Take each other's. Right."

Tahl shifted aside so that Alnor could move to complete the triangle. They sat in silence for a short while and then, without a word, let go.

"Yes, I see," said Alnor solemnly. "Asarta's magic isn't really in the bread and the water, not any longer. They're just tools we use, so to speak. But the true magic is in ourselves, in our blood, renewing and renewing itself through the generations. Twenty generations after Asarta, and twenty more after Faheel, and now another twenty to come."

"Can't say that yet," said the Ropemaker. "You've still got to make it happen, you two, Meena in the forest, Alnor in the mountains."

"First we have to get me there," said Alnor.

The Ropemaker nodded and fell silent, stroking his long chin.

"Problem," he said. "Can't get you through the forest without messing up what Meena's got to do. Not sure I could, anyway—still got a lot to learn. So . . ."

He stared out over the trees, frowning with concentration. The whole landscape seemed to fall still, sucked into the intensity of his thought. His raucous laugh split the silence.

"No way through," he said with a naughty-boy grin. "Not that I know. Different sort of magic. But . . . roc feathers, right? Let's have 'em."

A little reluctantly Tilja took the feathers out of her pocket and gave them to him. He ran them gently between his fingers as if he were stroking a small creature, and they sparkled with the true fiery look of the living roc.

"Nice," he whispered, and pursed his lips into a silent whistle. Tilja heard a rustle and caught a movement out of the corner of her eye. She looked, and saw Calico's tether undoing itself, and then Calico came nosing over, looking for once interested in what was happening around her. The Ropemaker plucked a grass stem and rubbed a few seeds out of it into his palm. He closed his hand and opened it, and the seeds were a fistful of wheat. When he poured them onto the ground they became a small pile, which didn't seem to grow any less as Calico lowered her head and munched away.

"Going to need the muscle," he said, as if he were explaining something.

He took the roc feathers and gently slid the quills into Calico's hide, just behind the shoulders on either side, with the plumes lying along her back. He stroked them again, and Calico shrugged herself and switched her tail as though a fly were bothering her. The feathers began to grow. Smaller ones sprouted on either side, and became fledgling wings, which, without her apparently noticing what was happening to her, she twitched and spread and shook into place as they grew and grew. Her sagging spine straightened to a shallow curve, muscles swelled and twitched beneath a suddenly glossy hide. When she raised her head there was a proud arc to her neck and a light in her eye. She whinnied with what sounded like excitement.

"That's more like it," said the Ropemaker, punching her on the shoulder. "No, you don't!" (as Calico twisted to snatch at his arm). "Born cussed, die cussed, eh?"

He slapped her back and there was a saddle there, with a flap behind for a second rider.

"All set," he said. "Up you get, then, young fellows. Wings out of the way, old lady."

Calico snarled, but raised her great pinions clear of her flanks, moving them easily, as though she'd had them since she was a foal. But she had grown by a couple of hands or more, and Alnor was too proud to be helped into the saddle. Meena didn't help by crowing with laughter as he hopped around trying to heave himself up, until something invisible seemed to give him a boost and he could sit and stare arrogantly ahead of him, the young warrior prince ignoring the jeers of the rabble. Tahl, sensibly, let the Ropemaker lift him into place. When Calico laid her wings flat they covered the riders' legs. The Ropemaker handed Tahl the tasseled rod.

"Bit of trouble back home, you told me," he said. "May need this. Time comes, give it a shake. Right, then, off you go, old lady."

He slapped Calico on the rump. She sat back on her haunches, spread her wings and sprang into the air, with Alnor clinging inelegantly to her mane and Tahl's arms round his waist. Calico seemed to know exactly what to do. They watched her pounding upward until she found a thermal and could soar, circling round and round until she looked like no more than an unusually large bird spiraling in the evening sunlight.

"That tassel," murmured the Ropemaker, still staring upward. "Bit of stuff I picked up from Dorn when he went. Keep an eye on the lad, Tilja. Can't tell what it might do to him."

At last Calico broke from the spiral and arrowed north.

19

The Lake

"Men get to ride, women have to walk, then?" said Meena, pretending to sulk about it.

"Looks like it," said the Ropemaker. "Start in the morning, sleep in a tree, home for supper tomorrow. Get yourselves an appetite for it."

"What are you going to do?" asked Tilja.

"Have to think. Don't like the look of any of this. Not my sort of thing. Stuck with it, though. This woman you told me about—said she'd help . . ."

"That's right, Aileth," said Meena.

"Have a word with her, for a start. Going to take a while . . ." He fell silent, gloomily rubbing his long chin.

"Suppose I came back one day—" Tilja began, hesitantly.

"You want to?" he interrupted.

"I don't know. I've been thinking about it. I want to go and stay with Meena for a bit, but . . ."

"Go on—say it," said Meena brutally. "I'm not going to last forever in that old carcass."

She managed somehow to speak in the exact fierce tone she might have used before she had eaten Faheel's grapes. It sounded appalling coming from those young lips. Tilja put her arm round her and hugged her and held her close, more for her own comfort than for Meena's. She could hardly speak.

"I'm going to stay with you, I promise," she croaked.

"No, you're not—not if you're needed here, soon as you're old enough. I've been watching you changing, Til, more than you realize, I daresay. It's like he was saying about his magic when *he* started—it was what he was for. It'll be a waste of you, having something like what you've got in the Valley, where there's nothing for you to do with it. It'll eat into your heart, knowing what you could be doing. Right, aren't I—like it would be for you, mister, not being able to do your magic?"

Through her tears Tilja could see the lean face of the Ropemaker watching her. He nodded slowly.

"And you'd like her back, wouldn't you?" Meena insisted. "She'd be a bit of use to you?"

He nodded again.

"Mind you, if you could do something about this leg of mine I'm going to have when I get home," she suggested. "And if Alnor could see right . . ."

Oh, yes! Tilja thought. Why hadn't she . . . but the Ropemaker was shaking his head sadly.

"Not up to it," he said. "Like to help, but . . . mean messing around with time again. Don't know enough, not yet. You two, you're young now—don't know how he did that—tweaked something, somehow, way beyond me. Be in the rope somewhere—daren't touch it, not till it's finished. Tricky, don't you see?"

"I suppose so," said Meena with a sigh. "Well, we'll just have to make the most of what we've got, as usual. You're leaving us, then."

"Better. Stuff happening in the Pirrim Hills. Pines aren't holding it—not since what you did at Lord Kzuva's palace. Gets through, those three ladies are going to have their work cut out. Give 'em a hand, maybe. Got to start somewhere, eh? This bit's under control—try and keep it that way, then move on. Just do a spot of hunting for you first, right. Back soon."

With a twist of his wrist he unloosed his turban. His amazing hair shot out round him in a swirling cloud that shrank, thickened, became beast-shaped and solidified into a gaunt angular creature, somewhere between a fox and a wolf, but with a fiery orange hide. It grinned at them, its long tongue lolling from between savage jaws, and loped into the dusk.

While they waited they fetched water from the old cistern and rebuilt the fire. By the time it was truly blazing the creature was back, dragging the body of a small deer over its shoulder. It laid it down, shook itself like a dog shaking water out of itself, but instead of a spatter of droplets it shook out the same swirling cloud as before, which then gathered itself back into the shape of the Ropemaker. He took out a hunting knife and deftly gutted, skinned and jointed his prey, then sliced the liver for Meena and Tilja to roast on pointed sticks while he lashed a spit together so that they could turn the larger pieces over the heat.

When they had eaten, the Ropemaker rose, belched and stood looking down at them. The firelight flickered off his bony features. For once he looked like what he really was, a man with immense, strange powers.

"Needn't keep watch," he said. "Put a fence round you. Don't you touch it, Tilja—won't stand that. Sleep well. Good luck."

He vanished.

"And the same to you," said Meena to the space where he had been.

They woke at first light. Meena rose and groped her way blearily toward the nearest bushes, but stopped in midstride. Tilja saw her push with her hands against empty space.

"Wait a moment," Tilja said, and walked up beside her, and on, feeling only the slight, indescribable flicker of a piece of structured magic falling apart. Meena, still pressing against the unseen obstacle, almost fell over.

"Might've warned me," she grumbled, and stumbled on. In the early mornings she was always most like old Meena, sulky and hazed with sleep.

———

The sun had barely risen when they made their way into the forest by the same route as before, and then walked and scrambled and walked all morning. At first it was worryingly slow going. Though Meena could sense the general direction, she didn't of course know any exact route, in the way that she had known the route from Woodbourne to the lake. Sometimes they could walk side by side over almost level ground, between majestic old trees that soared up, branchless for thirty feet or more, with a leaf canopy above dense enough to inhibit undergrowth. Here they could talk, or sing for the pleasure of it. But then they would reach a place where a patch of even older trees had been struck down by some winter gale, knocking their neighbors over in their fall, leaving an impenetrable barrier of tangled trunks and branches. Or else the ground would become more broken and they would find themselves trapped at the bottom of a narrowing valley ending in crags too steep to climb, and they would have to turn back and look for another route.

Around midday they had just made their way dispiritedly out of such a place when Meena halted and peered at the ground, moved to her left, peered again and knelt.

"See there?" she said, pointing at a patch of bare earth.

Tilja knelt beside her to look. The print was very faint. It was extraordinary that Meena should have noticed it at all. Not slotted, like a deer's. Too small for a horse. Anyway, a horse here? . . . No.

"A unicorn," she whispered. "How did you . . . ?"

"Felt something," said Meena. "They've been here—not just once, neither, or I wouldn't've noticed. It's one of their paths. Must go somewhere. Let's hope."

She rose and walked on, slowly at first, but then more confidently. After a while she started to sing, not any known song, such as they had been singing together earlier, but the same almost shapeless, wavering, quiet chant that Tilja had last heard her singing when the raft had been floating down the canyon and

Meena had sat with Alnor's head in her lap and sung to the unseen unicorns among the trees. The invisible path wound to and fro, weaving past the obstacles that had so held them up that morning, but steadily—Meena said—heading toward the lake.

Nothing else happened all day. Tilja found it very wearisome—not the hours of walking—she was used to that after all these weeks—but the endless, dull sameness of trees, the shadowy stillness, with never an open vista, never a glimpse of sky, and besides that an even vaguer oppression which after a while she guessed must be coming from the forest itself. She had never felt it at Woodbourne, but there she had only twice gone deep in among the trees, and both times she had been too taken up with surface events to think about her own feelings. Moreover, since then she herself had changed, grown, become aware of what she was and what she could do, and with that had come a greater awareness of things she might not have noticed before. So, now, just as in the pinewoods in the Pirrim Hills, she knew that she was sensing the magic of the forest itself. This time, though, it was not trying to overwhelm her. It was simply there, pressing in against her, a different kind of magic from any that she could deal with, diffuse and huge.

One of Faheel's friends, she wondered? She didn't think so. It didn't feel like anybody's friend, and didn't respond when she tried, in her mind, to tell it about Faheel. It was itself.

She would have liked to talk to Meena about this, but Meena didn't want to talk. She wanted to sing. She actually said as much when Tilja spoke to her during one of their rests.

"No, leave me be, love. I'm just about getting through to them, maybe."

She was talking about the unicorns, Tilja guessed, or perhaps the cedars. There was no way she could help with that, except by not interrupting. All she could do was trudge wearily on.

Sleep in a tree, the Ropemaker had suggested. The trees were not of the sort you could climb, but they managed it in another way. Toward dusk they came to a cedar grove where something, lightning, perhaps, had riven one of the old giants apart all down one side but left it standing. The crack was wider and deeper at the base, leaving a small cave in the heart of the trunk. Beasts must have laired in there from time to time. There were a few bears in the forest, and solitary wolves, and other hunters, but none, by the smell, had been there recently. They broke and dragged fallen branches to the place and built a crude barrier across the entrance—nothing that would keep a hungry bear out but enough at least to make it wake them as it demolished the obstacle.

The floor inside was soft and dry, and Tilja was tired enough to fall into deep and friendly sleep as soon as she lay down. She was dragged out of her dream by Meena squeezing her arm.

It was pitch dark, but she knew at once where she was. Meena squeezed again, gently, and Tilja moved her other hand and touched Meena's to show that she was awake, and then lay still, listening. She wasn't afraid—there had been nothing alarmed or urgent about the way Meena had woken her—but something was moving around close outside. Then a completely familiar noise, somewhere between a snort and a snore—a horse. Out here in the depths of the forest? Calico come back to take them home? A likely tale—and anyway Calico's snort would have been much deeper and more disgruntled. This was light, interested, inquisitive . . . and now, staring out at the darkness above the barrier, Tilja began to imagine she could see a faint change in the color of the night, like moonlight—only there could be no moon. It had been rising, fingernail-thin in the east, when they had woken that morning.

The noises moved away. Meena gave a sigh of pleasure.

"Lovely," she whispered.

"Do they really shine in the dark?"

"You saw it too? I thought I was imagining it. And the cedars are waking up, too. I can hear them beginning to mumble."

They slept again and woke in the dim forest daylight, cleaned themselves up and ate the last of their food to save carrying it, and then set out with lighter hearts. They walked steadily all morning, without feeling the need to rest. Meena sang almost all the way, more loudly than the day before, and mixing in bits of ordinary song, just as she had done on the raft, so that Tilja could now join in and carry on to the end of the song while Meena's voice, after a line or two, went floating away into the cedar song, weaving in and out through Tilja's tune.

She was halfway through "Cherry Pits" when she saw her first unicorn.

Still singing, Meena nudged her elbow and glanced to the right, a gesture and look that said, *Over that way, but don't stare.* Cautiously Tilja half turned her head and out of the corner of her eyes caught a flicker of whiteness in the shadows. It vanished and came back and this time for a moment she saw it clearly, moon-white against the dark depths of the forest, small as a child's pony, with a flowing mane and tail, but straight-backed and light-boned as a deer, the arched neck carrying the head high, to balance the weight of the ivory horn. Then it seemed to sense her astonished gaze and twitched itself out of sight among the tree trunks.

Soon another appeared on the left, and this time she was careful only to glance and glance away, and it stayed there, moving along with them, coming and going among the tree trunks. The first one reappeared, and a mare and foal joined it, and then more, so that after a while there was a troop of them on either side, a line of that unearthly whiteness threading its way through the forest.

For a long while Tilja was so absorbed in wonder that she was barely listening to Meena's singing. At last she heard it, one particular note like a cry of pain, except that it was a pure sung note, wild as birdsong, throbbing with joy. She turned and stared. Meena's cheeks were streaming with tears. She couldn't possibly see the faint tracks they had so far been following, but her feet seemed to know the way.

The forest ahead grew darker and became a solid wall of

cedars, much younger than the giants they had been passing, with interlacing branches sweeping to the ground, impenetrable except at one narrow opening that became a winding path barely wide enough for the two of them to walk side by side. Now Tilja guessed where she was, though the path seemed different from the one along which she and Dusty had wrestled with the logging sledge almost a year ago. Glancing over her shoulder, she could see no sign of the unicorns, but Meena hadn't faltered in her song so she knew they must still be there, following, out of sight beyond the last bend. Round yet another corner lay the lake, still as a sheet of steel. The grassy clearing where they had found Ma was a short way off to their right.

Still singing, Meena stopped and turned, holding her spread hands in front of her as if she was asking for some special favor. Tilja understood the gesture at once. This was not for her—she was an intruder. This was for Meena. But she could stay and watch, or Meena wouldn't have let her come as far as the lake. She turned and scrambled away beneath the branches beside the water, found a comfortable place with a good view of the clearing, and sat down.

Meena had almost reached the arena. The air was so still that whispers of her song came floating across the water, and when she halted and turned to face the lake Tilja could hear it clearly.

This seemed to be what the unicorns had been waiting for. One after another they emerged from the opening and paced solemnly along beside the lake, moving not like ordinary animals, tame or wild, but like a team of dancers entering to begin some stately dance. There were twenty-three of them, and the single foal. Their reflections gleamed, perfect, in the unruffled surface.

They gathered in a wide circle around Meena and stood and waited. Her voice had dropped so low that Tilja could no longer hear it as Meena sank to the ground and spread her arms in a gesture of welcome. The unicorns came right up to her and lay down, without any jostling, but arranging themselves in two exact rings, their bodies spreading out like the petals of an open flower. Tilja understood that she was watching something wholly magical, not the man-magic of Talagh, or of the ring, but the kind of magic by which Faheel had made friends with mountains and with oceans. She was filled with delighted amazement that she, Tilja, whose touch could undo powerfully woven charms and destroy great magicians, was allowed to watch this happen.

After a long while the song ended. Meena bowed her head. The unicorns backed away into their circle and returned to her, one at a time. Each lowered its horn and touched her above the heart. She in her turn laid her fingers on each muzzle, both gestures clearly blessings of farewell. The foal came with its mother, seeming to know exactly what to do. Its horn was about as long as Tilja's middle finger.

When they had finished they turned and came just as solemnly back along the lake, but before they reached the opening something seemed to startle them. They bolted and were gone. Meena hadn't moved. She was sitting as before, with her head bowed, deep in her trance. She didn't look up when Anja appeared running along the far side of the lake, shouting excitedly. A moment later Ma came out of the trees, leading Tiddikin by the bridle. Tilja ran, and met them on the other side of the clearing.

"The cedars told us!" cried Anja, gasping for breath every few words. "They've woken up! I heard them talking. So did Ma! They said we'd find you by the lake, and we did! Are you all right? Da's gone to fight the horse people! Calico came back! She's got *wings*! She's gone too! And those boys! Where's Meena? What's that girl doing by *our* lake?"

Tilja didn't answer, but gave her a hug and kiss and ran to meet Ma. Ma knelt and held her tight, both of them sobbing quietly. Her hug was as awkward as ever.

"Oh, I'm so happy to see you!" Tilja said as soon as she could speak. "Is Da all right? The river told us the pass was open and there'd been fighting in the Valley."

Ma let go, rose and dried her face on her skirt. "Horsemen

came through the passes, just like we said they would. People always start to believe you when it's too late. Da's gone to help try and fight them back, of course. That was ten days ago. We've been coming up to the forest every day to see if the cedars had anything to tell us, but they've been asleep, oh, almost since you left. And then this morning they started to wake up, just mutters and mumbles at first, but—Anja can hear them better than I can, and she swore they were saying you and Meena were coming back through the forest."

"Nothing about the fighting?"

"No, but . . . I suppose that's Meena, over there?"

She asked the question so matter-of-factly that Tilja blinked. Then she remembered what Anja had said and realized that if you've seen what you know to be a cantankerous brute of a horse come flying into your farmyard, ridden by two boys, one of whom you last saw as a blind old man, then it mightn't be hard to believe anything, let alone work out what had happened to Meena. Anja must have made the connection too, she now saw. She was kneeling beside Meena, bombarding her with questions, giving her no time to answer, and Meena had her arm round her and was laughing aloud.

Tilja had no idea how Ma's meeting with Meena would go. It must be very strange for both of them, she guessed, even stranger than it had been for Tilja herself, finding her grandmother had become a sort of elder sister. They stood and looked at each other for a while; then Meena stretched out her hands and Ma took them and they kissed each other gently.

"I suppose I've got a third daughter now," said Ma.

"If you like," said Meena, laughing. And then, still laughing, but with a note of the old sharpness beneath the words, "You'll have to make the most of it, *Ma*. Soon as Alnor comes back and we've done what we've got to, I'll be telling you what's what again, like always."

20

Home

It was sunset when they came out of the forest, a fiery sky to the west, and a soft pink light glinting off the northern snow peaks. Tilja stopped and gazed down at the long-loved farmstead. It looked shuttered and dark and still. All the way from the lake she had been twanging with worry about Da. According to Ma, the boys had arrived two days back in the last light, told her their news, and at dawn flown off to the army. Ma didn't think there could be much that two boys, even on a flying horse, could do against a horde of mounted warriors, but Tilja was confident in the Ropemaker's magic. That wasn't enough, though. Da had left ten days earlier, taking Dusty with him. Neither of them knew anything about war, and there must have been fighting already. Anything could have happened to Da, and she knew it and Ma and Meena knew it, and all the while they had trudged between the trees it had been impossible to think about anything else.

But now, as she stood and looked out over the darkening Valley, she found she could put that aside as her whole being brimmed with happiness to be home. No, she could not stay here forever. Yes, everything could still go agonizingly wrong. But this was the place she belonged, at least for now, as a fox belongs in its lair. Home.

Anja, perched on Tiddykin's back, pointed northwest.

"Look! Look!" she cried.

They looked. Black against the flaming sky, already far too large for any bird, wide wings spread into a long glide, Calico too was coming home. Now Tilja could see the riders on her back, and how in flight she tucked her legs up beneath her, as if she were jumping a hedge—something that, as far as Tilja knew, she'd never attempted in her life. She circled twice, the second time so low that they could hear the whistle of her plumes. Tiddykin looked up and whinnied, apparently recognizing her despite her strange behavior. She answered with a ringing neigh and settled into the farmyard with a mighty battering of wings that sent all the loose straw litter swirling up in a flurry that caught the last rays of the sun and glinted gold as it rose above the shed roofs.

Tilja and Meena picked up their skirts and ran down the spare ground and across the meadow. Anja slid down and scampered after them. They reached the farmyard to find Calico stuck in the stable door, unable to go any further because her wings wouldn't go through. She was starting to flap them with all the panicky indignation of a hen being stuffed into a coop. A glancing blow sent Tahl crashing into the water butt. Alnor shouted. Calico heaved and flapped and squealed. A little more of this and she'd have the stables down.

Tilja was over the gate before she knew it and running for the far door. She grabbed a handful of yellownut and thrust it under Calico's nose. Calico paused and sniffed at it, unbelieving—yellownut after all these months. She lowered her head, but Tilja had moved her hand and she had to take a pace back to reach it. Then another, and another, until she was out.

Tilja gave her the yellownut and heaved the door shut while the horse chewed it. Anja was already pestering Tahl.

"What happened?" she was saying. "Where've you been? Why are they kissing like that? That's my grandma! Grandmas don't kiss people! Not like that!"

"I know how you feel," said Tahl. "That's my grandpa."

"Did you see my da? Did he kill a lot of people?"

"Tell you later. Is there anything to eat? We're starving. There was food at the camp, but Calico had got it into her head she was coming home."

"Barn rat with wings," said Tilja. "Da's all right, then?"

She put it like that because his face hadn't changed when Anja had asked him.

"Fine," he said cheerfully. "I told him you were on your way home, so he started back yesterday as soon as the fighting was over. We got him on one of the rafts. The river's in spate, so he could be back tonight."

"Fighting?" said Anja. "Tell me! Tell me!"

"Food," said Tahl, "or I'll eat *you!*"

Despite his obvious weariness he seemed in tearing high spirits. Ma took Anja off to start getting a meal together while Tilja rubbed Calico down, wearing gloves so that she didn't touch the magical wings with her bare hands. There was a strange mark, like a burn, on Calico's right flank. When she'd finished she coaxed Calico into the barn, which had much bigger doors than the stable, bribing her shamelessly with yellownut to get her to behave, and then tethering her as close as she safely could in front of a full manger. Tiddykin got a good share of yellownut too, because she'd waited so patiently and then done whatever was asked of her without it. By the time Tilja reached the kitchen the others were sitting down to eat.

Home felt like a shoe that didn't quite fit, a shoe the right size and shape, but with odd little bumps and hardnesses that the foot isn't used to, a shoe that needs wearing in. Nothing in the kitchen had changed, that she could see. It was the people—Anja cocky and bossy as ever, especially now that she was so excited at their homecoming, but different. When Tilja had given her the mother-of-pearl hair comb she had bought for her in the market at Ramram, and somehow ferried home unbroken, through all her adventures, Anja had been delighted with it, but instead of rushing off and looking for something she could see her reflection in and then flaunting it in front of everyone and pestering them for admiration, she had first thanked Tilja rather gravely, almost as a grown-up might have done, and actually said it must have been a nuisance to carry it all that far. Yes, Anja had changed, because for several months now she had been the elder daughter, and one day Woodbourne was going to be hers, and she had begun to understand in her bones what that meant.

That hurt. Tilja didn't want it to, but it did. She had accepted with her mind, and believed that she had accepted with her heart, that her own life was going to be elsewhere, but it wasn't wholly true. Not yet.

The change in Ma was different, subtler, harder to pin down and then understand. Tilja first noticed it when Anja was prattling on about going up to the forest "every, every day" to see if the cedars had woken up. Ma made the usual gesture with her hand to tell her that that was enough, started to say something herself, and stopped. That would never have happened in the old days. Either she wouldn't have spoken or else she would have known before she started exactly what she intended to say, and said it. She seemed to have lost some of that confidence.

Once she noticed, Tilja saw other tiny signs of this change, slight hesitations in familiar actions, an odd, quick smile that didn't seem to mean anything at all, fiddlings with loose wisps of hair. Perhaps, she thought, it was something to do with the magic dying out of the forest. Once that had happened, what was the point of Ma being at Woodbourne at all, instead of Grayne? What was the point of all those Urlasdaughters before her, trudging out year after year through the winter snows to sing to the unicorns? Twenty generations of certainty, gone. Oh, the cedars were talking again. Only that afternoon Meena had sat by the lake with the unicorns spread round her, singing to tell them she was home, and was reweaving the magic for another twenty generations. But nothing would ever bring back the old certainties into Ma's own mind. So she fiddled with her hair.

At first the boys were too busy wolfing their meal to talk much, so they hadn't begun on their story before they heard

359

Brando's yap of welcome from his kennel by the door. Tilja rose eagerly and turned to fetch the lantern, but Anja was there first and snatched it up.

"Anja," said Ma, firmly. "Da would like to say hello to Tilja first. He's been very worried about her."

"I've been worried about *him*," said Anja, but handed the lantern over. Tilja lit it with a spill from the stove and carried it out into the yard, where she found Da wiping Dusty down with a fistful of straw, as if all he'd been doing was a day's plowing. He turned and gazed at her in silence.

"I told you I'd come home," she said.

Without a word he picked her up as if he were about to lift her onto Dusty's back, just as he'd done almost a year ago, sending her out to look for Ma by the lake. He held her for a moment, studying her face, and set her down.

"You're tired," she said.

"Not as tired as I might have been. I'd've had five days on the road, but for the raftmen. You've grown. It's been a while. Done what you went for?"

"Yes, in the end. I hope so, anyway. We'll know when the snows come. Da, I haven't just grown, I've changed. But this is still home."

"Good."

That was all, and all she'd expected, but she could feel his happiness echoing hers, so it was enough.

Tired though they all were they talked far into the night, exchanging their adventures.

"And don't leave anything out," said Anja. "Da always leaves stuff out. I want to know *everything*."

"Do my best," said Da.

"Good," said Anja, and fell asleep, and after that slept and woke and asked questions and was asleep again before they were answered.

Just as Anja had said, Da couldn't help leaving most of his

story out. His hands spoke better than his tongue. But piecing his mumblings together, Tilja made out that as soon as the pass was open, in high summer, the raids had begun, but had been driven off without too much loss. Then there'd been a lull, until eighteen days ago the lookouts on the crags had reported an army of horsemen massing on the northern plain, and the message had gone out for all able-bodied men to rally below the pass.

They had made their stand at the foot of the mountains, on a long meadow, rising to a ridge, and flanked on one side by precipitous stony woodland and on the other by the ravine carved out by the melting glacier. All one day they had held off the attacks of the horsemen, but during the night a large troop of the enemy had somehow climbed down into the ravine and swum their horses down the swollen river, so when they woke next morning the men of the Valley had found themselves surrounded.

There was nothing for it but to turn about, facing both ways, and stick it out long as they lasted. For a while there was heavy, close fighting, and then the horsemen sounded their horns and drew off, readying for the final assault. The men of the Valley waited, knowing they were done for. Da was seeing to Dusty ("Suppose I was saying good-bye to him," he muttered) when all of a sudden the horse gave a great squeal and reared up. Men were shouting all along the line, and he looked round and saw the enemy, all over the place, struggling to control their horses. . . .

"And there, rushing in above them like, like I don't know what, was—"

"Calico!" yelled Anja, wide awake for the moment.

Da laughed with the rest of them. The interruption somehow seemed to loosen his tongue.

"That's right, chicken," he said. "Only I didn't recognize her, didn't even spot her for a horse, not at first, nor that she had riders on her, because hardly had I seen her before the fire came down, ropes of it, wriggling around in the air and lashing out at the men below. And men and horses were screaming and bolting around, and the fire ropes went snaking off after 'em, dragging the men out of the saddles.

"The thing circled round close by us a couple of times so now we could see it was a horse, a horse with wings, and a couple of fellows on its back, one of them holding the reins and the one behind making the fire ropes. Then it came on at us and I ducked down, thinking we were for it too, but the fire laid off while it went over and then it shot out ten times as strong the other side, where the main lot of the enemy were. The lie of the ground had stopped 'em seeing what was up beyond us, so they'd almost reached our line when it fell on 'em. They heaved round and raced yelling for the pass and the flying thing swooped to and fro, harrying 'em on.

"We'd mostly turned to watch what was happening, and now the fellows who'd got behind us came hammering through, taking no notice of us, no more than if we'd been a row of bushes or something, so we opened up and let 'em by and they raced on and joined the scrimmage at the foot of the pass. But there must've been a couple of hundred of 'em—more—they left lying on the ground, and riderless ponies careering about. And we just stood there, not knowing what to make of it. One moment we'd thought we were dead men, and next it was all over.

"There's a lot of good men we won't see again. Young Prin down at Siddlebrook's one of 'em, sorry to say."

"Prin!" said Ma. "But he's only sixteen, no, seventeen now. Oh dear!"

Da shook his head, leaned back in his chair and reached for his cider.

"But what happened next?" asked Anja. "What about Calico? I've got to know about Calico."

"You won't get any more out of him," said Ma. "Ask Alnor or Tahl. They know."

Tilja's eyes were heavy with sleep. She looked round the familiar kitchen. With just one lamp burning, and the glow and flicker from the open stove, it was a place of gleams and shadows. Only the old table was a pool of light, with a pile of fruit and nuts at the center, and the remains of a loaf, and cheese, and on the pewter platters a scatter of peelings and husks. Meena and Alnor had moved to the settle by the wall and were sitting in the corner at its darker end. Tahl was on the other side of the table from Tilja. The lamp was between them, so his face was hard to see, but his hands were bright-lit as they fiddled with the curious silken tassel that the Ropemaker had given him. Tahl glanced over his shoulder at Alnor, waiting for him to start.

"Why don't you let Tahl do it?" Meena suggested. "He'd only keep interrupting you."

"Instead of Alnor putting me right when I've finished," said Tahl. "Where'd I better start?"

"Flying away from us on the other side of the forest," said Meena. "We can tell them the rest of it later. Last we saw you were way up in the sky, heading off north."

Tahl didn't even pause to gather his thoughts. The story came bursting out of him.

"First off the only problem we had was staying on," he said. "Calico knew where she was going. Alnor tried using the reins a bit, but she wasn't having any, so we just let her fly until we got here. She was heading for her stall, like this afternoon, when Alnor managed to hitch her to a post, and by then Selly and Anja were here, and Anja got her quiet by giving her a feed in the yard, and we had a bite to eat while Selly told us about the horsemen coming through the pass and all the men going off to fight them.

"We were dog tired, and we wanted to be off early, so we wolfed our supper and fell into bed. Selly got us up and we were all set to go as soon as it was light. Trouble was, Calico wouldn't budge, no matter how much we yelled at her and kicked her ribs. She was home and she was staying home.

"Then I remembered this. The Ropemaker said I might need it, but I didn't know what for, so I'd just put it away, but now I thought it might be a special sort of whip for telling a flying horse who's master, so I took it out and gave a her a flick with it. That did the trick, and some!"

He twitched the tassel and each thread became a wriggling line of flame, brighter than the lamplight, flowing across the table without quite touching the surface. They withdrew the moment he twitched the tassel again.

"There's a scorch on Calico's right haunch," said Tilja.

"Sorry about that," said Tahl, his laugh belying the words. "I hadn't got the hang of it, then. It does what I want, just because it's me wanting it. Look."

Another flick, and this time the fiery threads flowed out close together, like a loose-woven cord, which coiled around the pile of walnut husks Tilja had been constructing on her platter while she was listening to Da's story. The husks burst into flame and burnt until they were ashes.

"Anyway it did the trick with Calico," said Tahl, still laughing. "One squeal and she was up and away. I gave the thing another shake, trying not to touch her this time, just to tell her I'd still got it, but it did better than that. The fire threads shot out and round behind her, like a dog snapping at her heels, telling her she'd better behave. Could have done with that once or twice on our journey, right? She got it at once.

"She was really flying now, and Alnor wasn't having any trouble making her go where he wanted, so I put the thing back under my jacket, but of course I was thinking about it, wondering what else it could do, when the fellow's name clicked into my mind . . . Dorn. . . . You'd told us about him using his fire whip on the walls of Talagh, remember, Til, and again in the barn in Goloroth? That's what it was. And that's why the Ropemaker had given it to me—to use against the horse tribes in the fighting. So I told Alnor to steady Calico best he could and then hold on tight, and I leaned over and spotted a tree in a field and I took the whip and gave it a shake and said, 'Burn that!' *Aaaah!*"

Tilja couldn't see his face, but there was something in his

voice, something in the wildness of his excitement, and in the long sigh of exhilaration at the end, that bothered her. And there'd been that curious pause as he had spoken Dorn's name. Tilja remembered the Ropemaker's words—*Bit of stuff I got from Dorn. Better keep an eye on him.*

She rose, taking her plate, moved round the table and scraped the ashes into the trash bucket, then came quietly back and stood behind Tahl.

Anja had been falling asleep again, but the movement woke her.

"Go on," she mumbled, still with her eyes half shut. "I'm listening. What's happening?"

"This," said Tahl, flicking ribbons of fire across the table toward her.

She screamed. Tahl flicked again, laughing wildly. Tilja leaned over his shoulder and closed her naked hand around the blazing source of the fire. There was the now-familiar quick shock of numbness, and when she opened her fist a twig and a handful of twisted grass stems tumbled onto the table.

"What did you want to do that for?" shouted Tahl, scrambling up and turning toward her. His face was taut with fury. She thought he was going to strike her. She grabbed his wrist and he went rigid. They stood like that for a moment while she channeled the quick sluice of magic through herself, realizing with relief that Dorn himself wasn't in it. It was just leftover Dorn stuff, like a dead man's clothing.

She let go of Tahl's wrist and he slumped back into his chair and put his head in his hands.

"I'm sorry," he whispered, and again, "I'm sorry. I couldn't stop it."

Only when he'd spoken did Tilja realize how intense the silence had been while the shadow of Dorn had come and gone through the kitchen. Now she could sense the others relaxing, and daring to breathe.

"It's not your fault," she said. "The Ropemaker told me it was

365

a risk. But it was worth it, wasn't it? If it hadn't been for you, Da would be dead by now, and farms would be burning all across the Valley."

"And that's true," said Da.

"You know what I'm thinking," said Ma in a low voice. "Now that we've all seen a bit of real magic, we understand that we're better off without it, here in the Valley. It belongs in the forest and the mountains. It has no place here, among us."

"And that's true too," said Da.

"But what happened next?" said Anja. "What happened in the battle?"

Tahl raised his head and attempted a smile.

"Alnor's turn," he said.

"If you wish," said Alnor, formal among near strangers. "There is not a great deal to tell. We landed twice at farms to ask where our people were gathered, and arrived around midmorning. We could see the fighting, and I spotted Dusty in the middle of it, so I didn't wait. I had no trouble with Calico—she must have warhorse blood in her somewhere, I think. I just shook the reins and gave her a kick with my heels and she came swooping down and gave a great ringing neigh as we were going in. 'Neigh' is the wrong word. It was more like a cock crowing, a cock the size of an elephant."

"That's the roc," said Tilja. "It did that when we were leaving Talagh."

"I expect so," said Alnor. "Anyway, there is more magic in old Calico now than just flying. Right through the din of the battle every horse must have heard her—one moment they were charging up the slope and the next they were all over the place, out of control."

"That's right," said Da. "Dusty too. And till then the horsemen could've done almost anything they wanted with their ponies."

"Then we were over them," said Alnor. "And Tahl started to use his whip. Leaning over, I could see the fire ropes just licking

366

the riders out of the saddles without even touching the animals. We went round a couple of times and then flew over and did the same on the far side, and harried them around for a bit, but there didn't seem any point in going on with that once they were all crowding into the pass, so we came back to look for Solon and see how the battle had gone. He had hurt his arm—he didn't tell you . . ."

"Kick from a horse," muttered Da.

"So we talked with some of the war council and decided to fly up the pass and make sure the horsemen kept going. In fact we went right over onto the far side and burnt their tents, so they knew we could get at them there too, if we wanted. We'd have liked to come straight back to Woodbourne, but Calico had done a lot and we were tired too, so we spent the night at our camp, and then flew over the pass again this morning to check. We didn't find a soul in sight in a day's journey from the pass, so we turned round and came home. Anything else, Tahl?"

"The whip," said Tahl in a low voice. "It wanted to burn the horses. I wouldn't let it."

"Sounds like you're well shot of it," said Meena. "Well now, I suppose you stay-at-homes are wanting to know what we've been up to since you saw us off on the raft. It's mostly going to be Tahl and Tilja, for the first half, anyway, because it's confusing for Alnor and me after what's happened to us. And then there was a bit when the other three of us were asleep, and only Tilja knew what was going on. It's going to take a while—there's a lot of it to tell. You sure you're up to it, Til?"

"We can wait till tomorrow," said Ma.

"I can't," said Anja.

"Thing is, there's something we've got to do, Alnor and me," said Meena, "and it's only going to be worse for us if we hang around. So we'd like to get this over, if Til's not too tired."

"I'm all right," said Tilja.

In fact the story seemed to tell itself, just as it had when she'd told it to the Ropemaker. Perhaps it was easier for them to

367

understand because they had all just seen a piece of true, dangerous magic doing its work in Ma's kitchen, until Tilja's touch had
unmade it. Even Anja, when she next woke, asked almost no
questions, but stared at Tilja with wide, amazed eyes, as if her sister had been as strange a creature as the great roc that had carried
her to Talagh. It must have been midnight before she reached the
point where Meena and Alnor had eaten their grapes on the
southernmost tip of the Empire, and from then on they joined in
the telling. Tahl too by now had recovered his spirits, so they
could pass the tale round among the four of them. Clearing the
table while one of the others was talking, Tilja noticed a glint of
gold among the litter of grass stalks into which Dorn's whip had
disintegrated. *Yes, of course*, she thought. *For a piece of magic that
powerful.* She picked up the single strand of the Ropemaker's hair
and wound it carefully round the little finger of her left hand.

When it was over Da rose and stretched.

"Bed now," he said. "Who's sleeping in the attic?"

"Just Tahl," said Meena. "Alnor and me are going out to the
barn. And there's no need to look like that, Selly—tales I could
tell about when you were my age, and you always thought I didn't
know. Anyway, like I said, it isn't that. There's something we've
laid on us to do, and we might as well get it over. Right, love?"

"It is decided," said Alnor quietly. "It is for the Valley. Do you
think we would not do otherwise if we had the choice?"

"And we'll need the makings of a fire," said Meena.

They had all heard the story. Only Anja didn't understand
what was happening. Somberly they helped pack rugs and firewood into two loads, but Meena and Alnor refused any help with
carrying them out to the barn. Tilja was fighting with tears by the
time they opened the door.

"Oh, cheer up, everyone," said Meena, waving the lantern she
was carrying to and fro like a dancer at the midwinter fire feast, and
laughing as if she meant it. "Look at it this way. Suppose someone
had come to us four months back and told us just you can be young
again till you get home, d'you think we wouldn't've jumped at the

chance? This time we've been having, we wouldn't've missed it for anything in the world! Right, love?"

She turned and staggered through the door under her load. Alnor paused in the doorway, smiled an odd, teasing smile, so that for a moment he looked just like Tahl, and followed her out into the darkness.

Tired though she was, Tilja woke from ancient habit when Da got up shortly before dawn to go and see to the animals. The little finger of her left hand was throbbing uncomfortably, and she realized that the Ropemaker's hair must still be wound round it. Perhaps it was that that had told her so clearly in her sleep that there was something unfinished. As she slid out of bed her movement woke Anja, who, instead of snuggling complainingly back under the covers, sat straight up.

"Where are you going?"

"Shhh. Go back to sleep. There's something I've got to do."

"Magic?"

"Sort of."

"I'm coming too. Please. I've got to be there."

Tilja was on the point of telling her to lie down again when she realized that what Anja was saying might possibly be true.

"All right. Put some clothes on. We're going outside."

When she opened the door it was still dark, but the first gray light in the east outlined the roofs across the yard. Through the gap beside the barn she could see, close beneath the dark edge of the forest, a single orange spark, the glow of a fire. It was too bright to have been burning all night—the firewood Meena and Alnor had carried wouldn't have lasted. Sighing, she took Anja's hand and led her to the stables, where she left her by the door. Groping in the pitch black, she found a pannikin on the shelf, scooped it into the bin that contained the yellownut, carried it out and gave it to Anja, then led her up to the barn.

"Wait here," she said, and again by touch went in and found and untied Calico's tethers and led her out. She waited while

Calico stretched and eased her wings with a tremendous rattle of plumes and then folded them along her flanks.

"Aren't they beautiful!" said Anja.

"Yes, but I'm afraid I've got to take them away."

"Oh, you mustn't! I want to fly, too!"

"So do I, but it's like Ma said. Magic doesn't belong in the Valley, only in the forest and the mountains. If we let Calico keep her wings it will spoil everything. I don't know how, but somehow or other it will, in the end. No more talking to the cedars, no more unicorns, no more Urlasdaughters at Woodbourne . . ."

"I suppose so."

"All right. Now you give Calico the yellownut, a little at a time, just to keep her mind off what I'm doing. That's right . . ."

As Calico nosed forward for the yellownut Tilja ran her bare hand along the spine of the great wing. For an instant she could feel the hardness of a bone as broad as her wrist beneath the silky plumage, then the flicker of numbness, and then just air. One golden feather wavered toward the ground. She picked it up, went round to the far side and picked up the other feather. That wing had already vanished with the first. She unwound the Ropemaker's hair from her finger and rewound it round the quills of the feathers.

Calico was nuzzling into the pannikin for the last crumbs of yellownut. Realizing she'd had it all, she raised her head and gave her shoulders an irritable shake, then looked round, so obviously puzzled that Tilja laughed aloud.

"What's that about?" said Anja.

"She's wondering what happened to her wings. She knows something's changed, but she can't think what. These are for you."

"Oh . . . what are they?"

"Let's put her in her own stall and I'll tell you there."

They settled onto a pile of hay, close together, not just for warmth, but because they were long-parted sisters, with feelings for each other no one else could have, ever.

"Those are roc feathers," said Tilja. "The roc gave them to me, so that the Ropemaker could use them to help me. He couldn't have if I'd just found them, or stolen them somehow. That's because a roc is a magical creature in its own right, like a unicorn, or the merman who towed us away from Faheel's island. They aren't made magic like the ring, or Dorn's whip.

"Now I'm giving them to you, because someday someone is going to need them again. Not you, I hope, nor your daughter who can hear what the cedars are saying, when her time comes, nor many daughters' daughters after that. But one day one of them is going to need to go to the Ropemaker and ask him to help the Valley, just as we went to look for Faheel.

"So you've got to keep the feathers safe, and pass them on to your daughter when the time comes, and tell her the story we told you last night. I'll tell it to you again, because you were asleep some of the time, and if I can I'll come and tell your daughter when she's old enough to understand.

"I saw what the Ropemaker did, but I've no idea how he did it, so I can't tell you how she must use the feathers—that daughter's daughter who's going to need them. Perhaps her hands will know, because the feathers will tell them, and that hair round them. That's one of his. It's full of his magic. I think she'd better go into the forest, because that's where the magic is, and the forest is our friend. There'll have to be a horse, and a man or a boy from Northbeck. And then—I don't know—perhaps she must do the exact opposite of what I do, taking all the magic that's in her, and all she can suck out of the forest, and passing it out through her hands into the feathers and the horse. And at the same time she must say the Ropemaker's name. Ramdatta.

"It is a secret name. None of you, not you or your daughter or any of the daughters after, must ever tell anyone that name, except the one who's going to have Woodbourne after you."

"Ramdatta?"

"That's right. Do you understand?"

"Of course I do. It's important. It's for the Valley."

"That's right."

They sat for a while in silence, Tilja vaguely but deeply content at the completion of things with this homecoming, Anja turning the feathers over, studying them, stroking them gently with her fingertips. When they rose and left the stables, day had broken.

Crossing the yard, Tilja turned and looked east through the gap between the stable and the barn. Two figures were coming slowly along the track, a rather stout old woman and a slighter man. The woman was limping, leaning heavily on the man's arm. He seemed to be staring in front of him, but from the way he carried his head it was at once obvious that he was blind.

Anja shouted, raced to the gate and climbed it. Twisting round on the top bar, she cupped her hands round her mouth and yelled.

"Wake up! Wake up, everybody! Meena's come home!"

She swung herself down on the other side and raced to welcome her grandmother.

Epilogue

A woman led a lame horse across an unpeopled landscape. For much of the way all seemed peaceful,
but then she would come to an area where build-
ings were shattered or gutted with fire, field after field of standing crops burnt black, and bodies, both human and animal,
sprawling in their blood and now rotting unburied. Ahead of her
lay the heavy line of the forest, and close beneath it the remains
of one last farm. So Saranja came home to Woodbourne.

Six years ago she had left, swearing to herself she would never
return. For five of those years she had been the house slave of
one of the warlords beyond the East Desert, until he and the two
children she had borne him had died when his keep was stormed
by his brother's army. In the chaos she had escaped, and continued to stagger on through the darkness. When dawn had broken
she had found herself already in the desert.

Six years ago she had almost died, crossing it, though then she
had carried food and water. Now she had nothing. But she did
not turn back. Death would be better than the life she had been
living. This time, though, the desert seemed to let her through as
if it had chosen to do so. It provided her with two freak thunder-
storms and a water hole large enough to support a colony of birds
which, having no predators, laid their eggs on the ground. With
those, and things that she had learned from her first crossing to
recognize as food, she had come through.

And then, seeing what had happened in the Valley, she had known that she must go and find out if anything was left of Woodbourne.

Not much. When a thatched and timbered building goes up in flames, very little remains but the central chimney stack, standing amid a pile of ashes and a few rafter ends.

No voice answered her call. She hadn't expected one. Her brothers would be fighting the raiders, or dead, her mother and aunt hiding in the forest with the animals.

She scuffed with her feet among the fringes of the heap. It was a way of preventing herself from weeping, because she felt she had no right to. Of her own will she had cut every connection with Woodbourne, even grief. All that was over.

Something glinted in the ashes. She stooped and eased out a golden feather, perfect, looking as if it had been shed that very morning. She pulled it free, and another came with it, attached at the quill by a twist of golden hair. She laid them together and ran her fingertips along them. The idiot story flooded back into her mind, the story that she had never believed, thinking it just a mechanism by which her mother could bind her for all her life to Woodbourne, as she herself had been bound, because Saranja had once made the mistake of admitting that she sometimes imagined she could hear the cedars talking.

With a sigh she turned to the horse, a useless old gelding she had found yesterday—or rather he had found her, wandering out of nowhere and nosing up to her for food, and had then simply followed her. She hadn't driven him off, because he was company of a kind, and also fresh meat that she didn't have to carry. She had imagined till now that he followed her so persistently only because he didn't want to be the only living creature in the landscape.

If it's you, you'll need a horse as well as the feathers.

"Waiting for me, weren't you?" she said. "Now all we want is some fellow from Northbeck."

She looked back along the way they had come. A man was

limping up the road toward her, leaning heavily on his staff. Without thought her fingers caressed the golden feathers as she waited for him, until she realized that her hands were full of a peculiar glowing warmth. She looked down. Feathers and hair seemed to shine with their own light. There was no need to go up into the forest. If she could do it at all, she could do it here.

The man came into the yard. He was about forty, slight, dark, with a look of arrogant energy beneath his obvious weariness and pain. There was a bloodstained bandage round his left calf.

"Ribek Ortahlson," he said.

"Well, I'm Saranja Urlasdaughter. Hold his head, will you."

She moved round to the horse's flank.

"I've no idea if this will work," she said.

She whispered the name.

"Ramdatta."

Her hands knew what to do.

Peter Dickinson is the author of many books for adults and young readers and has won numerous awards, including the Carnegie Medal (twice), the *Guardian* Award and the Whitbread Award (also twice). His novel *Eva* was a *Boston Globe–Horn Book* Fiction Honor Book. *Eva* was also selected as an ALA Best Book for Young Adults, as were Dickinson's novels *AK* and *A Bone from a Dry Sea*. His most recent book for Delacorte Press was *The Lion Tamer's Daughter and Other Stories*, which was chosen by *School Library Journal* as a Best Book of the Year. Peter Dickinson has four grown children and lives in Hampshire, England, with his wife, the writer Robin McKinley.